EARLY READERS ARE RAVING

on Goodreads

"Oh man, it's been a while since I went through a book in one sitting."

———

"Outstanding."

———

"When can I expect another book? Holy crap, this was a great read."

———

"Quirky, funny, and likeable."

———

"I couldn't put [it] down."

———

"Suspense, romance, and intrigue make this a fast, entertaining read."

———

"A lot of fun."

———

"I can't wait for the second book in this series."

SCHOOL FOR PSYCHICS

BOOK ONE

K. C. ARCHER

Simon & Schuster Paperbacks

NEW YORK LONDON TORONTO SYDNEY NEW DELHI

Simon & Schuster Paperbacks
An Imprint of Simon & Schuster, Inc.
1230 Avenue of the Americas
New York, NY 10020

First Simon & Schuster trade paperback edition April 2018

SIMON & SCHUSTER PAPERBACKS and colophon are registered
trademarks of Simon & Schuster, Inc.

For information about special discounts for bulk purchases, please
contact Simon & Schuster Special Sales at 1-866-506-1949
or business@simonandschuster.com

The Simon & Schuster Speakers Bureau can bring authors to your
live event. For more information or to book an event, contact the
Simon & Schuster Speakers Bureau at 1-866-248-3049
or visit our website at www.simonspeakers.com.

Manufactured in the United States of America

1   3   5   7   9   10   8   6   4   2

Library of Congress Cataloging-in-Publication Data has been applied for.

ISBN 978-1-5011-5933-6
ISBN 978-1-5011-5935-0 (ebook)

To UB, AG, EM, ES;
to all the unforeseen forces at work on this book,
and in the universe

SCHOOL FOR
PSYCHICS

CHAPTER ONE

THE STRIP. IF THERE WAS ANY PLACE IN THE WORLD as appropriately named, Teddy Cannon didn't know what it was. The Las Vegas Strip had been created for the sole purpose of stripping money from tourists, stripping clothing from women, stripping dignity from drunks, and stripping romance from weddings. And Teddy loved everything about it.

Her cabdriver pulled into the entrance of the Bellagio, past the hotel's famous fountains. He idled behind a stretch limo painted candy-apple red. It was slick and shiny and shockingly tasteless, even by Vegas standards. Teddy watched as a group of twentysomethings careened out of the limo, chanting, *"Vay-gas! Vay-gas!"* In the center of the group was an especially plastic-looking blonde wearing a tight dress, a tiara, and a pink party sash emblazoned with *Birthday Girl*. She'd probably spent her entire paycheck on that dress. Tonight she would drink too many cosmos and do something she would come to regret in the morning. There was only one place Teddy wanted to hang out with girls like that—at a poker table. They were easier to read than a copy of *Us Weekly*.

The driver tapped the meter. "Twenty-two fifty." Teddy resented having to shell out money for a cab, but she didn't have a choice. She'd sold her beloved 2004 Volvo the day before. She'd gotten five grand for it, enough to bankroll tonight's gambling.

Teddy nodded but didn't reach for her wallet just yet. Instead she returned her attention to the entrance to the hotel, trying to get a read on the crowd.

"What's the matter?" the driver asked. "You nervous?"

"Me?" She adjusted her wig. Damn, it was itchy. "Never."

"Well, you should be. Let me tell you something. These casinos, little lady, they don't lose."

She met his gaze in the rearview mirror. "Neither do I." She paused. The rest of the sentence echoed in her mind: *You sexist jerk*. But she silenced her snarkiness, offering a more acceptable comeback: "Because I don't play like a 'little lady.'"

He laughed so hard that his considerable belly shook. Teddy knew her own belly wouldn't shake like that. Because it was fake. One hundred percent cotton, with zero percent jiggle factor. "If you say so," he said. "Las Vegas—everyone thinks they're a winner!"

Not everyone. Just me.

"You from around here?" he asked

"Yeah."

"Funny. You don't look Vegas."

Meaning, she supposed, she didn't look like a stripper, a cocktail waitress, a showgirl, or even that plastic blonde. She couldn't decide if it was a compliment or an insult. *Wrong, in any case.*

Teddy Cannon was the epitome of Vegas. She'd grown up just a dozen miles away. And like the town itself, she was entirely self-invented.

In seventh grade, she'd been given the task of researching her ancestors and presenting an oral report about her heritage. She'd put on a sad face, hoping to play on her teacher's sympathy and skip out of the assignment altogether. "But Mrs. Gilbert," she'd said, "I'm *adopted*. I don't know anything about my ancestors."

Mrs. Gilbert, who was eight months pregnant at the time and supported by ankles that had swollen to the size of footballs, was crankier than usual. "Oh, for God's sake, Teddy. Just make something up."

It had never occurred to her that she could. She'd researched her options and decided to become Irish. Not the cherub-faced, flame-haired, grinning-men-in-green-suits Irish. No, she was Black Irish. A perpetual outsider. A member of a cunning, brawling, down-on-their-luck people. Years later, she certainly looked the part. Medium height and slight of build, sharp angles rather than soft curves. Raven-haired and eyes so pale they appeared almost silver.

Not that anyone would recognize her now.

She wore a long ash-blond wig that hid her pixie-ish hair, and contact lenses that turned her silver eyes brown. Weighted undergarments packed thirty pounds and several years onto her slender twenty-four-year-old frame. She'd found clothing at a local thrift store: starched white blouse with faint perspiration stains under the arms, black rayon skirt that pulled at her hips, faux-leather leopard-skin pumps. Lots of cheap jewelry. She wanted to look like someone who'd made an attempt to doll herself up and didn't realize she'd failed. She'd blend right in here.

Her disguise ensured that no one would give her a second look. Because if anyone—namely security—did, she'd be screwed.

The cabdriver had been her first test. She'd passed.

She paid the fare, leveraged herself from the backseat, and headed for the casino's revolving doors. Her panty hose rubbed between her padded thighs, emitting a distinct cricketlike chirp as she walked. Odds-on favorite for the most obnoxious noise in the universe.

She stepped inside the Bellagio and moved through the lobby. She hadn't left her apartment in weeks. God, the money, the greed. Bet more, win more! Shrill bells. Flashing lights.

She tried to avoid flashing lights on principle, as they could trigger a seizure. She'd been diagnosed with epilepsy as a kid, and she took medication to prevent the wild, unpredictable episodes that would take hold of her (once, even, in the parking lot of the Luxor). She'd skipped her pills this morning. They dulled her senses. On meds, even walking from her parents' couch to the fridge felt like moving through water instead of air.

She looked at the ATMs to her right—available to those who had anything left to withdraw from their bank accounts. Some of that cash would end up in her pocket, if she made it past the overhead cameras. Getting past the facial recognition software would be tricky. She tucked in her chin and kept her gaze low.

As she walked toward the tables, the words from MGM's chief of security replayed in her head: *Permanently banned from every casino on the Strip.*

The curse—delivered all those months ago, along with a restraining order—squeezed the air from her lungs. She slipped her hand into her purse, feeling for the prescription bottle just in case her body got the better of her, and walked on.

It wasn't like she was there to storm the casino's vault *Ocean's Eleven*–style. She just wanted to play a couple hands of poker. She had to play. She had to win. And she definitely, absolutely could not get caught. Teddy wouldn't think about the life-altering consequences if she did.

Except that was all she *could* think about.

First there was the Sergei factor: Sergei Zharkov, a Vegas bookie who boasted connections to the Russian Mob. A bookie with the crooked grin of an underfed coyote. Who had pet names for each of his guns. Not someone you wanted to owe $270,352. Sure, Sergei had been great fun when she was winning. A laugh a minute. But once her luck dried up—well, let's just say it had been a long time since she'd seen that trademark grin of his.

But that wasn't the worst of it. The worst was also the most stupendously stupid and seriously selfish thing she had ever done, atop a long list of majorly questionable decisions: she had forged three withdrawals from her parents' retirement savings account. She'd taken $90,000, a deposit on the money she owed, to buy a little time. Show him she was good for it.

Sergei had given her until the end of the week to pay him back in full. If she failed . . . If he decided to go after her parents for the rest of the cash . . . Teddy straightened her shoulders, refusing to let panic dig its ugly claws into her.

A casino security guard strolled right past her, not even sparing her a glance. Good. Her plan was working. She could still fix everything. Take care of Sergei. Keep her parents safe. Pay all the money back before anyone found out what she'd done.

The poker room was crowded, noisy. An attendant directed her toward an open table. Teddy took a seat. Texas Hold'em, no limit. She could play anything, but this was her favorite game.

She cleared her throat and put on a syrupy Southern accent. "Can I buy some chips from one of y'all?" She emptied her purse on the table, sending her prescription bottle, coins, and receipts everywhere. That was her play: make everyone think she was dumb and drunk. Teddy extracted the crisp hundred-dollar bills and stuffed the rest of the debris back in her purse.

The dealer, a reasonable-looking guy in his forties, rolled his eyes and exchanged her cash for chips. A cocktail waitress magically appeared at her side and asked what she wanted to drink. "Thanks, sugar," Teddy said. "Can I have another rum and Coke, please?" *Another*, as though she'd been drinking all night. It was a nice touch, if she did say so herself, and Teddy hoped the other players at the table had caught it. Devil in the details and all that.

Teddy rested her forearms against the table's gold leather bumper, ran her fingers over the expanse of green felt. The nerves that had seized her just minutes earlier vanished, as they always did when she prepared to play.

Teddy cracked her knuckles. This was it. Her last shot.

The dealer sent her a nod. "Ready?"

Was she ready? It had been months since she was in a casino. Five months, three days, and two hours, to be precise. She positively ached to play. "Absolutely."

The blinds placed their opening bets. Fifty and one hundred, respectively. Teddy shifted forward as the hole cards were dealt. She picked up total trash: eight-three off-suit. Fine. She'd fold early and get a read on the table.

There were eight other players, plus the dealer. A few men in expensive suits, out-of-towners on business, she guessed. Sure, they wanted the bragging rights of a big win, but Teddy doubted they would risk the wrath of their wives at home to get it. Next: an attractive Chinese woman in her forties wearing a chunky diamond ring. She looked slightly bored. Maybe killing time while waiting for a show to start. Seated to the woman's right were two guys in their fifties—regulars, probably. Solid players who knew the dealer by name.

The last player slipped in just after Teddy did and took the chair to her left. Like her, he rested his forearms on the leather bumper while he played. He'd rolled back the sleeves of his blue dress shirt to expose forearms that were tanned and corded with muscle. She keyed in on his hands. Hands that looked strong and capable. She watched as he toyed with his chips. She felt her body flush. Damn. She didn't have time for this.

Teddy allowed her gaze to drift upward. Wide chest, broad shoulders. No tie, shirt unbuttoned enough to catch a glimpse of more skin. Then her gaze reached his profile, and she sucked in a breath. He was flat-out gorgeous. The kind of guy who, under normal circumstances, would instantly make her to-do list. Cheekbones, green eyes, a strong nose just crooked enough to keep him from being too pretty, like he'd been in a few fights but the other guys always came out looking worse.

As though aware of her silent assessment, he turned slightly and acknowledged her with a tilt of his chin. He was even better-looking dead-on. Teddy forced her attention back to her cards. Tonight she had only one man on her mind: Sergei Zharkov.

The next hand she drew better hole cards, picking up a pair of tens. She met the opening hundred and stayed in the game. One of the businessmen dropped out and so did one of the locals. Everyone else stayed in for the flop. The dealer turned three cards: five of clubs, jack of spades, seven of hearts.

The Chinese woman raised another hundred. The remaining players got out of the way and folded, leaving it up to Teddy.

Teddy knew the woman was bluffing.

"But how do you know that?" her old friend Morgan had asked a year or two ago (whined like a six-year-old, really, if Teddy was being honest) after accompanying her to a casino and losing nearly a grand. "How do you *know* they're bluffing?"

Teddy could lecture all day long about tells. Watch their eyes—did they glance at their own chip stack or look away? Study their mouths—were their jaws relaxed or tense? If they touched their chips, it meant this; if they touched their cards, it meant that. But the real answer, at least for Teddy, came down to instinct. She knew because she *knew*. She never tried to explain it to anyone, because she thought it would sound ridiculous. It was kind of like how kids learned to count on their fingers without being shown. Just a way to work out a problem. She couldn't tell exactly what people were thinking, but she could always tell if they were lying. For when they did, a feeling of anxiety so acute, so alarming, took over—it was as if every molecule in the universe were telling her to trust her gut.

"You know that feeling when you're walking down an alley and you think you're being followed?" Teddy asked Morgan. "When you get into an elevator with someone who looks like a creep? When the voice inside your head shouts, *THIS IS WRONG!* and you have no choice but to listen?" But Morgan never understood, exactly. Anyway, Teddy learned early that it was easier to keep her explanations to herself.

From a young age, Teddy's gut had taught her a hard truth: everybody lies. Her father lied when her mother asked about her cooking; her classmates lied when the teacher asked about their homework; her supposed friends lied when she asked about their weekend plans. She couldn't live in a constant state of anxiety, but she also couldn't live with the constant heartbreak of knowing that the people she trusted were untrustworthy. So she'd done her best to shut out the feeling everywhere except the poker table. Her medication helped dull the feeling, too, but focus was harder. That's why she'd skipped her pill tonight. Because tonight she needed every edge to win.

Not a single casino had ever been able to prove she cheated. That's because she didn't—technically.

Teddy looked at the woman and called the raise. The turn showed an eight.

Without checking her cards, Teddy pushed in another pot-sized raise, which was more than the rest of her stack. Teddy sat very still, considering the woman across from her.

"All in." The woman said.

That feeling overtook her—her pulse raced, sweat formed on her palms. The woman had nothing. She was bluffing.

You can't play me. I'm basically a human lie detector.

"I think I'm gonna go all in, y'all. Is this how that works?" Teddy said as she pushed her remaining chips into the pot. Then Teddy smiled as the woman mucked her cards.

* * *

An hour passed, and then another. No big winners, no big losers. Teddy took down more pots than anyone else.

God, she missed this—the waxy flutter of playing cards, the clatter of chips, and the clubby insider jargon that defined the game: the blinds, the flop, the turn, the river. But most of all, she missed who she was when she played. She felt . . . plugged in. Switched on. As though some essential part of her came to life only when she was seated at a casino table. She positively *thrived* here. Which made it even more obscenely unfair that she'd been banned from every casino on the Strip.

The dealer lightly clapped his hands and stepped away from the table, indicating a shift change. Teddy tipped him and stood, taking the opportunity to unstick her skirt from her panty hose. As she waited for the new dealer to step in, Teddy glanced around the room. Her gaze landed on a man sitting by himself at the bar. She didn't think she'd ever seen him before, but something about him caught her attention and held it. He was a big guy—NFL-linebacker big. Midfifties, African American, casual dress. But nothing else about him was casual. Unlike other patrons, he struck her as purposeful, as though waiting for something or someone. He looked suspicious, and she was sure her instincts would kick in to warn her. But they didn't. Then he abruptly picked up his drink and left the room.

*   *   *

Things were going well: she was winning—almost fifty grand up— and no one seemed to have recognized her.

A cocktail server made her rounds. "Gin and tonic," the guy said, then gestured toward Teddy's empty glass. "And a rum and Coke."

Teddy jerked her attention back to the table. "What? Oh, no, thanks. I'm fine."

"You certainly are."

A line? When I'm dressed like this? Do you think I'm an idiot?

She didn't need her instincts to know that he was a player. Her gaze slid to his left hand. No ring, but that didn't mean anything. Not in a town like Vegas.

She looked at the server. "Coke's fine. Extra ice, skip the rum."

"Suit yourself." The guy held out his hand. "I'm Nick, by the way."

"Te—" she started, then caught herself just in time. "Anne."

He smiled, cocked his head to one side, and drew his brows together as though deep in thought. "TeAnne? Interesting. I don't think I've ever met anyone named TeAnne before."

She played along. "Well, it's an unusual name. A family name, actually. My mother's TeJoan and my father's TeJack."

"Ah." He grinned. "That explains it."

She settled back in her chair. She knew how Vegas worked. She wasn't naive enough to believe any of this was real. A guy like Nick could have any woman in the room. At the moment, she had all the sexual allure of a middle-school teacher with swollen ankles. No, he was trying to throw her off her game, win back some of his money. It wasn't personal, just strategy.

"And you're just plain ol' Nick," she said.

"Yup. Just plain ol' Nick."

"Well, just plain ol' Nick, nice stack of chips you've got there."

"Not as big as yours, though."

"You don't play as well as I do."

"True," he said. "Got any pointers?"

"Sure. Quit while you're ahead."

"That's what you should do, TeAnne. Quit while you're ahead." Except he wasn't smiling when he said it. Teddy flushed for a different reason altogether. Did he work for the casino? Or Sergei?

Teddy refocused her attention on the table. She noticed that the businessmen had left, replaced by two of the plastic blondes who had pulled up in the limo earlier. A fat stack of chips sat between them. It was time to get to work. She had been playing tight all night. No big moves, no showy hands. But with the addition of the plastic blondes, the mood at the table shifted, like when she'd hit the accelerator on her old Volvo. Stakes shot up with each hand. Her winnings grew. The rest of the players leaned in.

*   *   *

A little after two in the morning, Nick caught her eye. The last few heavy losses had been his, but he wasn't backing down. She peeked at her hole cards and made up her mind: he was her next target.

She pushed every round. Raised big before and after the flop and again at the turn. She studied Nick. Again, Teddy waited for the feeling of anxiety to take hold, but nothing. Her body turned cold, so cold her skin pebbled. There was a faint metallic tang on her tongue.

She spun around to find that the African-American guy she'd noticed earlier had returned. She tried to focus on the game, but now she couldn't get a read on anyone. She couldn't tell who was holding, who was bluffing. Her head pounded. Not a seizure—not now. She reached for the meds in her bag, her throat suddenly dry. Her hands shook and she spilled pills on the carpet. She bent down to gather them.

When she looked up, she saw Sergei drifting by the tables, checking out the action. Teddy swallowed. He hadn't noticed her, not yet, but if there was anything her bookie was good at, it was sniffing out weakness. Sure enough, his gaze landed on her. There was no recognition in his eyes, but his frown told her he was thinking. Teddy did not want to be the one to make Sergei Zharkov think.

"Ma'am?" the dealer said. "Your bet."

Every sensation she experienced was magnified, the blast of the AC on her already cold skin, the itch of her wig, the feeling of pills in her hand. She could hear conversations from tables away as if they were unfolding next to her. Teddy's vision swam as she tried to focus on her cards. A pair of jacks with one on the board, giving her three of a kind. She was up $50,000. A minute ago she'd thought her cards were enough to win, but now she wasn't sure. She was playing blind. She shoved her entire stack of chips into the pot. It was an ugly move, but it was the only thing she could think to do. A gasp sounded around the table. Over one hundred thousand riding on a single card. The pit boss strolled over to watch. So did a pair of casino security guards.

The other players folded fast. All eyes shot to Nick. He waited a beat. Then, his gaze fixed on Teddy, he met her bet. "You know," he drawled, "it's funny. All my life, I've been lucky with the ladies."

"That's how the saying goes," Teddy said. "Lucky in love, unlucky at—"

The corner of his lip twitched as if he was fighting a grin. He flipped his cards.

Two queens. A third sat on the board.

She'd lost it all. Everything. Gone.

CHAPTER TWO

TEDDY STUDIED THE CARDS SPREAD BEFORE HER. SHE didn't want to believe it, but there they were: three queens. Nick had taken her for everything.

The edges of her vision went dark, and for one mortifying moment she thought she might pass out—just fall face-first on the center of one of the Bellagio's best tables. She did a quick mental check: no tingling in her fingers, no nausea. It wasn't a seizure, just plain ol' terrifying panic, brought on by the psychotic amusement-park ride that was her life.

"Hey," she heard Nick say, as though speaking to her from a great distance. "You okay?"

She caught his eye and quickly looked away. "Fine," she said, pushing back from the table. If this were an amusement-park ride, she wanted off. Her legs felt like Jell-O, just as they had when she'd been twelve and ridden the Tower of Terror at Disneyland with her dad.

Oh, God, my dad.

She didn't want to think about him. Teddy searched for a comeback to brush off Nick's concern, but she had nothing. She didn't even know what her next move would be—all she knew was that she had to get out of the casino. Now.

"I'm done for the night, I think," she said, gesturing toward her cards.

From the corner of her eye, Teddy caught another glimpse of Sergei. She grabbed her purse and moved toward the exit that would take her out of the poker room and onto the casino's main floor.

"Just a minute, ma'am," the pit boss called after her. She glanced back to see him standing with one finger pressed against his earpiece—an earpiece that connected him to the security team monitoring the overhead surveillance cameras. He was nodding and frowning.

She'd been made. Goddamn facial recognition software. Didn't matter if she wore a rainbow wig.

Teddy shoved her way through the poker room, picking up speed as she went. The fat suit slowed her down, the dense foam slipping around her thighs and stomach. When she felt her wig falling off, she didn't even bother trying to grab it. She was too terrified to care.

The theater doors flew open, releasing the late show. Teddy threw herself into the crowd, letting the flow of people carry her to the front exit. For thirty blissful, life-affirming seconds, the tactic worked brilliantly. She could see the casino entrance and, beyond it, the glittering neon expanse of the Vegas night.

Until Sergei smiled his crooked smile and blocked her way.

He really needs to see a dentist.

Teddy veered right, heading for the ladies' room. She would ditch what was left of her disguise and make a run for it.

Just as she reached the restroom door, someone grabbed her by the shoulder. She tilted her head to see the NFL linebacker who'd been watching her so intently back at the poker table. He steered her into a service area blocked off from the general public by a tall rattan trifold screen.

Over/under on someone thinking this guy is kidnapping me if I start screaming?

Before she could open her mouth, he stopped her. "I'm not going to kidnap you," he said, his voice even. The calmness of his demeanor startled her. She tried to twist free. If this guy was going to hurt her—

"Teddy, I'm not going to hurt you."

Her jaw dropped open. Had her fear been written so clearly on her face? And how did this guy know her name? Then it hit her: he wasn't some pervert or hustler—he was a cop. "What do you want?" she said.

"For starters, keep your mouth shut."

He didn't act like any cop she'd met before. Even if he didn't read her the Miranda, she knew that everything she said could and would be used against her. Especially since she'd broken the restraining order that banned her from entering the Bellagio. She would be wearing an orange jumpsuit for the next six months.

Teddy could already picture her mom's face, red from crying. She could hear her dad's "I'm disappointed in you" speech. Teddy hated letting her parents down. But it seemed like that was all she had done her entire life. She imagined them visiting her in jail and felt her stomach drop again: there wasn't anything that could make her sink any lower in her parents' eyes. Well, maybe something: it started with Sergei and ended with Zharkov.

As she tried again to free herself from the man's grasp, a new thought formed: *If this guy really were a cop, I'd be in handcuffs by now.*

"I'm serious this time. Let go of my arm or I'll scream," she said.

"I wouldn't suggest it." He pulled her out from behind the screen, and she looked up to see Sergei heading straight toward her. The angry pit boss and his security team were close behind. Teddy took a sharp breath. She was trapped in plain sight.

"Easy," the linebacker said, his voice low and soothing, as though he were talking to a skittish horse. "Just stay quiet and they won't notice us."

Was this guy delusional? Though the light peppering of gray in his hair pegged him as middle-aged, he was big, and with one good swing, he could probably knock Sergei flat. But two armed security guards and a pit boss, too? Unless . . . Her gaze snapped to his jacket, searching for some sign of a bulky holster strapped across his chest. She did *not* want to be caught in a casino cross fire.

Her thoughts were so tangled she almost missed what happened next. Which was . . . *nothing*. Sergei slowed. His grin faded. Teddy looked into Sergei's eyes, expecting to see the same cold fury she had encountered minutes ago. Instead, his eyes were blank, pupils like black holes. Teddy looked from him to the pit boss and his crew—all wore identical vacant expressions. Her gaze swung to the linebacker, watching as the group passed by. His stare held the same pointed intensity with which he'd watched her play poker.

Her heart picked up. She didn't want to believe, but had this guy just cast a spell? Like real-life magic? She'd have been more freaked out if she hadn't been so impressed. As soon as the men were out of earshot, Teddy broke her silence. "What the hell was that?"

He released her. "We've got two, maybe three, minutes before they remember who they're looking for."

"How did you—"

"Later. First things first: I'm not here to arrest you."

She took a shaky breath. "You're a cop, though, aren't you?"

He nodded. "Ex-cop. Retired detective from the Las Vegas Metro PD."

She tilted her chin up defiantly, despite the fact that she in no way had the upper hand. "If you're a cop—or ex-cop—then why should I trust you?"

"I would start at the beginning if we had time, Teddy. But we don't. I'm Clint, by the way. Clint Corbett." He held out his hand, and when Teddy ignored it, he sighed. "I'm not here to arrest you. I'm here to recruit you."

"For a poker game or something?" Teddy asked. "You must know by now that I'm banned from the Bellagio. As well as most casinos in Vegas. So I wouldn't be very useful."

"Not for poker." He looked around the hallway. "I work for a school in San Francisco. And we want you."

Why me?

Teddy didn't voice her thought, one that had haunted her since she'd found out she was adopted, since she had realized she'd been given up as a baby. After her parents died, no one from her extended family, none of her parents' friends, even, had come forward to claim her. But it seemed like Clint heard it anyway.

"You're one of the best candidates I've ever seen."

"I'm not all that great at school," she said, as if her problems were academic, not borderline criminal.

Clearly, he has no idea I was kicked out of Stanford for starting that gambling ring.

"I'm not talking about Stanford," he said. "I'm with the Whitfield Institute for Law Enforcement Training and Development. I'm offering you a chance out of this mess."

"Law enforcement?" She gave a choked laugh. The idea was so absurd that a measure of relief poured through her. So much for reading her mind. "You obviously have no idea who you're talking to."

"Theodora Delaney Cannon, I know exactly who I'm talking to."

"Hey, look, thanks for your help with those thugs, and for the offer"—she made a vague gesture—"at the Whitfern Institute, but you've got the wrong person. I don't like cops. Cops don't like me. It's a relationship built on mutual disdain."

"Haven't you ever wondered why you're so good at guessing your opponents' hands? Predicting their next moves? Haven't you wondered why you can do things other people can't?"

Of course she had. Every day of her life. Rationalization had been her default. Believing otherwise meant confronting something inexplicable.

"There's no simple way to put this," he continued, "so I'll just say it: we train psychics."

Teddy stared at him. Psychics? She wasn't psychic. She just had good instincts, that was all. And right now her instincts were telling her to run. She returned her attention to the casino floor. If she bolted, she might able to get away clean.

Clint stepped in front of her, his massive frame blocking her exit. "You, Teddy Cannon, are psychic."

She shook her head. "If you had any idea how—"

"How screwed up your life is? I know, Teddy. It's because you've never learned how to handle your power."

He didn't move. After everything she'd been through, now she was trapped in a service bar with an enormous, crazy—

"Why do you think you win so consistently at poker?" he said. "Because you get lucky? No. You win because you read the other players at the table, and I'm not talking about tells. You know who's bluffing. You *know*. Every time, all the time."

"Not all the time. Seems to me I just lost pretty big back there." But even as she said it, she was uncomfortably aware that she *had* been winning, just like she always did, until he turned up.

"What do you think I did back there?" Clint said.

At that moment, it started—the familiar trembling. She felt the old pins and needles in her hands and feet, the chills. A seizure wouldn't be far behind. Emotional stress always did this to her. She reached up to drag her fingers through her hair, encountering the sticky glue and bobby pins from the wig.

"I need to get out of here," she said, digging in her purse for her pills.

"You're not epileptic, Teddy. You're psychic. Like me. This is just how your body reacts to sensory—and extrasensory—overload when you don't know how to channel the energy."

"You're crazy," Teddy said.

He tilted his head to one side, studying her the way her teachers always had. The way her parents did. (And her parents' friends and her friends' parents and basically every adult who had known her for longer than twenty minutes.) The look that conveyed how much potential she might have had if only she hadn't, well, been herself. "You're out of moves, Teddy. Sergei will come after your parents next. You do understand that? You lost tonight. Someone's got to pay."

Of course she understood. And no, she could not, would not, put her parents in danger. She'd already put them through enough.

"Teddy," Clint said, pulling her attention back to him, "listen carefully. At the Whitfield Institute, we work with psychics like you from all around the country. We train them in law enforcement techniques and teach them how to channel their gifts to make the world a better place. If you accept, I'll make sure that your record is wiped clean and that Sergei will never bother you or your parents again. I'm giving you another move—not Sergei, not jail, but *school*."

"I already told you," she said, "I'm not psychic."

He looked at her. "You can stay and face Sergei and casino security, or you can follow me out. I'm parked under the main entrance awning. Dark blue Taurus sedan, California plates. I hope you make the right choice."

Since when is getting into a car with a stranger the right choice?

Teddy watched Clint leave the casino. If she defaulted to rationalization now, she'd have to admit that epilepsy had never accounted for all her symptoms; her medication had never worked like it was supposed to.

Psychic.

Teddy tried to dismiss what he'd said. And she might have succeeded if she hadn't felt something coursing through her body—not anxiety, not the signs of a seizure, but something different, something new. Hope.

CHAPTER THREE

"WAIT UP!" TEDDY RAN TO CATCH UP WITH CLINT, scanning the crowd for the dark blue Taurus by the curb. She rapped her knuckles on the driver's-side window. Rapped so hard she hoped to startle Clint, but he simply pushed the button to lower the glass. "Let me see it," she said.

"See what?"

"You said you were a cop. I assume you've got ID to prove it." She would have checked to see if he was lying, but she still couldn't get a read on Clint.

Clint pulled a small leather case from his pocket and flipped it open. His Metropolitan Police badge filled the left side of the case; his police ID, stamped *Retired*, filled the right. He also had a CCW—a permit to carry concealed weapons. Teddy grabbed her phone and snapped a photo. She typed a message, hit send, then trotted around the car and got in.

"Care to explain what that was about?" he asked.

Teddy held up her phone to show him the text message—leaving Bellagio with this asshole—along with a photo of Clint's badge and ID. "I sent that to two of my friends. You're also on the casino's surveillance cameras. So good luck trying to pull any shit." He didn't need to know that she had just texted the photo to herself.

Clint checked his side-view mirror, then swung out into traffic. "I know how surveillance cameras work."

She checked her own side mirror, half expecting to see Sergei running after her. Or maybe one of the Bellagio's security vehicles, lights flashing. Instead, they slipped seamlessly onto the Strip, merging with the other late-night traffic. Teddy sank deeper into her seat. The car was quiet, nothing but the steady hum of tires against pavement, until Clint broke the silence by turning on the radio. Sitting down, he was far less intimidating than he'd been in the casino.

She corrected herself immediately. Not once in their brief encounter had she felt threatened by Clint. Sure, she'd been creeped out when he put a hex—or whatever that was—on Sergei and the others, but she'd believed him when he'd said he wasn't going to hurt her. Actually, there was something about him that made her feel protected. And, she might as well admit this, if only to herself: she was intrigued. As she watched the road, Teddy realized she hadn't given him her address. "At the next light, you'll need to make a left—"

"I know where you live," he said.

"Of course you do. Let me guess—you read my mind."

"No, I read your file."

Her brows shot up. "I have a file?"

"You were banned from every casino on the Strip. Of course you have a file. What I found interesting was that you never got caught cheating."

"Goddamn right. Because I didn't."

"The casinos thought you did. So many players complained about you that the casinos assumed you'd developed a new system for doing so."

"Whatever happened to innocent until proven guilty?"

"It's private property. They can ban anyone they want," he said. "The point is that's why you caught my eye. It's not unusual for untrained psychics to get into trouble. But you've been keeping a low profile lately. Avoiding your Serbian friend, maybe?"

"I had things under control," Teddy said. "Until you showed up."

Clint ignored Teddy's jab. "I really should have found you after you got kicked out of Stanford."

Teddy's body tensed. Stanford. The day she'd opened the big envelope had been one of the happiest in Teddy's life. But that hadn't lasted long. "I still don't buy this whole psychic nonsense."

"I'm going to have to prove it again, aren't I?" Clint said.

Does this guy really think I'm going to fall for that David Blaine crap?

"David Blaine's a hack," he said. "And he's a stage magician, not a psychic."

"I—," Teddy started. "I don't know who you think you are, but you can't just go around butting in on private conversations in people's heads."

"You're the one who wanted proof."

He had her there. "Okay," she said. "I'll play along. If there really are psychics, why would they even bother to go to school? Why wouldn't they just play the lottery and get rich?"

"Fair question. Let me ask you one. Why play poker? Why *not* the lottery? Or the slot machines?"

Because she couldn't predict numbers out of thin air. But she could read people. At Stanford, all she'd had to do was have a quick conversation with the quarterback before kickoff to know how to bet. Despite his bravado, when she'd felt that familiar anxiety, she'd known the quarterback was lying and that his game would be off.

"You'll find that psychics aren't that easy to read," Clint said. "You'll have to break down a few walls before you know if they're telling the truth." He smiled. A warmer smile than she had expected from him.

So he knew that she couldn't use her lie-detector skills on him. Interesting. "Just on you or on all psychics?"

"I have extra defenses in place. But our brains are wired differently. You'll find that you can't read us as easily as you do your opponents at a poker table." Keeping one hand on the wheel, he dug inside the glove compartment and retrieved a glossy brochure. The cover featured an impressive-looking redbrick building situated on a craggy rock overlooking the sea. *Whitfield Institute for Law Enforcement Training and Development,* the caption read. Did he think a slick brochure was going to impress her? Or did he just want to convince her the place was real?

He shook his head. "I get it. Back when I was approached, I was every bit as stubborn as you. Maybe more."

"You went to Whitfield?"

"It wasn't around then, but someplace like it, yeah." He tapped the brochure. "The point is, we don't just train people to work with local law enforcement, although obviously, that's the route I took. We place students with Homeland Security, FBI, CIA, private security details, the military, customs . . . you name it. And they go on to do important work."

The car slowed, then came to a stop. Clint shifted into park. She looked up, startled to find they'd already arrived at her parents' tidy suburban home. A knot formed in her stomach. What was she going to tell her parents? Sergei would stop at nothing to get his money. She had screwed up before—not just by getting kicked out of school but by pissing off bosses at crappy waitressing jobs, getting evicted from lousy apartment after lousy apartment, and more—but nothing compared to this. They'd have to take out another mortgage on the house.

She turned to thank Clint for the ride and found him studying the house with an odd expression. "They were good to you? The people who raised you?"

The people who raised me? They're my parents. She hoped he wasn't going to start asking whether she had ever tried to track down her birth parents and their families. Besides that assignment for Mrs. Gilbert's class, she hadn't asked any more questions. She didn't need to know. She had made a policy early in life of not wanting anyone who didn't want her in return: boys, Stanford, families . . .

"Yeah," she said. "It's not their fault I'm running from a loan shark."

"That's not what I asked."

"They were better than I deserved."

He nodded, seemingly satisfied. "Speaking of your parents: the school is top-secret. You can't tell them about it."

"What am I supposed to say? I'm moving to San Francisco to join a commune?"

Clint smiled. "The cover most students use is training for a classified government job."

"Convenient," Teddy said. She gathered her purse and opened the passenger door. "Thanks for your help tonight. It's been . . . interesting."

Clint reached over and put his hand on the door, stopping Teddy from getting out of the car. "The next time something like tonight happens, I won't be there to bail you out."

She stiffened, imagining herself in a prison uniform, her parents renting an apartment on Balzar Avenue with bars on the windows. "Yeah. I got it."

"The world needs people like us to show up, Teddy." He handed her the brochure. "There's a plane ticket in there. Flight leaves this morning at seven for San Francisco. I suggest you be on it."

"As in seven a.m. today? As in five hours from now?"

"I tried to approach you earlier, Teddy. But you were hiding in your parents' garage."

Teddy rolled her eyes. "It's not a garage, it's an apart—"

"I told you there was one last move. Not Sergei, not jail, but school. If you choose to attend Whitfield, we'll take care of your debts and make sure Sergei stays away from your parents." He held her gaze for a moment longer, then shrugged. "Think of this as a scholarship offer. You give us four years, we'll take care of everything else."

Teddy walked away from the car, wondering if he was telling the truth. She made it two feet before she had to ask him what had been nagging her since they left the casino. "Earlier tonight," she said, "what happened in the casino. You . . . you told them to do that, right? Sergei and the pit boss. You told them to just turn around and walk away?"

"Told them?" He arched a single brow. "Did you hear me say anything?"

"You know." Feeling foolish, she tapped her temple. "With your mind."

He held her gaze. "If you really want an answer, come to Whitfield."

With that, he drove away. Teddy stood on the curb, watching his taillights disappear around the corner. She loitered a moment longer, hoping there would be something, some sign, to help her make this decision. The cops pounding on the door. One of Sergei's men driving past her house. Clint waiting by the curb to take her to the airport. But there was nothing. Just the warm desert air, accompanied by the sound of real crickets. All that was left was her—her and her thoughts.

CHAPTER FOUR

TEDDY WALKED AROUND HER PARENTS' HOUSE TO the two-door (detached) garage. And just like that, ten yards later, she was home. As she fumbled with her keys, she remembered the day her dad had installed a real door with a real lock—his effort to make her feel like a real grown-up—instead of what she actually was: a twenty-four-year-old woman who lived in her parents' two-door (detached) garage.

She unlocked the door and walked into the remodeled space, which now held a separate living and sleeping area, with a small kitchenette tucked into the corner. It was nicer than some of the dumps Teddy had lived in. And the rent was *very* affordable.

She tossed the Whitfield brochure on her desk. *Why does that name sound familiar?*

She needed a long, cold shower. Then she needed pancakes. When she was a kid, her dad had cooked pancakes every Sunday morning while her mom slept in. The tradition had continued into her teens. Teddy and her dad discussed only the most important topics over pancakes—football, heist movies, disappointments and heartbreaks, adoption, epilepsy. Pancakes made everything better.

She stripped out of her costume, kicking it all into a corner.

As she showered, she thought about what Clint had said. If she were psychic, wouldn't she have been able to predict her debacle at Stanford? Sergei? Avoid this whole mess in the first place?

Breakfast wouldn't help answer that question. Exhausted, she slipped into bed, hoping that by morning she'd have a plan. And that maybe by tomorrow night she'd be laughing at the idea of a school for crime-fighting psychics. Oh, she'd laugh right up until Sergei tracked her down. She didn't have to be psychic to know that whatever he was going to do to her would be bad.

One last move.

She grabbed the brochure and her laptop from her desk and carried both to her bed. She settled her computer across her lap and typed *Whitfield Institute* into the search box.

The school popped up immediately. Lots of photos of building exteriors, of students sitting in classrooms. It was all stock-photo stuff, except none of the students or teachers faced the camera; the photos showed only the backs of their heads. It felt as though the webpage were a mock-up, details to be filled in later. Next she Googled Clint. Now, this was a little more interesting. Apparently, Clint Corbett wasn't just any cop. He was a Good Cop. Article after article featured his fancy cop certificates, shiny cop medals, and earnest cop plaques for solving cases that other cops believed were unsolvable. The Whitfield Institute wasn't mentioned by name.

Curious, she dug a little further and found a YouTube video with footage dated 1982. Apparently, Clint had played football for USC. Not surprising, given his build. She started the video: "Corbett jumps the route and intercepts the pass!" the sports announcer shouted. "Thirty, twenty, ten. Touchdown, USC! Corbett does it again! It's like he can read the quarterback's mind! Don't know how he does it!"

Teddy smiled. "He's psychic, dummies."

Her plane tickets checked out, too. Round-trip, leaving San Francisco at seven a.m., with the return date left open.

Teddy set her laptop aside. She drew her legs up and wrapped her arms around them, resting her chin atop her knees. Minutes ago, she'd been exhausted, but now sleep seemed impossible.

The idea of starting over in San Francisco was becoming more appealing by the second. The few friends she had left in Las Vegas from high school were busy "adulting"—going to brunch, having babies, buying sensible sedans, being normal with their jobs, partners, and families. And that left her even further out than she had been in school.

Teddy's medication sat on her bedside table. She glanced at it but didn't move to open the bottle. What if Clint was right? What if she wasn't epileptic but overstimulated? Because—and here was a terrifying admission—he had described exactly what her seizures felt like. Not a misfiring of neurons but a sensory overload.

Psychic.

Even though the medication made her feel as dull as a rock, some essential part of her continued to rebel against it. Against everything. She could not settle into the life her friends had embraced. Deep down, she knew she could never be happy like that. Maybe that was why she seemed to sabotage every attempt at a normal life. Getting expelled from Stanford. Leaving one job after another. Failing at relationships. Racking up insane gambling debts. The depths to which she was sinking kept getting lower and lower. She looked at the ridiculous costume piled in the corner and shuddered. If she hadn't already hated herself, she did now. Nothing like stealing from your parents to make you feel like the worst sort of person.

At least Whitfield Institute offered a possibility that she might finally be able to turn her life around. Fool's gold, knowing her luck, but a possibility was better than nothing. Something had to change—and if she was honest with herself, she knew that something was her. Clint's words came back to her now: *The world needs people like us to show up, Teddy.*

She saw a light turn on in the main house and wondered if her dad was awake. Lately, she'd been coming home to find him puttering around the house, fixing a broken lamp, flipping through the pages of some American history book. Teddy knew it would be so easy to walk over, to strike up a conversation, to mix the batter for pancakes.

It would be harder to tell him about the money she owed, about Sergei, about Clint and the school in California. Her dad would listen with his usual measured care before launching into the "I'm disappointed in you" speech. He'd tell her to do what she thought was right. But if she told him all of that, she'd have to also tell him that she'd stolen from him. And she wasn't ready to own up to that.

Teddy must have drifted off to sleep, for she woke abruptly, feeling dazed and disoriented. The wispy remnants of a familiar dream stayed with her—an image of a young woman standing before a yellow house, a cottage, really, beckoning her inside. A soft lullaby had drifted through the air.

Teddy rolled over. Her bedside clock read five-thirty. She shook her head clear of the dream and leaped out of bed. When she'd fallen asleep, she hadn't been sure what she would do about Clint's offer. But now she knew this really was her last move. She could show up. She was going to Whitfield.

Teddy pulled out her phone and summoned a Lyft. She gathered her makeup and toiletries and dumped them in a bag. She threw her clothes into a suitcase. She paused only long enough to stuff her costume and padding in a trash bag; she'd toss that out herself.

Finally, she placed her official Whitfield Institute letter of admission (personally addressed to Theodora Cannon—a thorough, if presumptuous, touch on Clint's part—and stuffed inside the pamphlet along with her plane ticket) on the kitchen table, where her parents would find it, along with a handwritten note. The letter didn't mention psychic stuff, so Teddy felt like she wasn't breaking any rules by sharing it with them.

Mom and Dad,
*   Didn't want to mention this until I knew, but look—I got*
in! I'm giving school another try. Heading out this morning. I'll
call as soon as I can.

Outside, the Lyft driver gave a quick honk, and she paused, thinking back to Clint's insistence that the world needed people like him. She corrected herself. *Like us.*

Until now, she had thought of herself as someone who needed people, not someone who other people needed. But for a brief moment she let that idea carry her away. She knew she wasn't Wonder Woman or Superman or anything, but maybe she could learn to make a difference, in a small way. She reread her note and added a quick postscript: *Next time I come home, you'll be proud of me.*

CHAPTER FIVE

TEDDY DODGED BETWEEN GROUPS OF TOURISTS who filled the bustling San Francisco pier. Ignoring the shops hawking cable car ornaments, Golden Gate snow globes, and T-shirts proclaiming the wearer had just escaped from Alcatraz, she made a beeline for the nearest coffee shop. She'd dozed a little on the plane, but it had been a short flight. She'd barely closed her eyes before touching down at SFO.

She ordered a triple mocha espresso, hoping the combination of caffeine and sugar would knock the sluggishness from her brain and eliminate her headache. It wasn't bad yet, just a dull pain behind her right eye: her body's normal way of reminding her that she hadn't taken her meds in over twenty-four hours. Only this time she'd deliberately forgotten to take them. All based on a highly nonmedical diagnosis from a cop who didn't even know her.

You're not epileptic, Teddy. You're psychic.

She touched the small bottle of pills tucked inside her jacket pocket, just in case. She felt more herself today, off her medication and in her own clothes—multiple ear piercings, leggings, combat boots, leather jacket.

There was a blast of a boat horn, a final call for anyone who wanted to board the ferry to Angel Island. Last night—wait, was it really just earlier this morning?—when Clint had told her the school was in San Francisco, she'd assumed he meant *in* San Francisco. Not on some tiny offshore island, little more than a pencil speck on a map of Northern California. But there had been a ferry pass clipped to her plane ticket, and so here she was.

Teddy capped her coffee and raced down Pier 41 to the dock where the ferry waited. Well, she ran as fast as she could, given that she was dragging her suitcase, carry-on duffel, and purse, along with the steaming mocha, all while dodging tourists. She was the last to board before the crew hauled in the carpeted plank and pulled away from the wharf. She dumped her gear at her feet against the rail. As the boat's engines hummed, she watched the city skyline recede. She hadn't been to San Francisco since her disastrous stint at Stanford.

"It's pretty, isn't it?"

Teddy turned to see a young woman in her early twenties standing beside her. She was small—elfin, almost. In fact, Teddy thought it looked like this girl might have spent more time reading *The Lord of the Rings* under her bedcovers than walking outside in the sun. Dark circles shadowed her eyes.

"I've never seen San Francisco from this vantage point," Teddy said, looking out over the horizon.

"You're on your way to Whitfield, too?" the girl asked.

Teddy turned to her, wondering if the girl was psychic.

The girl smiled and tilted her head toward the pile of luggage amassed at Teddy's feet. "It's pretty easy to tell who's planning on staying for months and who's just day-tripping," she said, pointing from her own luggage to the other passengers. "I'm Molly Quinn, by the way."

Teddy glanced around the deck and saw that Molly was right. Most of the people on board were tourists: couples and families equipped with backpacks, bikes, and water bottles, prepared to explore the island for an hour or two. Only a few had the number of bags that identified them as students.

"I'm Teddy."

Molly wasn't what Teddy had pictured when she'd imagined the typical Whitfield student. She'd half-expected (all right, dreaded) a group of kids in capes, tarot cards spilling out of their pockets and crystal balls cupped in their hands. But Molly looked normal enough, besides her pallor.

"What made you decide to come to Whitfield?" Teddy asked.

Molly looked away, appearing to study the foam churned up in the ferry's wake. "I didn't exactly choose to come. It was this or jail. Turns out I'm considered a threat to national security."

Teddy laughed, then stopped when she realized it wasn't meant as a joke. "You? Really?" Teddy thought this woman looked as dangerous as a mouse.

"Well, I sort of hacked in to the CIA's mainframe."

Teddy did a double take. Molly Quinn didn't look like a computer hacker. Surely she was bluffing. Teddy braced herself, expecting that anxious feeling to creep through her body as Molly talked, but it never came. She remembered that Clint had said psychics would be harder to read. And then something strange happened: an image appeared before her eyes, just a flash, like a frame from a movie: Molly huddled in front of a computer. The image was gone as quickly as it had arrived. Had she been in Molly's head? She wanted back in, to see that image again—was it a memory? Dazed, Teddy tried to rejoin the conversation.

"I wanted to prove myself." Molly shrugged. Teddy guessed that even mice could chew through the right wires to destroy the system.

Molly looked Teddy up and down. "Let me guess. Psychometrist?"

Teddy didn't know what a psychometrist was.

Molly continued, "I'm an empath. Do you know what that is?"

Teddy shook her head.

"It's someone who can tune in to the emotions of others, but on an extremely heightened level. I can feel—literally—everything someone else is feeling: pain, grief, joy, boredom. Like right now I can feel that you're excited but also frustrated—like you can't get a handle on all the information you'd like. Don't worry. Lots of students have close to no psychic knowledge when they first arrive."

Teddy didn't like how easily Molly had figured her out. She wasn't used to talking about her feelings with anyone except her dad, and even then pancakes had to be on the table. So she just smiled and changed the subject. "How does being an empath help you hack in to a computer?"

"It doesn't, not really. I have a degree in computer science, so I know my way around tech," Molly said. "Obviously, that helps. But those upper-level coders, the guys who work for the CIA . . ." She paused, shaking her head. "They're so proud of all their tricky little bits of code, their so-called impenetrable firewalls. It's ridiculous how cocky they get. It's like they leave a trail of fingerprints, and I just follow that inside."

While Molly talked, Teddy tried to recall that image of her. But this time nothing happened. Whatever connection there had been was gone.

Guess there's a reason psychics go to school.

"So how'd you get caught?" she asked.

"Well, I got cocky, too. I left a note. You know, a 'Hey, if I got in, who else is reading this?' kind of a thing. They traced the breach back to my laptop. Then these guys from Whitfield showed up."

Teddy wondered if she and Molly were more alike than she'd thought. Had all of Whitfield's students run into trouble before enrolling? She wondered if Whitfield was some sort of academy for wayward psychic millennials. That wasn't what she'd signed up for.

Molly looked at Teddy, her expression mirroring Teddy's own. Then Molly shook it off and gave another smile, gentle but strained. "Don't worry," she said. "Whitfield's actually pretty amazing. I wouldn't have come back if it hadn't been."

"Come back?"

"I was here first semester last year, but I took time off to deal with some personal stuff. Luckily, they're giving me another chance."

They both leaned against the railing, watching as a small island, covered by scrubby pine and ringed by steep coastal cliffs, rose dramatically from the center of the bay.

"That's home," Molly said.

The ferry bumped up against the dock. Passengers milled toward the exit plank, preparing to disembark. When they stepped off the ferry, Teddy was surprised to discover a port large enough to accommodate the ferry and several private boats. A few shops offered the tourist catchalls of water, first-aid kits, sunscreen, hats, and T-shirts, as well as bike, scooter, and kayak rentals. An information booth directed people toward trails and campground sites. Teddy spotted a Cantina serving food and drinks on a dock overlooking the bay. She liked the idea that there was somewhere to get drunk on this island if she needed to self-medicate with a margarita.

"That's our ride," Molly said, pointing to an unmarked tram.

Teddy picked up her belongings. She followed Molly toward the tram, dumped her things on the back, and then stopped. A group of people had gathered in front of a statuesque woman holding a small black dog. She was beautiful, but everything about her was big: hair, boobs, butt, thighs. She was wearing so much fringe that she looked like a giant lampshade, and she was yelling.

"Wilson says that cheap dog food you switched to is giving him gas. He should be eating organic. And throw in a probiotic. You should do that, too." Her fringe swayed as she pointed to a man—the owner, Teddy guessed. "Also, he wants to go back to the dog park," the woman went on.

"W-what?" the man said. "No, he can't. The last time I took him, he got into a fight—"

"—which wasn't his fault," the woman said. "He says the other dog was a total asshole." She put the dog down. The woman had blond wavy hair that reached the small of her back, which she swooped from shoulder to shoulder when she spoke, as if for emphasis. That, with the fringe and the bracelets, made Teddy wonder if she had taken a wrong turn at the intersection of Haight and Ashbury. Teddy almost laughed. Could this woman actually talk to dogs?

The dog's owner didn't find the woman funny. He tugged the dog in the opposite direction as the dog lurched toward a nearby flock of seabirds.

Frowning, the woman called out, "Wilson, stop projecting! Those birds did nothing to you!" The gulls circled overhead. "You're welcome," she said as they flew away.

Then she turned to Teddy and introduced herself as Jillian Blustein.

"Are you like a modern-day Dr. Dolittle?" Teddy said after introducing herself.

"Well, I also have been dabbling in palmistry," Jillian said as she grabbed Teddy's hand and turned it over. "You have a strong life line . . . or laugh line. I can never keep those straight." She gave a good-natured sigh, as if it didn't really matter. "But yes, I'm an animal medium."

Teddy laughed this time and then regretted it. "Sorry," she said. "You must get that a lot."

Jillian waved it away. "I'm used to it. People have been looking at me funny since I was a kid." She threw her arms in the air, making the fringe on her jacket wave. "Me. Blending in. You can imagine what a disaster that was?"

"Never worked for me, either," Teddy said.

"So are you walking or riding?" Jillian asked.

"What?"

"To Whitfield. It's only a mile or so from here."

"Sounds like you already know your way around."

Jillian shrugged. "I arrived a few hours ago. It's a nice walk. Come on, I'll show you."

Teddy called out to Molly to ask if she wanted to join them, but she was already settled in on the tram, so Teddy followed Jillian down a well-worn dirt path that curved south away from the docks.

"What's your story?" Jillian asked.

My story? Teddy shrugged.

"You know, psychically? How you got here?"

Teddy was so used to keeping her cards close to her vest, so to speak, that her first instinct was to deflect. Instead, she decided to do something she hadn't done very often, at least with strangers, since that moment when Mrs. Gilbert told her she could just make something up. Teddy told the truth. "I got into a little trouble at the poker tables in Vegas. Clint Corbett sort of bailed me out. He offered me a spot at Whitfield, and I took it."

She held her breath, waiting for a response. If Jillian was going to judge her as a lowlife, so be it. She'd pick up her chips and move to another table.

But Jillian's eyes grew big. "Clint Corbett personally recruited you?"

"Is that like a big deal or something?"

"It is a really big deal," said a voice behind them. "He's the dean of students."

Teddy swung around to face the man who had just spoken. His black hair sprouted in messy spikes off his head, as though he'd just tumbled out of bed.

"Do you make a habit of waiting behind trees?" Teddy said.

His head tilted to one side as he studied her. "Sorry, I didn't mean to startle you," he said. "My name is Jeremy Lee. I'm new at Whitfield."

"We're new, too." Jillian smiled. "I'm an animal medium, by the way. What can you do?"

"I'm a psychometrist," Jeremy said. "When I touch objects, I get a sort of flash. Sometimes it's a glimpse of the future, sometimes it's a glimpse of the past."

Jillian nodded as if she met psychometrists every day. "One time," she said, "I went on this road trip through Arizona, and I met this woman who could—"

Teddy tuned out the conversation as their surroundings changed. She had no idea what she *was*. The whole thing sounded like the beginning of a bad joke: *An animal medium and a psychometrist walked into a forest . . .*

The path led through a thicket of trees, and when they emerged, Teddy caught her first glimpse of Whitfield. It sat perched atop a cliff overlooking the bay, its impressive redbrick facade towering over the horizon. Whatever was beyond that facade would change Teddy's life forever. She stopped.

"What's wrong?" Jillian said, turning and seeing Teddy standing alone. If Molly were here, Teddy thought, she would know what Teddy was feeling; she would understand that Teddy felt excited and terrified and sad and happy and a thousand things at once. She thought again about what Clint had said: *The world needs people like us to show up.*

Teddy glanced back at the path to the dock. She could turn and run. But then she thought about the note she had left for her parents. She turned the collar of her leather jacket up against the breeze.

"Nothing," she said. "I'm coming."

CHAPTER SIX

WHEN THEY REACHED THE TOP OF THE HILL, TEDDY paused to look up at the school's official entrance: a massive iron gate topped with an arch that read *Whitfield Institute*. That was when she finally put it together—the school was owned by one of *those* Whitfields. The luxury-resort Whitfields. Why a Whitfield wanted a school for psychics was beyond her.

The whole setup reminded her of a fancy college—until she noticed the barbed-wire fence in front of the entrance and the accompanying armed guards. That would surely keep any tourists out. Teddy watched as Jillian and Jeremy passed through the security checkpoint. She stepped forward to follow but was stopped by a guard with a clipboard.

"Name?" he said. The guy was about six-six and looked to be about 250 pounds of solid muscle. The only man she'd met so far was Jeremy, and this guy made Jeremy look like a toothpick.

"Teddy—I mean, Theodora Cannon."

He checked something off in his paperwork. "ID?"

"I was just wondering where I can find the cabanas," Teddy said as she handed him her license. "This is, after all, a Whitfield property." She thought she might be able to get him to crack a smile.

But he only scrutinized her license and handed it back to her, then flipped to a page on his clipboard, turned it toward her, and pointed to the bottom. "Sign here," he said, handing her a pen.

"You mean 'Sign here, please,'" she said.

He made a slight movement of his head, and the two other guards turned toward her. "Miss, if you don't sign it—"

"Okay, okay," she said. "Just tell me what it is."

"It's a nondisclosure agreement. You're not permitted to tell anyone what you see, hear, or learn once you pass through these gates."

Teddy wanted to ask what would happen if she refused, but she was pretty sure she wouldn't like the answer. She scribbled her signature. "See you by the pool," she said, and walked through the gate. She actually wouldn't mind seeing him by the pool. All that muscle and maybe a pair of tiny European swim trunks. *It's been a long time, okay?*

She was surprised to find herself in a courtyard that could be described as East Coast Ivy League meets Eastern Zen Garden. The brick buildings were shaded by plantings of cedar, yew, and Japanese maples. Across the courtyard, she noted a bamboo pagoda and a fountain, as well as meditation benches. A few low footbridges traversed paths of flat river stone and pools of artfully raked sand.

If the garden was meant to inspire a sense of tranquility, she had no time to enjoy it. She had fallen farther behind Jillian and Jeremy; she'd totally lost track of Molly. She spotted a few stragglers near a building with *Fort McDowell* emblazoned on a plaque. She followed them into a large auditorium where thirty or so people were scattered about. She spotted a hot guy slouched in the corner. He was wearing ripped jeans and a white T-shirt with his dark hair covering his eyes. Anywhere else, Teddy would have written him off as a cliché.

Teddy slipped into a seat as a man moved to the podium. When she turned around, she saw the hot guy staring at her—a look that generated so much heat she felt herself blush. She couldn't remember the last time she'd blushed. Probably around the last time she wore a training bra.

"Welcome, first-year students," the man at the podium said. "My name is Hollis Whitfield." Teddy would have described him as distinguished. He wore a perfectly tailored navy suit. Not a single silver hair out of place. Definitely one of *those* Whitfields. "I have led the expansion of my family's company as president for thirty years. But I am proudest of my philanthropic work, especially here at the Whitfield Institute. I always knew that with the right guidance, men and women of your talents could be our nation's greatest assets."

Teddy wondered about the talents of the hot guy. She hoped he wasn't a mind reader, though she was sure her thoughts were written plainly enough on her face for all to see.

"Five years ago," Whitfield continued, "I had the distinct privilege of becoming a founding member of this institution, working beside representatives from our country's military and law enforcement personnel. If you've made it this far, congratulations. You are now part of an elite group of individuals with talents that the world is only just beginning to recognize, let alone utilize. Before I turn the microphone over to our dean of students, Professor Corbett, I want to say one more thing: today marks your first day of a remarkable journey. We are here to guide you. But you will guide our future."

Clint followed Whitfield to the podium. He looked even larger onstage than Teddy remembered. His presence commanded even the most bored-looking students' attention.

Clint cleared his throat. "As Hollis mentioned, this is a selective program which trains individuals to serve the highest level of government. The purpose of Whitfield is known only to a select few. We were founded, and continue to be funded, by both the private sector and the U.S. government. We are unlike any other school in the country, maybe in the world. And our sole mission is to train psychics to become successful members of law enforcement, military, and other related fields.

"You are here to protect your country. In many ways, we are the last line of defense. We're the ones people call when traditional police work isn't suited for the job. We're the ones the military looks to when they need individuals to go not only above and beyond the call of duty but also above and beyond the call of human cognition. We're here to do what's right when it's not only hard but seemingly impossible. I will teach you how in monthly Empathy 101 classes, which will start later in the semester."

Teddy couldn't exactly envision a life in public service. Hell, she'd been a public menace most of her life. She glanced around to see if anyone had stirred, but the students seemed glued to their seats.

Clint went on, "Before we continue, I want to introduce you to two other individuals who will direct your first-year training: Professor Amar Dunn, who will be teaching Introduction to Seership." Clint pointed to a man wearing a sport coat over a band T-shirt. The professor waved. "And Sergeant Rosemary Boyd, our military liaison, who will be teaching your tactical training." A woman with short brown hair stood and nodded. Sergeant Boyd was definitely going to be a pain in the ass: Teddy didn't have to be psychic to see that coming.

Teddy let out a breath. This place seemed like it was going to be a lot more work than Clint had let on back in Vegas. She was going to need an extracurricular activity to let off steam. Teddy casually leaned back and turned her head to the right. She saw the hot guy smirk.

"I'm aware that you took different routes to get here," Clint continued. "Some received glowing recommendations from government officials; some of you ran afoul of the law. None of that matters now. You are all first-year recruits, and that means you start at the same place—the bottom. If you want a space here, you'll have to earn it. Tomorrow you will each face a series of physical, mental, and psychic-ability exams to determine your suitability for the Whitfield Institute. If you don't pass those exams, you will be sent home."

Teddy felt as though her chair had just been kicked out from underneath her. No one had told her about any entrance exams. She had assumed her admittance was automatic—Clint had recruited her, after all. Why hadn't he mentioned that she had to pass a series of exams to get in? And exactly what was she supposed to tell her parents if she returned home within forty-eight hours? *Oh, Whitfield Institute? That bit about you being proud of me? Just kidding.*

She toyed again with the idea of bailing. Was an unreliable human lie detector really going to cut it on the front lines? But before she could make a move, someone sat down beside her. Teddy looked over to see the hot guy slouch down in the seat next to hers. Up close, he was even more gorgeous. Tattoos covered his olive skin, wrapping down his arms and up his neck. He looked like the kind of guy who'd enjoy breaking rules.

He leaned toward her. "See something you like?"

She'd known guys like this before. All ego. She rolled her eyes and returned her attention to Clint.

"Everything we do here is classified," Clint continued. "You will not discuss events that occur on this campus with anyone. Not your mother, not your partner, not your best friend. That's why each of you signed a nondisclosure agreement. We have taken precautions to ensure your discretion. If you stay, you will be confined to this island until Thanksgiving, and if you leave, you will be held to this contract. Furthermore, you will turn in all electronic devices for safekeeping—that includes laptops, tablets, cell phones, and any other gadget that connects you to the world outside this institution."

Teddy definitely hadn't signed up for that; a general rumbling in the audience told her that the other recruits were just as distressed by the news. Teddy looked down at her outfit, wondering if she could stash her phone somewhere. Bra, maybe.

"This is for your own safety," Clint said. "We will not risk having the names or faces of any of our recruits or staff showing up on Snapchat or wherever people are posting online these days. You will receive your official ID—which you will wear on your person at all times and swipe into and out of buildings—only after you've turned in your devices. Do not lose your ID. Do not lend it to anyone. Do not alter it in any way. And if any of you decides to play Edward Snowden and leak what's happening here, I guarantee you will not make it to Russia. We will catch you, and you will be tried for treason. That means years in a federal penitentiary. Trust me, even this place won't prepare you to survive there." Clint laughed. "As if the world would believe you, anyway."

Clint wrapped up with general housekeeping matters, like room assignments, how their belongings would be delivered, where and when dinner would be served. Then he dismissed them.

Teddy rose, turning her back on the hot guy. Right now he was the least of her problems.

Jillian found her in the crowd. "That was intense," she said.

Teddy looked past her at two girls in the corner who were whining about how unfair it was that the faculty got to keep their cell phones.

"I gave up mine years ago," Jillian said. "Did you know carrier pigeons were the original text message?"

"Um, yeah. Totally," Teddy said, playing along. "Listen, I'm going to go check my phone before I turn it in."

She ducked into the hallway to leave a voicemail for her parents in which she explained that she would be incommunicado for a few months, but they shouldn't worry. She knew they would anyway. With a sigh, she turned off her phone and dropped it in a bin by the door with everyone else's.

"If we end up in another Sector Three situation, we can't even text our loved ones final goodbyes," said one woman to another in the line ahead of Teddy. The woman tossed her phone into the bin and then twisted her braids into a pile on top of her head. She wore a denim jacket almost as beat up as Teddy's leather one, with the sleeves rolled up, revealing a string of silver bracelets that shone against her dark skin.

"What's Sector Three?" Teddy asked.

The woman looked around. "Who are you?" she asked.

"Teddy, a girl who doesn't want to say final goodbyes any time soon. I'll take any scoop I can get."

"My grandmother told me there was this secret government facility in the eighties that trained psychics for the military, and then the whole thing went to shit," the woman said. "Mind you, my grandma also believes that they kept real live aliens at Area 51, so, grain of salt and all that."

Teddy couldn't get a read on the woman, but she was beginning to understand that this would be her new normal. She would have to learn to live in a world where people could lie to her and get away with it. At least while she was at Whitfield. "So your grandmother was a psychic?" she asked.

The woman looked Teddy over and smiled. "I come from a long line of psychics. I'm the first at Whitfield, though. I'm Dara, by the way."

They walked toward a fold-out table at the front of the auditorium, where Jillian stood alongside a group of students. She picked up a folder with her name scrawled across it. Inside was her ID and a stack of papers.

"Guess who got lucky in the roommate lottery?" Jillian said, and pointed at Teddy.

Teddy smiled. She could deal with Jillian. Though the endless enthusiasm might get on her nerves eventually. Teddy scanned the room for Molly and saw her talking to Jeremy quietly in the first row, her hand on his arm. She'd wanted to ask Molly more questions about Whitfield, since she had been through the introductory phase before, but her conversation with Jeremy looked heated—like Teddy wasn't the only one who'd already identified a potential extracurricular.

"Come on," Teddy said to Jillian. "It says here we're in Harris Hall, room seventeen." She slipped her ID badge in her pocket.

*   *   *

Their belongings were piled on the steps of the building next door. Teddy and Jillian dragged their luggage up three flights of stairs and along a brightly lit hallway to room seventeen. Jillian swiped her ID in the card reader. The door clicked open to reveal a space the size of a utility room: two metal-frame twin beds that were practically guaranteed to squeak; desks and chairs that looked like office rejects; gray blankets that made Teddy's skin itch from the doorway; white walls. Teddy figured dorms were the same, no matter if the school was Stanford or Whitfield.

She ran a hand along the wall. "If you worked for a paint company, what would you call this color? Oncology waiting room?"

"It's not so bad," Jillian said. She tugged up the metal blinds at the window. "Look, we've even got a view of Alcatraz."

"I wonder if the prisoners there had better accommodations."

Jillian laughed. "Well, we'll hang some posters."

Teddy picked up a folder from one of the desks. Inside was a schedule with her name on it, as well as a sheet of paper labeled: *Whitfield Institute Code of Ethics*. The form described a range of behaviors and substances that were strongly discouraged on campus: no drinking, no drugs, no red meat, no caffeine, no refined sugar, no physical relationships between students, no infiltrating the minds of faculty or other students without permission. In other words, no fun.

"Goodbye, hamburgers," Teddy said, passing the form to Jillian. "We're supposed to sign to acknowledge that we've read it and then turn it in tomorrow morning."

Jillian squinted at the small print and shrugged. "It doesn't say anything here about *agreeing*. But honestly, Teddy, I've been a vegan since I was eight. It will really clear up your aura." She grabbed a pen from her backpack, scrawled out her signature, and then handed the pen to Teddy. "Sign it and we'll deal with the more important stuff."

"What would that be?"

"Going downstairs for dinner. Then maybe encountering some individuals to enhance our psychological well-being through emotional and physical contact."

Teddy looked at her and paused. "Emotional and physical contact?" It took her another second before she put it together: Jillian Blustein wanted to get laid. "Isn't that against the rules?"

"It never hurts to look." Jillian winked. "Come on, let's see what's on the menu."

*   *   *

Teddy expected the worst—soggy, tasteless cafeteria food. But the buffet was like something out of a pricey spa, featuring the sort of self-righteously organic, New Age, feed-your-soul food that people were thrilled to overpay for: roasted squash salad with mustard greens; braised lentils with simmered onions and carrots; spiced quinoa with charred eggplant.

They sat down at a long metal-topped institutional-style table across from Molly and Jeremy. The two were debating the finer points of something called mental defense. "You have to build a wall," Jeremy said. "It's all about the wall." Teddy had no clue what they were talking about. All she wanted was to build a wall between her and that hot guy from the assembly so she could avoid any temptation. But when she stood to check out the dessert table, there he was.

"Hey," he said.

Teddy thought about the list of discouraged activities. If she ignored him, maybe it would be easy to stick to her promise. She focused on a strawberry acai yogurt bowl, reading the list of ingredients over and over.

"I'm Lucas, but everyone calls me Pyro," he said.

Teddy couldn't resist. "Did you pick that nickname yourself? Real cool."

"I think you mean 'real hot.'" He winked. "That was corny, wasn't it?"

Teddy laughed. "Very."

"So what can you do?" he asked. "You know, psychically."

She shrugged. "I think I'm a faulty human lie detector." Clint had been right: psychics weren't easy to read. She hadn't picked up anything since she'd been at Whitfield, other than that image from Molly.

He smiled. "Should we play truth or dare?"

"Sure," Teddy said. "I dare you to show me what you can do."

Pyro's gaze moved slowly down her body.

She crossed her arms over her chest. "Psychically, dipshit."

His smile grew wider as he lifted his right hand and briskly rubbed the pads of his fingers against his thumb. Then he touched his fingers to the hem of the white cotton tablecloth spread over the dessert table. The tablecloth started to smolder, then a spark appeared.

Startled, Teddy stumbled backward away from the fire.

A second pass of his fingers and the flame was extinguished, leaving nothing but a burn mark. "It's called pyrokinesis. Controlling fire with your mind. Hence the nickname."

It had to be some kind of trick. Unable to hold his gaze, Teddy turned her attention to his tattoos. Most of them were run-of-the-mill religious icons. She spotted a sword and a snake, too. But the ones that crept up his throat—now, those were interesting. Dozens of tiny flickering flames seemed to sway and spark with every word he spoke, until they disappeared beneath the collar of his T-shirt. Teddy wanted to follow that fire and see where it ended.

"Are you one of those recruits who 'ran afoul of the law'?" Teddy asked.

He frowned, and the chemistry between them seemed to wane. "I was in the police force when Clint first approached me." Teddy took a step back. But he reached for her hand and rubbed his thumb over her wrist. She tried to jerk her arm away from the heat—like when she once touched a stove she didn't realize was on—but with each pass of his thumb, she began to welcome the warmth like a caress.

"Make it up to me?" he asked.

She arched a brow at that.

He continued brushing his thumb across the inside of her wrist, tracing mysterious patterns that felt too good. It would be easy to say yes. But this was the new Teddy. She didn't want to mess up before she even had a chance to succeed at Whitfield.

"Your turn," he said, voice low. "Hint: you're also supposed to choose dare."

Teddy scoffed. "Not tonight. You read the Code of Ethics."

He shrugged. "It's a list of discouraged activities. Not rules."

"I'm trying to be good," she said.

"Too bad," Pyro said.

She'd hoped for at least a mild show of disappointment, but something told her that wasn't part of his game.

He turned and left. She couldn't help but stare as he walked away. The guy was cocky as hell, but it sure looked like he could back it up.

And damn, the view was fine.

CHAPTER SEVEN

TEDDY WENT TO BED ALONE. WELL, NOT TECHNICALLY alone. There was Jillian. After a few hours tossing and turning, she finally adjusted to the sound of her roommate's light snoring and Whitfield's not-so-luxe accommodations.

For the second night in a row, Teddy dreamed of the yellow cottage. She followed the flagstone walkway toward the green door. She could see paint flaking around the edges of windows. She could hear the woman singing the familiar lullaby. Teddy reached out to turn the doorknob, and an alarm went off. The incessant beeping drowned out the song, shaking Teddy from sleep. She fumbled with the clock on her nightstand.

"Nobody should rely on an alarm," Jillian said.

Teddy covered her head with her pillow. "They should when they have an appointment at the clinic at seven-forty-five," she said.

She opened one eye to find Jillian in the middle of the room in tree pose. Naked. Teddy hadn't expected to see a tree in the morning, but she also hadn't expected to see . . . It was really too early to think about gardening.

"Jillian, please put all of that away."

Jillian untangled her limbs and pulled on her robe. "It's a very natural way to do yoga."

Teddy sighed. "Just warn me next time." She had forgotten what it was like to live with roommates. Roommates who weren't your parents, anyway.

Teddy sat up and immediately wished she hadn't. Her stomach clenched, and her vision swam. She felt shaky. This was prescription medication withdrawal—far worse than yesterday. She stood. The world tilted left and then right. When the room finally righted, she grabbed her towel and staggered to the shared bathroom down the hall.

On the way, Teddy caught sight of herself in the mirror. She looked like crap. She had cut her hair short after high school and kept it that way ever since. Normally, it worked for her—a deliberately messy look that gave her more edge, like a twenty-first-century Audrey Hepburn who had stopped by a dive bar for a Scotch on the way to an indie-rock concert. Today her hair looked more like a nest for birds who had been rejected from other, nicer, better people's bedheads.

She heard the water turn off in another stall. It was only seven, and she'd already seen one person naked. She tried to run into a stall before the person emerged. Instead, she managed to run right into him.

Because it was a him. *The* him. With only a towel wrapped around his waist.

"Whoa." He grabbed her shoulders and held her at arm's length. "You don't have to throw yourself at me."

Teddy searched for a comeback, but she was barely awake. "I'm just trying to, you know, to—"

"Shower?" Pyro offered.

"Shower," she said, and shot past him into a stall, where she turned on the water and tried unsuccessfully to think of something other than Pyro's half-naked body.

* * *

She arrived late for her appointment at the clinic, behind Fort McDowell. A middle-aged receptionist passed her a lengthy health questionnaire and a pen. In some ways, the reception area of the lab looked just like every other doctor's office, with two computer stations for the receptionist and medical assistant, a seating area, and several ferns. That was if she ignored the collection of psychic pamphlets on the coffee table where women's magazines were supposed to be.

Teddy glanced at the receptionist hopefully. "I don't suppose you've got a secret stash of caffeine hidden around here somewhere?"

The woman frowned. "Sorry. You know caffeine interferes with psychic ability. We do have some lovely decaf herbal teas at the beverage station. Hydration always helps."

Teddy declined. The woman's advice sounded like one of those awful bumper stickers you saw on alternative-fuel station wagons: *Proud to Be Pagan. Envision World Peace. Hydration Always Helps. Caffeine Is for Dummies.*

Teddy took a seat and tried to focus on the questionnaire. Once she'd filled in her own health history, the Don't Know box became her go-to. Paternal history of cancer—Don't Know. Maternal history of diabetes—Don't Know. Paternal history of high cholesterol—Don't Know. Maternal history of infertility— probably not, given her existence, but Teddy checked Don't Know to be on the safe side. The only information Teddy knew about her birth parents was that they'd died in a car accident when she was a few months old.

Then came the interesting stuff: Paternal and maternal history of schizophrenia. Depression. Bipolar disorder. OCD. Autism. Sliding from there into telepathy, clairvoyance, precognition, and a host of other psychic terms she barely recognized. Don't Know. Don't Know. Scary, though. Did it imply that mental disorders and psychic ability were related? She didn't know, but she hoped not.

A male doctor wearing a long white lab coat ushered her into a private office. He introduced himself as Dr. Eversley. He took her vitals, then gestured for her to sit while he reviewed her questionnaire. "Epilepsy?" he said, his brows arching in surprise. "How'd you wind up with that diagnosis?"

Teddy described the bombardment of sensations that had overwhelmed her as a child and the seizure-like states she'd fall into in response. The epilepsy medication had been the only thing that blunted her hypersensitivity to touch, movement, sights, and sounds.

"Interesting." He nodded. "And the last time you took your meds?"

Teddy calculated. "A little over forty-eight hours ago."

"Any seizures since then?"

"No."

"And how do you feel now?"

"Sort of . . . seasick." She described her current symptoms, watching as he recorded them on a notepad.

"So your current discomfort is primarily physical? Nothing mental? Do you feel disoriented? Sometimes that's an effect of stopping medications cold turkey."

"I matriculated into a school for psychics, so, yeah, I feel disoriented."

He didn't smile. "And since then—no flashes of insight, no sudden knowing, no psychic impressions of any kind?"

Teddy thought back to the image of Molly at the computer. Had that been a flash of insight? It had lasted only a second.

"Psychic abilities manifest differently in different people." He frowned as he flipped through the rest of her questionnaire. "There's nothing here about your genetic history."

"I'm adopted."

"Ah." He scrawled a note in her file and closed it, tossing it on his desk. "Unfortunate."

Teddy stiffened. "What's unfortunate about being raised by two people who want you around?"

He stood and crossed the room. She heard a rustling of paper as he rummaged through a medical supply cabinet. "I meant unfortunate from a research point of view. It's difficult to categorically establish a genetic link to psychic ability if we don't have that information."

"You think my biological parents were psychic?"

"These abilities tend to run in families. It's possible that your birth parents were psychic. But the abilities can also manifest in individuals who have no history at all."

She knew how lucky she was. She'd been raised by parents who were kind and almost relentlessly supportive. Though she didn't really get their sense of humor and they didn't get hers (her parents didn't think *Monty Python* was funny—who doesn't think *Monty Python* is funny?), they loved her and she loved them back.

She'd read once—probably in some guidance-counselor-approved leaflet that her parents had brought home—that many adopted children created elaborate explanations about their biological parents. She had imagined them as world adventurers, zoologists, even corporate executives. But the thought of them being psychic—and perhaps having passed that astonishing trait on to her—was thrilling. It didn't provide any concrete answers, but it was something.

"So that's what all these tests are for?"

"We're trying to gather enough information to prove that a gene marker even exists." Dr. Eversley returned with a metal tray full of empty vials, rubber stoppers, hypodermic needles, and gauze pads.

Teddy eyed the tray. "Since I don't know my family history—" she began.

"Doesn't matter. That's secondary information." He swabbed a spot in the crook of her arm. "The research that Hollis Whitfield sponsors makes this team a leader in the human genome field."

He tied the tourniquet and then slid a needle into her vein. Teddy looked up at the ceiling.

Yesterday Clint Corbett had explained that the Whitfield Institute was a public-private partnership. She'd assumed that meant everything was split down the middle. So the scientific research belonged to Whitfield, while the public-service-bound psychics benefited the government. She supposed that made sense, but she couldn't help wondering why a nonpsychic billionaire would be interested in psychic research?

"So we're just science experiments?"

"The more we know about the science of psychicness, the more we can help everyone, psychic or not," Dr. Eversley said.

"Whitfield's research—is it public? Published in a medical journal or something?"

"Public?" Dr. Eversley chuckled. "The lab is as high-security as you can get. No one goes in or out without clearance. Don't worry, the information we collect is perfectly secure." He withdrew the needle and stoppered the vial, then labeled it, placed it in a numbered slot in a refrigerated cabinet, and locked its door.

"That's it," he said, applying a small bandage to her arm. "You're free to go."

Teddy stood, but Dr. Eversley stopped her at the door. "One more thing. I'm recommending that you postpone your psychic-ability exam until tomorrow. That will give the epilepsy meds another twenty-four hours to completely vacate your system."

Teddy's head felt like it was filled with concrete—she didn't feel like she could pass an IQ test, let alone a psychic-ability exam. She could have hugged him.

*　　*　　*

Outside, Teddy walked across a large campus green, back toward the central courtyard. The grass was cut so she could see the straight lines left by the mower, razor-sharp. *Meditation Lawn,* a sign read, *Please Remove Shoes.*

Teddy had tried meditating once before, after a humiliating loss at the poker table. It had been after she had been kicked out of the MGM but before she had been banned from New York, New York. She had sat cross-legged and everything, but she just couldn't clear her mind.

She pulled out her schedule. She had an appointment in thirty minutes with Dr. Sands, the school psychiatrist. She wondered what she would confess to this stranger: that she was struggling with the symptoms of withdrawal; that she was puzzled by her birth parents' genetic background; that she was scared she wouldn't be able to hack it here.

Teddy took a deep breath. *I can do this.*

She took off her shoes and sat on the meditation lawn. She tried to ignore the pounding headache and the relentless nausea, tried to clear her mind. And promptly fell asleep.

*　　*　　*

Teddy arrived late to her next appointment. Again. "I'm so sorry," she said to Dr. Sands, who welcomed Teddy back to Fort McDowell and ushered her into a comfortable chair upholstered in white damask. "I was trying to meditate, and I fell asleep."

"It's fine." Dr. Sands, the kind of naturally elegant, soft-spoken woman who made Teddy feel sloppy, sat down in a similar chair and made a note on her clipboard.

Normally, Teddy didn't care about being a little late or being judged for it. But she couldn't help wondering if this was the kind of thing that could get her sent home and get her whole deal with Clint revoked. If she would have her kneecaps broken by one of Sergei's men just because she fell asleep on a goddamn mediation lawn.

"It's not going to count against me, is it?" Teddy asked. "I'm still trying to adjust to being off my meds and—"

"Apology accepted." Dr. Sands put down the clipboard and smiled. It was a genuine smile, the kind that would put a normal person at ease. But Teddy wasn't a normal person.

"I'm not usually like this," Teddy said.

"Like what?"

"You know—overly apologetic."

Dr. Sands sighed. "This isn't that kind of session, Teddy. I'm tasked with assessing whether or not you're a good candidate for Whitfield. I'm going to ask you some questions to get us started. Where were you living when you were recruited?"

"In an apartment. By myself."

Dr. Sands held her pen above her clipboard, as if waiting for Teddy to elaborate.

This lady totally knows I live at home.

Why had she lied about it? Teddy hadn't accounted for the fact that her whole life was probably spelled out in her file.

"It was in my parents' garage," Teddy added quickly, "but I had my own entrance. And I paid rent."

When I didn't gamble it away.

"Tell me a little bit about how you handle stress," Dr. Sands said.

"I held my own against the best poker players in the world. You think I can't handle the classes at Whitfield?"

"I didn't say that." Dr. Sands made another note. "Have you ever had a vision or a vivid or recurring dream?"

Teddy let out a breath, relieved that the conversation had changed direction. She thought of the dream that had awakened her that morning. "Sometimes I dream about a house," she said.

"And how does it make you feel?"

It makes me feel safe.

"It's familiar. Like I might have been there or something."

Dr. Sands made another note.

"Did I say something wrong?"

"There are no wrong answers, Theodora."

Teddy tried not to squirm, but something about these overstuffed chairs made her feel like she was about to be swallowed whole.

"Any other unexplained incidents? Moments when you felt like you could predict the outcome of a situation?"

Gambling.

"I sometimes know when people aren't telling the truth," Teddy said.

"And does that affect your relationships?"

She'd always known the Tooth Fairy and Santa Claus were bogus. She'd never had a long-term boyfriend. She kept friends at arm's length. Never mind the "Do I look okay in this dress?" question; the million other small lies that people told throughout the day were enough to drive her crazy. She could tell when her parents were disappointed in her, even when they said they weren't. "How could it not?" Teddy said.

"And what happens when you know someone's lying?"

"I feel . . . anxious." Teddy swallowed. "As a kid, I hated that feeling. Medication helped. But I tried to, I guess, not put myself in situations where I'd feel that way."

"So you didn't have many close relationships before Whitfield? How do you think that will affect your ability to work with a partner?"

Teddy's throat tightened. "Clint said that it wouldn't be the same around psychics. And I haven't felt like that since I arrived at Whitfield."

Dr. Sands made a few more notes. "I think we're done here."

Done? Like done *done?*

Teddy had to make one last move in this game she suddenly found herself playing. She cleared her throat. "I can read a table. I know how to egg another player on in order to increase the pot. I know how to bet. I can feel it in my bones when it's time to fold. And I know—" She ran her hands through her hair. "God, I know it's not time to fold yet."

Dr. Sands took her time placing her notepad on the table next to her. "It's clear that the choices you've made have led you down a path that—" Dr. Sands frowned. "Well, it's a path most parents wouldn't be happy to see their child take. You're impulsive, disdainful of authority, and have difficulty trusting others. I believe those behaviors grew from an instinct to protect yourself from getting hurt." She looked up at the ceiling, and blinked. It was a trick she'd picked up somewhere, to stop tears from sliding down her face. "They're learned behaviors, Teddy. So you can unlearn them. That, combined with Dean Corbett's recommendation—"

Teddy swallowed. "Does this mean I passed?"

Dr. Sands looked amused. "There's no passing or failing. There is simply gathering the information we need to decide if Whitfield is a good fit for you."

Bet on me.

Teddy had to bite back the words. She waited in silence, her heart beating erratically, until Dr. Sands spoke again.

"I'm technically not at liberty to say whether or not I'll recommend you for admission. But between us, I think you'll find Whitfield a lot more comfortable than your parents' garage."

Teddy felt light, as if the shame she'd carried since Stanford—since before that, even—had finally loosened its grasp on her heart.

"Thank you," she said, grabbing her jacket.

"Teddy," Dr. Sands said, "you still have to pass the psychic-ability exam with Professor Corbett and Professor Dunn."

"Oh, that." Teddy swallowed. "Piece of cake."

CHAPTER EIGHT

SPEAKING OF CAKE, TEDDY WAS STARVING. SHE WAS pretty sure the Whitfield Institute wouldn't serve cake—sugar probably did something to some receptor that interfered with psychic ability. Still, she headed over to Harris Hall to double-check.

Teddy spotted Jillian, Jeremy, and Molly, along with a few other now-familiar faces, at one of the dining hall's long tables. No Pyro, she noted. Too bad.

Teddy surveyed the entrées. She could hardly believe she lived in a world without cake. She chose a microgreen salad and sat down next to the other first-year recruits.

"Well?" Jillian said, leaning forward. "How'd your test go?"

Teddy finished chewing something green that didn't taste nearly as bad as she expected. "Good news," she said, "I'm sane after all."

"Not your psych exam. Your psych-*ic* exam."

"Deferred until tomorrow morning."

Jillian cocked her head. "Bummer."

Teddy didn't need to read Jillian's mind to see that her roommate was dying to talk about her own exam. "Spill it," Teddy said. "Did you nail it?"

Jillian grabbed Teddy's arm, knocking the fork out of her hand. "God, I did! I was *amazing*."

Jillian started at the beginning. First, Clint had brought in an orange tabby who communicated something about a dark, damp place she feared. After Jillian relayed this to Clint and Dunn, it was confirmed that the cat had been rescued from a drainage pipe. Next, Clint had introduced a very depressed golden retriever who had been a service dog for a blind woman who had died. The only thing Jillian got wrong was the timing—she told Dunn and Clint that the woman had passed two years ago, but in fact it had been eight moths.

"Dogs don't really have an accurate sense of time passing," Jillian said.

"Of course," Teddy said. "Otherwise we'd call them clocks." She turned to Molly. "Tell me about *your* exam."

"Draining," Molly said.

"But you passed?"

"Clint already knew what I can do from last year. But he still put me through my paces." Molly trailed off as if reliving something she wanted to forget. Teddy noticed Jeremy raising his arm as if to comfort Molly, then pulling it back when Dara appeared.

Teddy did what Jeremy apparently couldn't: she put a hand on Molly's shoulder. But concern for Molly was eclipsed by fear for herself. Clint had been serious about cuts. She glanced at the doorway, where she saw a group of first-year recruits saying their goodbyes. This same time tomorrow, she could be doing the same.

Dara slammed her lunch tray down next to Teddy's. "Can you believe this?" she said, as if they'd been in the middle of a conversation. "It's already happening."

"What's already happening?" Teddy asked, sneaking another look at the group by the doorway.

"The whole Misfits-Alphas thing."

Teddy glanced around the table. She'd assumed Dara meant the students leaving campus. "What are you talking about?"

Dara sighed. "This upperclassman named Christine said it happens every year. It's worse than high school. Whitfield Institute attracts two types of people. The Alphas, who think their psychic ability makes them vastly superior to everyone around them." She tilted her chin toward the table to their left. Teddy noted a group of well-groomed recruits who looked like extras from an old episode of *Gossip Girl*.

"And the Misfits," Dara continued. "People whose psychic gifts always made them feel like freaks." Her lips curved upward. "Remind you of anyone?"

Teddy thought about it: so far, she'd met a free spirit with the ability to talk to pets; an emotionally unstable ex-CIA hacker; a bad boy with the ability to set fire to . . . anything. She took Christine's point. These might not be the people she would choose as friends, but they were all she had.

"So what gift made you feel like a freak, Dara?" Jeremy asked.

"Death warnings," Dara said. "I can tell when someone's about to transition to the other side. Like about thirty percent of the time."

There was a collective pause at the table.

Dara smirked. "Don't worry, none of you are about to drop dead in your tofu." She took a bite of her bread and cultured butter. "I think."

*　　*　　*

After lunch, the first-year recruits reported to the basement of Fort McDowell for their first tactical training session. Even though everyone was dressed exactly alike—navy cotton T-shirts printed with the Whitfield Institute logo, black sweatpants, black sneakers, and ankle-high black cotton socks—it wasn't difficult to distinguish the groups Dara had labeled. The Alphas stood at the base of the bleachers, stretching and jumping, while the Misfits leaned against the wall. By now, their numbers had shrunk dramatically—from the thirty or so recruits Teddy had seen two days ago in the auditorium, twelve remained.

Pyro walked into the basement, late. Teddy stared. He wore a tight white T-shirt and basketball shorts, as if the uniform were beneath him.

Jillian nudged Teddy with her elbow. "Found something you like on the menu?"

"We ran into each other this morning in the, um, shower."

Before Teddy could say more, Sergeant Rosemary Boyd marched into the gym, clipboard in hand. She stopped in the center of the track. "Recruits front and center!" she said.

The Alphas instinctively lined up in front of their superior.

"Guess subservience is in their DNA," Teddy said to Jillian as she and the other Misfits made their way toward Boyd. Pyro took longer than the rest to fall into place, sidling up next to Teddy. "Nice uniform," she whispered.

Boyd strode up and down the line, eying each of them. "It's my responsibility to ensure that each of you graduates with the physical skills necessary to serve. I don't care about your 'special' powers. If you aren't able to jump a fence, you're not qualified to protect this country."

"Why jump a fence when you can just light it on fire?" Pyro said.

Boyd whipped her head toward him. "Name?"

"Lucas Costa."

"Why aren't you in uniform?"

Pyro shrugged. When Boyd looked down the line of recruits, he turned to Teddy. "Welcome to Shitfield," he whispered.

Teddy laughed. And her laughter drew Boyd's attention back to them.

"Unless I ask for specific information, Costa, you may reply to me in one of three ways: 'Yes, ma'am,' 'No, ma'am,' or 'No excuse, ma'am.' Anything else will get you on that ferry back to San Francisco. Now let's try again. Why aren't you in uniform?"

Pyro fixed his gaze on a point over Boyd's head. Seconds ticked past. Boyd shook her head and lifted her clipboard.

"No excuse, ma'am," Pyro said.

Teddy let out a breath as Boyd lowered her clipboard again. "Give me fifty." Pyro dropped as Boyd continued her speech. "I love comedy, I really do. In fact, nothing's funnier to me than watching a smart-ass blow his last chance. Tell me, were you kicked off the force because you were funny, Costa?"

So that's why he's here.

Boyd stepped away as Pyro finished his push-ups. "There are twelve of you left," she said. "Divide yourselves into two squads."

They split naturally into the groups they'd already favored: Misfits and Alphas. Before Pyro's clash with Boyd, Teddy had wondered what side he would pick. Sure, he acted like one of them, but he also used to be a cop. Now she knew where he stood: the Misfits included Teddy, Jillian, Dara, Pyro, Jeremy, and Molly. Teddy hadn't had the pleasure of meeting any of the Alphas yet, but three men and three women stood across from her—all of them annoyingly fit.

"Ladies and gentlemen, there is good in this world, and there is evil. Out there, you will be facing drug dealers, traffickers, rapists, murderers, and terrorists. There is one word, and only one word, for those people. Enemy. In here, the opposing squad is your enemy. If you fail, the enemy wins. I don't care about trying. I care about winning. Got that?"

The idea of stopping a violent criminal made Teddy's heart pound. She'd always been on the other side of the law. Now things were about to change. She was going to change.

"This course is designed to replicate everyday obstacles," Boyd said, directing their attention to the structures in the center of the room. "The sort of obstacles that law enforcement and military personnel might face. You'll move through the course as a unit. Clear?"

Boyd explained the mechanics: belly-crawl under thirty feet of wire, rope-swing across a pit, walk an elevated balance beam, traverse a set of monkey bars, drag a two-hundred-pound dummy to a point of safety, climb up a wall, and rappel down the back in less than twenty minutes. Teddy cast a look at the rest of her squad. With the exception of Pyro, they all looked worried. Especially Molly, who surveyed the wall with wide-eyed, panicked horror.

Boyd lifted her stopwatch and pointed to the Alphas. "You first."

The Alphas flew through the course with a grace that was beautiful to watch. The only glitch occurred at the rope swing when Ben Tucker, an Alpha who looked like a rich kid from a John Hughes movie, shot forward without sending the rope back to the next member of his team.

When they finished, the Misfits lined up at the starting point. Teddy wiped her palms on her gym shorts. She could only hope her team-mates had been studying the Alphas' run as carefully as she had. Boyd blew her whistle and they took off.

They made it through the belly crawl and across the rope swing, each Misfit deliberately hurling the rope back to the next squad member. So they had been paying attention. Jeremy wavered on the elevated balance beam, but Molly grabbed his hand to help him. Teddy made it across the monkey bars before her arms gave out. Pyro, Dara, and Teddy caught the two-hundred-pound dummy and dragged it to the point of safety.

Teddy joined her group as they raced toward the massive wall, the final obstacle. Pyro bent down to give the other recruits a knee up. Dara caught the top of the wall, hurled herself over, and raced to the finish line. Jillian followed. Then Jeremy. When Teddy placed her foot on Pyro's thigh, it slipped, nailing Pyro in the groin. He crumpled. "I'm so sorry," Teddy said.

"You owe me one," he said, and then pushed her up toward the wall with his hand on her ass.

"This makes us even."

"Not even close," he said.

Teddy made it to the top of the wall, swinging her legs over to rappel down the other side. Only Molly and Pyro were left. They were going to make it.

Then Teddy looked up to see Molly frozen at the top of the wall, her limbs rigid, her delicate features frozen in fear.

"Thirty seconds!" Boyd bellowed.

Pyro was already halfway down the wall before he saw Molly stuck at the top. He yelled to Teddy, "I need you to hold her rope while I carry her down. I won't leave a teammate behind." Teddy hesitated. Her instinct was to drive forward, to take care of herself first. She stood for a moment, trying to decide which way to move. By the time she glanced back, it was too late. With Pyro's help, Molly was halfway down the wall. With nothing else to do, Teddy ran across the finish line.

"What happened back there?" Jillian asked.

"Molly froze." Teddy heard footsteps pounding behind her and turned to see Pyro crossing the line, carrying Molly in his arms, just as Boyd blew her whistle.

Teddy looked around, hoping to see happy faces. "You might have passed the test," Boyd said. "But you lost to the other squad by a full two minutes. That means your enemy won."

Teddy's gaze shot to the Alphas, who stood grouped together on the sidelines. A tall girl, her shoulder-length brown hair pulled back in a tight ponytail, laughed.

Boyd continued, "In the real world, there are consequences when you fail. You die. Your partner dies. An innocent victim dies. Nobody will die in my classroom when you fail, but there will be consequences.

"The winning squad goes back to the dorms to shower and relax. Losing squad reports to Harris Hall for kitchen patrol after dinner. That means mopping floors, scrubbing appliances, cleaning toilets, washing plates and silverware, peeling potatoes, and whatever else the dining staff tells you to do."

The Misfits walked off the track in silence, heads low.

"It could be worse," Dara said.

"How so?" Jillian asked.

Dara gestured to the window, where the gates to Whitfield loomed. "We could be going home."

CHAPTER NINE

TEDDY AND JILLIAN RETURNED TO THEIR ROOM, EX-
hausted after cleaning every single one of the dining hall's long tables.
Teddy threw herself down onto her cot with a sigh.

"Aren't you going to the party?" Jillian asked, spraying a cloud of
patchouli.

"I'm wiped." Teddy couldn't remember the last time she'd gone to
sleep this early. Probably the same time she'd last been forced to do
chores. "Also, FYI, you smell like my grandmother's attic. Actually,
no, you smell like the chest in my grandmother's attic that belonged to
her grandmother."

"The third-years are hosting," Jillian said. Her bracelets jingled as
she turned to face Teddy. "And patchouli's an aphrodisiac."

Teddy groaned. "I don't want to know that."

"I bet I can convince you to come with me," Jillian said.

"I bet you can't."

"There's a rumor that there's going to be contraband at this party."

Teddy made a face. "You think you can tempt me with drugs?"

"Not drugs," Jillian said. She picked up Teddy's leather jacket and
threw it at her. "Cheeseburgers."

*　*　*

Twenty minutes later, dressed in a black V-neck, her favorite pair of
jeans, her leather jacket, and her best (and only) combat boots, Teddy

followed Jillian to the southwest corner of campus and over the serpentine brick wall that encircled Whitfield's perimeter.

The rest of the Misfits had arrived already. The Alphas were there, too. Teddy deduced that the others must be upperclassmen. After two days at Whitfield, Teddy still expected to encounter weird psychic behavior among the otherwise normal twentysomething students. Maybe levitating a keg. But all she saw was a makeshift bar set up in one corner of the clearing and a lanky guy pouring drinks into red plastic cups.

Jillian mumbled something about an aura calling to her and walked toward the campfire. Teddy scanned the crowd for Pyro. There he was, leaning against a tree. And could that boy lean. He was talking to Liz, a petite blond Alpha from their year. Jillian had told Teddy that Liz was a clairvoyant gymnast from Kentucky. If she'd been as good at seeing the past as she was at seeing the future, Liz would have known that Teddy had seen Pyro first.

Liz flicked her blond hair over her shoulder. Teddy wasn't going to pretend to be some team-spirit type just to impress a guy. If Pyro lost interest in her because of what had happened in Boyd's class, that was his problem. She wasn't going to waste another second thinking about him. So she did what she always did at parties: made her way to the bar.

"Welcome to our top-secret institution's top-secret hootenanny," the bartender said in a Texan drawl. He introduced himself as Brett Evans, a third-year.

"Teddy, first year. Or possibly no year by this time tomorrow."

"Then you have no excuse not to celebrate tonight." He winked, handing her a drink.

"Who said I was looking for an excuse?" She cast one more look at Pyro and Liz and downed the drink. Vodka and something sweet. She handed the cup back for a refill. "Doesn't this party kind of violate every one of Whitfield's Code of Ethics?"

Brett laughed. "We haven't been shut down since I've been here. And the tradition was already in full swing when I arrived, so . . ."

"But the staff is full of military personnel and psychics; they must know what you're up to."

Brett considered her for a moment. "This place has more twists than a pretzel factory. But I don't poke a possum, even if I'm pretty sure it's dead."

"In English, please?"

Brett refilled her cup. "That's Texan for drink now and ask questions later."

Out of the corner of her eye, Teddy saw Pyro making his way toward the bar. So she grabbed Brett and dragged him to the makeshift dance floor.

There were bursts of drunken laughter from a group of the first-year Alpha guys. Teddy had learned their names at dinner. The all-American eighties teen dream was Ben Tucker, the de facto leader of the group. Supposedly, he was telepathic. His chief suck-up was Zac Rogers, a college soccer player who received psychic messages through dreams and planned to fast-track to a position with Homeland Security after Whitfield. The third was Henry Cummings, another clairvoyant.

Kate Atkins, the tall brunette, stood off to one side of the dance floor. She was an icy midwesterner from a military family who didn't seem to have an at-ease switch. A claircognizant, Kate had flashes of insight that allowed her to know things without regard to source, logic, or facts. Ava Lareau swayed in the middle of the crowd. She was a medium from Mississippi, and Dara swore she dabbled in voodoo, which was strictly forbidden at the school.

Teddy looked up at Brett as they danced, wanting to ask him more about Whitfield's traditions, but his eyes were elsewhere. Teddy realized that he was staring at Jillian, who was dancing to the beat of her own drum. "Ask her to dance," Teddy said, nodding toward her friend. "She doesn't always smell like mothballs."

Brett smiled. "All right."

Teddy returned to the bar, where she bumped into Molly, the one person she didn't want to see: she still felt terrible about what had happened on the track.

"Shot?" Teddy asked, lifting the vodka bottle.

"I'd rather not compromise my position," Molly said. She took a swig from a water bottle.

Teddy rubbed the back of her neck. "I guess it's obvious I've never been good at team sports."

"Well, I have this thing with heights," Molly said. "I've been working on it."

The two shared an awkward silence. Teddy wished she were the kind of person who would not have hesitated on the course. Like Pyro. Teddy hoped Molly could feel what she was feeling right then, because she wasn't capable of saying it out loud. "Anyway," Teddy said, "I was dragged here under the promise of burgers, and I have yet to find one."

Molly nodded toward a figure emerging from the woods: Jeremy, carrying a box from In-N-Out.

"My hero," Teddy said as she accepted a wrapped burger. She held it to her nose and inhaled. "Have I told you lately that I love you?" she said to Jeremy.

"Me or the burger?" Jeremy asked.

"I love you each in your own special way."

Jeremy blushed.

Dara walked up behind Teddy, grabbing a burger. "All right, leave some for the rest of us, Cannon."

Teddy took two more burgers and followed Dara to the campfire, where they sat down on a log to eat.

"You never mentioned how your test went," Teddy said to Dara. She wanted all the intel on the psychic-ability exam; she needed any help she could get.

Dara chewed her bite of burger longer than necessary. "I come from a long line of psychics," she said. "Like great-great-great-great-great-great-grandmother long. My family expected me to go into the 'business,' but I didn't show any aptitude until a year ago, when I saw my grandmother's death. That was really messed up. My mom was relieved, though. That was doubly messed up. So I've gotten only one real death warning, and now I'm here."

So Dara was still figuring out her psychic abilities, too. "They must think you have potential, otherwise you wouldn't be here," Teddy said.

Dara shrugged. "I guess. Hand me another burger, would you?"

Teddy passed another from her stash.

"So, speaking of contraband," Dara said, "there's a rumor that Brett has keys to the reception of the lab. He's running some sort of black-market setup where you can trade crap for Internet access. I don't know about you, but I couldn't go a whole year without checking Facebook."

Teddy had little interest in status updates, but that didn't mean she didn't miss being plugged in. "I thought there were computers we could use on campus."

"Have you seen those computers? They're PCs from the nineties. I'm talking dial-up action. And first-years can't even use them until second semester, when we have case assignments." Dara took another bite of her burger. "Also, I suggest becoming Jeremy's best friend ASAP, because he's the only one we know who's got a way off-island."

"How's that?"

"He's got a boat stashed somewhere. His family is from San Francisco, and apparently, they're loaded. Not quite Whitfield rich, but almost."

Teddy watched as Jeremy whispered into Molly's ear and Molly smiled. Jeremy didn't seem like the kind of guy to have a ton of moves, but he must have found one that worked on Molly. Teddy hoped she wasn't just in it for the boat.

Teddy put down her burger. "I'm going to get another drink. Want anything?"

Dara shook her head.

As Teddy made her way back to the bar, she cast glances for Pyro and Liz, but they were nowhere to be found.

"Looking for someone?" a voice behind her said.

"Not someone," Teddy said, turning to face Pyro. "Something." She held up her red plastic cup as evidence.

He leaned against a nearby tree. God, the leaning. "Come on," he said. "You've been watching me all night."

"You know, I had assumed you moved on," she said. Teddy thought back to Boyd's class. Talking about her feelings was harder than Boyd's obstacle course. She didn't want to make excuses, but she couldn't let him think she was the kind of person who would leave a teammate behind.

"And why would I do that?"

She shrugged. "Because I was ready to abandon my teammate to cross the finish line."

"I saw you tonight." His gaze flicked down her body. "And I reconsidered."

"Seriously, Pyro."

"I'm being serious," he said, crossing his arms over his chest. "It happens. People choke."

"Not you."

"Yes. Me. I left someone behind once." He shifted on his feet, visibly uncomfortable. "My first week."

"Tell me," she said.

He looked up at the stars as if searching for a sign, a reason to continue. "My partner, Anthony Mandarano," he said, looking back at her. "Just had his second kid—baby girl. It was just supposed to be a normal, regular 415." He turned away from Teddy. "When we arrived at the scene, we heard shots. Anthony told me to call for backup while he went through the back entrance. He—" Pyro turned back to face Teddy. His eyes were blazing. "He was shot while I was radioing for help. If I had gone with him, or if I had been the one who had gone . . ."

Teddy wanted to brush his hair from his forehead, touch his cheek. Instead, she said: "You were following protocol."

"Yeah, tell that to his kids."

"So that's why you're here?"

"I set the whole place on fire. The whole goddamn house. I didn't even mean to do it." He paused. "I was recruited after that." He shot her a sideways glance. "Like you, I'm guessing."

Teddy ignored the question, focusing her attention instead on the flames tattooed at the base of his neck and on his collarbone, and the long, lean cords of muscle visible through the thin white cotton of his T-shirt.

When she looked back at the campfire, she saw that the party was winding down. The music was playing low and slow; the dance floor had cleared out. The breeze coming off the bay had turned cool. She rubbed the goose bumps that sprang up on her arms. "We should go."

"Why? You drunk?"

"Nope. I just feel . . . good." That was true. The vodka had taken the edge off her headache.

"I wouldn't want to make a move on you if you were drunk."

"Oh?" She arched a brow. "You're going to make a move on me?"

"Definitely."

"What about Liz?" She hated trying to read guys. In that respect, this ignorance was bliss.

"I was just trying to make you jealous."

Dr. Sands's question from earlier that day echoed in her head: *How has your power influenced your relationships?*

Her psychic ability always made her feel alone. Alone even in a crowd of people, at a party.

"Convince me to come back to your room," she said.

Pyro lifted his right hand and slowly twisted his wrist, like a magician proving he had nothing up his sleeve. His fingers slowly grazed the hem of her T-shirt. Then he pressed his palm, fingers splayed open, against her stomach.

Heat.

She tilted back her head, closed her eyes, and parted her lips.

When she opened her eyes again, she found Pyro watching her, a smile on his face. A smile telling her that particular move worked every time. All right, so he was a player. She wasn't looking for commitment. "How far is your room?"

Pyro took her hand and led her back along the path to the dormitories. His room was on the first floor, right off the front lobby. He swiped his ID card, opened the door, and pulled her inside with him.

"Where's your roommate?" Teddy asked.

"Sent home this morning," he murmured before he pressed his mouth to hers.

Her hands rested on his shoulders, pulling him closer. Pyro wrapped one arm around her waist, drawing her more tightly into his embrace.

He held her firmly against him, not the least bit rushed. Kissing her as though they had all the time in the world. Her knees went weak. Her balance lost, she stumbled backward, bringing him with her. "Just promise me you won't make any jokes about crossing the finish line together," she said.

Pyro caught her under the knees, lifting her to his bed. He pulled off his shirt and tossed it aside.

Teddy swallowed. His chest was lean and hard. And all of it beautifully, extravagantly inked. She hadn't looked properly when she had seen him in the bathroom earlier. Swirling fire covered his torso, disappearing beneath the waistband of his jeans, which hung low around his hips. His chest was an inferno, and when he reached for her, his hands were hot.

But again, no pain. Only a delicious, welcoming heat. She wanted to feel those hands everywhere. She toed off her shoes and kicked them aside, wriggled out of her jeans, and slipped out of her shirt. She was vaguely aware that the sheets were growing hot beneath her back, and she smelled smoke, faint but distinctive. Startled, she sat up. "Pyro—"

"It's all right," he said. "I've got it."

Leaning forward, he pressed his lips to her throat. He was right, Teddy decided, reveling in the sensation. Why worry?

Suddenly, Pyro tilted his face away from her, his expression alert. She heard shrill bells, accompanied by shouts and the thunder of running feet.

She sat up. "What?"

A hazy film of smoke floated near the ceiling. Teddy heard shouts in the hallway.

"I think we just set off the fire alarm," Pyro said.

CHAPTER TEN

SHE WAS BACK AT THE YELLOW HOUSE. SHE WANTED to go inside, walk upstairs, and look around. But the door wouldn't budge. She twisted the knob. She jammed the doorbell. She threw her weight against the door once, twice. She woke up drenched in sweat, panic coursing through her.

She was supposed to take her psychic-ability exam this morning. Wasn't she? Wait. Where was she? As her gaze flew about the room, the events of the previous night came rushing back. The party. The vodka. The smoke alarm. Pyro.

She scanned the bedside table. A small clock radio read 9:05 a.m. She was already five minutes late.

Teddy threw back the sheets and leaped out of bed. She staggered, pain slamming right between her eyes. The alcohol, which had provided such relief from her withdrawal symptoms the night before, now made her feel like her head was buried in concrete.

She gathered her clothes. The soft rattle of pills reminded her that she'd tucked her meds in her pocket as a precaution. She lifted the familiar bottle, chewing her lower lip as she studied it. Maybe going cold turkey had been a mistake. One or two pills might knock back the discomfort.

"Don't do it," Pyro said. "I'm sure the doctor told you those things mess with your brain." He closed his eyes again and muttered something that might have been "good luck." Or at least rhymed with "luck."

"Thanks," Teddy said.

"For last night?" he asked, sitting up in bed. As he did, the sheet dropped.

Damn.

"For the advice," Teddy said. She bit her lip again. "About last night . . . just to be clear, I'm not really looking for anything serious. I don't really do the girlfriend thing."

He grinned. "Good. Because I don't really do the boyfriend thing."

"Good. So thanks again."

"That one was for last night, right?"

Teddy rolled her eyes and tried unsuccessfully to hold back a smile. "Yeah, that was for last night." She grabbed her leather jacket and left.

Teddy kept her head down as she walked outside the building. Her stomach recoiled. In hindsight, attending the party probably hadn't been such an amazing idea. She certainly wasn't in the kind of physical or mental shape to face what might be one of the most important tests of her life.

*   *   *

When she stepped inside the classroom, she was officially fifteen minutes late. The stony expressions on Clint's and Boyd's faces told her she might as well walk right back outside. (*Boyd? Really?* Just her luck. She'd heard that everyone else had been tested by Clint and Dunn.)

"So you decided to join us after all," Boyd said.

Teddy ran through Boyd's list of acceptable responses: *Yes, ma'am. No, ma'am. I don't deserve to exist, ma'am.*

"Yes, ma'am."

Clint looked her over and shook his head. Not quite disgusted but close. He looked like a weary beat cop who was tired of hearing the same old bullshit from the same old bullshitter. He folded his arms. "I heard there was a party last night. And certain first-year recruits were there to celebrate their admittance to Whitfield."

So he knew about the party. Maybe that would make him just a *little* sympathetic to her current condition. After all, if everyone was there . . .

"Yes," she said.

"Violated nearly every line of Whitfield's Code of Ethics," he continued.

Teddy felt like she was a teenager again, being grilled for breaking curfew.

"Well?" he asked. "What do you have to say for yourself?"

"Am I grounded?"

Clint didn't smile. "Sit down," he said, gesturing to a chair on the opposite side of the table where he and Boyd sat. "Let's get this over with."

Teddy's old self threatened to make an appearance. She wanted to knock the chair over and tell Clint to go to hell. But Whitfield was her last move. She lowered herself into a chair.

"Whitfield policies mandate two instructors observe psychic-ability exams to document the events that transpire during these sessions," Clint said. "Normally, Professor Dunn would be here, but he's teaching a class this morning. Sergeant Boyd agreed to fill in." He shuffled a stack of papers. "We'll begin with a simple color wheel," he said. "Are you familiar with how this works?"

She shook her head.

"Then let me start with the basics. Psychics—all psychics, no matter how their ability manifests—connect to the world differently than other people. Psychics are able to glean information or manipulate the energy of a person or an object in a way that others find impossible. In short, they sense the insensible and know the unknowable. To accomplish this, psychics rely on their extrasensory perception, or ESP."

She must have made a face at the cliché, for Clint continued, "Don't be put off by the phrase, Teddy. ESP simply means gaining information beyond the basic five physical senses. Are you with me so far?"

Teddy nodded, though her thoughts were still muddled.

Clint gestured to a color chart attached to a spinning wheel—the sort of wheel employed by game-show hosts to award prizes. "This is our first test," he said. "I want to see if you can pick up psychic impressions. At the poker table, you could tell when people were lying, but can you learn to ascertain what people are thinking? It's quite simple. Out of your line of vision, I spin this wheel"—the wheel made a clicking sound as it spun, eventually stopping on yellow—"and when it lands, I will mentally project the color I'm seeing to you. All you have to do is say that color aloud."

Teddy put her fingers to her temple "I'm getting yellow here . . ."

"You already know how I feel about comedy, Cannon," Boyd said.

Clint set up a white partition screen to divide Teddy's side of the table from his own. She could see their faces but nothing else. The wheel was hidden from her view.

Game on.

She imagined she was in Vegas, back at the poker table. It was as if she could feel the felt beneath her fingers. She listened for every click of the wheel like she listened for every shuffle of the cards. All she had to do was guess a color. It was just odds in the end, right? She lived on odds. She listened as the wheel spun, slowed, and stopped. She waited for a color to appear in her mind's eye.

But there was nothing. No color at all.

"Black," she guessed.

Clint made a mark on a form and spun the wheel again. She shut out everything else, the wheezy sound of Boyd's breathing, the smell of Clint's aftershave, the hum of the air conditioner, everything except the click of the wheel.

"Blue?" she said.

Clint spun again and again. Teddy could tell from Boyd's face that she wasn't getting any of the answers right. After the last spin, Teddy asked for some water, and Clint pointed to a pitcher on a counter across the room. Teddy poured herself a glass and gulped it down. With her back to Clint and Boyd, she closed her eyes, desperate to regain her composure.

"You all right?" Clint asked.

She faked a smile. "Absolutely. I'm having a great time."

"Let's move on," Clint said. He put away the color wheel and showed her a deck of flash cards. "These are called Zener cards," he said. "Named after a pioneer in the field of psychic research. Each card features a geometric shape on the reverse. I'll put up the partition and shuffle the cards. Sergeant Boyd will flip over a card one at a time. You name the geometric shape I'm seeing. Got it?"

Teddy took a fortifying breath. She didn't think it was possible to concentrate any harder. Her head was pounding, her mouth dry. Still, she guessed card after card.

Boyd stood abruptly, giving the hem of her boxy jacket a tug. "I think that's all we need to see, recruit."

"Very impressive," Clint said.

Boyd spun around. "Excuse me? We've seen nothing to indicate—"

"Exactly. She got every single question wrong. Fantastically so. That's actually difficult to do. I've never seen anyone get everything wrong."

"Does that mean anything?" Teddy asked.

Clint leaned back in his seat. "You tell me."

"I'm sorry, Corbett, but Ms. Cannon shows absolutely no sign of any psychic ability whatsoever. I think we can safely say she failed the exam."

"She didn't fail. Well, technically, she failed," Clint said. "But that doesn't mean she failed."

Boyd sighed and folded her arms.

Clint ignored her. "Teddy," he said, "what were you focusing on during the tests?"

"What do you mean?"

"I mean, where was your mind during the first two tests?"

Teddy bit her tongue. "On the wheel. And the deck."

"That's what I thought." He smiled.

"I don't know why you're smiling when you just said you've never seen a recruit perform so badly on an exam," Boyd said.

"Teddy," Clint said. "Why do you play poker and not slot machines?"

It took Teddy a second to put it together. And then she felt like an idiot. She took a sip of water from the glass next to her.

"Do you want to tell the sergeant or should I?" Clint asked.

"I read people," Teddy said. "Not wheels or cards."

"Exactly," Clint said. "She shut me out so completely by focusing on the testing devices that she effectively blocked any psychic communication between us. Meaning she failed. But spectacularly."

"I don't see where you're going here, Corbett," Boyd said.

"Where I'm going, Rosemary, is now I'm going to give Teddy a chance to focus on me."

"You think she's a telepath?" Boyd said.

Clint nodded.

A telepath? She could tell if certain people were lying, sure, but her life would have been a hell of a lot easier if she'd known what people were thinking all the time. She could read players, evaluate their behavior, and even guess their actions. But know their thoughts? *You've got to be kidding me.* Teddy stifled a laugh.

"You seem to be the only one finding this amusing, recruit," Boyd said, tapping her clipboard.

"I'm not kidding, Teddy. Just do what you did in Vegas." Clint met her eyes.

"But we're not playing poker. What am I supposed to look for?"

Clint smiled. "Something . . . interesting."

It wasn't a decision to reach out to Clint's mind—it had been a habit since before she could remember—but the force of meeting his consciousness was like nothing she had encountered before. Was it because she was off her meds?

She'd glimpsed one image of Molly, but now she seemed to be turning the pages of a flip-book. She was bombarded with what felt like thousands upon thousands of . . . She wanted to say they were memories. Clint featured prominently in a lot of them. There was a younger Clint in a football uniform, then a military uniform, then a police uniform. Walking through a barren desert. Talking to the same Rosemary Boyd in front of her. Watching Teddy at the casino in Vegas. As soon as she felt had purchase on one image, another would appear. Teddy felt dizzy. If only she could slow them down.

She saw an image of a young Clint, maybe age eight or nine, on a lawn, a black and white dog at his side. In the next, she saw Clint hook the leash on the dog's collar in the yard. In the next, she saw him go into the house. She saw what he did not: that the dog pulled on his leash. That he jumped the fence to chase a red car down the street, into traffic.

In her mind, Teddy yelled: *Stop!*

The image began to fade. Clint's mind grew darker and colder. She wanted to dive back into his consciousness—to see more, learn more—but when she tried to reach out again, she felt as if she had slammed into a metal wall. She opened her eyes, breaking the connection. When she looked up, Clint was standing above her. "Are you okay?"

Teddy looked up at him, confused.

"You cried out for us to stop."

"What did you see, Cannon?" Boyd said.

Teddy turned to Clint. "When you were young, your dog was hit by a car. You felt like it was your fault. It wasn't. You didn't notice that the leash broke."

Clint looked at her, then sat back down. "It seems like a trivial thing to worry about a dog all these years later."

Teddy swallowed. "What just happened in there, Clint? It was like

I could see everything you've ever thought in your entire life."

"Huh," Clint said. He leaned forward, studying Teddy for a moment. "I thought you might be a telepath because you could tell when people were lying." He cleared his throat. "I also practice telepathy, Teddy, but it's aural. I can hear thoughts. I can hear what you're thinking at this exact moment, but I don't have access to anything beyond that." He leaned forward. "What you just demonstrated—what we've never even seen here at Whitfield—was something called *astral* telepathy. You have access to thoughts not only on the physical plane but on the astral one as well. And it seems like you can see them. You can see not only everything I'm thinking at this moment but everything I've ever thought, and one day, maybe, even everything I'll ever think. Astral telepathy provides access to all thoughts, conscious and unconscious, deliberately transmitted or not."

You've really *got to be kidding me.*

Boyd cleared her throat. "I'm sorry, Corbett, but the rules are clear. Protocol states that a new recruit must pass two of three psychic tests. You asked me to stand in and witness the exam. Procedure must be followed. It's only fair."

Clint sighed. "Sergeant, I'm sure we can make an exception here."

Red splotches appeared on Boyd's cheeks. "I wonder if other students were afforded the same treatment as Ms. Cannon." Teddy wondered if the sergeant was remembering her poor performance on the course. Did Boyd think she wasn't up to rigors of Whitfield?

"With all due respect, Sergeant, this is not your area of expertise. Once Professor Dunn hears what happened today, he'll agree with my recommendation."

Boyd nodded. "I see my services are no longer needed." She turned and exited the room, closing the door not loudly enough to be an intentional slam but strongly enough to send a message.

Clint waited a moment. "Congratulations," he said to Teddy. "You passed. But don't get too excited. What just happened here was the easy part. What comes next is harder. It takes discipline. Dedication. Commitment."

She wasn't exactly excited; what she felt was more like relief. "I can do that."

"Which part of showing up fifteen minutes late after dragging yourself out of bed with a hangover is supposed to convince me of that?"

"It's the meds—"

"Excuses won't work anymore. Bottom line, Teddy, and you'll excuse the poker terms, but I need to know that you're all in."

"I am."

Clint stood. "If you decide to stay, you won't catch any more breaks. Boyd was right: being a Whitfield student means playing by the rules. And you'll have to study hard to pass your midyear exam in December. If you don't, you're out. Got it?"

"Loud and clear," Teddy said.

*　　*　　*

Teddy needed some time to think. She'd heard once that fresh air could help a hangover, though she'd never bothered to try it before (her preferred cure being hair of the dog). She flashed her ID and slipped through the campus's checkpoint station, following the rocky coastal path away from the dock.

A flash of something metallic caught Teddy's eye. Pausing, she peered over the rocky ledge to the sea below. Half-hidden by the jutting cliff was a sleek speedboat bobbing on the incoming tide. Someone stood on the stern, cleaning the motor, an assortment of tools spread at his feet. She took a step closer and realized it was Jeremy. So that was where he stashed his boat. If not for that flash, she would have walked right by and never seen it. She carefully maneuvered down the ledge, settling atop a rock to watch Jeremy work. He was methodical, carefully arranging each tool.

He looked up. "Ah," he said. "Hello."

"Nice boat," she said.

He grimaced. "I know I'm not supposed to have one. Because of the rules about leaving the island. But my family lives in San Francisco, and it's nice to visit them. Well, not my family. My dad and my stepmom. So maybe you wouldn't say anything about the boat?"

"What boat?"

He swung around and pointed. "That boat right—" He paused. "Oh."

Not thirty minutes ago, she was trying to convince Clint she could toe the line. And here she was, already breaking another school rule.

"I can give you a ride back to San Francisco if you want," Jeremy said.

"What? Why?"

"You look unhappy. I assumed you failed your test."

"As a matter of fact, I passed."

Jeremy raised his eyebrows. "You did?"

"You don't need to look so surprised."

He shrugged. "Most people celebrate when they pass. You look like you're ready to check out."

She imagined speeding off with Jeremy in his boat. Maybe she'd walk from the pier to some little shop and get a job in San Francisco, then find a room in some apartment with a bunch of grungy twenty-two-year-olds fresh out of college.

"Can I ask you something?" she said.

He shrugged. "Sure."

"Why are you here?"

"Because I want to serve my country."

He said it so quickly that it took her aback. She wanted to say: "You seem so sure." Instead she said: "You sound like Boyd."

Teddy could imagine how Boyd would react to hearing that she had left. So damn smug. That alone was almost enough to make her want to stay.

"I want to put my talents to use," he said. "And what could be a better than keeping us safe?" He fiddled with the lid of his toolbox. "My mom was in Tower Two. As a psychometrist, I could have seen something. I should have studied the clues." He said this with the same flat emotion with which he had offered Teddy a ride back to the mainland. With the same emotion she imagined one would say "I like tuna fish sandwiches" or "It's cold outside today."

"I don't believe," he said, pausing as if considering his words carefully, "that the future is set in stone. I don't believe that we aren't supposed to change it. We wouldn't have these gifts otherwise."

Teddy thought about that as she rattled the bottle of pills in her pocket. She had talents, too. She didn't have any idea how they could be put to good use, but the thought of finding out, the possibility of sharing Jeremy's certainty . . . She realized that Jeremy Lee had inspired her. Him, of all people.

"But like I said," Jeremy added, "if you want a ride back to the main—"

"No," she said, swallowing hard. "I want to stay."

"You mean right here?" he asked, pointing down at the slab of rock she was standing on, overlooking the water.

"No," she said, laughing. "Here." She spread her arms toward the campus. Clint had made it clear that if she wanted to succeed at Whitfield, she had to be all in. Teddy reached into her pocket, took out the bottle of pills, and flung it as hard as she could out into the water.

"What was that?" Jeremy asked.

Teddy dusted her hands. "Old habits," she said, and she didn't look back.

CHAPTER ELEVEN

TEDDY AND FIRST DAYS OF SCHOOL DIDN'T REALLY, WELL, mix. Think oil and water, toothpaste and orange juice, Taylor and Katy. On her first day of kindergarten, Teddy punched her teacher in the face. On her first day of high school, she got drunk after fifth period and threw up on the bus ride home. On her first day of Stanford, she placed her first bet before her first class, screwing up everything before a professor could even call her name from the roster. On first days, that feeling of anxiety plagued her. When people tried their best to fit it, they always lied.

On the first official day of classes at the Whitfield Institute for Law Enforcement Training and Development, Teddy was determined to break the pattern. She woke up early. She showered. She put on a clean shirt. She ate breakfast (if you could call chia seeds breakfast; really, weren't they tadpole eggs?). And then she followed the rest of the first-year students to Fort McDowell for her first class, Introduction to Seership.

Ivy had taken over most of the stucco facade, and red bricks lined the roofs. It seemed strange that a subject as unconventional as seership would take place in a building with such a regimented history.

Next to her, Jillian shivered. "This place gives me bad vibes."

"Ghosts?" Teddy asked.

Jillian nodded. "Something."

Teddy turned to see writing on a wall plaque outside the entrance. She ran her hand over the embossed metal.

IN RECOGNITION
OF THOSE WHO PASSED THROUGH ANGEL ISLAND
AND WERE NOT WELCOMED,
OF THOSE WHO WERE TURNED AWAY,
OF THOSE WHO WERE TREATED UNFAIRLY
BECAUSE THEY WERE DIFFERENT,
AND BECAUSE THOSE DIFFERENCES WERE FEARED.
MAY WE REMEMBER THAT IT IS OUR DIFFERENCES
THAT MAKE US STRONGER.
ANGEL ISLAND, 1910–1954

From behind her, Dara said, "Angel Island was the Ellis Island of the West. Mostly Chinese, Japanese, and Korean immigrants came through here. During World War Two, it was basically an internment camp. In the fifties, California voted to make it into a park." She nodded to Jillian. "No wonder it gives Ms. Medium the creeps." Dara wrinkled her nose. "Though I thought she could only talk to animals?"

Teddy guessed none of them knew the extent of their powers—at least not yet.

She turned back to the plaque. The American government had turned on its own citizens. She technically would be working for the government one day; what if she disagreed with their policies? Would she still have to serve, as she had promised Clint?

* * *

Those questions stayed with her as she took her seat and waited for Professor Dunn. And waited. He entered the classroom—his T-shirt today listed the dates of AC/DC's 1980 *Back in Black* tour—and launched into his lecture without introduction.

"You may think," he said, "because you're here to study seership, that I'm about touchy-feely mumbo-jumbo. But you would be wrong." His harsh words were at odds with his laid-back appearance. Teddy bit her lip in an effort not to laugh. She kept her eyes on Dunn, refusing to look at Jillian, who would be crestfallen. Jillian loved mumbo-jumbo.

Dunn continued, "We're going to be approaching the art of parapsychology through science. Because this is a science." He began to walk through the aisles, looking at each of the recruits. "Without a foundation in the science of psychic ability, there's no way to expand on the power you already have. And if you don't expand that power, you will fail your midyear exam in December. And if you fail, you're out."

Besides her knack of guessing when people were lying, which seemed to be irrelevant when dealing with psychics, Teddy had only once demonstrated any psychic ability—the day before, with Clint. She looked around the room, trying not to feel like an imposter. She would have to figure it out before that exam.

You're not dressed in a fat suit and a wig, pretending to be someone else. This is the real you. You belong in this room.

Dunn went on, "Psychics see, smell, touch, feel, taste, sense, know what is unknown. And that is the definition of seership: seeing the unseeable—not with our eyes but with our minds. Only then will we know the unknowable. That practice begins with meditation—"

There was an audible groan from the back of the class. "I thought you said we weren't doing any hippie-dippie crap?" Zac Rogers yelled out.

"What makes you think that changing your neurochemical makeup is 'hippie-dippie'? The more focused your brain, the more focused your psychic ability. I have degrees in astrophysics and neurochemistry from Berkeley. I spent a decade in India studying with a swami. I use both Eastern and Western science in this classroom. That's how we get the full picture on what it means to be psychic."

"But what about the cool stuff?" Zac said. "You know, like mental attacks?"

"That's a very specific—and advanced—type of telepathic communication. And there's no way to master that until you master the basics of telepathy. And you can't master the basics of telepathy until you master meditation."

Dara asked what a mental attack was, exactly, and Dunn looked thoughtful. "We're getting ahead of ourselves, but it's when one mind breaches another mind through uninvited mental connection."

Teddy thought back to the casino. Was that what Clint had done to Sergei and the guards? They hadn't seemed like they were under attack. They didn't resist. They didn't struggle. They had just done what Clint had wanted them to do.

"Today we're talking about the brain and its structure." Dunn walked back to the front of the classroom and pulled down a large-scale diagram of the human brain. "You're going to become very familiar with this over the next month."

After class, Teddy wished that the rest of the time had been as exciting as Zac's interruption. Instead, she had a notebook full of brain facts to memorize and an hour of meditation homework. On top of that, Dunn had instructed the first-years to recount their dreams to their roommates each morning, then record them for future analysis of precognition and premonition.

Teddy looked to an equally befuddled Jillian as they exited Dunn's classroom. "Not what you expected, either, huh?" she said.

Jillian shook her head.

The two began to walk toward Harris Hall for lunch. A thought had been nagging at Teddy all morning: she hadn't spoken to her parents. After every bad first day, her parents had been there to talk. Even though there was a no-tech-on-campus rule, she had heard there were phones in the office available for students to use. As they passed the main office in Fort McDowell, Teddy told Jillian to go on ahead.

The woman who sat behind the front desk looked as old as the fort itself. Teddy cleared her throat. "Excuse me?"

"Yes?" the woman said.

"I heard there were phones in the office available to make personal calls?"

"Do you have a phone card?"

Teddy shook her head.

The woman sighed and slid a piece of plastic across to Teddy. "This should have ten minutes left on it. Phones are the second door on your left. Buy a phone card next time you're in town."

Teddy opened the door and took a seat at one of the phone booths. Luckily, no one else was in the room. She hadn't used a pay phone since maybe . . . ever? She punched in the digits on the card and then dialed the familiar numbers of her parents' home line. It was early in the afternoon, and her mom was sure to be home.

The phone rang once, twice, and then after the third ring, her mom's voice came on: "Hello?"

"Mom?"

"Oh, Teddy! Is that you? We were so worried. We didn't know . . . You left a note, but . . . Oh, sweetie."

"Mom, I'm fine." There was something about those words that made the events of the last two days feel very, very real. She had followed a stranger across the country to study at a school for psychics— because she was *psychic*. What was more, she had learned there was a possibility that her birth parents had been psychic, too.

Her mom sounded relieved. "So how is it, this new school?"

"Good." Teddy wanted to ask about her birth parents, but she'd been through it before—her mother and father didn't know much. The story was always the same: car crash. And every time Teddy brought it up, she knew it hurt them. So she just told her mom some meaningless nonsense about liking her instructors.

"You have a real opportunity there, Teddy."

"I know," Teddy said, trying not to roll her eyes. She knew her mother would somehow sense the action even through the phone.

"Teddy—" her mom began, but their conversation was interrupted by a beep, signaling that the phone card was running out of time.

"Gotta go, Mom."

"One last thing," her mom said. "We only get so many chances in life. Stanford was a chance. This is another. Learn from your mistakes. Don't make the same one twice."

Through the window, Teddy saw Pyro wave. Was last night a mistake, too? In that moment, she decided her life would be all about studying until the midyear exam. She would do everything in her power to succeed at Whitfield. To not blow this last chance.

"I won't, Mom." She hoped she wouldn't.

"Okay, good. I love you."

The line went dead; she'd run out of time. But Teddy still said "I love you, too," before hanging up.

CHAPTER TWELVE

TEDDY TRIED TO KEEP HER PROMISE TO FOCUS ON schoolwork. The early days of October brought damp fog and lower temperatures to the island, and the daily grind of classes became routine. Meditation. Theory. Forensics and Police Procedure. Trips to the shooting range. Self-defense. No lecture elicited the same thrill as Professor Dunn's first one. Teddy had forgone other thrills as well—namely, a certain bad boy with tattoos and a talent for setting school linens on fire. December, and with it the midyear exam, loomed.

The first-year recruits sat on yoga mats in the Seership classroom, waiting for Dunn to show up—late, as usual. Teddy clicked her pen again and again. "How can a guy who's supposed to be in a constant state of Zen always be late?" she said to Jillian.

"I think he's brilliant," said Ava, who was sitting behind them.

"You know you don't have to kiss the professor's ass when he's not in the room, right?" Dara said.

Ava flipped her hair over her shoulder. "Whatever."

When Dunn finally walked into the room, he dropped his backpack on his desk and began without preamble. "Last class, we discussed how the pineal gland is believed to be the seat of psychic power."

On the wall behind him were two diagrams, one of the brain and the other a picture of a human body with the location of chakras, which apparently weren't touchy-feely mumbo-jumbo. "Consider this location from a metaphysical as well as a scientific approach: the pineal gland is controlled by the sixth chakra, which, as you know, is considered the chakra that rules extrasensory power." Dunn looked around the room.

Jillian, Dara, and even Pyro swore they could feel a tingling in each chakra when they focused their mind. Teddy had yet to experience anything, but she was operating on fake it till you make it.

"If you've all been meditating regularly, putting theory to practice should be an easy transition," Dunn said.

There was a stir in the classroom. At last! They were finally going to *do* something psychic. Teddy just hoped she wouldn't embarrass herself.

Dunn went to the chalkboard. He drew two circles and then connected them with a line. "Physical telepathy—the ability for two minds to consciously and deliberately send and receive messages. Think of it like two tin cans connected by a string. One person sends a message down a channel for the other to receive. In this instance, brain waves act like sound waves."

Teddy leaned forward. Telepathy. This was supposedly her jam, although she hadn't yet told any of the other Misfits. Her psychic ability wasn't flashy: she couldn't start fires, or predict a death, or talk to animals. She sometimes felt like the remedial student in a class of overachievers, especially here, in Seership. All she had was her instincts. Now she could finally prove why she deserved to be at Whitfield.

Dunn continued, "As you know, I am opposed to judgments of any kind. We are all on different spiritual journeys, and one path is as valid as another. However, the purpose of Whitfield Institute is to train students to utilize their psychic ability in a position that serves the greater good. To that end, the ability to communicate telepathically will play a crucial role in your future careers. You will be tested on this skill in your midyear exam. Those of you who fail will be asked to leave."

She couldn't fail.

Dunn assigned each of them a partner for the first exercise. Teddy was hoping for Jillian or Dara or Molly or even Pyro, despite the obvious distraction.

"Cannon, you're with . . ." Dunn scanned the room. "Molly Quinn."

"Thank God," muttered Kate Atkins.

Teddy was about to take umbrage on Molly's behalf. After all, Molly was a little quiet, but she wasn't bad. Then Teddy realized Kate was talking about her.

"You have a problem with me?" Teddy said to her. Teddy had yet to see Kate crack a smile.

"I like working with people who have some sense of discipline," Kate said, her eyes moving from Teddy's leather jacket to her badass boots.

"And I like working with people who don't have a stick up their—"

"Each team will receive a deck of playing cards," Dunn said. "One student will select a card at random and act as the projector, then use telepathy to communicate that information to their partner, the receiver.

"There are many different ways to perform this task, but here at Whitfield, we begin with auditory telepathy. I want you all to imagine that you and your partner have walkie-talkies inside your head and you have to tune in to the same channel in order to hear each other. Agree on a number, visualize it in your mind. The key here is to use your breathing and meditation to sync to that channel and to your partner's consciousness." He paused, gazing about the room. "This exercise requires a complete state of mutual trust and respect. Active emotional vulnerability coupled with firm belief in your partner's psychic talent. There's no way to communicate without it."

Molly gave Teddy a look. Teddy guessed even Molly wasn't thrilled to be her partner.

Dunn distributed packs of playing cards. Excellent. This she could do. She tore the plastic off the package and shuffled the cards, the weight of the deck beautifully familiar, the cards themselves slick in her hands. She alternated her fancy shuffle with pivot cuts, her hands flying around the deck. That was when Ben Tucker spoke: "Where did you learn to do *that*?"

When Teddy looked up, she noticed half the class staring at her. She shrugged, self-conscious. These people didn't need to know about her past. "Some of us didn't spend our teenage years hanging out at the mall," she said.

"Let's just get this over with," Molly said, as if about to get a cavity filled.

I don't suck. You suck.

Teddy put the deck on the table. "After you."

Molly nodded and picked up the cards. "I'll project."

"Remember," Dunn announced from the front of the room, "get on the same channel. Imagine the walkie-talkie in your mind. Sync up your breathing and connect consciousnesses before you begin. Physical contact helps to start."

Teddy reached out her hand to Molly. "Should we pick a channel for our psychic radio?" Teddy asked.

"Sure," Molly said, taking Teddy's hand. "How about three?"

In her head, Teddy closed her eyes, imagining a set of old yellow walkie-talkies that her dad had bought her when they'd gone camping on her ninth birthday. She wondered where the walkie-talkies were now—probably somewhere in the basement. In her mind, she turned the dial to the number 3, trying to sync to Molly's breathing.

Teddy opened her eyes as Molly slipped a card from the middle of the deck, looked at it, set it facedown, and then stared, wide-eyed, at Teddy. But Teddy didn't hear anything. Not even static. Ben Tucker, another telepath, was the first to successfully receive a communication. All around, Teddy heard other classmates naming cards, followed by whoops. A familiar feeling of defeat rose within her. The same feeling she'd gotten when she'd lost big at poker, when she'd been fired from another crappy job, when she'd called her parents to tell them she was coming home from Stanford. But Teddy closed her eyes again, determined.

She gave up on the walkie-talkie idea. Instead, she pretended she was at a poker table. That Molly was an opponent across from her. She reached out to Molly's mind, hoping to see the card. She'd landed on something the first day they'd met; maybe she could again. But instead, when she reached out to Molly's mind, her mouth went dry and her skin grew hot. She saw a wall of gold . . . or was it sand? Teddy imagined brushing against it, feeling the coarse grains between her fingertips. She imagined the strongest wind scattering the sand, blasting it apart; she saw the wall—a dune, really—crumble before her. Then:

Whoa.

Beyond the wall, emerging from the inky darkness in her mind's eye, she saw the card.

Four of clubs.

Her palms were sweaty—no, she was sweaty everywhere, hair plastered to her forehead. Something clicked, and that old plugged-in feeling she had chased at the poker table gripped her. It felt like she'd stuck her finger in an electrical socket. She could see every card held by every student in the room.

Ace of diamonds, three of hearts, six of clubs, jack of spades, queen of hearts.

She felt a jolt before the cards faded away, and she was bombarded by new images. She saw Pyro in the cop car, the night his partner was shot, crying. She saw Jeremy Lee on the morning of 9/11, trying to call his mother on the phone. She saw Molly hacking in to the CIA mainframe. These were memories, she realized. There were more of them, ones she couldn't comprehend, couldn't place. Ava shoplifting from an expensive department store. Liz taking steroids before a competition. Molly—

Like a computer losing power, her mind's eye went dark. And then everything else did, too.

*　　*　　*

Teddy blinked and looked at the ceiling, confused about how she had ended up on the floor. The last thing she remembered was that she was in class, sitting with Molly . . .

Oh, God.

Teddy sat up quickly only to find Molly also sprawled across the floor. In fact, everyone seemed to be rubbing their foreheads, dazed. And then everyone turned toward her. Before she could think of what to say or do, the room tilted sideways. Her stomach heaved, brilliant white lights exploded before her eyes, and excruciating pain reverberated through her skull.

Oh, God, not now. Please not now.

She knew the symptoms. She was about to have a seizure. She was epileptic, after all.

She stumbled to her feet and lurched toward the door. She barely made it into the hallway, the hum of voices growing louder behind her, when Dunn grabbed her elbow. "Teddy, are you all right?" he asked, his brow furrowed.

She managed a nod. If she could just get to her room, there was a chance she wouldn't—

"That was an incredible display of astral telepathy," he said. "I haven't seen anything like that in years."

Teddy clutched the wall. "I didn't mean to."

"Clint mentioned, but . . ." His words swam together; he was speaking gibberish now. Teddy gave another nod. When she moved her head, the edges of her vision began to blur; the hallway was tunneling before her.

This is really going to hurt.

And then everything went dark again.

CHAPTER THIRTEEN

TEDDY OPENED HER EYES. SHE WAS LYING DOWN, tucked into a bed that wasn't hers. The room, with its pale blue walls and flimsy white curtains, wasn't hers, either. A glance out the window revealed the bright afternoon sun. She blinked, confusion giving way to worry. It didn't matter whose bed she was in. She had to get up. She was late for Seership.

"You're awake." Molly stood at the door to the room. "Feeling okay?"

Whenever Teddy had a seizure, there were gaps of unaccounted time. It took a few minutes for her brain to put together the pieces now: she'd already been to class. The events of hours earlier slammed into her. Professor Dunn's lecture, Dara and Ava arguing, Kate goading Teddy on, a deck of cards.

An entire classroom of people had seen her stagger into the hall and pass out. Teddy's head throbbed. She was embarrassed. She tried to avoid Molly's gaze and focused on the items mounted on the wall just to her right: hypodermic needle container, emergency call button, blood pressure cuff.

"I'm at the infirmary?"

"It was quite a fall," Molly said, stepping closer.

"How bad was the seizure?" Teddy asked.

"Seizure?" Molly's brows drew together. She came to a stop beside Teddy's bed.

"I—" Teddy began, then she stopped, trying to remember. She recalled a pounding headache, the flashing lights, the dizzying disorientation—everything that indicated a seizure was imminent. "Tell me what happened."

"We were practicing telepathy," Molly said. "Things got . . . strange." She shifted uncomfortably, as if unsure whether she should reveal the rest.

"We're at a school for psychics; everything is strange," Teddy said.

Molly let out a breath. "You didn't just receive the thought I projected—you went into *everyone's* heads. Just jumped right in. It's kind of a faux pas among psychics, actually. They have a line about it in the Code of Ethics. You should have heard Liz Cook go on about it."

"Am I in trouble?" Teddy asked. She immediately thought of Clint and his warnings, of Boyd and her obvious desire to see Teddy out of school for any minor infraction.

Molly looked confused. "Trouble? Are you kidding me? Everyone thought you were amazing—well, except Liz. Dunn said there's a name for what you did. It's called—"

"Astral telepathy. Clint told me when I took my exam," Teddy said.

"Why didn't you tell anyone?"

Teddy shrugged. She'd done it only the one time. "I have no control over it, Molly. Part of me isn't fully convinced I'm not epileptic."

"Dunn said that wasn't a seizure. It's just what happens when you're psychically overstimulated. Your body shuts down. Something like that used to happen to me, too." Teddy thought she saw Molly shudder. "We all react to our abilities in different ways."

Teddy stared at the ceiling as she tried to process what Molly had said. Even though Clint had told her the same thing months ago, she found it hard to let go of the past. Especially after what appeared to have been a seizure. For as long as she could remember, she had thought she was the victim of shitty brain chemistry and neurons that randomly and repeatedly misfired. Five-five, dark hair, pale blue eyes, epileptic.

Because for those few brief seconds, when she'd slammed through the mental barriers that separated her from her classmates, Teddy hadn't felt like a victim. Instead, she'd felt completely in control. And even more than that—she had felt *powerful*. Well, until she'd passed out. So why had it taken her so long to believe that maybe something wasn't *wrong* with her but *right*?

It was the same feeling she had when she was riding high at a poker table. When she knew that the player across the table was bluffing. When she could see the unseen. It wasn't the risk she liked, it was the certainty. She shivered as the realization began to form in her mind that what she loved best about poker hadn't made her a gambler at all but, at heart, a psychic.

Teddy blinked away tears. Her throat squeezed shut and her breath caught. She was too overwhelmed to hide her feelings anymore.

"I'm happy for you," Molly said.

Teddy turned, stunned to see the tears she'd struggled to hold back also brimming in Molly's eyes.

"Empath, remember?" Molly pointed to her temple. "I can feel what you're feeling. Not that I want to. I don't. I really, really don't. I just can't help it sometimes."

"I feel . . ." Teddy struggled to catalog the emotions careening within her: anger, fear, joy, sadness, and something else, something more important than all the others. "Relief."

"No kidding." Molly gave a choked laugh. "So knock it off, all right?"

The two were quiet for a minute.

"Did I miss anything important in class after"—Teddy gestured to her head—"you know?"

"No, you pretty much caused a standstill. Especially after you discovered that Liz used steroids."

"I said that out loud?" Teddy groaned. "I don't remember doing that." She tried to recall the information she had gleaned while inside her classmates' minds, but it was fragments, too jumbled to make sense of.

"Remember any other juicy tidbits about the Alphas?" Molly winked.

Teddy tilted her head. As she looked at Molly, a memory came flooding back. Well, not a memory but a feeling. The last psychic impression, before contact had been broken, had been with Molly. Molly, upset—or had she been frightened? She definitely hadn't wanted Teddy in her mind: that, Teddy was sure of. She remembered brushing up against a wall, like in Clint's mind. Clint's wall had been steel; Molly's . . . was it sand?

Molly shifted in her seat. Teddy had to remind herself that Molly couldn't read her thoughts, just her emotions. Teddy rubbed her forehead. "It's kind of been a long day," she said.

Molly looked tired, too. Teddy guessed her own emotional whirlwind had taken a toll on Molly. Teddy smiled, trying to change the subject. "I'll let you know if anything comes to me later."

Molly was about to say something when she was interrupted by a series of coughs at the door. Jeremy, deliberately trying to get their attention. "I thought I would bring Teddy notes from the Forensics class she missed," he said. "I was looking for you, Molly, since you skipped, too."

"I was going to find you later, but I wanted to check on Teddy first," Molly said. They were turning into *that* couple—the kind who couldn't be out of each other's sight longer than ten minutes. Considering Molly's empathic abilities, codependency seemed both annoying and unhealthy.

Teddy slid her legs off the bed. She was ready to get out of this place. "How'd I get to the clinic, anyway?"

"Pyro brought you," Jeremy said, stepping into the room.

Teddy had been avoiding him since their night together. "What do you mean?" she asked. "Like on a stretcher?"

"The whole class followed you out to the hall. Total mayhem. Even Dunn couldn't get it under control. So Pyro basically just told everyone to back off, then picked you up and carried you in here," Jeremy said.

Teddy, who'd been poking around under the cot for her boots, straightened and looked at Jeremy. "He did?" Her lips twitched and threatened to curl into an idiotic grin.

Molly flushed bright red. "You're forgetting the empath thing," she said.

Teddy blushed, too.

"Should I also be blushing?" Jeremy asked, handing Teddy the boot she hadn't managed to find.

As Teddy tied her laces, Jeremy subjected them to a brief forensics lecture, warning them that they had a quiz the next day. Speaking with clinical precision, Jeremy explained rigor mortis, or how the stiffness of a corpse could help determine the time of death; algor mortis, how the body's temperature helped pinpoint the time of death; and livor mortis, how the settling of the blood helped to determine the position of a body at death.

In short: decomposing bodies? Really effective mood killer.

Jeremy's recap was interrupted by Nurse Bell at the door. "Professor Corbett wants to see Ms. Cannon. You're fine to get up and walk around now." She nodded toward Molly and Jeremy. "So that means visiting time's over."

"You think Liz's already reported me?" Teddy said, only half joking. Being called to Clint's office wasn't part of her kick-ass-at-school-until-exams plan.

"It's highly probable," Jeremy said.

"Jeremy," Molly said. "That's not funny."

Part of Teddy wanted to ask Molly and Jeremy to stay. But she'd broken the rules. Again. Now she'd have to face Clint . . . and the consequences.

CHAPTER FOURTEEN

WHEN TEDDY REACHED CLINT'S OFFICE IN FORT MC-Dowell, she hesitated. Should she knock? Wait until he called?

"You can come in, Teddy," he said.

How does he always know what I'm thinking—

"If your thoughts weren't so loud, I might not have such an easy time hearing them."

He was sitting in a chair by the window, wearing an old police academy sweatshirt and reading glasses. The gym-professor look seemed at odds with the array of psychic bric-a-brac that lined the crowded office.

"Heard you had quite a morning," he said, putting down a file. He gestured to the wooden chair in front of his desk, so Teddy sat. She was definitely in trouble.

"Did Liz talk to you?" she asked.

"Ms. Cook gave me quite an earful."

"I didn't mean to"—Teddy threw her arms up—"do that astral telepathy thing."

They looked at each other a moment longer, before Clint cracked a grin. "I heard it was awesome."

Relief surged again in Teddy's chest—that new, welcome feeling—and she couldn't help smiling, too.

"Ms. Cook and Professor Dunn told me their versions of events. I'd like to hear yours." Clint leaned back in his chair. "Tell me as much as you can remember. What you felt, what you did, what you saw."

Teddy shifted. "It just sort of . . . happened."

Clint leaned forward until his elbows rested on his desk. "Close your eyes and try to put yourself back there in your mind. Sometimes it helps to repeat actions that occurred the first time. What were you doing when you started?"

Teddy thought a moment. "Shuffling cards."

Clint opened a drawer and handed her a worn pack. Teddy began shuffling the deck, the action so familiar that it allowed her to relax. She recalled her frustration as she'd tried to connect with Molly using Dunn's walkie-talkie exercise. How she'd doubled down, and something had clicked into place. And then she could see everything. Not just playing cards but thoughts, feelings, memories, secrets. Then the connection had broken and she'd collapsed.

"Why do you think the connection broke?" Clint asked, leaning forward.

"I felt," Teddy began, remembering the grit of sand underneath her fingers, packed and rough, "a wall." She scanned Clint's face for a sign of encouragement. "It sounds stupid, but I brushed up against a wall made of sand." She cut the deck and shuffled and then repeated the process. "You have a wall, too, I think, but it feels different. Smooth, cold, like steel." When her words ran dry, she looked up to find Clint watching her.

"I hoped that, given the opportunity, you'd be able to unlock your potential here at Whitfield." His choice of words struck Teddy as odd. Almost parental. Of course, he had personally recruited her and fought Boyd to ensure her place at Whitfield.

His forehead creased. "It must have been Ms. Quinn's wall that broke the connection. Interesting. I didn't know she had gotten that far in her defense training." Clint walked over to a small chalkboard in the corner of his office. He was in teacher mode. "The kind of psychic ability I think of myself an expert in is mental influence—I can manipulate others through psychic communication."

So that's what he did in Vegas.

"Yes, that's what I did to your pursuers in Vegas," he said without turning around. Teddy gritted her teeth. She didn't like that he could read her thoughts so easily.

"If you want to keep me out, you better pay attention." Clint drew some circles and arrows on the board. "The theory behind astral telepathy is based on what you're learning with Dunn. Tin cans. You and your classmates are practicing sending messages down a shared cord. Except astral telepathy works more like . . ." He paused, searching for the metaphor. "Free Wi-Fi. Like you're a hub that other networks hook up to wirelessly and automatically. You can go into others' minds without agreeing to use a cord. Until you run into a firewall." He drew a horizontal line between the two circles, cutting them off. "Trained psychics—meaning those trained in mental defense—will all have some sort of firewall blocking you from entrance." Clint continued to add to the diagram, wrapped up in his own train of thought.

Teddy took the moment to study the objects on his desk. Several large crystals, physics textbooks, psychic pamphlets. But one object stood out to Teddy: a screw encased in glass. It was so menial—so unpsychic but so well preserved—that it seemed out of place.

"Usually, we teach mental defense in the second year. But who knows what else may be possible? Likely the astral telepathy means you can also master astral projection and telekinesis."

"What, like moving things with my mind? Like *Carrie*?"

He continued, barely registering Teddy's questions now. "Dunn would explain it better. Think of it this way: inside every physical body is an astral body with an astral self, the seat of your mind and soul. For most people, including psychics, astral bodies are tied to physical bodies. Today your astral body became untied. It visited your classmates' conscious and then subconscious minds. If you can learn control, you can learn how to project your astral body—on both planes. How to use it to move matter on the physical plane. How to use it to travel on the astral plane. The possibilities are endless."

She wasn't really following what Clint was saying. Did he mean teleportation was a thing? Teddy rubbed her forehead. It was still sore from earlier, and Clint's explanation wasn't making it any better. "So what happens next?" she asked. "I just keep working on that astral thing?"

"Definitely not." He laughed. "Pacing, Teddy. You don't put a new diver on an Olympic platform and tell him to jump."

"But—"

"Just because you've demonstrated an ability to perform astral telepathy doesn't mean that you're ready to use it. Mastering psychic skills take time, practice, and moral responsibility. That's why Whitfield is a four-year program. We don't want our recruits rushing headlong into anything without first building a solid foundation."

Teddy shifted in her seat. She'd just learned that she could fly, psychically speaking, and Clint wanted to ground her.

"Here's what I'm willing to do," he said. "Second-year recruits work closely with tutors to develop their specific psychic abilities. I'll begin your tutorial process now, but only if you agree to do it my way."

"What does that mean?"

"It means we start at the bottom and work our way up. Before we do anything, you need to learn mental defense."

"You mean I need to build my wall."

"Exactly." Clint made his way back to his desk. "And then maybe we'll start with telekinesis. We don't have any telekinetics at Whitfield at the moment, and the ability is highly sought after in government service. Mental influence as well. It's a psychic skill that walks a delicate ethical line and should be used only when absolutely necessary. In the wrong hands, it can be deadly."

Teddy shivered, his words leading her to imagine the worst: What if someone could influence her? Tell to walk off the cliffs overlooking the bay? Or stop breathing? The lighthearted exercises in Seership could be so easily twisted. She had to remember that this wasn't a game. The ultimate goal wasn't to beat the Alphas; there was something larger at stake.

"You and I will meet for private tutorials once a week. Until then, work on your mental defense: start building your wall. It can be made of anything, but make it strong, Teddy. Throughout the day, as you're walking to class, talking to your peers, eating lunch, imagine placing a barrier around your mind. Do it until it becomes second nature. That's the first way you can stop someone who wants to gain access where you are most vulnerable." Clint looked directly at Teddy as if reassessing her.

Teddy avoided his gaze, her eyes moving again to the screw on Clint's desk. "Got any other loose screws?" she said. "Or just this one?"

Clint picked up the screw. Underneath the glass, Teddy could see a date and a symbol engraved in gold. It looked like the number 3, overlapped in a series of concentric circles, underneath the year 1994.

"Special football award or something?"

Clint looked down. "No." He took a deep breath. "It's to remind me that when you're missing one piece, a piece as small as a screw, the machine will fall apart." He looked back at Teddy. "One gap in your wall, and you'll fall apart, too. Next week we'll meet here. Same time."

Teddy knew she had been dismissed. She got out of the chair, then paused. "Thanks," she said, stopping herself from adding *for believing in me,* because it was just too cringeworthily corny.

"It doesn't matter how much I believe in you," Clint said. "You have to believe in yourself."

Okay, that was even more *cringeworthy.*

"Work on your wall. And get out of here already," Clint said, returning to his paperwork. "It's last call at Harris for dinner. And I'll see you tomorrow for our first Empathy 101 class." Teddy had almost forgotten that the next day they would begin a new class—Clint's famous seminar.

*   *   *

Teddy headed straight to Harris Hall. The dining room was full of the usual laughter and conversation that accompanied meals at Whitfield. But the second she stepped inside, the noise level abruptly dropped. Whispers whipped across the tables. Some students leaned forward to confer with classmates, while others craned their necks to get a better look at her.

Every person in the room was psychic. Why single her out for freak status? She lifted her chin, meeting their curious looks with a ferocious don't-mess-with-me glare.

As Teddy settled into a seat at the Misfit table, Jillian raised a shot glass brimming with wheatgrass juice. "All hail my roommate, psychic goddess." The others raised their glasses.

Teddy reddened. "It wasn't a big deal."

Jillian lowered her glass. "You should be proud of yourself. I am. For weeks, *weeks*, I've watched you struggle. We all thought you must have pulled strings or something to get in here."

"The point is," Dara added, "when opportunity knocks—"

"Jillian's probably inside doing naked yoga," Teddy said.

"The point is," Dara repeated, "when you suddenly become legend at a school full of legendary people, you take advantage of it." She nodded toward a table full of upperclassmen who were staring at her. "Scare them a little, would you?" Dara asked. Teddy laughed.

"How did you do it?" Jeremy said, setting out a pen and paper from his backpack as if to take notes.

"Turns out I'm an astral telepath," she said. "Clint's going to help me control it. Don't worry, I won't always be reading your thoughts."

"Hold on," Molly said. "You're studying with Professor Corbett one-on-one?"

"He rarely takes on individual students," Jeremy added.

Out of the corner of her eye, Teddy looked at Pyro, who had been silent since she sat down; she willed him to help her change the subject. Though he'd been the one to rescue her earlier, now he put his hands up as if to say "Don't look at me."

Fine. If that's how he wants to play it.

Teddy turned back to her dinner tray. She was starving. She'd skipped lunch, but it was more than that—she felt drained.

"Anyway, Teddy's a star, and we should celebrate," Jillian said. "I'd like to toast with something shaken, stirred, or on the rocks." She slid a glass of wheatgrass to the edge of her tray. "Let's go to the Cantina."

Dara laughed. "What do you say, Teddy? Are you game?"

She was exhausted, but she needed to take her mind off of walls and astral bodies, Liz Cook's complaints, and Molly's secrets. And the only way Teddy knew how to do that was via booze and boys. Teddy tried to catch Pyro's eye again, but he was focused on his wheatgrass. "I'm in," she said.

CHAPTER FIFTEEN

IT WAS A BREEZY NIGHT. THE WIND BLEW OFF THE bay as Teddy and her friends crowded around a table at the Cantina. The stars were bright, the margaritas were cold, her friends were loud. She felt like she could sit in this spot forever.

Since they weren't supposed to mention Whitfield when they were off campus, Dara turned their conversations into a drinking game: anyone who let anything slip about their lessons had to take a shot. Even the most oblique reference was off limits, as there were civilians nearby. One man in particular caught Teddy's attention. He was hanging out by a railing, but he was standing so close and so still that it seemed possible he was listening to their conversation.

"What about you, Teddy?" Dara asked.

"Me?" she said, only vaguely aware that they had been talking about boys. Or maybe not. The margaritas had made the conversations sound fuzzy and distant.

Dara tsked, impatient. "Have a crush on anyone?" she said.

Teddy looked at Pyro, beside her. She placed her hand on Pyro's lower back, then felt him tense. She promptly removed her hand. They hadn't exactly spoken about that night, but she assumed Pyro would welcome a friend with occasional benefits. Apparently, she'd misread things.

Teddy took a long sip of her margarita. "I'll let you know when I do."

Jillian laughed. "As if it wasn't the two of you who set off the fire alarm in the dorm our first week."

Pyro grabbed one of the shots lined up in the middle of the table and pushed it toward Jillian. "That counts."

"I didn't say the name of the dorm," she protested. "We could go to any school."

He nudged the shot a little closer. "Hey, I don't make the rules."

"Whatever," she said.

"I'll take one, too," Teddy said. She downed the shot in a single gulp.

Teddy missed the table when she slammed her shot glass back down. It went tumbling onto the wooden floor, and then off it rolled as if on a mission. She rose, intending to chase it. But the glass came to a stop when it reached the polished dress shoe of the man she'd noticed earlier.

He bent to pick it up and handed it to Teddy. She opened her mouth to say thanks, but when she looked at his face, she stopped cold.

She knew this guy.

Teddy closed her eyes for a second, trying to place him. Athletic. But not in a vain gym-rat way. No, this guy was almost rugged. He wore a blue oxford shirt with the sleeves rolled up. She glanced down at his hand, wrapped around the neck of a Dos Equis bottle. As she stared at the corded muscles of his arm, it came to her.

"Oh, God," she said. "It's you."

He smiled. "Plain ol' Nick."

"What are you doing here?" she asked. She'd lost all her money to this guy that night back at the Bellagio. She assumed she'd never see him again. Yet here he was on Angel Island. Nothing about it made sense. Her mind swam from the alcohol. Had he been Sergei's plant at the table months ago? Meant to push her to bet more? Was Sergei tracking her now? She suddenly wished she were sober enough to understand how a coincidence like this could happen.

He held up his bottle. "Having a beer."

"You know what I mean," she said. "What are you doing *here*?"

"I work nearby."

Now, that was weird. Who worked on Angel Island? "What are you—a park ranger?"

He laughed. "Hardly."

"You're very . . . vague."

"Am I?"

"There you go again."

"Hey, Teddy!" Dara called.

"So it's not TeAnne?" he said, his mouth serious but his eyes smiling.

"It's actually Teddy," she said, putting a hand on his chest to steady herself. "I'm usually not like this—" She stopped herself mid-thought. "You have a hell of a memory."

"It's part of my job," he said, and she noticed that he didn't back away, didn't remove her hand. Not like Pyro. This was promising.

"Which is . . . ?" she prompted, and then stopped herself. "Never mind. Don't tell me. I like the mystery." She tried to take a step closer but lost her balance. He caught her with one arm, and their faces were so close she thought he was going to kiss her. She closed her eyes.

But then nothing. He removed his arm, set his beer on the railing, and used both hands to straighten her shoulders. "You okay?" he asked.

"Better than okay."

"I think your friends are waiting for you."

She glanced over her shoulder and saw Pyro glaring so hard that it seemed like he might set the whole deck on fire.

You can't have it both ways, friend without benefits.

"We're celebrating," she said, stalling, trying to think of something else to say. She didn't want Nick to go, not yet.

He grinned, revealing the perfect dimple next to his perfect lips.

She was bad. Bad to plan to leave with one guy and then switch to another. But this seemed like fate. And psychics were supposed to believe in those kinds of things. Otherwise why would perfect Nick be at a hole in the wall on a small island off the coast of San Francisco on tonight of all nights?

"What are you celebrating, Teddy?"

"I can't tell you."

"Or you'd have to kill me?"

"No, I'd have to drink." Teddy looked down at her hands as if to count. "Like twenty shots as punishment."

"Teddy," he said.

"Nick," she said.

"If you don't go back to your friends, that guy is going to come over here and try throwing a punch. And I don't want to have to hurt him."

Teddy didn't think of herself as the swooning type, but holy shit. Nick made her knees go weak.

"Besides," he added, "I have to go."

Take me with you.

But before she could say another word, he kissed the top of her head and was gone.

Teddy stood there for a few moments, watching him disappear into the night. Did he just dad-kiss her? On top of her head? She felt a hand on her shoulder and looked up to see Pyro at her side.

"What the hell was that all about?" he asked.

Good question.

Teddy let out a breath. It was a puzzle she would have to solve later. For now, Pyro was right here, his hand on the inside of her elbow. "Just someone I knew from Vegas," she said. "You know the saying."

"We need to talk." Pyro said. There was something about Whitfield that lent itself to melodrama. They knew each other too well; living, eating, training with the same people every day heightened every interaction.

Great. Another talk. She'd had enough talks today. And talks after tequila were *really* great.

"You ignored me for weeks," he said. "And then tonight . . . I'm not just some"—he lowered his voice—"booty call."

Are Pyro's feelings hurt?

"I've been busy," she said. "You know, studying."

"When I saw you collapse today in Seership, I was worried," he said.

She'd thought Pyro was a player, but this conversation was veering into relationship waters. "I really appreciate what you did for me," she said. "But I told you, I'm not looking for anything serious." She leaned in to kiss him on the cheek, but he turned away.

"Teddy!" Jillian called. "Next round's on me!"

She couldn't worry about Pyro's feelings. She had to look out for herself. She squeezed his hand and then returned to the table.

*　*　*

That night Teddy again found herself visiting the yellow house. She could hear a woman's voice singing the familiar lullaby. She walked down the flagstone path and toward the front door. She had never been inside the yellow house; she always woke up before she could enter.

This time she grasped the metal of the handle and pushed.

Teddy found herself inside an entryway with faded wallpaper. With each step, the mahogany floorboards creaked with age. A low table housed everyday debris: photographs, keys, letters. Teddy followed the sound of the woman's voice through the entryway and into a small white kitchen. The woman hovered over the stove, waiting for a steaming teakettle to sing. As if sensing Teddy's presence, the woman turned around, and then—a series of sharp, shrill beeps.

Teddy jerked upright. Her alarm clock read 7:05 a.m. Jillian's bed was empty, which meant she was probably already in the shower. Teddy heard the muted voices of her classmates in the hallway, followed by the groaning and clanking of ancient pipes as toilets were flushed and faucets turned on. A typical morning at Whitfield.

But she couldn't shake the dream. It had felt so real. The sounds—the song, the floorboards, the kettle. It was as if Teddy had actually been in the house.

Maybe it was the alcohol from the night before. She remembered the shots. She remembered the awkward conversation with Pyro. She remembered throwing herself at that guy from the casino who had improbably shown up on Angel Island. And she realized something else: he had recognized her immediately, despite the fact that she hadn't been dressed in a wig and a fat suit.

Jillian returned to the room fresh from her shower, wrapped in a paisley bathrobe. Though they had been exchanging fragments from their dreams (most of Jillian's featured a menagerie of animals), Teddy had found herself keeping her own secret, instead making up random images to make her roommate laugh (most of them featured Ryan Gosling). Something about the yellow house felt too private to share with her roommate.

"Ryan Gosling getting you down?" Jillian asked.

"I've already thought of three comebacks about Gosling and the word *down*. You make things too easy." Teddy swung her legs over the side of the bed. Her head was pounding. "Must have been something to do with drinking last night."

"Funny you said that, Teddy. I had a strange dream last night, too. I was a dog, or I think I was a dog. Maybe a very small coyote. Definitely in the canine family. And I was in the desert. But not because I wanted to be there. There was a big explosion. And, oh." Jillian shivered. "It was horrible."

Teddy didn't have time for dreams about dogs this morning. "I'm sorry, Jillian," she said as she grabbed her shower caddy and headed to the bathroom. "I can't be late."

*   *   *

Teddy's dream stayed with her as she showered and dressed, as she ate breakfast with her friends, as she walked to Fort McDowell for the first Empathy 101 class with Clint.

The lullaby endlessly replayed in her head until the door slammed and Clint walked into the classroom. He threw his beat-up satchel on a large desk and sat down beside it, one leg casually swinging beneath him. He wore khaki pants and a blue button-down shirt, cuffs rolled up and collar unbuttoned. He appeared totally normal. Nothing the least bit psychic about him. In other classes, Teddy gossiped with her fellow Misfits until the teacher began a lecture. But here, the room stayed pin-drop quiet.

Teddy had tried to visualize her wall, like Clint had asked. She could choose steel like his, or sand like Molly's, but neither felt right. Clint looked at her. She knew he could tell.

"Empathy. Let's start with a definition."

"Feeling sorry for someone," Ben said without raising his hand.

Clint shook his head, leaning back on the desk. "I had a lot of different partners when I was a cop. But two of them stick out in my mind—and these were good cops, guys I liked and respected. One of them was dyslexic. He couldn't turn in a report without me or his wife checking it over first for spelling mistakes. The other guy was color-blind. He'd lied to get the job; I don't know how he even made it onto the force. But despite his false application, he was a great cop. I'm not dyslexic, and I'm not color-blind—but I understood their brains were wired differently than mine."

"I'm guessing it didn't work the other way around, did it?" Pyro called out.

Clint laughed. "Right. My psychic ability helped us close case after case, but they couldn't understand that my brain was wired differently, too. Both of them requested a different partner within six months."

Behind her, Teddy heard Ava Lareau clear her throat. "I'm sorry, Professor Corbett, but I don't see what any of this has to do with empathy."

"Empathy is the ability to understand and share the feelings of others. To be able to put yourself in their place. Ultimately, it's up to you if you disclose to your partner about your abilities, but if any of you is harboring some private fantasy that you're going to jump into a position at the CIA, Homeland Security, or local law enforcement and be embraced because everyone there was just dying to have some hotshot psychic join their team and solve cases they'd been stumped on for years, you're wrong."

Clint stood up and pointed a single finger ceiling-ward. "So that's number one," he said. "You need to *empathize* with your colleagues. It has to be frustrating as hell to learn you arrested the wrong guy—or worse, let the right guy walk. Whether or not they realize you had extracognitive help, they'll resent you for making them look like idiots. But it's not about you, people, it really isn't. Accept that and move on. That's the kind of empathy you need to learn to keep your job.

"Number two," Clint went on, "and this is more important: all of you have demonstrated an ability to psychically connect to another psychic. That's good, but you need more than that when you're dealing with a potential suspect. You need *empathy*. And I'm not talking about pulling that Officer Friendly bullshit where you cuddle up to someone and convince him to waive his constitutional rights. I mean getting to the core of another person's feelings, thoughts, and motivations. Be ready to access that skill on a dime. Not just fast—instant. That's the kind of empathy you need to be good at your job."

Teddy glanced over at Molly, whose face looked white in the dim classroom. As an empath, she had no choice to feel—and Teddy knew she hated it.

"We'd all like to believe we're good people," Clint said. "But the truth is, empathy is a fragile reaction. In times of extreme stress, the psychological capacity that humans have to empathize with others is often eliminated. That's why you'll see people kicking others off life-boats to save themselves. The only way to counter that is to diligently practice empathy every day. That's the kind of empathy you need to be a good person."

He asked the students to find a partner and share an experience during which they'd felt vulnerable. Molly tapped Teddy's elbow, and Teddy nodded back.

Clint moved through the room as the class shuffled off into pairs. "As your partner is speaking, I want each of you to connect to your partner's emotions. Actually feel them. Mine them for all you can get."

Other students had claimed the more private corners, so Teddy and Molly found themselves squarely in the center of the classroom. They sat down cross-legged on the floor, facing each other, their spines straight.

"You first," Molly said.

Teddy could talk about her birth parents, her so-called epilepsy, struggling to come to terms with her new psychic abilities. But she didn't know how to put those experiences into words. They felt too raw, too new.

Instead, she described the time a few years ago when her best friend from high school had come back to Vegas to visit. Her friend had recently married; she was expecting a child soon. As Teddy talked, Molly voiced each of her varying emotions. The joy at seeing her old friend, the nostalgia while reminiscing over old times. Teddy's pang of guilt at not being able to finish college, as her friend had done. Her mixture of envy and happiness at her friend's description of married life.

Then it was Molly's turn. She sat there for a few moments, as if trying to decide which part of her she was willing to share.

"I know it's hard," Teddy said. Which was bullshit, because she had taken the easy way out.

Molly shook her head. "It was hard to be a kid and just . . . feel everything all the time. Especially adults' emotions. My dad had just died, and my mom was on her own. She was doing her best, but she was depressed. Didn't help that I was a handful. Crying all the time. One night when my brothers were acting wild, I got hysterical—sensing my mother's sadness, I think. But she couldn't deal with me and my brothers at the same time, and so she locked me in a closet. I was stuck in there for hours."

Teddy closed her eyes and tried to put herself in Molly's place, in the dark, alone. Molly went on, "I've always been scared of everything. Heights. Spiders. Darkness. It's hard to be brave when you feel how scared everyone is—of things big and small—all the time."

For a second, Teddy caught a glimpse of a hallway, heard the sound of crying from somewhere above. But then it was gone. Teddy's parents had always been happy to have her around, even if she was a troublemaker. In fact, they'd done that thing so many adoptive parents do—assured Teddy again and again that she was special because she'd been chosen.

Teddy opened her eyes to find Jeremy watching Molly, visibly concerned. Molly turned to look at him quickly before she continued, "I'm working now on learning to shut out people's emotions. But high school was a nightmare. College, too. Even this place can be overwhelming. I took a break last year because I still wasn't ready to be around so many people. That's why I like computers." She laughed. "Just data, no fear. But I've been working with Professor Dunn. He's teaching me how to control it."

"I'm glad," Teddy replied, her throat dry. "Your wall helps, though, right?"

Molly looked at her, eyes wide. "What?"

"In Seership, that day I broke through your wall. You know it was an accident. I didn't mean to invade your privacy."

Molly nodded. She looked even more drained than usual. Dark circles showed under her eyes, her pale brown hair was lank, and her skin had an almost ghostly pallor. It was like each day at Whitfield sucked a little more out of her. Teddy made a silent vow to check in on her more often.

"All right, people." Clint's voice carried across the room. "That's enough for today. Remember: empathy won't just make you a better psychic; it'll make you a better government official, a better colleague, a better friend, a better spouse, a better human being. So keep working at it."

Teddy stood up and extended a hand to Molly. "Want to go grab a coffee down by the docks?"

Molly looked to Jeremy, who was still watching them. "Can't," she said. "I promised Jeremy I'd hang out with him."

"All right, maybe another time."

"Yeah," Molly said. "Another time."

As the students gathered their belongings, Clint called Teddy's name. "How's your wall coming?" he asked.

"It's coming," she said as she made her way toward the door.

Alone, Teddy walked to the meditation lawn. Even though she hadn't been able to tackle the thirty minutes of meditation that Dunn advised the students to perform each morning and night, Teddy slipped off her shoes, threw down her bag, and sat down on the damp grass. She turned her palms up on her knees and began to breathe deeply. She cleared her mind. She then waited for the idea of a wall. It wouldn't be sand or steel. She blinked, letting in a bright flash of light. *Yes,* she thought. *Light. Electricity.* So strong that no one could even touch it, let alone manage to break through. She would build a wall of pure power.

Teddy imagined the light crackling. She breathed in deeply and visualized sending more energy to her electric wall until it jumped in waves, giving off sparks. She spent an hour on the lawn turning the shield on and off. She didn't notice the students walking by, she didn't notice the sun start to set, and when Teddy finally got up and walked back to her dorm, she felt calm, as if she finally had gained some control over her mind and her body.

CHAPTER SIXTEEN

THE END OF OCTOBER CAME TO ANGEL ISLAND FASTER than a dealer could yell "No call bets" at craps. Midterm exams were still far enough away that the students at Whitfield felt like there was time to celebrate. Conveniently, October brought an occasion for it: Halloween.

The Whitfield Institute took Halloween seriously. Like, too seriously, considering it was a government institution for adults. And while its celebration could never reach Vegas proportions, it captured a certain level of Vegas enthusiasm. The highlight of the evening was a costume contest—everyone on campus was encouraged to dress up, even teachers.

That was how Teddy ended up in the dining hall, next to Jillian, wearing a plaid shirt and jeans covered in blood (okay, fake blood): she'd gone with a *Walking Dead* theme. Recruits from all years crowded into the dining hall. As Teddy took a sip of her nonalcoholic fair-trade fruit punch, she thought about how quickly life at Whitfield had taken on a rhythm—she went to class, she did her work, she strengthened her mental shield, she met with Clint, he tried to break her mental shield, she got her ass kicked by Boyd, she meditated, she tried (and failed) to replicate her astral ability in Dunn's class, she went to bed exhausted, and she woke up the next day and did it all over again. She'd done her best to keep her nose clean, play nice, follow the rules. It wasn't that hard to *want* to fit in. She liked the other Misfits.

And there was a part of her that had grown to enjoy organic nonalcoholic fair-trade fruit punch.

She looked around the dining hall. The staff had even gone to the effort of decorating, cheesy cobwebs gracing every surface, complete with plastic spiders. The coveted prize for winning the costume contest was a weekend pass for two off-island. Teddy knew she didn't have a shot at it. She'd discovered she was merely one of a zombie horde.

Jillian had done better, transforming one of the diaphanous rolls of fabric that hung above her bed into a toga in order to become the empress from a tarot deck. Thankfully, she had let up on the patchouli, instead dusting herself from head to toe in shimmery body powder.

"So are you meeting with Brett?" Teddy asked.

Jillian shrugged. "We just have some loose plans."

"Yeah, sure," Teddy said, rolling her eyes and taking another sip of punch.

"And what about you and Pyro?"

Now it was Teddy's turn to shrug. Their interactions since that night at the Cantina had been awkward, to say the least.

"Speaking of," Jillian said.

Out of the corner of her eye, Teddy could see Pyro making his way over to them. Of course he hadn't dressed up.

"And who are you supposed to be?" Teddy asked.

"The man who haunts your dreams?"

"Very funny," Teddy said.

"You want to make tonight a little more interesting?" Pyro asked, nodding to her cup and pulling out a flask.

Teddy thought for a moment. She remembered her promise to Clint. She had to at least try to follow the rules on campus. "I'm good," she said.

He smiled. "Let me know if you change your mind."

She saw Clint standing with the instructors by the punch table across the room. Even they had gotten in the swing of things. Professor Dunn had dressed as the Dude from *The Big Lebowski,* while Clint looked relaxed and comfortable in his college football jersey.

Dara, wearing a fur coat, too much eyeliner, and a pink polo dress, sidled up to Teddy. "You know what I like best about tonight?" she asked, taking a fake drag from her unlit cigarette. She looked just like Margot from *The Royal Tenenbaums.*

"What?" Teddy took another sip of punch.

"That Boyd's not here. Imagine her predicament. What if she dressed like a troll and nobody noticed she was in costume?"

The Misfits' intense dislike of Sergeant Rosemary Boyd had only magnified. Boyd ran her classes with an iron fist and was responsible in large part for the rivalry that ran between the Misfits and the Alphas. It was as if she wanted the competition between them to spiral into something like tribal warfare.

Teddy laughed, catching Clint's eye. He was watching her. They'd been working consistently on mental defense, but Clint had been able to penetrate her mind each and every time he tried. She imagined a current crackling in her fingers, traveling up her arms. She closed her eyes, marshaling that electricity. Then, as if it were thread, she pictured spinning the bright white light into a web inside her mind, shielding her thoughts. Clint raised his cup to hers and returned to his conversation with Dunn. As if he could hear her silent vow to keep him out of her damn mind.

Ava Lareau bumped Teddy's arm, almost spilling her drink. Ava was one of those girls who thought lingerie and animal ears made the best Halloween costume. Teddy guessed she was dressed as either a call girl or a cat.

"Anyone seen Brett lately?" Ava asked, her eyes right on Jillian. "He promised to meet me here, but I haven't seen him yet."

Teddy just hoped that Jillian wouldn't take the bait. Everyone knew that Ava was determined to be the best spiritual medium among the first-year recruits, and that she perceived Jillian as a threat. She'd gone on the offensive, doing everything she could to undermine Jillian's confidence and class rank. And when Ava had discovered that Jillian had a crush on Brett Evans, she'd launched a campaign to openly flirt with him any chance she could. Jillian had retaliated by doubling her efforts to get Brett to notice her instead, occasionally pulling down her dress to reveal another inch of cleavage.

Ava's eyes narrowed as she turned her attention to Jillian's costume. "Oh," Ava drawled. "I just love what you did with that curtain. Very Scarlett O'Hara."

"I like your costume, too," Jillian said, smiling. "Clever idea to appear practically naked in front of your professors. Let me know if it works for you."

Ava flushed. "If you see Brett, tell him I'm looking for him." With that, she turned and left.

Dara put her hand on Jillian's shoulder. "He's over there," she said, pointing toward a table where a group of upperclassmen—including Brett, dressed as the Long Island Medium—were reading fortunes. "Jeremy and Molly tracked him down earlier. They're still trying to make that trade for Internet access. Remember? Brett has a key to the lab? The whole black-market thing?"

Jeremy and Molly, dressed in coordinating doctor and nurse costumes, blended easily into the crowd. But Brett stood out. It was hard to miss a six-foot-tall guy in leopard-skin stilettos, a tight leather skirt, a bleached-blond wig—and five o'clock shadow.

Despite the getup, Jillian looked so lovestruck that Teddy decided to accompany her friend across the room to keep her from doing anything stupid. As they drew closer, however, it was clear that Brett wasn't exactly in character. "I mean, I understand that *some* people need the rules and restrictions," he said. "But *I* don't. Just the opposite. All these regulations are curtailing my abilities. Makes me feel like I could start a fight with a possum. Why put us through all this training if we can't use—"

"Hey," Molly said, cutting off Brett's rant the moment she noticed Teddy and Jillian nearby.

"Hey," Jillian said breathily. "You owe me a dance."

"I do?" Brett said.

Jillian grabbed Brett and led him onto the floor.

Teddy sneaked off to get a refill of nonalcoholic punch. She chatted with Dara and an upperclassman, but no matter how she tried to relax and enjoy herself, there was a distinctly middle-school feeling about the party. Bored, Teddy practiced putting her wall up and down as she watched her peers grind on the dance floor.

That was, until she saw him.

Nick, killer dimples and all, walked into the Whitfield dining hall. Teddy had tried not to think about him much after that night, it had been too cringeworthy—she had made a move on him, and he'd dad-blocked her!—and now he was here and talking to Clint like they were old friends.

She felt like she'd been hit with a ton of bricks, because she realized the truth. They *were* friends. Or colleagues, at the very least. Nick knew all about Whitfield, all about her—and he had known since the moment she'd first laid eyes on him in the Bellagio. She'd been freaking played.

There'd been a reason she couldn't read plain ol' Nick's hand that night in Vegas. And the reason had been not so plain ol' Clint Corbett. How could she have been so stupid? Nick must have been—what? CIA? FBI? Homeland Security? Vegas PD? Here Clint was, telling her to play by the rules, when he was the one who'd set up a long con to trick her into coming to school. The guy in charge of the ethics class.

Teddy ran through the options in her mind. She could confront Nick and Clint in front of all the instructors and other students. Or she could get drunk first and then confront them. But Pyro (or, more specifically, his flask) was nowhere to be seen. Time for Plan C.

She turned to Dara. "Do you know who that guy is talking to Clint?"

"No clue, but I'd like to."

Teddy sighed, exasperated. "Never mind."

Dara nodded to where Molly and Jeremy were sneaking out of the dining hall. "I think Molly and Jeremy managed a trade for lab keys. Want to see if we can grab some Internet time?"

Two words were at the forefront of Teddy's mind: *Google search*. If Nick knew so much about her, the least she could do was find out more about him. She was done playing by the rules. If Clint didn't have to follow them, then she didn't have to, either. "Hell, yes."

Dara and Teddy made their way to the back of the dining hall to catch up with Molly and Jeremy. "Mind if we tag along?" Teddy asked. "Desperate for some Internet."

The two looked at each other, hesitating a moment before Jeremy responded. "That would be fine."

They left through the back of Harris Hall and cut through the meditation lawn to the lab. Jeremy fished a key from his pocket and opened the door. For a second, Teddy expected an alarm, a flashing light, something, but nothing happened. Inside, it was just the same office space, the two shiny Macs powered down for the night.

Outside, they heard footsteps. Boots on gravel. A shadow slipped across the glass of the door. Dara sucked in a breath. "Of course, we're going to be the ones who get caught doing something *one time* that the *entire school* gets away with."

"Shhh," Molly whispered.

Teddy's heart pounded. Was she about to throw her entire life away, her shot at Whitfield, just to get revenge on Nick and Clint for setting her up in Vegas? Clint had forced her hand, but he'd done it to give her a second chance, Teddy could see that now. Her convictions had seemed stronger back in the dining hall.

The noise grew closer, and then the lab door creaked open, revealing . . . Pyro.

"Hey, heard you guys got Internet."

"Jesus H. Christ," Dara said. "You nearly gave us all coronaries."

"I just wanted to see how the Chargers are doing. Heard Rivers got hurt."

"Is that English?" Dara asked.

"Football," Pyro said.

"There are two computers in the reception and two more in Eversley's office," Molly said. "I'll use one in there, it'll likely have a password on it, but I can break in, no sweat."

"I'll keep watch," Jeremy said.

Dara and Pyro booted up the computers in the reception.

"I'll come with you," Teddy said to Molly, who looked at Jeremy as if for permission. "Is there a problem?" Teddy said to him. Maybe Molly was nervous. Using two unlocked computers was different than breaking in to Eversley's office.

"Go," Jeremy said. "We don't have much time. Ava and Liz have the next spot. I have to meet them after at Harris. Brett's been letting the entire school in and out of here all night."

Molly reached for the office door. Locked. Molly tried the key again, but it didn't work.

"This," Teddy said, "I can do." She grabbed a paper clip from a desk drawer, fashioned one end into a shallow hook, and inserted it into the lock. After a couple of jiggles and twists, the lock clicked.

"Something you picked up in Vegas?" Molly asked.

"Maybe one day I'll learn to do it with my mind."

They entered the dark lab. Teddy fumbled for a light switch. The fluorescent bulbs flickered on. There were two computers on one side of the room and a patient table on the other. All around them were floor-to-ceiling cabinets.

"Kind of a depressing office, huh?" Teddy said.

"Tell me about it." Molly was already at work on one computer and Eversley's password.

"Just tell me it's not something like ILOVEBOOBS or PSYCHICSSUCK."

But Molly didn't seem in the mood for jokes. She took out a USB drive and plugged it into the computer. "This program does the hard work for me." In a few seconds, she was in. "Not too bad—49ERSFAN#1!—didn't peg Eversley for a sports guy, though. He and Pyro should hang out."

"You came prepared." Teddy typed the password onto the second computer in front of her, watched the screen come to life. *All right, Nick,* Teddy thought. *Let's see what you've got.*

Jeremy appeared at the door. "About fifteen minutes or so?"

Molly nodded, furiously typing away, the number of windows and boxes and programs running simultaneously on her screen astounded Teddy.

"Wow, that looks intense."

It took Molly a second to realize that Teddy was talking to her. "Oh. Sorry, I'm trying to help a friend. Nothing serious, I promise." She glanced at the clock. "We don't have a lot of time."

Teddy went back to her computer, clicking on the file STAFF & FACULTY LIST—UPDATED. And she'd thought this would be hard. She clicked on the search bar and entered *Nick*. There were three Nicks on campus. One who worked in janitorial. One in security who had been at the school since 2015. And one Nicholas Stavros who had joined the faculty a month ago as an FBI liaison. She closed the document and looked over at Molly, only to find that Molly was staring right at her. "What?"

"N-n-nothing," Molly stammered. "I just—" She swallowed. "I have to tell Jeremy something, and then I think we should wipe the history on these computers and get going. I'll be right back." She stumbled out of her chair and left the room. Sometimes Molly seemed fearless, like when she was being all super-spy, hacking a computer, and other times it seemed like she needed Jeremy in order to put a sentence together.

Just as Teddy closed the faculty file, she noticed another one on the desktop marked FIRST-YEARS: MEDICAL REPORTS. She opened it and saw a list of her classmates' names, including her own.

She couldn't resist clicking on her own name. Teddy opened the folder and clicked the first file. Lab tests. DNA samples. She couldn't decipher most of it. She scrolled through to the bottom to see if Eversley had written some kind of note or summary. She heard footsteps down the hall, Molly's voice at the door: "Someone's coming."

"One second." This was important. More important than finding out about Nick. There! At the top of the page: FINDINGS.

"Teddy, *now*." Molly was shutting down her computer.

Teddy scanned the page: *Evidence suggests that there are both maternal and paternal DNA markers present in subject's makeup—*

Then the screen went blank.

"Hey!" Teddy said.

Molly hit a button and powered it back up. Then performed a command. "I'm deleting your history. We have to go."

Teddy pushed away from the desk and followed Molly from the room, her head reeling.

Maternal and paternal markers. Psychic markers? Eversley said that they hadn't hadn't proved the existence of such things.

Pyro grabbed Teddy at the door. "You okay?" he asked.

"Yeah," Teddy said. "Just got some news from home. Need a minute to digest."

Teddy looked around the room. Dara was waiting by the door. Molly was packing up her hard drive. "Where's Jeremy?"

"Bathroom," Dara said, shrugging on her fur coat. "Let's go. This place gives me the creeps at night."

Teddy turned to Molly. "I thought you said that we had to leave? That someone was coming?"

"We do," Molly said, zipping her bag closed. "But I'm not responsible for Jeremy's bladder."

They heard a noise—a slam, followed by a lock clicking shut. Molly put her finger to her lips.

"Do you think someone else is in the building?" Dara asked. "We can still get out of here before—"

"I gave Jeremy the key," Molly said. "We're waiting for him. We can't lock up without him."

"And we don't leave anyone behind," Pyro said.

Steps in the hallway, getting closer, then Jeremy's even voice: "Ready?"

"You know you scared the crap out of us, right?" Teddy said. "What is with everybody tonight?" Her nerves were on edge. She just wanted to get out of here. "Come on, if we hurry, we'll make it in time for best costume."

"I hardly think you'll win, Teddy," Jeremy said. "Your costume is not very original."

Teddy snorted. "Look who's talking."

"Please," Molly said. "Enough." She stopped Jeremy as he was locking the door. "Got everything?" Jeremy put the lab keys in his doctor's bag, adjusted his stethoscope, and nodded.

The group walked back across the meditation lawn.

"That was risky," Teddy said to Pyro.

"It was worth catching up with my partner's family." Pyro looked down. "His kids got so big."

"I thought you were just checking sports scores."

Pyro shrugged, avoiding Teddy's eyes.

She didn't want to press him for more, but this was rare—Pyro being Lucas, the cop who watched his partner give up everything for the job, for him. She reached out to touch his arm, then caught herself. She couldn't lead him on. "You wanna talk about it?"

He shook his head. "I just want to forget about it." He walked on without her.

She was reeling, too. Teddy leaned against the cool stucco of the dining hall facade, where she was shrouded in darkness, invisible. She looked up into the clear San Francisco sky. What she'd read in her file. Maternal and paternal psychic markers. Both her parents were psychic, too. It changed everything she knew about herself, her life.

And then she saw Nick passing beneath the lamppost on the corner of the path. Instead of feeling lost or confused or sad, she felt anger. He'd tricked her. And lied about it. "Hey!" she said, shoving him. In a split second, he'd pinned her against a tree. "Stop! It's only me," she said.

Nick let out a breath and released her. "Next time you do that to a federal agent, you might get your head blown off."

"FBI," she said. "I should have known."

"What are you doing here?" he asked.

"I go to school here, remember? You tricked me into it."

He folded his arms. "I was just doing my job."

"I assume that's what you were doing the other night at the Cantina, too, huh?"

"Yeah. New assignment."

"As what? Barfly?"

"FBI liaison. And teacher."

She stared at him, her poker face revealing nothing. She couldn't let him know that she already had that information. "Why you?" she asked.

"Because I'm good."

"How good?"

"Good enough to know that you and your friends just sneaked into an office where you didn't belong."

Teddy kept her expression even as she tried to figure out her next move. "If you're that good, you'd know that half the campus sneaks into that office."

"But they don't get caught."

She swallowed hard. She couldn't risk getting into trouble. Not when she had so much more to learn. About being psychic. About her birth parents. She looked back at Nick. She could play this. Find another move. Like she always did. "When do you start? Your first day as a Whitfield teacher, I mean."

"I don't start until next semester."

"So, technically, you don't have to report me. You don't really work here yet." Teddy reached out and put a hand on his arm. He looked at her hand and then back at her. "Technically—" he began.

"I'd consider us even," she said.

"Even?" he asked.

"For Vegas," she said. "It was a dirty trick. For both you and Clint."

"Okay," he said, as if it were no big deal.

Teddy blinked, surprised. "Okay?"

"I won't report you," he said. "But not because I regret what happened in Vegas." He took her hand off his arm and started to walk away.

"Why, then?" she called.

"Read my mind," he said, and disappeared into Harris Hall.

Teddy followed a few minutes later. "There you are," Jillian said. "I've been looking all over for you. I can't find Brett, either. They're about to announce the winner of the costume contest."

Dunn took the microphone at the front of the room, announcing that the prize for best costume went to Brett Evans. The room erupted in cheers and catcalls. When Brett didn't appear to claim his prize, lewd shouts suggested where he might have gone (and with whom). Jillian picked at the hem of her dress, eyes downcast. Teddy scanned the crowd but didn't see him. Hopefully he wasn't off somewhere hooking up with Ava. For now she had more important things to worry about: a score to settle. Teddy was a player, and she'd let herself be played.

CHAPTER SEVENTEEN

IT WAS JUST AS WELL THAT PROFESSOR DUNN WAS late to class the following morning. Normally, Seership began with deep-breathing exercises designed to focus the mind, but the morning after the Halloween party, Teddy ducked into the classroom to find the Misfits and the Alphas assembled together—an unprecedented occurrence.

"What's going on?" she asked.

"Someone broke in to Eversley's office," Ben Tucker reported. "It's not like everyone doesn't use the front-office computers—I mean, I gave Brett a box of cigars for time last week. We're not supposed to know about it, but the news is all over campus. Apparently, once Clint catches whoever did it, they'll automatically be expelled."

"Expelled?" she said. "For trespassing?" She'd been the one to pick the lock.

"No, not just for that," Ben clarified. "Whoever broke in also stole vials of blood."

That didn't make sense. Neither she nor Molly had taken anything from Eversley's office.

"They're already trying to track any students who were near the lab last night," Ben said. "They're supposed to go straight to Boyd's office for questioning."

Boyd would be more than happy to see the backside of Teddy. If Boyd found out Teddy had broken in . . . Teddy shared an uneasy glance with the other Misfits. Her mind shot to Nick. She couldn't count on his silence now. Not when there'd been a theft. She had to find him. Convince him they were innocent.

"I'm sure it was just some stupid Halloween prank," Dara said.

"It wasn't just the blood," Ben Tucker said. "One of the lab computers was hacked." Teddy risked a look at Molly, whose gaze was focused on her lap.

"Why would someone steal blood?" Pyro said.

"Eversley's research was top secret," Kate said. "I couldn't begin to guess."

But Teddy could. He had said that the Whitfield Institute was a leader in the field of human genome research. And if what she'd read last night was correct, they'd discovered the genetic markers for psychic ability. Any number of people might be interested in that information.

"Brett's missing, too," Ava said.

"What do you mean?" Teddy asked, looking at Ava.

"No one's seen him since last night. He didn't turn up for breakfast, and he missed his tutorial this morning."

Ava appeared more thoughtful than upset. Teddy glanced at her roommate, who looked devastated.

"Maybe he's the one who stole the blood," suggested Jeremy.

Teddy considered other possibilities. Brett Evans was one of the school's biggest success stories. A highly respected third-year, he had a plum internship waiting for him next year at the FBI. But she *had* overheard Brett complaining to Jeremy and Molly that the pace of his studies at Whitfield was holding him back. So maybe he'd gotten tired of everything and walked away. But in the middle of the night?

"He's not dead," said Dara. "I didn't see anything at all." She paused to take in the appalled glances of the other recruits. "Oh, please. Spare me. You know you were all thinking it. Wherever he is, he's okay."

The door swung open and Dunn entered. The students waited thirty seconds before bombarding him with questions about the break-in, the theft, and Brett's disappearance.

Dunn held up his hands to quiet the class. "I don't know anything," he said. "And if I did, I wouldn't be able to tell you." He plunked a large physics textbook down on his desk. "We're starting a new subject today."

Teddy closed her eyes, focused on her breathing, and slipped into her meditative state. She put the threat of expulsion, Boyd, Nick, Clint, Brett, all of it, out of her mind. Admittedly, she was nowhere near the divine state of nirvana Dunn went on and on about, but after a lifetime of tumbling from one crisis to the next, the ability to calm herself felt pretty damn good.

"To date, we've focused our energies on forming a simple mental connection with our partner," Dunn said after a few minutes. "One person looked at a playing card, or a photograph, or an object, and transmitted that information via an auditory message. A rudimentary psychic task."

More often than not, Teddy had managed to successfully connect with her peers (though she was better with her fellow Misfits than the Alphas, and much better at projecting than receiving). And she'd stuck with her promise to Clint: she'd practiced only physical telepathy, the basics. She hadn't tried anything like the astral telepathy that had brought the class to a standstill.

Professor Dunn continued, "Now you are ready to move beyond a simple psychic connection. What I'm talking about is expanding our mental communication. Instead of sending messages, we're looking now to begin a discussion."

He went on to explain their task: to set a concrete goal and psychically ask a partner to accomplish it, a job that would require far more stamina than anything they'd done to date.

"Nothing foolish," Dunn sternly warned. "We do not squander or misuse psychic ability. It is paramount at all times that we treat our partners and ourselves with respect. An acceptable task might be to request that our partner open a door. Retrieve a book from a bookshelf. Write a word on the message board."

"Excuse me," Ava said, raising her hand, "but I'm a medium. I don't see how I'll ever need to use this. The spirits I communicate with are dead. They couldn't open a door if they wanted to."

"Perhaps," Dunn said. "But as we've discussed, the specific manifestation of your psychic ability isn't important at this juncture. Your first year is about developing correct meditation practices and enhancing your ability to connect with others."

Dunn further explained that the ability to perform this skill was crucial to passing the midyear exam. The reminder ruined Teddy's state of mental calm. If Boyd didn't get her for trespassing in the lab, she could be out by December anyway.

Dunn directed the recruits into two rows. "Look to your left," he said. "That's your partner for this exercise."

Teddy tried to catch Molly's eye, beside her. But Molly fixed her gaze on her meditation mat.

"I'll project instructions first," Teddy said. "You receive."

Molly nodded.

"And we need to talk about last night," Teddy said.

"Not here," Molly said.

Teddy looked around, lowered her voice, and spoke quickly. "What were you doing on that computer? Do you think someone lifted the vials before or after we left? We can tell Clint that we were in the lab for those twenty minutes, but we have alibis for the rest of the night. He won't be happy that we broke in, but we didn't steal anything."

Molly, if possible, looked even paler than usual, eyes even larger, circles underneath even darker. "I don't need an alibi, Teddy, because I won't be telling anyone I was there."

Teddy tensed. "Nick knows we were there last night; he stopped me."

"No one stopped *me*. Anyway, I don't even know Nick."

"Nick. Nick Stavros," Teddy said, exasperated. "The new FBI liaison."

Molly shushed Teddy. "Keep it down. Maybe we should just focus on the exercise. I don't want to fall behind."

"Listen, I've learned the hard way that lying to Clint doesn't work." Molly wasn't thinking straight. Surely it was better to admit they'd been sneaking time on the Internet than to get expelled for stealing the samples. "Does this have something to do with what you were doing on the computer?"

Molly was logical. She wouldn't risk losing her place at Whitfield again. They'd survive this class, and they'd talk through a plan once everyone had the chance to cool off. Teddy tried to let go of her frustration. She glanced around the room, considering her options for their assignment. Once she'd decided on an appropriate goal—asking Molly to sit on a chair near the window—Teddy said, "Fine, we'll just focus on the exercise. What channel? Three again?"

"Sure," Molly said.

First Teddy lowered her wall. She wouldn't be able to connect with Molly without disarming her mental defense. She watched her electric barrier fade in her mind, then pictured the small yellow radio, imagined turning the dial to channel three, until she heard Molly's voice.

Come in? Over, Teddy telegraphed, jokingly.

"I hear you, Teddy," Molly said.

At least they'd gotten this far. Teddy took a deep breath, refocusing on her directive.

Please go sit in the chair by the window.

There was no response. Teddy tried again. And again.

Window. Chair. Sit.

She felt the rough brush of sand. In her mind's eye, the walkie-talkie faded away, and Teddy saw endless dunes of gold. Molly's wall? Teddy opened her eyes and looked at Molly, stunned to see a film of sweat glistening on her forehead and her features fixed in an expression of intense mental strain. Molly was actively blocking her—why? Just because she was pissed?

Teddy closed her eyes again, refocusing on the landscape of Molly's mind. Inside, the wall of sand had only grown higher. Teddy pushed her mind against it, searching for a weak spot. She imagined a gust of wind reshaping the edges of the dune, like the first time she'd broken through Molly's defense, but grit clouded her vision. Next, she visualized a tidal wave washing the sand away in a sweep. The dune began to collapse. Teddy heard Molly gasp as a score of images rushed forward. Teddy tried to hold on to the few she could: the boat. Jeremy holding his doctor's bag. Molly in her nurse's costume. Jeremy leaning forward as if to kiss her—

"Stop it!"

Teddy's head snapped back as though she'd been struck. The connection shattered. She opened her eyes.

"Don't do that!" Molly shrieked. "I didn't give you permission to enter my mind like that!"

Teddy hadn't intended to enter Molly's mind. She'd just been trying to complete Dunn's exercise. She'd pushed her way through only when Molly had blocked her. But now hardly seemed like the time to point that out. Not when Molly was clearly upset and the rest of the class was staring at them.

"You can't keep doing that! It's why no one ever volunteers to pair up with you!" Molly's eyes grew wide as she realized what she'd said. "Excuse me, Professor Dunn, I'm not myself. I think I need to go to the infirmary." Without another word, she pivoted and raced out of the classroom, letting the door slam behind her.

Teddy rocked back. She hadn't meant to do it; she just couldn't stop herself. Aware of the heavy silence that filled the room, she looked up to find the other recruits' expressions displaying varying degrees of sympathy and satisfaction. But no one—not even Jillian—rushed to deny what Molly had said.

"You crossed a line," Jeremy said. "Again."

Teddy flushed with anger. She wanted to blame Clint. He'd promised her that they would work to control her gift. But the only thing they'd done so far was work on her stupid wall. Mustering as much dignity as she could, she lifted her chin and left the room without looking back.

She needed to talk to Clint now. She wanted to get ahead of the situation—both of them, actually: the trespassing in Eversley's office, and this morning, in Molly's mind. The others would forgive her—Jillian and Dara and Pyro and Jeremy would, at least. Molly? Teddy wasn't so sure.

*　*　*

Teddy's racing thoughts carried her through Fort McDowell and up the two flights of stairs to Clint's office. She heard voices inside.

"How many samples were stolen?" Clint's voice boomed.

"Three." Nick. She shouldn't have been surprised that they would be together, trying to get to the bottom of this. Nick investigated crimes for a living, after all. And that's what this whole thing was, after all—a crime. "Evans, Federico, and—"

"Cannon."

Cannon? They were talking about the stolen samples. Why would someone want her blood? Clint's voice went quiet then, and she couldn't make out what he said, but she distinctly heard her name again.

"And Brett Evans is gone," Clint continued.

"Yes, sir," Nick said. "Rumor has it that he was in possession of a key. Makes for a pretty short suspect list." Nick's arrival on campus had been well timed. An FBI agent appearing just when Whitfield needed one most.

Teddy had decided two things before she knocked on the door: she wouldn't tell Clint that Molly had hacked Eversley's computers, which meant she couldn't let on that she had discovered her parents were psychic; if finding out more about them meant more time at Whitfield, she could wait.

The second decision was that she would enter the room with her wall in full force. She closed her eyes, summoning the electricity. It buzzed up her fingers. She wrapped it once, twice, three times around her mind. She imagined turning up a dial to full force, making her wall so strong that her hair crackled and stood on end. And then she opened the door and walked into the office.

She spoke before either man could stop her: "I'm going to say some things, and you both are going to listen. One: I haven't forgiven either of you for what you did in Vegas. That was low. And I'm still mad as hell about it." Her eyes stung from either anger or hurt, she didn't know. She'd trusted Clint. And even if he had his reasons—good reasons, Teddy supposed—he'd manipulated her. "Two: I was in the lab last night. Nick knows. I didn't take anything. And three: we need to figure out a way to control this astral telepathy thing, because it's seriously interfering with my life."

"You knew she was there last night?" Clint asked.

Nick shot Teddy a stare so cold that she practically felt crystals forming on her skin. "I was waiting until I had more details before I confirmed a list, sir. Ms. Cannon was just one of those names."

"Who else?" Clint asked.

"That's not for me to say," Teddy said. "But trust me: we didn't steal those samples. We were in there for fifteen minutes, tops, between eleven-thirty and eleven-forty-five." Teddy's vision swam. Clint was trying to break down her mental defense, as he had so many times before. She could feel him right at the edge of her mind; she could hear her own thoughts, a collection of damning phrases about Molly's USB device, the computer in the lab room, the windows on the screen. If Clint heard, she'd be done for.

She summoned every bit of energy she had. With his every push, the electricity sparked. She turned the dial even higher, making the wall burn brighter, stronger. Teddy called on her frustration over losing the money in Vegas, at being duped, betrayed, converting every ounce of anger into powering the wall. She was sweating from the effort. So was he.

Clint said, "I don't know whether to be disappointed that you broke school rules again. Or impressed that you're managing to repel me with such staggering mental force."

"Look, I'm coming clean." She looked pointedly between Nick and Clint. "I only wish you had done the same."

"If you're talking about Agent Stavros's involvement in your recruitment, it's standard protocol." Clint adjusted some papers on his desk. "And if you expect to be rewarded for coming forward about your infraction, you're mistaken. We'll discuss your actions with the rest of the administration. As of now, it's an open investigation."

"What does that mean?" Teddy asked.

"First, it means you have a lot of work to do in the dining hall." Clint said. "Second—stay out of it."

Like hell she'd stay out of it. If someone wanted her blood, she was damn well going to find out who. But she'd been lucky to get off with just chores. No Boyd. No goodbye to Whitfield.

"And Teddy," Clint called out to her as she was leaving his office.

"Yes?"

"Now that you've finally mastered your wall, you can start learning to control that astral telepathy thing that's been interfering with your life."

As she walked down the hall, Teddy heard Clint mutter something about her interfering with *his* life.

CHAPTER EIGHTEEN

A MONTH AFTER THE BREAK-IN, BRETT EVANS STILL hadn't returned to campus. Jillian seemed to be taking his disappearance especially hard, but she hadn't confided a single thing to Teddy about her feelings. Molly wasn't speaking to Teddy, so Jeremy wasn't, either. Things with Pyro had cooled way down. Nick had been avoiding her. Dara was the only person who would sit with Teddy at meals. Their conversations revolved around the various death warnings Dara received for her grandparents' friends and a few D-list celebrities, which rarely turned out to be prophetic.

Though only a few people were still talking *to* her, Teddy knew everyone was talking *about* her. The investigation into the theft of the blood vials was ongoing—and it seemed like everyone knew that Teddy had confessed something to Clint. So, with fewer friends and more free time, Teddy decided to focus all of her energy on becoming the best damn psychic she could possibly be. It was that or obsess about why someone had wanted to steal her blood sample.

"I've been thinking about the best strategy to control your trips into someone else's mind," Clint said one afternoon in tutorial. "Have you ever heard about the concept of memory palaces?"

Teddy shook her head.

"I thought that since you're from Vegas, you would have. Some players use them to help count cards for blackjack."

"Poker, remember?"

Clint rolled his eyes. "A memory palace is an imaginary location where you can store mnemonic images. In your case, it would be a place where you'd store actual memories. The technique works best when you imagine a location that you're familiar with and know in detail . . ."

Teddy couldn't help but think of the yellow house that haunted her dreams, which had been occurring with regularity; when she was especially tired from a long day of school, the images were particularly vivid.

"The memory palace is the inspiration behind this technique. Since you're using this to help store another's memories, we're going to have to diverge from the device at this point."

"What do you mean?" Teddy asked.

"It's impossible to navigate everything that's happening in someone's astral body. You're going to build a structure to help organize it, so you can control what images you want to see. Instead of being bombarded with thoughts and memories, you can place them in rooms, look through them at your leisure. But what I'm wondering, since this is all theoretical, is how you can be able to access the subject's house."

Teddy adjusted herself in the seat across from Clint's massive desk, her eye catching the screw in the left-hand corner. "I'm not following."

"Once you've made it past your subject's fortifying wall—if that person is psychic, you should assume there will be one—you're going to have to summon his or her house, so to speak. You'll have to synthesize what you know about the subject into a unified, concrete structure—everything you know about him or her combined into one design. Then enter it. I'm assuming the better you know the individual, the more detailed the structure will be." Clint cleared his throat. "I think we should try it."

"Like now?"

Clint rolled up his sleeves. "Like in Dunn's class. You picture an image—a walkie-talkie, right?—to help build your connection between minds. I'm going to lower my wall, and you have to lower yours, and then you're going to try to organize what you see inside my head into one structure—my house. Then imagine your astral self walking into it. And then find a memory. Sound good?"

"Yeah, totally—just make an imaginary house out of everything I know about you and walk through it and find a memory and then tell you about it. After that, why don't we hold hands and go for a unicorn ride on a rainbow?"

"Teddy," Clint said, eyebrows raised.

"Okay, okay." She hadn't performed astral telepathy since Molly had freaked out on her a few weeks ago. She wasn't scared, exactly. She just hadn't had any favorable experiences using this supposedly amazing skill.

"Focus," Clint said. "I'm lowering my wall."

Teddy dimmed her mental wall until it was just a low hum of electric current. She considered everything she'd learned about Clint—his messy office, his dad jokes, his old jersey. The memory of his dog. The screw on his desk. A piece of paper on his desk caught Teddy's eye: *Lab Report*. Her thoughts went back to her blood sample. She couldn't think about that now; if she wanted to get this right, she had to focus.

When she reached out to his mind, she wasn't confronted with a cacophony of images; instead, she saw . . . nothing. From inky darkness, a shape started to emerge. She felt the urge to blink but forced herself not to. She walked toward a white picket fence, an orderly lawn. It wasn't the same place she'd seen in Clint's memories, the one with his dog. What emerged was a small two-story white house with a gray shingled roof. In the window, a light was on.

In her mind's eye, she saw herself walk up the steps, reach for the doorknob, and open the front door. When she turned toward where the kitchen should be, she didn't see a kitchen at all. She walked into a memory.

The first thing she registered was that it was night. And that she was in the desert. She could feel the hot air on her skin. She could smell smoke in the air. The charred aftermath of an explosion. There was nothing but miles and miles of arid, empty space. Teddy somehow understood that what mattered wasn't on the surface at all but underground. A bunker. A number three surrounded by concentric circles etched on the bunker door. She heard bullets in the background and ran back toward the door to Clint's house. And suddenly found herself in the worn chair in Clint's office, looking right at him.

"What did you see?" he asked. "I felt you in my mind, but I couldn't see what you were looking at. What were you trying to see?"

She turned the power of her wall back up to high. She didn't know why she lied, but she did: "Your dog. Another memory of your dog. You were playing catch."

Clint smiled. "It worked! The house?"

Teddy nodded, still unsettled from her trip into Clint's memories. "It did." She reached for a pitcher and a glass of water on a side table. "Do you live in a place with a gray roof? Neat lawn?"

Clint rubbed his chin. "Interesting. That's what my house looked like to you?"

Teddy nodded again, taking another sip of water.

"No, I've never lived in a house like that. It sounds nice, though."

"It was nice," Teddy said. "It looked like a home." She looked around the office. Clint was distracted, happy with her performance. She hoped to take advantage of it. Find out what she could about the lab. "Mind if I change the subject?" she asked.

"If it's about the break-in, Teddy, all students have been given the same information—"

Even without reading her thoughts, he'd known what she would ask. But she didn't have the same information. She knew the names of the three students whose blood samples had been stolen. That coupled with what she'd just seen . . . "It's about my genetic markers."

"How do you know about genetic markers?"

Teddy thought for a minute before the lie came, too easily. She hated lying. But she didn't have a choice. She had to know. "When I bumped into Eversley in the hall the other day, I must have connected with his mind. I saw that he knew I had both maternal and paternal genetic markers. That's what he's researching here at Whitfield. Gene markers for psychic ability." She could sense a shift in Clint. She noticed sweat on his brow, his fingers tensing. Signs she knew how to read from the poker table.

She wanted him to make the last connection: that she had realized her birth parents were psychic.

He didn't—or at least he didn't voice it. His gaze flicked to the screw on his desk. "You need to focus on the task at hand. Your parents' genetic makeup doesn't have any bearing on what you're doing in this room."

Teddy released her frustration with a sound that was part groan, part growl. All right, so maybe what Clint was saying was true.

"It's not a roller-coaster ride, Teddy. You're building a foundation here, remember? Just lay one brick at a time."

His words didn't cool the simmering impatience that coursed through her. She had lived her entire life oblivious to her past. Now that she was finally beginning to understand it, she wanted know everything *immediately*. Now. Yesterday.

Teddy glanced at the screw on Clint's desk. A screw that was so important he had it encased in glass. He really did believe in the power of small things, small steps.

"Fine. Let's try something new," Clint said. He pulled a Ping-Pong ball out of his desk drawer. "A plastic ball filled with air *wants* to move."

Teddy raised an eyebrow.

"Yes, I know. It has no brain, no central nervous system. It can't want anything. I'm simply saying that an object in motion tends to stay in motion. The physical properties of a Ping-Pong ball offer almost no resistance to energy. It doesn't matter whether that energy is psychic or physical force. The ball simply acts upon that energy and moves." He threw the ball, sending it skittering across his desk. "Now you try."

Teddy reached for it.

"Not with your physical body. With your astral body."

Is he crazy?

"First of all, how? Second of all, what does that even mean?"

"Imagine your astral body extending through your physical body to push the ball."

Teddy took a deep breath. She centered herself, drawing upon Dunn's meditative techniques for focus. She reached out to the Ping-Pong ball the same way she'd reached out to Clint's mind a moment ago. She pictured a shadow of her hand stretching forward, a shimmer of fingers wrapping around plastic.

Nothing.

"Try, Teddy."

"I am." Again she willed the ball to move. It just sat there. Clint kept telling her to try harder, to summon her power. She did, again and again—with no result.

"You really, really want the Ping-Pong ball to move. But all that wanting it to move—and resulting frustration when it doesn't—is about *you wanting the Ping-Pong ball*. Just move the Ping-Pong ball. The Ping-Pong ball does not take directions. Does that make sense?"

"No."

"Look, Teddy." Clint shifted in his chair and tried again. "You've made it a battle of wills. You versus the Ping-Pong ball. The Ping-Pong ball doesn't care about you. Just move it."

Teddy took a moment to consider what he'd said.

Stop thinking. Just do it. Nike should start marketing to psychics.

She rolled her eyes. "Okay, fine. I'll try one more time." Teddy took a deep breath and imagined her astral arm reaching out of her body, pushing the Ping-Pong ball across the desk.

It wavered.

Clint scooped the ball up from the desk. "The end goal of this exercise is to draw upon both your telepathic and telekinetic ability. Today it's a Ping-Pong ball, but one day it could be a bullet."

Teddy couldn't imagine moving a bullet. An object in motion with its own speed and force. "Like in *The Matrix*?"

Clint laughed. "Yes, like in *The Matrix*. But there's a whole principle of astral quantum physics behind it." He held up one hand. "First, telepathy. When you reach out to someone's mind and encounter his astral body, you access all his thoughts, memories, and feelings out of order, right? You see time in a nonlinear way. As you develop your skill, you may start to see the future, memories that haven't even occurred."

"I guess," Teddy said, remembering what it was like when she went into someone's head.

"What if you can extend this philosophical principle from telepathy to telekinesis? If you treat time as nonlinear on the physical plane, too? You could free yourself from the constraints of time itself, potentially change how you experience time—meaning you could actually change its speed. That combined with the ability to move an object . . ." Clint trailed off.

"Means that I'd be able to slow down time in order to bend a bullet's path."

"Exactly."

A knock on the door interrupted them. She checked the clock. Their two-hour tutorial was already over, and another student stood in the hallway, waiting to meet with Clint.

Before Teddy turned to leave, Clint tossed the Ping-Pong ball in her direction. She caught it with one hand.

"One brick at a time," he said.

CHAPTER NINETEEN

EVEN THOUGH WEEKS HAD PASSED SINCE HALLO-ween, Boyd seemed to take the theft personally. And in turn was personally trying to ruin the first years' lives by ensuring they could never walk again. After a merciless cycle of lunges, squats, and walkouts, they now were running laps on the track. "Faster!" she yelled.

Teddy tried to block the sergeant's shouts, not an easy feat when the only other sound was the heavy breathing of the recruits surrounding her. Her lungs burned; a cramp pierced her side. And she still had two more times around the track to go.

She finished the course in the middle of the pack—not great but good enough. She put her head between her knees, gulping air as Boyd tore in to the recruit who stumbled in last.

Molly, as usual.

They had barely spoken since the events of Halloween, but watching Molly crumble as Boyd yelled at her made something inside Teddy soften. She opened her mouth to tell Boyd to lay off, but the sergeant seemed to sense even potential insubordination. She whipped her head around to face Teddy, as if daring her to speak. Teddy remembered the first day of class, the list of acceptable answers: *Yes, ma'am. No, ma'am. No excuse, ma'am.* Teddy wanted to use other words. One in particular that started with the letter *F*.

Boyd returned her attention to the rest of the class. "All right, recruits, line up for a couple of announcements." The students formed a line and stood at ease, feet shoulder-width apart, chest out, chin back, hands clasped behind their backs. Alphas on Boyd's right, Misfits on her left.

"I heard that there are still rumors floating around about Halloween," Boyd began. "We will find out who stole from this institution. And they will be punished."

She paused, letting the threat sink in. "Next. We're starting a new physical fitness unit. By now you should be at the level of fitness expected of those who choose to serve. If you aren't, the gym's open twenty-four hours a day." She shot another glare at Molly, then hit a wall switch. The heavy vinyl curtain that divided the gym into two workspaces groaned open to reveal a large obstacle course that looked like it had been designed by a sadist: climbing walls, swaying ladders, hurdles, balance beams, rope netting, seesaws, punching bags, monkey bars, and too many other instruments of aerobic torture for Teddy to name.

Next to her, Pyro shifted uneasily. The course looked *hard*, and Boyd appeared far too delighted with it for the outcome to bode well for anybody, even a former police officer.

"Oh my God," Dara said, still panting from their run. "At what point do we just give up?"

The sergeant strode across the gym to stand at the entrance to the course. "This is an official SWAT tactics course, designed to replicate the kind of obstacles you might encounter in the field. You will face similar physical barriers during your midyear exam in a few weeks, so I suggest you take this exercise seriously."

Teddy's wistful hope that the sergeant might give them time to acquaint themselves with the course's various obstacles was instantly crushed.

"Team challenge!" Boyd bellowed. She went down the line, assigning each of the Misfits, and then each of the Alphas, a number. "You will complete your section of the course before signaling your teammate to begin. First team to successfully reach the end of the course wins." She paused, giving Teddy a hard stare. "Remember, in my class, there are *always* consequences for allowing your enemy to win."

Teddy was second to last in the Misfit lineup. She looked over her portion of the course, mentally preparing to tackle it. Boyd blew her whistle, and the challenge began.

Teddy watched as both teams erupted in shouts of encouragement. Pyro led the Misfits. He was up against Henry Cummings, for whom exercise meant a round of golf at his father's club.

Pyro took off fast and didn't slow down. He shot through a pipe, crab-walked over a strip of netting, climbed up a steep incline wall, grabbed a rope, and hurled himself toward Dara.

The Misfits flew through the course. Teddy watched, caught between awe and excitement. Her teammates were kicking some Alpha ass. Dara finished fast, and so did Jeremy. The Alphas remained a solid three obstacles behind. Their lead wavered a bit when Jillian was matched with Liz Cook, who flew over the balance beam as though walking on air. But Jillian was stronger. She burst through a maze of foam pads far faster than Liz, and smacked Teddy's hand.

Teddy ran, Zac Rogers trailing behind her. She swung across monkey bars, sprinted up and down a seesaw, and high-stepped through a tire course. She couldn't believe that only a short time ago, she'd spent every evening balancing a bag of Tostitos and salsa on her stomach while scrolling through dumb Instagram feeds in her bed. Now she felt—strong. Sure, her muscles ached from Boyd's torture, but she could rely on her body in a way she never had before. All those years she'd never played team sports because of her epilepsy diagnosis. And now, as she pushed off the wooden board and propelled herself forward to tag Molly waiting at the next station, she felt a high similar to what she felt while playing poker.

She loved to win.

Teddy tagged Molly, finishing her round of the relay. Molly took off running. To everyone's surprise, she handled her obstacles like a pro, running, leaping, crawling, climbing, gaining speed as she went. Molly scampered up to the top of the climbing wall and grabbed the rope to rappel down the other side. The Misfits erupted into pre-celebratory cheers. For once, finally, they were going to win.

"Don't do it!" Kate Atkins shouted to Molly, hurling herself over the obstacles as she raced toward the climbing wall. "Look down! You'll fall and break your neck!"

Molly froze, the rope caught in her hand.

Teddy stared at Kate, dumbfounded. Everyone knew that Molly was scared of heights. It seemed impossible that anyone could be so mean.

"It's too high!" Kate shouted.

Molly's face drained of color.

Teddy clenched her fists so hard she felt her fingernails bite into her skin. She was going to get Kate for this.

Kate reached the top of the wall and pulled the rope out of Molly's hands. She rappelled down the other side, landing in a crouch. As Molly slowly, painstakingly, made her way down, the Alphas celebrated their victory.

Teddy caught Kate's upper arm. "What the hell was that?"

Kate jerked her arm free. "That's called winning, Cannon. You ought to try it sometime."

Rage surged through Teddy. Unbidden, she felt her electric wall flare in her mind. She wanted to humiliate Kate the way Kate had humiliated Molly.

Pyro stepped between them. "Chill, Teddy. It doesn't matter."

"It doesn't matter? How can you say that? She cheated!"

Suddenly, Boyd was by her side, too. "Let me make one thing perfectly clear, recruit. There is no rule prohibiting the use of verbal tactics against a classmate."

"But that's not fair!" Teddy protested.

"Fair?" Boyd's eyes went cold. "You expect the enemy to play *fair*?"

Teddy swallowed hard, biting back her words. She wanted to take Boyd down, too. But she stood there, breathing hard, trying to remember that this wasn't worth getting kicked out of Whitfield. She couldn't risk another infraction. Not with the pending investigation.

Boyd continued, "It's my job to prepare you for the field. I can goddamn guarantee the enemy will exploit every weakness they can. When you're in pursuit, the enemy won't let you scale the smaller wall because you're delicate—and I'm talking to you, Cummings."

Henry Cummings studied the floor.

"The enemy doesn't care how many Zen meditations you do. The enemy doesn't care how hard you try," Boyd said. "If given a chance, the enemy will slit your throat. You need to pay attention in my class. That's the only way you're going to survive out there in the real world. Am I making myself clear?"

Both the Alphas and the Misfits mumbled their assent. Teddy's throat was burning.

"Dismissed," Boyd said.

Teddy gathered her things and rushed for the exit. All she wanted was to get out of there and find a way to blow off steam before she exploded. It seemed arbitrary what rules were upheld in Boyd's class. That Teddy had almost been rejected from Whitfield all those months ago on a technicality, but Kate was lauded for belittling a fellow student? That wasn't right. Just as she reached the door, though, she felt a hand on her shoulder. Teddy whirled around, ready to snap at whoever had the audacity to approach her. But it was Molly. She looked Teddy straight in the eyes and uttered a single word: "Thanks."

The first words Molly had spoken to her in weeks. Teddy shrugged as if to say it was nothing. But one look at Molly's face reminded her that Molly was an empath; she knew exactly what Teddy was feeling. Molly was the first and only person who had understood her.

CHAPTER TWENTY

AFTER THE SHOWDOWN ON BOYD'S OBSTACLE COURSE, the recruits at Whitfield went on lockdown. Exams were around the corner. In the history of the institution, only one class had managed to survive their first year with all its members. Looking around at her fellow Misfits as they sat in a drafty classroom in Fort McDowell, Teddy was determined to return to Angel Island in January.

The only bright spot in their rigorous schedule: a short reprieve off-island for Thanksgiving break. Both Misfits and Alphas were counting down the days until they could say goodbye to Whitfield and its vegan fare (well, except Jillian). But what waited for Teddy in Vegas? Casinos, poker, Sergei. The old Teddy.

She dragged her thoughts back to Clint's lecture, the last before the holiday. Clint had picked up on the room's restless energy and begun telling a story. "So I knew we had the right guy in custody," he said.

"But you didn't have any physical proof," said Zac Rogers, "right?"

"Right," Clint said. "A psychic's word—even when you're one hundred percent certain you're right—isn't going to hold up in court. So we had to let him go."

Liz Cook frowned. "Couldn't you have done something?"

Clint turned to her. "Like what?"

"You know, get him to confess. He was a child molester. Couldn't you have used your skill at mental influence to force him to reveal everything?"

Clint shook his head. "That's coercion. I can use what I know to encourage a confession, but I can't force one. That's not how the system works.

"In this situation, though it may be hard to empathize with a defendant, try to understand *why* he or she behaved in a certain way. Combined with the extrasensory insight you have as a psychic? That's invaluable. That will allow you to get a genuine confession in a way that no one else can."

He waited a bit, letting that sink in.

Zac shifted in his seat. "So let me get this straight. Even if I know someone's guilty, I'm supposed to just sit there and watch a rapist or a serial killer or a terrorist walk out the door? Unless I can try to feel sorry for him and talk about his feelings?"

Clint bristled. "If you can't get a confession? Or you're not willing to put yourself in a place to get one? You don't have a choice. You have to try. And no matter what type of case you're working on, the cardinal rule of psychics in police work always holds."

Clint stood and strode to the dry-erase board behind him, writing in bold letters: A PSYCHIC CAN NEVER USE HIS POWER TO TAMPER WITH EVIDENCE OR TESTIMONY TO BENEFIT THE OUTCOME OF A CASE.

"Sometimes the end justifies the means," Jeremy said.

Teddy looked at him. She couldn't help remembering what he had told her about his mother's death on 9/11: he couldn't do anything before the planes hit the Twin Towers.

"Not when the means are illegal," said Clint.

Jeremy held Clint's gaze for a long moment, then turned his attention to his textbook, brushing his fingers along the frayed edge as he muttered softly, "I just don't like to see innocent people get hurt." Molly, sitting beside him, placed her hand over his.

Clint sighed. "Nobody does." With that, he shot a glance at the clock. "For those of you heading home for Thanksgiving, enjoy your weekend. We'll reconvene Monday afternoon."

Teddy had gathered her things and moved to follow the rest of her classmates when Clint stopped her.

"I didn't see your request for a pass to leave campus on my desk," he said.

"I'm staying here to study," she said. The thought of an empty campus held a certain appeal. No awkward encounters with Pyro, or Nick, or Kate, or Molly, or Boyd . . . The list was getting long.

He pulled out another Ping-Pong ball from his pocket. "Practice over break, okay?" The ball flew in an arc toward Teddy.

She caught it, barely. Hand-eye coordination wasn't her strongest suit. Turned out neither was moving Ping-Pong balls with her mind. "Clint?"

He stopped at the door and frowned at the strain in her voice. "Yeah?"

Teddy chewed her lower lip. Since their last meeting, she'd been trying to shake the images she'd seen in Clint's mind. She wanted to talk to him about it, but she didn't know how. At last she said, "That guy. The child molester. Did you ever catch him?"

A flash of brilliant white teeth. "Of course I did. But the right way," he said.

*　*　*

Later that evening, she burrowed into an armchair in the library, books spread out before her, the Ping-Pong ball clutched in her hand. Jillian, Molly, Dara, and Teddy had each claimed a corner of the room, the four of them struggling to finish their Forensics research paper before break. "So," Jillian said, "there's this coyote on the island who's so heartsick. When he cries, he sounds like a preteen girl screaming at a One Direction concert."

"Hmm," Teddy said. But her thoughts kept ricocheting back to the glimpse she'd had into Clint's consciousness. The coyote, the bunker, the desert, the smoke. *Coyote.* She'd heard that before.

She set down her pen and looked at Jillian. "Hey. Speaking of coyotes. Remember that dream you had a few weeks ago?"

Jillian, her nose in her textbook, didn't bother to look up. "If you're talking about the one with Al Gore, that was told in confidence."

"Okay, enough with Gore. I meant the one where you were"—she really felt like an idiot saying it aloud—"a coyote?"

"Yeah, what about it?"

"Do you recall anything else? Any details?"

Jillian raised one eyebrow. "Sand." That could have been anywhere. Teddy was about to dismiss the dream when Jillian continued: "I was in the middle of the desert. And all around me, I felt like, the world was ending." She shivered. "And I remember seeing an inscription."

Teddy ripped out a page from her notebook, scribbling the symbol she'd seen in Clint's office and in his mind.

"Yeah, that's right," Jillian said.

"Why are you drawing the symbol for Sector Three, Cannon?" Dara said, leaning forward.

Molly's head snapped up. "I thought we were trying to get this report done."

"Give me a minute," Teddy said, waving her off. "I think Clint knows something about Sector Three. He was involved with it somehow."

"Well, he wasn't at Sector Three, I can tell you that for sure," Dara said.

"Why not?"

"Because Sector Three had no survivors."

Jillian frowned. "No survivors? Then how does anyone know—"

"My grandmother also gets death predictions. People here wouldn't approve of what she does. But she has a shop. Headdress. Crystal ball. The whole shebang. She told me a story about this one guy who came to New Orleans for Mardi Gras in the eighties.

"He told my grandmother he worked for a government contractor at the time. The contractor had clearance to enter this military base once a week and deliver food, drinks, ice, propane, whatever the mess hall needed."

"The base was in the desert?" Teddy said.

"Yeah. Somewhere in Nevada." Dara lowered her voice. "Anyway, the vision she first got was normal—most of what happened on the base was just boring military stuff. Combat training, weapons drills, vehicle maneuvers, things like that. But all of a sudden, she got this picture of this guy getting blown up on his delivery. She wanted to warn him, so she drew the symbol that she saw in her vision for him. And she told him to stay away from there if he wanted to live. And the guy basically flipped out. Told her that he'd had it up to here with psychics and he was never going back to Nevada."

"So Sector Three trained psychics?" Teddy asked.

Dara shrugged. "I guess so. That's what my grandmother always assumed. No one else in our community ever talked about it. There was no mention of the facility in any records. She got another vision months later. Just bodies. Everyone there had died. That's why I said no survivors."

An explosion. Teddy had seen the aftermath of an explosion in Clint's thoughts. But did that mean—

Boyd chose that moment to stroll through the library. They watched as she perused the rack of DVDs available for checkout, finally selecting one and leaving the library again.

Dara leaned forward, mischief dancing in her eyes, her story temporarily forgotten. "*Showgirls* or *Sharknado?*"

Jillian didn't quite manage to choke back her laugh. But Molly flinched as though struck. White-faced, she sat motionless at the table. Even at the mere sight of Boyd, Molly seemed to shut down.

"Hey," Teddy said softly. "Molly. I know it's hard, but try not to let Boyd get under your skin like that."

"You don't understand," Molly said. She grabbed her books, shoved them into her backpack, and fled their table.

Jillian blinked. "I hope she's okay."

Teddy looked up and saw Jeremy stop Molly at the library door. The two stood huddled together. At times Teddy couldn't tell if Jeremy was part of the problem or the solution. His presence seemed to calm Molly but also agitate her. Relationships. She didn't get them.

Jeremy came in and bypassed their table to sit down next to a pretty, athletic African-American woman with long brown hair.

"Who's that?" Teddy asked, pissed on Molly's behalf that he was talking to another girl.

Dara followed Teddy's gaze. "Christine Federico. She's one of the top third-years."

Evans. Federico. Cannon.

Teddy's shock must have shown on her face: Dara cocked her head, waiting expectantly for her to say something. Teddy opened her mouth and waited for her brain to catch up. It didn't. The gears simply spun. What linked Teddy to Brett Evans and this girl? Though Clint had effectively blocked any further discussion on the topic, Teddy couldn't dismiss the notion that the theft hadn't been random.

"Sometimes I see her in the meditation lawn," Jillian said. "I feel bad she's staying here for Thanksgiving."

"She is?" Teddy said. Her brain started to whir again—maybe Christine knew something about the theft. And though she had planned to do schoolwork over break, she now had another research project in mind: Christine Federico.

Jillian yawned. "I'm so glad I'm going home for the weekend. Need to recharge. You want to join, Teddy? Some time away from campus might do you good."

Teddy shook her head. "No, I've got stuff to do over break."

Did she ever.

CHAPTER TWENTY-ONE

BY THANKSGIVING DAY, TEDDY WAS REGRETTING HER decision to stay at Whitfield over break. For all of her idealistic plans of bumping into Christine around campus, Teddy hadn't seen the girl once. She went to the meditation lawn each morning; hung out around the gym; stayed in the dining hall until the hot pumpkin soup the staff was serving in honor of the holiday went cold. And despite her fear of slipping back into her old bad habits, she missed the idea of being home for the holidays. Even if that home was Jillian's parents' split-level in New Jersey, with a menagerie of bizarre animals, hippie parents, and a full vegan dinner.

Teddy walked to the main office in Fort McDowell, the Ping-Pong ball in her pocket. She hadn't managed to move it with her astral body, or whatever Clint had said, but she had taken to carrying it around with her. She'd come to think of it as a sort of talisman, a symbol of what she might accomplish.

Because there was basically no one on campus, there was no line to use one of the phones. She called her parents but wasn't surprised to get the answering machine. Thanksgiving in their family began with a morning hike in Red Rock Canyon. Her mom considered it early penance for all the food they'd devour later.

Teddy left a message and hung up. She decided to follow tradition as best she could, so she walked back to her room and suited up for a jog. Following the trail around the island's perimeter, Teddy tried to put home out of her head. She pushed herself to run faster and longer, through the burn in her chest, the cramps in her legs. She didn't know if she was running toward or away from something—all she knew was that if she kept moving, she'd eventually be too tired to think.

* * *

Exhausted, Teddy couldn't even bring herself to put in an appearance at the on-campus Thanksgiving celebration. Instead, with legs feeling the approximate texture of the cold canned cranberry sauce her mother usually served, she passed out on her cot, thankful for sleep free of Jillian's snores. When a knock came at the door, she was surprised to see that it was Pyro. They hadn't been alone together since that night at the Cantina. Teddy hadn't realized that he'd also decided to spend the holiday on-campus.

"Come on," he said, leaning against her door. "It's even more pathetic if you don't show."

She suspected she wasn't alone in feeling moody and out of place. The handful of students who remained sat together at a single table, decorated with perfunctory gourds. All except the one she'd hoped would be there: Christine.

Teddy and Pyro were the only first-years; the rest were upperclassmen, and the difference in conversation was noticeable. Where Teddy and her peers discussed nothing but the midyear exam, the upperclassmen compared their internships and debated the qualifications of the new FBI liaison on campus. Whenever Nick's name came up, Teddy felt Pyro's gaze shift toward her. She kept her face blank and her wall up. It was none of his damn business.

Just when Teddy had made the decision to return to her room, Christine took a seat across from her, wedging in between two upperclassmen.

"Sorry I'm late," she said to her friends. "Had to finish a report."

"Don't tell me you're working on those Russian theories again," a blond third-year woman said from down the table. "You know that Cold War remote-viewing stuff is garbage."

This is your chance, Cannon. Be cool.

She didn't want to scare Christine off by seeming overeager. Teddy thought of the dining table as being like a poker table. She needed a play to get the most information. First-year suckup? Aloof but interested?

"You're a remote viewer?" Teddy asked.

Christine nodded. Teddy found she didn't have to act at all as she listened, fascinated by Christine's report.

"It's funny," Christine said, "I'm in here, but everything important is happening outside these walls." She paused, shaking her head. "I've seen it. I know."

Teddy found it hard to stay invested in Christine's rant when all she wanted to do was ask about the blood samples. But how did you ask a stranger about her genetic makeup without coming across as creepy?

"Brett agreed with me," Christine continued.

"Brett Evans?" Teddy said, the name slipping out of her mouth before she could stop herself.

Christine turned to her. "He was my best friend."

"Was?"

"*Is.* I only meant he's no longer here."

"He was really nice to me when I first came here. At the party."

Christine nodded. "He's a nice guy."

Teddy wondered how far she could push Christine. Should she bring up the lab? "He was nice to everyone, trading for Internet and stuff."

Christine rolled her eyes. "That wasn't nice. That was stupid. But Brett was always a sucker for extra cash. If he had twenty bucks in his pocket, he could turn it into a hundred, and then he'd show up in Wyoming three weeks later with a new horse, fresh from a wild bender. He was like that."

"So has he called from Wyoming yet? What's the horse's name?"

Christine smiled. "Nothing yet."

"Do you know where he is?" Teddy asked.

Christine shook her head. "Brett could be anywhere. Surfing in Hawaii. Backpacking in Tibet. He's pretty impulsive that way. But one place he isn't is back home in Austin."

"Oh?"

"He didn't get along with his grandparents. Strict religious types. They raised him after his parents died. He couldn't wait to leave."

"How did his parents die?" Teddy asked. She knew the question sounded crass before she even finished asking it. She'd met plenty of people whose parents were divorced and a few who had lost a single parent. But never had she met someone her age whose mother and father had both passed away, like hers had.

"Actually, the same way I lost mine," Christine replied. "Car accident. I think that's one of the reasons he and I bonded: we both understood what it was like to lose our parents in an instant and at such a young age. What it was like to not feel like we belonged with the people we were supposed to."

Teddy froze. Her mind raced to calculate the odds: three Whitfield students out of a population of under one hundred, all of who had lost their parents as infants. No, not a coincidence, not when their three names were on a list.

"Did you ever learn more about those accidents? Ever think that was a coincidence?"

Christine clenched her jaw. "You know, I don't think I really want to discuss this anymore. I barely know you. Excuse me."

With that, Christine got up from the table and left the dining hall. Teddy had completely blown her chance to question her further.

Hey, Christine, what makes you, me, and Brett so special? What happened to our parents?

Like that was going to happen.

"What the hell was that about?" Pyro asked.

Teddy shook her head, trying to clear the conversation from her mind. She'd had Christine right where she wanted her. "I don't know. I mean, nothing. It doesn't matter."

Pyro put his hand on her shoulder. For a moment, she wanted to lean in to him, but she caught herself. She wasn't going backward. Only forward. "I've got some studying to do," she said, getting up from the table.

It was the truth, kind of. She wanted to go over what Christine had said. About Brett and her parents. Car crashes. It was too coincidental. She said good night to Pyro and returned to her room. Alone.

CHAPTER TWENTY-TWO

THE NIGHT BEFORE THE MIDYEAR EXAM, TEDDY dreamed of the yellow house. It was always in the back of her mind somehow, but since the night when she'd gone inside, her dreams had taken on a different tenor. Everything felt more vivid, more real—the colors brighter, the sounds louder, the smells stronger.

Tonight the desert sky was full of clouds, like a storm was brewing. Wind blew desert brush across the ordinarily manicured front lawn. The windows were boarded up. Teddy sensed that something was wrong. She'd never encountered the house like this.

Teddy reached for the green door, paint now chipped away, and walked in. She stood in the foyer. The wallpaper was stripped from the walls. On the low table, once loaded with knickknacks, stood a single photograph in a silver frame. Teddy stopped in front of it and reached down to pick it up. She studied it. Three men and a woman. They were all wearing army jackets emblazoned with a number three surrounded by concentric circles—the symbol for Sector Three.

Clint Corbett's face grinned at her from the photograph, his arms loosely draped over the shoulders of people he must have considered good friends.

She stepped closer to get a better look. The man to Clint's left was almost a full head taller than Clint and wiry, with dark eyes, sharp cheekbones, a prominent nose. His strong features were made even more distinguished by a slender scar that ran along his jaw from ear to chin.

On Clint's right stood another man and a woman. They stood close, in a manner that suggested they might be a couple.

The man was good-looking, but even from the picture, Teddy could tell that his nose had been broken more than once. His dark hair was slicked back off his face, revealing ears almost too big for his head. He looked kind, almost goofy. His eyes were dark but held an intensity that made Teddy step back.

The woman next to him looked familiar, and for a brief, disconcerting moment, Teddy thought she was staring at a photo of herself: same dark hair, same angular features, same slightly pointed chin. But she had never worn her hair that long, almost halfway down her back. She'd never had an army jacket. Teddy studied the picture, noticing more details: how the woman's silver necklace, furnished with a large purple stone, stood out against the military garb; how her eyes shone as she looked at the man next to her.

The moment of recognition set in, sending Teddy's emotions reeling.

My mother. My parents.

But not the mother she knew, who was a middle-school math teacher and drove a ten-year-old Camry. This was her birth mother. Teddy put her hand on the wall to steady herself, catching her finger on a nail as she did. She pulled her hand away and saw the blood welling up.

Her heart beat a wild tempo against her ribs.

*   *   *

Teddy jerked upright in her bed, her sheets twisted around her ankles.

"What's wrong?" Jillian looked over at her from her bed, her hair tousled from sleep.

"A dream." Teddy was drenched in sweat. She looked at her hand, feeling the sting as if it had happened to her just then. Teddy's heart stopped when she saw the bright red spot on her finger.

"Was it Ryan Gosling?"

Teddy collapsed back against her pillow, blinking up at the ceiling as she tried to piece together the sharp fragments of her dream. The house. The photograph. The jackets. Her parents? In the dream, Teddy had been so certain. But in the cool morning light, she began to doubt what she had seen.

"Get up before you fall back asleep," Jillian said. "You don't want to be late to the exam."

December 18 already. The days since Thanksgiving had blended together in a monotony of classes and studying. Teddy tossed back the covers and swung her legs over the side of her bed. For three whole minutes, she'd actually forgotten that in a matter of hours, the first-year recruits would face their most difficult challenge to date. It seemed less important now, considering everything else that had happened.

This morning she would tackle a grueling four-hour written exam testing her knowledge of police procedure, courts and the prosecution process, forensics, and evidence analysis. But the true test of their ability would come later: a rigorous, hands-on tactical course meant to challenge their physical and psychic skills.

Fittingly, the exam was scheduled on the school's last day before winter break. Those who passed the exam would pack a bag, enjoy the holidays, and then return to Whitfield after New Year's Day rested, refreshed, and ready to begin the second semester. Those who didn't would clear out their dorm room and go home for good. Teddy refused to even consider that option—especially now that she knew Clint could have a link to her past. A past that he'd been keeping from her.

She showered, tossed on her leather jacket, and walked toward the dining hall. She pictured herself successfully running the course. Overcoming obstacles. Returning fire. Apprehending and interrogating a suspect. She captured every image in her mind.

She could do this. She could absolutely do this.

She had to.

CHAPTER TWENTY-THREE

FOUR MONTHS OF CONSTANT WORK, OF STAYING ON
the straight and narrow and keeping her nose as clean as possible, all
came down to one more exam. The first-year recruits had finished a
morning of grueling written tests; the practical test was next.

The students, dressed in their black-and-blue athletic uniforms,
were ushered into a boat and then into a van as they traveled to an
undisclosed location. Teddy's brain had melted from the seemingly
unending list of multiple-choice and essay questions about forensic
procedure and the pineal gland, and the drive gave her time to collect
her thoughts. She kept her face pressed against the window. Eventually, the streets of San Francisco gave way to the hills of Northern
California, and the van turned in to a military facility. Sign after sign
warned visitors to keep out, but the van barreled forward. Teddy tried
to replay the major lessons she'd learned this semester: Dunn's breathing techniques, Boyd's torturous workouts, Clint's empathy lectures.
Clint: she couldn't think about him without her mind spiraling out
to other questions, about her parents, Sector Three, and the past he
had kept from her. Her thoughts were jarred as the van hit a pothole,
rocking the car. Next to her, Dara swore.

They drove past a razor-wire fence, through an electronic gate, and
into a compound of enormous metal warehouses. The car stopped in a
circular drive where Clint, Dunn, and Boyd stood waiting. The first-
year recruits exited the vehicle and gathered around their professors.

Teddy shifted her weight between her feet, anxious about the next part of the exam.

The fog still sat low on the horizon, obscuring the skyline. It seemed like they were in another world, an alternate universe of metal warehouses and clouds. "Welcome, recruits," Clint said. It was cold. He wore a cap pulled down over his ears. Teddy couldn't help thinking of the hat as a kind of costume that made him look more serious, more official—something that he really wasn't. She stood her ground, preparing for what was coming next.

Teddy watched as a SWAT officer signaled to Clint, who pulled the cap off his head and put a handful of folded papers inside. Without looking, Professor Dunn reached inside the cap and withdrew a name. "Zac Rogers."

Boyd reached in and withdrew the next. "Dara Jones."

"Team One," Clint announced.

Zac and Dara stared at each other, appalled.

The instructors continued, randomly pulling names to create teams. Jillian Blustein and Henry Cummings. Lucas Costa and Ava Lareau. Theodora Cannon and Kate Atkins.

Anyone but Kate, Teddy thought. Why couldn't she once—just once—catch a break? Teddy glanced across the group at Kate, whose lips tightened into a grim line as she returned Teddy's nod. At least Kate seemed as determined to succeed as Teddy.

Teddy watched as Ben Tucker and Liz Cook were paired up, which left Molly Quinn and Jeremy Lee. Lucky breaks for them.

Boyd explained that they were about to enter an obstacle course like ones used by local police departments, SWAT forces, FBI, CIA, and the military as a training ground designed to test and perfect combat techniques. Whitfield recruits were expected to meet the physical challenges of the course and go one step further, using the lessons from Dunn's and Clint's classes to complete tasks. One team member would run the obstacles while the other remained outside the facility, telepathically sending the instructions required to complete the course. In addition, special "enemy combatants" would be situated throughout the course. Teddy had heard that these were special-ops marines whose job it was to take down as many recruits as possible. The fact that there was no live ammo was little consolation. Teddy could only guess what else awaited them inside that warehouse—they were told to trust no one but their teammate.

Clint passed a radar gun and a padded radar-sensitive vest to each team. On the back of each vest was a brightly colored triangle. Teddy and Kate were the red team.

"There are four checkpoints. At each, you'll find a color-coded card that corresponds to your vest. Collect all four cards, as well as a color-coded key, which will unlock the exit door. If you don't, you fail. If your vest lights up, you've received a fatal hit, and you fail. If you shoot a fellow recruit, you fail. You have one hour to complete the course. If you don't make it through in the allotted time, you fail. Is that clear?"

Teddy thought, *A lot of ways to fail.*

"I'll stay on the outside," Kate said. "I'm better at projecting telepathic messages than receiving them. And we don't want to risk you going all astral on me in there."

Teddy hesitated. She knew Kate was right. Her astral powers were unpredictable. Still, Teddy wasn't great at taking direction, psychic or otherwise.

"Of course, I'm also better at running obstacles," Kate said.

"How good are you at keeping your mouth shut?" Teddy asked. "I'm going in." She shrugged on the vest, grabbed two pairs of handcuffs and a wooden baton that had been given to each group, hooked in to the straps, and holstered the radar gun.

Kate gave the belt on Teddy's vest an extra tug.

"Too tight," Teddy objected.

"Can you breathe?"

"I guess."

"Then it's not too tight. You don't want the vest bumping around while you run. It'll throw off your balance." Kate fastened the last buckle and stepped back. "Listen. I talked to a friend of mine who's an upperclassman. She said you'll find a couple of prehistoric assholes in there who consider the course a private boys' club. They go harder on the women than they do on the guys, so watch out for them."

Teddy nodded.

Dunn moved among the teams, distributing sealed envelopes containing maps and clues to be psychically transmitted.

Beside her, Kate swatted the envelope against her palm. "Hey, Cannon. We got this. You know that, right?"

"Yeah."

"So if anyone tries to hold you back in there, you have my permission to take them out."

For the first time in hours, Teddy smiled. "Where? The Cantina? Or just for a grain bowl at Harris?"

Kate scowled. "Channel?"

Teddy dimmed the energy she was diverting to her wall, now second nature.

"How about lucky number seven?" Kate said. She took Teddy's hands in her own. They started to breathe together, trying to sync their connection. Kate's mind was nothing like Molly's. It was easy to find Kate's rhythm: steady, regular, strong, constant like a metronome. Teddy pictured the now familiar walkie-talkie, turning the channel to seven, hearing first static, then Kate's voice.

I'm in, Kate said.

I know, Teddy said. *I'm not an idiot.*

Prove it.

A starter pistol split the air.

Teddy took a deep breath and jogged through the entrance of the first of three warehouses, labeled with a huge letter *A*. Inside, it was darker than she'd thought. She had to squint to make out her first obstacle. A couple more steps and it came into her line of vision. One hundred feet ahead was a vertical wooden wall with a knotted rope. She'd have to climb that before she got a glimpse of what else awaited her. But she could do that. As a matter of fact, after half a year at Whitfield, she was goddamn good at rope climbing.

She hurled herself upward and grabbed the rope. But it came loose, and Teddy pitched backward, grunting as she landed flat on her back. Her breath whooshed from her lungs and she fought to catch it.

The rope hadn't been attached to anything, and Teddy hadn't bothered to check it, as she'd been trained to do. Nearby, someone cursed. At least she hadn't been the only one to fall for it.

I thought you said you weren't an idiot, Kate telegraphed.

Teddy rolled over, got to her feet. She examined the wall, noting for the first time its notched grooves and discrete wooden footholds. She scaled to the top to survey the other side.

An obstacle course. But this one was far more elaborate than anything she'd ever run in Boyd's gym—from the top of the wall, she could see that they'd set up what looked like a small town inside the warehouse, ramshackle structures created twisting alleyways. People milled about the course, some dressed as civilians, others outfitted in combat uniforms. It looked like a two-bit dystopian movie set. One of Boyd's "real-world scenarios." Teddy's gut churned.

First checkpoint—flagpole.

Got it, Teddy said.

She spotted the flagpole at her three o'clock, just east of a pile of tires. For a second, she wondered about that obstacle but then remembered her task. She scanned the area again, plotted a path as she climbed down the wall. She lurched forward, shoving through a stack of wooden crates. Teddy reached the flagpole only to find coils of wire wrapped around the base, extending six feet into the air.

How the hell am I supposed to climb this? Teddy didn't realize she had telegraphed the thought until she heard Kate's response.

What? Talk to me, Kate said.

It's wrapped in wire.

Don't climb it. Climb something else.

Teddy saw a metal Dumpster a few feet to her left. She felt she ought to thank Boyd for all the fun and games, for she easily hoisted herself onto the lid. She planted her feet, bent her knees, and hoisted herself onto the pole just above the razor wire. Putting one hand over the other, she propelled herself to the top and reached for her first red card, stamped with *Checkpoint #1.*

One down, she said to Kate.

Teddy tucked the card into her vest pocket and skimmed down the pole, launching herself back onto the Dumpster. If only she had known how to do this in Vegas. Teddy smiled. That would have given Sergei a run for his money. Or rather, a climb for his money.

Behind schedule, Kate said. *Hurry up.*

She thought she'd been moving fast. *Got it. Next?*

Second checkpoint. Bravo warehouse, back office.

Teddy retraced her steps, exiting the first warehouse, which was probably A, Alpha, and entering the second, Bravo. Unlike Alpha warehouse, where the lights were dim, Bravo was pure chaos. Flashing strobes, smoke, alarms. Another one of Boyd's tactical drills meant to distract recruits and challenge their focus. Teddy took a deep breath. She had to find a back office in this mess?

Teddy raised her head and surveyed the ground. In between flashing lights, she saw a door above a catwalk on the southwest corner of the warehouse. When the next alarm went off, sending another surge of smoke through the space, Teddy sprinted toward the structure, raced up the steps, and threw open the door. The high-pitched buzz of radar guns sounded all around her. Crap. She'd forgotten to check for potential threats before she'd entered.

Teddy froze. From the corner of her vision, she spotted Zac crouched in the corner. His gun was trained on her.

She raised her hands in surrender, and he nodded at her. If he shot her, they'd both be out.

"Hell of an entrance, Cannon," Zac said.

What's happening? Kate said in her head.

Zac.

Trust him.

Teddy wasn't so sure. She held her finger to her lips, withdrew her weapon, and peered out the window, assessing the situation. Three enemy combatants were stationed atop the metal catwalk that ran along the right side of the building. Even if Teddy and Zac found their cards, they'd never make it out.

"Let's take them out first," Zac said. He lined up his shot, preparing to fire at the first man on the catwalk. The enemy had higher ground, but the lack of cover left them vulnerable to attack. The proper response was to open fire, get the enemy to abandon his position, then claim the warehouse.

But that would take time. Time that Teddy didn't have.

"Cover me," she whispered. "Kate said I could trust you."

"Are you crazy?" Zac said. "You'll never—"

She jumped out from her hiding spot, gun blazing, like the hero at the end of a Western movie. Zac opened fire. Teddy whirled around to see that two of the enemies were down, but the third one had his radar gun aimed at Zac. For a second, Teddy thought about letting the combatant take Zac out, until she remembered that he was paired with Dara. Teddy got off a quick shot, and the combatant's vest lit up like a Vegas slot machine. Zac gave her a thumbs-up, but there was no time to respond. Teddy ran back into the open office and began to look for her card. She rummaged through the paperwork, swept her arm over the files on the desk, and found her red card buried underneath.

Number two complete.

Kate responded: *Don't gloat. Fourth checkpoint. Exit through front of*

Bravo warehouse. Apprehend suspect. Female. Caucasian. Flannel shirt. Red cap.

But that wasn't right. Kate had missed the third checkpoint.

Third checkpoint. Third, Teddy said.

Fourth checkpoint's in the next warehouse. Third checkpoint's in motion.

Fine. What's the fourth checkpoint? Teddy said.

Exit through front of Bravo warehouse. Apprehend suspect. Female. Caucasian. Flannel shirt. Red cap—

I have a clear path out the back exit. On the move.

You're supposed to be listening to my directions, Cannon! Front exit.

Kate didn't know what she was talking about; she wasn't on the course. If Teddy had a clear exit, she was taking it. She was tired of following Kate's orders. That was when Teddy's anger got the better of her. The change in her mental state altered the pitch of her brainwaves, which in turn severed the telepathic connection: Kate was gone. She'd lost her. Teddy closed her eyes and tried to reach Kate again, but over this distance, it would be nearly impossible.

How had she come this far and blown it? Teddy took one more breath. And then another, trying to remember Dunn's exercises. She'd fall apart later. Right now she had a suspect to apprehend. They still had time. She'd get that done and then reconnect with Kate. She had to keep moving.

She shot out of the office and stopped, then remembered the message she'd received from Kate: *Exit through front of Bravo warehouse.*

It didn't make sense. She could see a clear path through the back exit, all the way to the next warehouse. Kate was wrong. She'd missed a checkpoint, screwed everything up somehow. Was she trying to sabotage Teddy?

That had been the only time Kate had given explicit directions since the beginning of the course. Kate had told her to listen to Zac. And he'd helped her. Teddy had to trust her teammate. Even though she didn't understand why, she turned around to exit through the front.

Teddy flew down the steps and was immediately hit by a flying tackle. She hit the pavement hard, with what felt like a bag of bricks falling on top of her. For a moment, she was so dazed she couldn't move. The man caught her wrists and pinned them above her head, squeezing hard.

It took another moment for the months of Boyd's self-defense training to kick in. Teddy let her eyelids flutter shut and her body go limp. The man's grip loosened, and Teddy instantly twisted her wrists to break free. She slammed her forearm into her assailant's throat.

Teddy shot to her feet. So did he. Her mind racing, she considered her options. He wasn't wearing a radar vest, so her gun was useless. She guessed this was meant to be a test of hand-to-hand combat skills. But how far were they supposed to take it? Teddy heard Boyd's voice in her head: *Your enemy doesn't care how hard you try*.

She thought about employing her baton, but it was no longer attached to her vest. She must have lost it somewhere on the course. Teddy hoped this guy wasn't one of the assholes Kate had warned her about. Maybe they were just supposed to spar a little bit, and then he'd let her go.

Then again, maybe not. Lowering his head, he charged, lifting Teddy off her feet and slamming her against the warehouse wall.

Her entire body throbbed, but the pain was nothing compared to her desire to take him out—not for a grain bowl, but for a knuckle sandwich. Grabbing him by the ears, she snapped his head forward while bringing up her knee and driving it between his thighs. She was from Vegas. She could play dirty, too.

The agent collapsed onto his side, moaning. Teddy snapped a pair of cuffs on him and stood. She brushed her hair out of her eyes. That's when she saw a flash of red in his back pocket. Bingo. Checkpoint number three. So that was why Kate had wanted Teddy to exit through the front of the warehouse; she must have been hoping Teddy would encounter the third checkpoint on the way to the fourth. Teddy swallowed. Her first instinct had been to doubt her partner—if only Kate had been more specific, Teddy would have listened. Then again, she had to admit, it cut both ways: if Teddy had trusted Kate, they'd still be connected, and she wouldn't be going through the course alone.

Teddy tucked the third card in her vest and went after the fourth. Her perp in flannel knelt on the ground outside Charlie warehouse. She held a radar gun at her side. Teddy tried to remember Kate's exact words: *Apprehend suspect. Female. Caucasian. Flannel shirt. Red cap.*

Teddy studied the woman, who stood head down, shoulders slumped. Something didn't add up. Teddy stepped closer, expecting the woman to raise her weapon, but the supposed perp's finger wasn't even on the trigger. This woman wasn't a threat; the fourth and final checkpoint was a nod to police procedure, a gift from Officer Clint Corbett, Las Vegas PD, retired. A reminder not to get so caught up in the insanity of the field that they forgot fundamental duties—first and foremost, to practice empathy. "Are you okay?" Teddy asked. The woman nodded. "Hand me your weapon," Teddy said, putting as much softness in her voice as she could manage. "Let me help you."

The woman dropped the radar gun, and Teddy moved with lightning speed to secure it. The woman sent Teddy an approving smile, transforming immediately out of scene. "Nice job, recruit. Your card is behind the door." She tilted her head at the front of the warehouse.

Teddy thanked her and grabbed the card for Checkpoint #4. She walked into Charlie warehouse, which was filled floor to ceiling with boxes. Rows and rows of boxes, with doors every dozen feet or so. Now came the difficult part. Teddy needed Kate's help to find the right key and the right exit.

Blocking out the noise and tumult surrounding her, Teddy took a series of deep breaths. She tried to replicate the metronomic quality of Kate's mind. She imagined the walkie-talkie, turning the channel to seven.

Checkpoints three and four in hand.

Silence.

She calmly repeated, *Checkpoints three and four in hand*.

Waited.

Checkpoints three and four in—

Their energies slammed together like sound waves coming into tune: first the frequencies clashed, and Teddy almost recoiled from the mental screech.

Yes! Kate's response came through loud, clear, and excited.

Key, Teddy said, a reminder that it wasn't time to celebrate quite yet. Then: *Time?*

Key. Charlie warehouse, third door on left. A beat, then: *Six minutes*.

Teddy had six minutes to get through the maze of boxes, find the key, and open the door. She took off, half expecting to be tackled again, or hit by a truck, or washed away by a tsunami, or whatever real-world torture Boyd could devise. She'd made it over a giant wall and through a catwalk with multiple shooters, survived an attack from an overgrown grunt, and an empathic apprehension. What was one more crazy obstacle? But Teddy made it clear through Charlie warehouse without any trouble at all. She walked to the third door on the left.

Key should be near door, Kate said.

Teddy looked around, brushing her fingers against the door. She checked the mantel, the knob, the jam. No red key. She dropped to her hands and knees, sweeping her hands over the floor.

Four minutes, Kate said.

Teddy skimmed a row of cardboard boxes, then unceremoniously flipped one over and searched underneath. It wasn't there.

Teddy heard a yell. She whipped around to see Molly, her face white, drenched in sweat, trembling.

Teddy's first instinct was frustration—with Jeremy. What had he been thinking, sending Molly through the course? He should have been the one to run the obstacles, not her. It took a second for Teddy to direct her frustration into something more productive: helping her friend.

"We can look for our keys together," Teddy said. Then she saw the red key clasped in Molly's fist. "Molly?"

It was like she didn't even hear Teddy. Her pupils were enormous, her eyes practically black instead of the normal green.

Three minutes, Kate said.

Teddy stared at Molly. She'd seen that look before. Teddy's mind flashed back to Vegas, to Clint and Sergei and the casino. There was nothing behind her eyes; she was blank: mental influence. Had another recruit resorted to this to avoid getting cut? "Molly, this isn't you. Give me the key."

Instead, Molly reached for her baton.

Teddy didn't want to fight Molly. But as her friend walked toward her, she didn't see another choice. If she knocked Molly unconscious, maybe she'd also break the connection to whoever had influenced her. As Molly swung, Teddy lunged forward.

Molly stepped out of Teddy's way. Her movement was almost robotic, mechanical. Teddy readjusted her stance, but Molly seemed to be two steps ahead.

Molly raised her arm again, and the last thing Teddy saw was the wooden baton before it connected with her temple.

* * *

Teddy. Teddy. Teddy. Two minutes. Teddy.

Kate's voice, a deliberate, insistent knock, intruded on her consciousness. Teddy blinked blearily and brushed her fingers along her temple, wincing at the lump that was already beginning to form. Molly had attacked her. Molly had taken her key.

One minute.

Teddy scrambled to her feet. The ground swayed beneath her. Nausea churned in her stomach. *No key,* she said.

Find it!

Impossible. Molly was gone, and with her, the key. Her heart drumming, Teddy raced to the third door. Maybe Molly had unlocked it, or dropped the key beside it, or . . .

The door was bolted tight.

Forty-five seconds. Kate's voice sounded thin and far away.

Teddy slammed her body against the door. Grabbed the handle and pulled hard. Kicked and slammed into it again. The door wouldn't budge.

Thirty seconds. Teddy, do something! Open—

There was only one thing she could do. The question was, could she pull it off? A metal door was a hell of a lot heavier than a Ping-Pong ball. If she was going to do this, she needed all her psychic energy. In her mind, she turned off the walkie-talkie, severing her mental connection with Kate.

Teddy took a deep breath and imagined the electric current traveling from the tips of her fingers and up her arms, gathering strength as it circled her heart. She was so angry—at Molly, Kate, Boyd, Clint, everyone who had led her to a door that couldn't be opened. She was so angry at herself for barreling toward an impossible task. Her whole body felt electrified, not just her wall but every cell of her being. It was only then, fueled by blinding fury at her predicament, that Teddy tried to imagine her astral body extending an arm to punch through the door. She hit it with every ounce of strength she possessed. Her limbs trembled with effort. She didn't just want the door open. She wanted the goddamn thing obliterated. She pictured it shattering. Twisting steel, fractured locks, and broken hinges. Flying debris.

Suddenly, she felt all that strength propelling forward. She was moving toward the door faster than she'd ever moved before, faster than was humanly possible. As she looked back, she saw herself standing still, grounded, stuck, eyes closed—had she left her physical body behind? The grating noise of grinding metal gears pierced the air. The steel hinges shattered, flying off the doorframe. The door shuddered, then collapsed outward, falling flat with a loud, dull *whomp*.

Teddy came back to herself, shocked, out of breath, sweating, limbs like sandbags. She dragged herself through the opening and landed on the other side. For a long moment, time seemed to stop. Teddy lay there, too stunned to move, let alone come to terms with what had just happened. Her fellow recruits, Alphas and Misfits both, gaped at her. Clint stared, Boyd looked shocked, and even the meditative Dunn was leaning so far backward he was practically falling over.

A siren blared the end of the exam.

They'd made it. Teddy looked at Kate.

Kate shook herself as though waking from a dream and then punched her fist in the air and whooped.

"I don't know what you recruits are celebrating," Boyd said, her tone desert-dry. "But the rules clearly stated you needed to open the door with a *key*. You didn't do that."

If Teddy had retained any energy, she would have cried. She fell to her knees, dropped her head.

"You fail," Boyd continued. "Both of you."

CHAPTER TWENTY-FOUR

TEDDY TRIED TO IGNORE HER HEADACHE AS SHE CON-sidered how to make her case. She paced her room, going over the speech she'd deliver to Clint. She knew it would do no good to let loose what she was really feeling—that if anyone should be leaving campus, it was the universally despised Sergeant Rosemary Boyd. As far as Teddy was concerned, she and Kate had not only met the re-quirements of Whitfield's midyear exam but exceeded them. She'd be damned if she was going to let Boyd send her home on some manu-factured technicality. Especially when there had been some sort of foul play. But she couldn't say that, of course, because it could get Molly in trouble, too. And there'd been so much chaos after she'd exited the warehouse, she wasn't even sure what had happened to Molly. Teddy refused to pack. If she packed, she was giving in, giving up.

As soon as she made that decision, the door opened: Kate. "Clint wants to see us in his office," she said.

"Kate, I—" Teddy began.

"What happened in there, Cannon?" Kate said.

"Molly attacked me. I think she was under some kind of mental influence. She stole our key."

Kate looked at her, incredulous. "Molly? Girl with arms the size of swizzle sticks? You're saying she got the better of you?"

"I think someone made her do it."

Kate tightened her ponytail. "Boyd's a military type. Excuses aren't going to work. Trust me. And no one is going to believe that Molly was influenced. Not one person in our class has that kind of power." Kate paused, considering. "And if you tell them that Molly sabotaged you, they'll expel her, too. Do you want that to happen? If this whole mess wasn't her fault, either?"

Teddy didn't even need to think. "No," she said.

"Then we focus on what we did right. They can't argue with the facts. We got through that door on time. Got it?"

Teddy nodded, impressed by Kate's plan.

The two walked to Fort McDowell in silence. Kate knocked twice on the door before opening.

"Clint," Teddy began, again wanting to explain herself, but he held up one hand to stop her.

"Wait until the others arrive." With that curt dismissal, he returned his attention to the paperwork that cluttered his desk. Teddy didn't want to wait. He'd been asking her to wait for months. Wait to learn how to control her power. Wait to learn about her parents. Wait to find out more about the theft. She was tired of waiting.

As if he could sense her growing restlessness, Clint sent her a pleading look. "Just be patient for a little longer."

Teddy amped up her wall's power. She didn't want him in her head. Not now. "You're not going to even acknowledge what happened back there?" she asked. Before Clint could answer, Professor Dunn and Sergeant Boyd entered. Clint greeted everyone and stated the purpose of their meeting. Kate spoke first, relaying her version of events, reciting word for word the psychic messages she'd sent Teddy. No conflict there. Yes, they'd had stressful moments when their connection had been broken, but she'd followed the rules as explained by Boyd.

Then it was Teddy's turn. The only hiccup came when Clint pressed her: "You're certain the key wasn't there?" As he questioned her, she felt his presence at the edge of her mind. She sent a small surge to her defenses; it was all she could manage.

"I'm certain," she said. "The key wasn't there." He didn't push further.

Clint and Dunn agreed that though it had been through unconventional means, Kate and Teddy had completed the requirements of the course. But to satisfy Boyd, who stridently maintained that rules had been broken and explicit instructions had not been followed, Clint suggested Teddy and Kate retake the exam—this time following the rules to the letter.

"We've never allowed this before," Boyd protested. "I don't like the precedent."

"We've never had a first-year recruit telekinetically force open a door before, either," Clint countered.

The only downfall to the proposed solution was that they'd have to remain on campus over the holidays in order to retake the test, which was scheduled a few days before Christmas; Teddy assumed Boyd had nothing better to do.

"If you'd rather go home permanently," Boyd said, "that can be arranged."

Teddy gritted her teeth, hoping the ghost of Christmas past would keep Ebenezer Boyd awake for a month. She would have to explain to her parents that she had to work over the vacation. They'd be disappointed, but they'd understand. They wanted this second chance to work out even more than she did.

"Teddy, hold up a moment," Clint said, as the others began to file out of the office. "What you did back there—" He stood up from his desk. "I've never seen a recruit make a jump in training like that before. A month ago, you could barely move a piece of plastic."

"Clint, I—"

"Let me finish," he said. "It scared the hell out of me."

She'd expected him to be proud of her. Not scared. She'd finally done what he'd asked her to do!

"Your ability is erratic at best. These bursts of intense power are followed by periods when you're unable to replicate the skill on even the smallest level. I . . ." He paused. "I think we need to slow down. You need to focus on foundational work in Dunn's class."

"After all that, you're the one quitting on me?" Teddy said.

"It's not quitting. It's reevaluating."

She tilted her head up, hoping that looking at the sky would somehow stop her tears from falling. She was tired. Exhausted. It was only then that Teddy realized she was still wearing her gear. Her vest was too tight, the straps rubbing her skin raw. Everything felt raw. "You're keeping things from me, Clint. Not only this kind of stuff. But stuff about my parents. About the theft." She looked at him, hoping that he finally would fold after months of holding his cards too close.

He looked her dead in the eyes. "You're forgetting that I'm in charge, recruit. Some information is need-to-know. So fall back."

He'd never called her "recruit" before. Boyd's list of acceptable responses ran through her head: *Yes, sir. No, sir. No excuse, sir.*

Each phrase tasted more bitter than the last. Teddy left without saying anything.

*   *   *

Later that night, Teddy left her room and wandered down to the beach. She watched the waves crest and dip from the shore. The campus had emptied out over the last few hours, students returning home after their exam results were posted. The first-year class, pending Teddy and Kate's retake, had passed. Even Molly and Jeremy.

"Mind if I join you?"

Teddy turned, surprised to see Kate. "Free country," she said.

Kate settled beside her, opened the backpack she carried, and withdrew a thermos. She filled two mugs and passed one to Teddy. "Merry Christmas to you, too."

"It's not Christmas yet," Teddy said, taking a sip. Eggnog liberally spiced with rum. It burned her throat going down, then a gentle warmth spread through her chest. Her unease lifted.

Kate shrugged. "My mom sent it early. I added the rum." They drank in silence for a few minutes.

"I'm sorry you're stuck here," Teddy said.

"Don't be." Kate studied her mug for a moment, frowning. "The second I saw you put on that radar vest, I wished it was me going in. Now I get that chance."

The admission surprised Teddy. It wasn't like an Alpha to show vulnerability. Maybe she'd been judging Kate too harshly, putting too much stock in the divisions Boyd had created.

"By the way, how's your friend doing? I heard she escaped to the infirmary as soon as we got back to campus," Kate said.

Teddy wasn't ready to see Molly yet—hell, she wasn't even ready to discuss the incident.

"I mean, I knew someone had to have taken our key," Kate continued. "I thought it might have been Ben. He's pretty competitive."

You're one to talk.

Teddy remembered how Kate had psyched Molly out in the gym. But she kept it to herself. Better to move on, focus on passing the exam.

"Molly is the last person I'd expect to do something like that," Teddy said.

"But she was partnered with Jeremy." Kate shrugged. "Maybe he told her to take the key."

"Jeremy? I thought you said no one in our class would be capable of that kind of thing." Jeremy was intense. But Teddy couldn't imagine him hurting anyone, especially Molly.

"I thought you couldn't do shit, but I watched you blow a metal door off its hinges today. I wouldn't dismiss anyone. Especially since someone has it out for you."

Teddy considered Kate's words. "How do we know I'm the one they're targeting?"

A smile flickered across Kate's face, then she shook her head, suddenly serious. Her brown hair, normally tightly secured in a ponytail, hung about her shoulders. "I can do some neat tricks. We all can. But no one else here can look into someone's head and see the past. Maybe someone here has something to hide. That makes you a threat, Cannon. And if I were you, I'd find out who."

A shiver ran down Teddy's spine. First the lab. And now this. If someone wanted her gone that badly, she didn't want to think about what could happen next.

CHAPTER TWENTY-FIVE

THE MORNING OF THEIR RETEST, TEDDY AND KATE suited up, determined to take out whatever obstacle came their way (and then take each other out for margaritas at the Cantina). They had reached an unsteady truce, working together in the mornings on the quiet and empty campus, running trails in the afternoon, and watching crappy Christmas movies on an old projector in the library at night.

To dispel any hint of unfairness, Clint, Boyd, and Dunn created an entirely new—and presumably more difficult—set of obstacles for Kate and Teddy to overcome. They did, with flying colors. Even Boyd was impressed. Or at least that was how Teddy interpreted her mild grunt followed by: "Not bad, recruits."

Buoyed by the success, Teddy felt ready to face Molly in the infirmary, where she'd been holed up since the exam. Teddy was still trying to work out what happened on the obstacle course. She knew there was a chance that it hadn't been Molly's fault. She wondered if Jeremy really could have been the one who influenced Molly's thoughts—or had someone else managed to hijack her mind while she was running the course? Whenever Teddy looked at Jeremy, she saw an awkward kid, someone who wasn't a threat.

"I wasn't sure you'd come," Molly said when Teddy arrived. She spoke so quietly, Teddy could barely hear her. It sounded like her throat was dry. It must have been a strain to talk.

Teddy's throat ached, too. "Neither was I," she said.

Molly stared out the window. "Were you kicked out of Whitfield?"

"Still here," Teddy said. "No thanks to you."

Molly turned to her, tears in her eyes. "I can only assume I haven't been expelled because you haven't said anything." She bit her lip.

Teddy didn't want to feel distressed on her friend's behalf, but she did. This wasn't how she wanted it to go. All those empathy lessons. Teddy wanted to be angry. Molly was the reason Teddy's exam had gone south. Why she was no longer talking to Clint. Why she was still on Boyd's shit list. "What happened in there? It was like you weren't you."

"I don't know," Molly said. "I don't remember. Everything after I entered the course is blank. Hours, gone."

Teddy had hoped Molly would provide more information. Something that would clarify what had happened, lead her to a suspect. "Did Jeremy—"

A tall, thin nurse, with hair so pale it looked almost white, walked into the room without making a sound. Teddy noticed her only when the door clicked closed behind her.

"Good morning, ladies," she said. She took Molly's chart from the foot of the bed. She made a note, then checked Molly's pulse and blood pressure, frowning at both. "I'm sorry," she said, turning to Teddy, "but Ms. Quinn needs rest."

"I don't want her to go," Molly said firmly.

"Your heart rate is 120, and your blood pressure is—"

"Please," Molly said. "Just five minutes."

The nurse hesitated. "Two minutes," she said, and left.

Molly waited until the door closed again. "Jeremy told me what happened afterward. I know how it looks, but I never meant to hurt you," she said. "Just the opposite. But I . . ." She stopped and scanned the ceiling as though she might find words there. "I have to tell you something," she began. She stopped, and her eyes changed focus, seeing something over Teddy's shoulder.

Teddy turned; the nurse was back. "I'm afraid time's up. You have to go, Ms. Cannon."

Teddy snapped, "We're not finished. I'd like to speak to Nurse Bell, please."

"Nurse Bell is away for the moment. And visiting time is over, Ms. Cannon."

Teddy stood up. Her conversation with Molly hadn't helped at all, especially with the nurse's interruptions. She turned back to her friend. "You sure you'll be okay?"

Molly nodded. "She's right, I should probably rest. I'm sorry."

*   *   *

The campus was empty. Teddy walked toward the evergreen pines, which stood like sentinels before Harris Hall, then she crossed the manicured courtyard back to her dorm, replaying the conversation with Molly in her head. Molly didn't know what had happened, but Jeremy had told her the details. How had he known? Teddy and Molly had been the only ones in that room. The only way Jeremy would have known was if he had been there or been inside Molly's head.

Caught up in her own thoughts, Teddy took a moment to realize that Kate was sitting on the front steps of the dorm.

"Are you going to Jeremy's parents' party?" Kate asked. She never bothered with small talk. Teddy still hadn't gotten used to her blunt conversational style.

"What party?"

"Their New Year's party. They do it every year—always invite a lot of big shots and military families. I've been when my family is stationed in the area."

"I wasn't invited."

"I didn't ask if you were invited," Kate said. "I asked if you were going."

"While it sounds like a lot of fun, going to a party full of government bigwigs, it's really not my scene," Teddy said.

"Well, if someone was hypothetically trying to get *me* kicked out of Whitfield, and having people over to his private residence, and there might be opportunities to snoop, *I* would theoretically want to be there," Kate said, getting up from the step.

"You mean like keep your friends close but your enemies closer?" Teddy asked.

"More like 'Know thy enemy and know yourself, and you need not fear the result of a hundred battles.'"

"Is that one of Boyd's mantras?"

"Hardly. It's Sun Tzu. *The Art of War*."

Teddy considered it. The party sounded boring AF, but Kate was right. "I don't have a dress," she said.

Kate eyed her. "I got you. But your feet are huge, Cannon."

Teddy shrugged. "Hey, combat boots go with everything."

*   *   *

An hour later, Teddy found herself in front of a Pacific Heights mansion. Teddy had assumed that Jeremy Lee came from money—he had a boat, after all—but she never would have pictured this. The exterior displayed tasteful Victorian beauty: pink stucco walls, wrought-iron balconies, plasterwork friezes, and carefully tended gardens. Ionic columns set off an elevated circular entrance. It looked like something out of a movie.

"If anyone asks you who or where your parents are, just say you live on base and they're on assignment," Kate said.

"Won't they ask which base or what assignment?"

Kate fixed Teddy with a stare. "This is a party with high-ranking officials from every branch of government. No one is going to ask what base or what assignment. It's implied if you don't say that it's confidential."

God, what was she getting herself into? "Are your parents going to be here?"

"No," Kate said. "They actually *are* on base on assignment."

Teddy smoothed out the skirt of the silver dress Kate had handed to her only hours before. It made her feel self-conscious; Teddy Cannon didn't do dresses. "So, you knew Jeremy before Whitfield?"

"I met him maybe once. He was rarely at these parties. He was away at boarding school or college or hiding in his room. And I didn't know he was psychic. Plus, even if he was there, you know—he's not much of a talker."

They began to walk up the front steps, and Teddy suppressed an actual gulp. This was nothing like her parents' suburban home. She'd been around this kind of money in the casinos, but that was at a poker table, where everyone was equal. Not a place where she had to make small talk.

"Okay, remember: don't do anything that's going to make you stand out. The entire point of this mission—"

Teddy held back a laugh. "Wait, we're on a mission?"

"Cannon," Kate said, "if we're doing this, we're taking this seriously."

"You got me in a dress, Kate." Teddy hadn't worn a dress since the last time she'd tried to go on a "mission," when she'd also been wearing a fat suit and a wig. "I'm taking this seriously."

Four months ago, Teddy couldn't have pictured working with Kate, let alone going to a party with her. "I'll have your back in there," Kate said, "but I'm not going down for you." They locked eyes for a moment. "Got it?"

"Got it." Teddy looked up the large staircase, past the tuxedoed staff hired to be valets for the evening. She studied the guests arriving—plenty of people in military uniform, women in fancy dresses. She'd been in training for more than four months to develop her combat, psychic, and crime-solving skills. Certainly she could tackle a cocktail party.

"Ready?" Kate asked.

"As I'll ever be."

*   *   *

The interior of the mansion was every bit as elegant as it appeared from the outside. Crystal chandeliers gently lit rooms arranged with love seats, chaises, and ottomans. Knickknacks sat on shelves that probably cost more than Teddy's deposit for college. Though this place was fancy, so they wouldn't be called knickknacks—they would be objets d'art.

Teddy tried not to gawk. But even the guests were intimidating. She spotted one U.S. senator, a petite woman she recognized as a news anchor from one of the cable networks, the mayor of San Francisco, and their very own Hollis Whitfield in line at the raw bar.

About an hour into the party, Teddy found herself in a conversation with a hair-sprayed matron in pearls. "So then I said, 'I never go there in the summer. That's when tourists go!'"

Kate elbowed Teddy in the ribs, nearly causing her to spill her drink.

"Excuse me," the lady said, looking between the two of them. "I think I see someone over there I must say hello to."

"Why are you talking to her?" Kate said to Teddy.

"I honestly have no idea," Teddy said. "And I haven't been able to sneak off, because those damn waiters keep trying to direct me to the bathroom on the first floor whenever I say I'm looking for a toilet. They must think I have an overactive bladder or a cocaine habit."

"Think about what you're looking for," Kate said.

"I don't know what I'm looking for! This was your idea, remember?"

"You're doing recon on Jeremy. Trying to figure out why he would want to take you down. And why he would have used Molly to do it."

"It's not like there's going to be a piece of paper on his desk outlining a master plan."

Kate rolled her eyes. "Whatever. Enjoy the free food."

Teddy hesitated. She couldn't believe she was going to do this. With Kate, of all people. The last time Teddy Cannon had asked for help wittingly was when she couldn't tie her shoes at the age of three. "I—" She sighed. "I need help."

"Okay," Kate said. "Let me into your head."

Teddy expected Kate to make a big deal of it. To lord it over her.

Kate asked, "Don't you trust me?"

Did she? Teddy grabbed Kate's hand. "Fine. Channel seven."

Teddy lowered her wall and pictured the walkie-talkie in her mind's eye. Having someone in her head was still uncomfortable. Like having a pebble in her shoe. *Especially if that pebble is a stubborn military brat who thinks she's God's gift to the Whitfield Institute.*

I heard that, Kate said.

Glad we're on the same page, then.

Teddy walked out of the main foyer and slipped through the kitchen, a route she had watched waiter after waiter walk. She hoped there was a back staircase that led to the family's private rooms.

Teddy found her way down a long mahogany-paneled hallway. Up one flight, she turned to the room on her left, which seemed to be a guest bedroom. An unopened suitcase lay near the foot of the bed. Teddy opened it. A hair dryer. Ladies' underwear. Definitely not Jeremy's. Or hopefully not Jeremy's.

This is useless.

It's not like TV, Cannon. The information isn't going to fall into your lap.

Teddy made her way back to the hallway. She went into two other bedrooms. Neither seemed to be Jeremy's. None had any clues.

We're sitting down for dinner soon, Kate telepathically wired to Teddy. *Hurry.*

Teddy went toward a partially opened door at the end of the hallway.

"I don't understand why I have to leave Whitfield before graduation."

She knew that voice. Christine Federico's. Teddy leaned closer. She couldn't make out what the other person was saying. It was a male voice. Calm. Quiet. Jeremy's? She couldn't be sure.

"What about Brett?" Christine asked.

Teddy hoped that her spying would reveal what had happened on the course, but if her time in Jeremy's house solved another mystery, she wouldn't complain.

She heard footsteps at the end of the hallway. She ran through her options: she could pretend she was lost, but that wouldn't explain why she was standing outside a door, listening to a private conversation. She would have to go inside.

Shit.

Language, Cannon, Kate said.

"Hey," Teddy said, walking through the paneled doorway into what looked like an office. Oak bookshelves lined the walls; a large captain's desk took up a significant portion of the room. "Got lost on the way to the bathroom."

Christine and Jeremy sat close together on a leather couch; they looked cozy. If Teddy hadn't been listening in the hallway, she would have been suspicious for another reason altogether. Jeremy looked up, surprised. "Teddy, what are you doing here?"

"I'm Kate's plus-one." Teddy shrugged.

"I should probably be going," Christine said. She gave Teddy a once-over, lingering on the combat boots.

"Don't let me interrupt," Teddy said. She backed toward the door.

"There's a bathroom down the hall," Jeremy said. "Two doors to the right."

"Thanks," Teddy said, turning around and walking straight into a uniformed, fully decorated officer.

"Jeremy," said a voice that made Teddy's hair stand on end. "Introduce me to your friends."

Jeremy sprang to his feet. "Yes, sir."

"We're at a party, son, you can relax." He turned to Teddy and stuck out a large palm. He was in his early seventies, at least. His silver hair was buzzed military-style. His face was tan and creased with lines, as if he'd withstood years in a desert and made it through the other side with all the knowledge of Moses.

That gut feeling she got around nonpsychics? The "alley, elevator, no good, get going, this isn't going to turn out well" anxiety that told her people were lying? One glance at this guy told her to get the hell out of there. Everything about him made Teddy want to run. She didn't have to look into his mind to know that.

"My classmate Theodora Cannon, sir," Jeremy said. Teddy shook the man's hand. His grip was too strong, as if on purpose. Teddy resisted every urge to squeeze back but knew she wasn't supposed to draw attention to herself.

"And this is Christine Federico; she's a third year."

The man turned and offered his hand to Christine. "General Paul Maddux. I'm a friend of Jeremy's father."

Teddy wondered if the general knew about Whitfield. Since it was a private-public enterprise, she was certain some members of the military were in the know.

Maddux turned to Christine. "Any plans after graduation?"

Christine gave Jeremy a quick glance, then shook her head. "I'm not sure where I'm headed next."

He turned to Teddy. "What about you?"

"I'm not sure—"

"General," Kate interrupted. "Kate Atkins, daughter of Major General Rodney Atkins."

Kate? How'd she find me?

"Everyone's getting ready for dinner, so I came to get Teddy. She has no sense of direction. We should probably get going." Kate grabbed Teddy's arm in a deathlike grip and steered her out of the room.

"You're hurting me," Teddy said, shaking free.

Kate stared at her, openmouthed. "The last thing I got from you was a surge of panic and then you cursing. You expected me not to find you? Wow. That hurts right here, partner." Kate patted her heart. "I can't believe Maddux is here. That guy is a legend."

Teddy's skin prickled. "He seemed creepy."

"If you can call a war hero creepy. He led some of the few definitively successful Vietnam missions. Since then he's practically written the book on how we handle guerrilla warfare."

They reached the main entryway, where several tables had been set up for dinner. Kate stopped Teddy and pulled her into an alcove underneath a tasteful watercolor of the San Francisco Bay. "Did you get any dirt on Jeremy?" Kate asked.

"No," Teddy said. "Unfortunately."

"I'd say we should go now, but it would look suspicious if we were walking around upstairs and then just disappeared," Kate said. "Let's stay for a course or two, then slip out before dessert."

"Mission failure," Teddy said.

Kate shrugged. "'When all is said and done, more is always said than done.'"

"Sun Tzu?" Teddy asked.

"Drake."

*   *   *

Teddy and Kate found seats at a practically empty table in the corner, alongside the hair-sprayed matron from earlier. Jeremy, Christine, and General Maddux entered the foyer ten minutes later. Teddy panicked when she realized that the only remaining seats were at her table. She braced herself for an uncomfortable meal with General McCreepy. But he acted the part of congenial guest, directing conversation as it drifted from holiday gifts to New Year's resolutions to, predictably, the weather.

And then the hair-sprayed matron just had to ask about homeland security.

Teddy saw Jeremy visibly tense. She knew his history, how he felt about America's role as the defender of the free world. How he felt about not being able to do anything to save his mother.

General Maddux didn't hesitate. "America's foreign policies and homeland-security tactics have left its citizens vulnerable to attack," he said. "We need the military now more than ever. We need men on the ground, drones in the air. I've been pushing to increase our presence overseas." He reached for his wineglass, his expression thoughtful.

This guy was a hawk. Worse, no one at the table questioned him. If she could only interrupt his train of thought . . . Teddy imagined knocking over his glass, the wine spilling across the tablecloth. She sent a current down her arm as her astral body reached out. She could almost feel the cool glass on her fingertips.

The glass wobbled. It was about to tip over and then instantly righted, defying the laws of physics.

Maddux finished his lecture. He looked at her and raised his glass. Had he known what she had done?

"The fact is," Teddy said, "I'd rather live in a free state than a police state. Your work will promote security restrictions and limit civil liberties. The alternative is—"

"The alternative is allowing acts of terrorism. Instead, we identify targets before they do harm."

"And who would identify these targets?" she asked.

"You're training to serve, Ms. Cannon. Who better than a carefully selected tribunal of our peers? One whose purpose has nothing to do with political expediency and everything to do with national security."

Teddy glanced around the table. "Am I the only one scared shitless at the thought of a military tribunal whose sole purpose is to undermine the constitutional right of due process?"

Jeremy fidgeted with his butter knife. "I can see its place."

"You can't possibly—"

He dropped his butter knife. "If it meant stopping something like 9/11, then yes, I could," he said, color high on his cheeks.

The general stood and smiled. "If you young people will excuse me." He reached into his pocket and took out his phone. "Duty calls."

Kate nudged Teddy under the table. "I think it's time for us to head out, too." She stood. "Thanks for dinner, Jeremy."

Teddy followed Kate out to the front steps, still fuming. "I don't know how you did it," Teddy said as they waited for a cab.

"Did what?"

"Grew up in a military family."

"They're not all like that. He's . . ." Kate hesitated. "He's sure of his own beliefs."

"So you agree with him?" Teddy felt her skin grow hot.

"I didn't say that. But doesn't it sound familiar, Cannon? Trying to find a way to stop people from committing crimes before they occur? If one of us gets a vision, we're supposed to act. Right?"

That was what they were learning to do at Whitfield. Teddy shook her head. "It's not the same."

"A debate for one of Clint's classes, to be sure."

A cab pulled up, and someone walked toward it to open the door.

"Thank you," Teddy said.

"My pleasure, Ms. Cannon," said a woman with hair so blond it appeared almost white.

It wasn't until they were in the taxi, on their way home, that Teddy wondered how the woman had known her name.

CHAPTER TWENTY-SIX

HOW TEDDY SPENT THE REST OF BREAK: ROLLING A Ping-Pong ball back and forth across her desk with her astral body, stalking Christine, wondering if Brett would turn up in Timbuktu, and avoiding Clint.

When she entered the dining hall on the first day of second semester, she saw Dara, Pyro, and Jeremy gathered around their usual table. Her heart skipped as she approached: she was happy to see them, even Jeremy. The realization hit her—she had friends. Really, really weird ones.

She looked at Jeremy, but he avoided her gaze. They hadn't talked since his party. She still didn't know what to make of the events of the exam, Molly's actions, or her account of them.

"We were wondering where you were," said Dara as Teddy took a seat.

"Turns out Jillian is a very effective alarm clock. I'm lost without her."

"When will she be back?" Dara asked.

"In time for today's assembly, I hope," Teddy said, sipping her organic orange juice. She turned to Pyro. "When did you get in?"

"Last night," Liz said, squeezing his shoulder. Teddy hadn't noticed her at the table. Pyro changed the subject, asking about Teddy's exam.

On the one hand, Teddy had never wanted anything serious with

Pyro. On the other, she couldn't deny that a part of her felt a tiny bit—not jealous but, okay, jealous. She described the retake, play by play.

"That sounds tough, Teddy," Dara said. "Hey, has anyone heard from Molly?"

"She seemed pretty shaken up after the exam," Pyro said.

And they didn't even know what had happened on the course. Teddy looked at Jeremy. He put his fork down. "The stress of the exam was a lot for her. After we got back to campus, she passed out. She didn't wake up after almost a week in the infirmary. I was really worried. But she's on her way back to campus. She said she feels like a whole new person."

Teddy still didn't know the whole story, but something about Jeremy's and Molly's accounts didn't add up. "Excuse me," Teddy said. "I'm going to wait for Jillian at the dock."

"I'll come with you," Jeremy said. "Molly might be there, too."

Teddy tensed as Jeremy followed her out of the dining hall. They walked in silence until they hit the quad.

"Look—" Teddy began.

Jeremy cut her off. "I know you think that I had something to do with what happened during the exam. I wanted to talk to you about it at the party, but you left before I could speak with you alone."

Was that before he made a move on Christine or after General McCreepy came on the scene? "Listen, Jeremy. I don't know what's going on between you and Molly, but I know what I saw in that warehouse, and what I saw wasn't my friend. I know what mental influence looks like." She thought back to Clint and the casino, the guards' and Sergei's blank stares.

Jeremy flushed. Teddy had never seen him angry before. Usually, he was a cipher, but now his fists were clenched by his sides, knuckles white. He paused and let out a long breath, then spoke. "You know she was asked to leave last year. But do you know why? She hurt someone, Teddy. It's in her file. Corbett ruled it an accident, and he let her come back. But her abilities get the better of her sometimes, send her into fight-or-flight mode." He softened. "I was trying to get her under control during the obstacle course. She wasn't listening to me. She attacked." He looked down at his hands. "I'm not a strong telepath. You've seen me in class. Mental influence is even more challenging. I was trying to protect you—both of you. It didn't work." He stared Teddy straight in the eye. "She wanted to run the course. Prove that she was stronger than last year. I should have been the one to go in."

In a way, what he said made sense: Molly's erratic behavior, why she didn't want Teddy inside her thoughts. Had Molly been hiding what had happened last year? Was she afraid that if Teddy found out, she wouldn't want to be Molly's friend? At that moment, Teddy wished she could get a clear read on psychics. But when she studied Jeremy's face, she didn't feel the anxiety that accompanied a lie. Short of breaking in to his mind, she would have to trust him.

"She really wants to stay at school," Jeremy said. "She's been trying to keep her stress low. Dunn has been helping her. And I would appreciate if you would help her by not bringing up the exam."

"You want me to pretend like it didn't happen?"

"If she's at school, we can help her. If she's out there . . ." He left the thought unfinished.

By the time Teddy and Jeremy reached the dock, Dara had caught up. Teddy was grateful for her presence; she didn't want to talk about Molly anymore. The three of them stood in the sun, stomping their feet and shoving their hands into pockets. There was a chill breeze coming off the bay. Teddy scanned the passengers milling about the upper deck of the ferry. She spotted Jillian and Molly standing together by the railing. Jillian was slumped, head down, while Molly stood tall, eyes on the horizon.

"I wonder what's wrong with Jillian," Teddy said.

Dara squinted at the view. "I wonder what's wrong with Molly. She looks almost happy."

Jeremy glanced at Teddy. "See? What did I tell you?"

When their friends reached the dock, Jillian collapsed into Teddy's arms. "It's my hamster, Fred," she said.

It took Teddy a second to remember which hamster Jillian was talking about. "Did he die?"

"*She,*" Jillian corrected. "And no, not yet. But she's going to. She told me. I wanted to be there when it happened. But, you know, I had to be here."

Teddy held Jillian as she cried. She glanced at Molly to see how she would handle such an outpouring of a sorrow. But instead of the pained look she usually wore when she encountered extreme emotion, Molly looked oblivious. Her expression was placid, content, even.

"You okay, Molly?" Teddy asked.

"You know," Molly said, as if it were the first time she'd ever considered such a question, "I really am!"

"Seriously, Molly," Teddy said, "what did they give you? Lexapro? Zoloft?"

Molly looked at her, surprised. "Medication interferes with psychic ability, Teddy. You know that. I've been working on this blocking technique with Dunn."

Teddy decided she wouldn't mention anything about what had happened before break. She didn't have the heart.

As they started toward campus, Teddy turned and caught a glimpse of another familiar figure exiting the ferry: a broad-shouldered man in a cable-knit sweater, duffel bag slung over his shoulder. She hadn't seen Nick in weeks. There'd been so much else happening on campus that his teaching this semester had slipped her mind.

"Looking for someone?" Dara asked. "Hey, isn't that—"

"No one," Teddy said. "It's no one. Come on, we're going to be late for assembly."

* * *

As they trudged to Fort McDowell, Teddy listened to Dara describing her holiday in New Orleans: she had received a death warning while shopping for Christmas presents at the mall. "One minute I was buying a pair of socks, and the next, I was flat on the floor," Dara said. "It must feel great being able to help someone," Teddy said.

Dara frowned, considering. "It's still new to me. I've only gotten a couple real visions—most of the time, it's just fragments. I have to put the pieces together, and I never know when or if it will happen. This time I had this flash of a girl on the ground of the parking lot, and she was wearing a watch. I was lucky. I found her just in time. Sometimes I can't do anything about it."

They passed a cluster of Alphas waiting in front of the building; Kate huddled next to Ava and Liz.

"Hey," Teddy said.

"Hey," Kate said. Her gaze lingered on Teddy before she turned away.

"Are you guys, like, friends now?" Dara asked.

"Kind of." Teddy shrugged.

The room buzzed as students gossiped about things that no longer really mattered to Teddy: questions they might have missed on the exam, how many hamburgers they ate over the holidays, Pyro's latest fling. Teddy found a seat at the back of the auditorium. She was surprised when Kate slid into the seat beside her. "What's up?" Kate asked.

Teddy was taken aback. Kate had chosen to sit next to her and not with the Alphas. It took Teddy a second to focus on Kate's question. "Um, it's Jeremy. And Molly," Teddy said, running a hand through her short hair. "Molly's acting like a Stepford wife. And Jeremy's trying to convince me that he *had* to influence her during the exam or Molly was going to attack me."

Kate nodded. "And you need me to . . . ?"

Teddy rolled her eyes. "Cut right to the chase, as always."

"Please, Cannon, you only open up when you need something."

Kate's accusation stung. But she couldn't deny it: Kate had put herself on the line for Teddy more than once since the exam. "Jeremy mentioned that Molly took a leave of absence last year after she attacked another student," Teddy said.

"Molly attacked someone before?" Kate looked almost impressed. "That changes things."

"There'd have to be a report or something, right?"

"Sure."

"So, maybe we could find it."

"By that you mean break in to the school records room while everyone is in assembly?" Kate said.

"You read my mind." Teddy smiled.

"And I thought that was your thing."

*　*　*

Assembly hadn't started yet. Teddy knew they wouldn't be missed. They made their way down the hall to the main office. Kate waited until the elderly secretary went to the bathroom before they sneaked behind her desk to the locked door of the file room. Teddy performed her Vegas key magic, and poof, they were in.

"I'll keep watch," Kate said.

Teddy was 95 percent sure that Kate wouldn't bail on her. She grabbed Kate's hand and took a deep breath. "Let's sync up. Channel seven." Teddy lowered her wall, imagined the walkie-talkie, and tuned the dial. It had become easier and easier to allow Kate inside her head.

Make it quick, Cannon. I don't want to miss the assembly.

Teddy nodded in acknowledgment, then stepped inside the file room. She needed to look at Molly's file, but she wanted to read so many others. What if her own included more information about her blood test? What if Brett's included information on his whereabouts? And she would risk getting caught to find out some more information on Jeremy.

Stay focused, Cannon.

Roger that.

Teddy walked around the room, searching through drawers until she found it: *Quinn, Molly.* The file listed Molly's date of birth, her address, her academic record. Her CIA profile. She hadn't been lying about hacking in to the mainframe. Teddy flipped page after page until she found a report from a hearing the previous year. In Dunn's class, Molly had thrown another student, a girl by the name of Erin Fridstein, against a wall, knocking her unconscious. Molly later claimed to have no memory of the event.

Dunn concluded that Molly's empathic reaction had triggered an out-of-character response. He suggested that Molly study blocking techniques. He insisted that Molly would be safer at school than anywhere else—without these techniques, she would hurt others or herself.

Let's go, Cannon, Kate said.

Teddy returned Molly's file to the drawer. Jeremy had been telling the truth. And now she intended to spend a few minutes looking through other files. She opened a drawer labeled *K–M.* As soon as she saw the file marked *Lee, Jeremy,* she heard Kate's voice in her head: *Abort! Abort!*

Teddy shut the file drawer.

Stay there. Don't move.

Why? Teddy asked.

Be quiet. I have to disconnect. I—

Kate ended their communication, and Teddy was alone with her thoughts. She swallowed, wondering how long she would be stuck inside the tiny windowless room. She crept toward the door. She could make out voices but not words. She heard the secretary's shaky voice and then a man's.

The door opened wide, and there stood the person she least wanted to see.

Nick folded his arms. "Did you get lost on your way to the auditorium?"

"I, uh . . . Kate and I were just practicing an exercise for Dunn's class."

"In a file room?"

"No windows," she said, pointing to the wall. "Perfect conditions for, um, stretching our telepathic communication."

"Why should I believe you?"

"You know what?" she said as she tried to brush past him. "I don't care if you believe me. I have to get to assembly."

He stood in front of the door, blocking her way. "The easy thing would be for me to report you. This is the second time I've caught you trespassing."

"So do it," she said. "Get me kicked out and ruin my life."

She hip-checked him and reached for the doorknob. Nick grabbed her arm. She tried to loosen his grasp with her free hand, but he grabbed that one, too. His face was an inch from hers. His gaze moved from her eyes to her lips and back. Teddy couldn't help but do the same.

"Stop that," he said.

"Stop what?"

"Looking at me like that."

"You stop looking at *me* like that."

"Like what?"

"Like you want to kiss me," she said.

He scoffed. "You're crazy."

Teddy smirked.

"You're a student."

"I'm old enough for whatever you have in mind."

Nick released her. "Get out of here," he said. He shook his head. "You're supposed to be in assembly." He reached for the doorknob and swung the door open. The fluorescent light poured into the tiny room.

"I'll see you in the auditorium in five minutes, Ms. Cannon," he said, loud enough for the secretary to hear.

"But—"

"Consider this your last warning."

Kate was down the hall, waiting for her. "That guy chased me out. There was nothing I could do. Are you in trouble?"

"Just a warning."

Kate let out a relieved breath. "Did you find out anything?"

Teddy nodded. "Jeremy was telling the truth: Molly did attack someone."

Kate was silent, seeming to try putting together the pieces. "It's still not adding up for me."

"Did you get something?" Teddy asked, hoping Kate had gotten one of her rare flashes of claircognizance.

"It's like that feeling when a word's on the tip of your tongue. Almost. But not quite. I'll let you know."

"You will?" Teddy asked. "Thought we were going back to the whole 'hating each other' thing."

"Oh, we will. But whoever messed with you on that course messed with me, too, and I don't let people who mess with me walk away that easily," Kate said. "Let's go. Assembly started."

When they returned to the auditorium, the assembly was well under way. It was an awards ceremony of sorts, with Hollis Whitfield honoring third-year recruits who had earned prestigious externships. Teddy sat down next to Jillian and watched as Kate sat down next to Ava. Teddy turned her attention to the podium, where Whitfield was shaking hands with a clairvoyant named Arjun Bahl, who had accepted a place with Homeland Security.

Students and faculty applauded politely. Whitfield continued, "And now, for the final externship, I'd like to congratulate Christine Federico on her placement at the CIA."

Teddy scanned the crowd for Christine as students and faculty clapped. A low rumble began to make its way around the room. Whitfield repeated her name, but there was no response. Christine Federico had not returned to school. Just like Brett Evans. Teddy swallowed hard as she thought about what else these students had in common. Dead parents. Stolen lab samples. Names on a list.

Just like her.

CHAPTER TWENTY-SEVEN

AFTER ASSEMBLY, THE FIRST-YEAR STUDENTS WERE told to report to room 203 in Fort McDowell. Teddy was quiet amid the unusually rowdy recruits; their excitement was palpable. Dara rocked back and forth on her heels as they waited to exit the auditorium.

"Did I miss something?" Teddy asked.

"We're starting a new class," Dara said. "Whitfield announced it at the start of assembly."

When Teddy had been in the file room. With Nick. "What class?"

"Something about casework," Dara said. "We're actually going to start solving some crimes. I feel like I need to buy a pair of aviators or something."

Finally, after months of Dunn's psychic exercises and Boyd's obstacle course, after forensics lectures and Clint's conversations about empathy, they were going to work actual cases. But Teddy couldn't share in the enthusiasm. Her mind was still reeling from the news that Christine hadn't shown, though others might dismiss her disappearance as coincidence.

"Oh," Dara said. "You also missed Boyd's update on last semester's theft." She explained that there'd been no further evidence of foul play; though the school had taken the incident seriously, they didn't believe that a student had been behind it. Instead, they increased security at the lab, replacing the locks with electronic key pads (so long, Internet access). But Teddy didn't buy Boyd's explanation. Shouldn't the school be *more* worried if someone outside Whitfield had stolen the blood samples?

Teddy followed her classmates up the stairs and down the hall to room 203 for Casework. The professor hadn't arrived yet, but a large stack of textbooks leaned precariously on the desk at the front of the room. *Criminal Profiling: An Introduction,* the cover read.

"Does anyone know who's teaching the class?" Dara asked.

"It's a profiling class. Probably Corbett," Zac Rogers said.

Others murmured agreement, but Teddy was pretty sure they were mistaken. There was a new FBI liaison on campus, and she thought it was a fair bet that he would walk into the room at any minute.

When he did, everybody in the classroom sat up straighter. She slumped down, avoiding his line of sight.

"I'm FBI Special Agent Nick Stavros," he said. "Some of you already know me." With that, he looked straight at Teddy, who folded her arms and sank deeper into her seat. "This might be your first experience working with a member of the FBI. But this is not my first experience working with psychics. I think it might be useful to explain how I ended up at Whitfield."

He opened his laptop and hit a key. An image appeared on the whiteboard at the front of the room. "This is Nogales, Arizona," Nick said. "A border town two and a half hours south of Phoenix." It was a small town in the desert, surrounded by scrubby foothills, miles of open road, and not much else.

Another click, another image. A young woman's body, white and bloodless. Teddy looked away from the image. So did the other recruits around her.

"Our first victim was found by two teenage boys messing around in the desert on ATVs. No ID or identifying marks. Her description— approximately sixteen to twenty years old, five feet four inches, one hundred twenty pounds, Hispanic—matched no specific missing persons report." Nick faced the room. "Normally, this would have been a local matter. But the woman was found on federal land, so I was sent down to lead the investigation."

Another click. A close-up of the victim's face. "The sheriff's office released this photo to various media sites, hoping for a hit. Nothing. Then this woman came forward."

The next image was a still shot taken from what appeared to be video of a police interrogation room: Nick stood on one side of a long table, accompanied by two seated uniformed police officers. On the other side of the table was a Korean woman wrapped in a shawl, her body bent with age.

"Hye Kim," Nick said. "She didn't speak English, so we brought in a translator. She claimed to be a psychic. She didn't know the victim's name, but she said the victim and many others had visited her dreams." He lifted a piece of paper that appeared to be a copy of an official police report and read: "'The women, and they are many, are watched over by the Virgin and guarded by dogs.'"

Teddy returned to the still shot of the interrogation room. The officers looked bored, but everything about Nick's stance in the photo radiated impatience. His arms were crossed, his body tense, his jaw clenched.

"I wrote off Ms. Kim. Total waste of time," Nick said. He dropped the report on the desk. "It's normal to have people come into the station who are, let's say, a few french fries short of a Happy Meal. Sometimes people will see something on TV or read something in the paper and get it into their minds that they know something about the case. We assumed that Ms. Kim was one of those people."

"What happened?" Jillian asked.

"Nothing initially," Nick said. "And then two more young unidentified women were found in the desert, not far from where the first victim was discovered."

"A serial killer?" Jeremy asked.

"We didn't know. The only thing we were certain of is that we had something bigger on our hands. I went back to Phoenix and had a beer with another agent, one who was older, more experienced, and a hell of a lot smarter than I am. You know what he told me?"

"Listen to Hye Kim," Pyro said.

Nick turned to Pyro. "Exactly. A guy I respected told me to listen to a *psychic*. I couldn't believe it. No offense to anyone here, but I thought psychics were con artists." He shook his head. "But I had nothing else to go on, so I gave Ms. Kim's statement another look." He clicked to the next slide, projecting Ms. Kim's words on the screen: *The women, and they are many, are watched over by the Virgin and guarded by dogs.*

"The dogs," Jillian said, leaning forward as though straining to hear the animals herself.

"Not everyone speaks dog, Jillian," Ben Tucker said.

The class laughed and Jillian blushed. "You could start looking for areas where there were large concentrations of dogs," she suggested.

"Churches," Ben said. "I'd start there."

"Yes," Nick said. "That's what I thought, too. I started checking out local churches. Ran background checks on priests and preachers and church employees. Nothing." His gaze moved to Jillian. "And then I thought about the dogs. So I went to training facilities, kennels, veterinary offices, and that's where I got lucky."

He hit the button again, showing an image of a modern facility with a sign out front: the Santa Cruz County Animal Shelter. He switched to another shot of the shelter, a different angle from a greater distance. Teddy spotted a small church with a statue of the Virgin Mary, arms outstretched, gracing the entrance.

"Remember, in casework, we never dismiss coincidences." Nick pointed to a dilapidated adobe structure set about a half mile off the highway, between the church and the animal shelter. "Our perpetrator was running undocumented workers, mostly women, into the country. Some didn't survive the journey." He faced the room. "Everything was right there if I'd just bothered to look at it. Two more people died because I refused to take Ms. Kim seriously at first. That will always be on me."

Silence fell over the room. Nick cleared his throat and moved on. "I'd like to say that ever since that moment, every psychic I met on an investigation has been an asset. But that would be a lie. Unfortunately, the majority of psychics who present themselves to the FBI really are con artists."

Until that moment, Teddy had been avoiding Nick's eyes. Now she looked straight at him. "If you feel that way," she said, "what are you doing here?"

He studied her. "When Clint Corbett told me about a program to vet psychics—to weed out the charlatans—I wanted to be part of it. Because my experience has taught me that working with *actual* psychics can save lives."

Teddy wanted to hate him at that moment. But he obviously cared about his job. About helping people. Plus, he was hot.

He dragged a hand through his hair. "Look, I don't have a goddamn clue how any of you do what you do. It's more than a little spooky to the average cop. And frankly, we cops don't like someone else knowing more than we do and making us look stupid." He extended his arms, palms up. "You know what I say to that? Tough. It's time to put our egos aside and work together."

Teddy knew that her peers would be won over by this speech. Most of them—at least the Misfits—felt like weirdos out in the "real world." They'd grown up knowing that what made them different should be kept hidden. And here was FBI Special Agent Nick Stavros telling them that their psychic abilities could actually save lives. In the end, that was all they wanted. Why else would they put up with the grueling physical tests and emotional trials—the bullshit insanity of Sergeant Boyd—to be here? Even the shocking knowledge that Clint and Nick had manipulated her into coming to Whitfield hadn't deterred Teddy. Infuriated her, yes. Convinced her she couldn't trust them, absolutely. Despite that betrayal, she had stayed.

"All right," Nick said. "Casework. Let's get to it."

He returned to his laptop and hit a key. The adobe structure in the desert disappeared. In its place was a photograph of a striking young man, a teenager in baggy shorts and a T-shirt. He was lean and long-limbed, with shaggy sun-streaked brown hair and a brazen smile.

"Corey McDonald," Nick said. He studied the photo for a moment, then swiveled back to look at the class. "Instant impressions. Throw out the first word that comes to mind."

The answers varied. Athletic. Attractive. Young. Rich. Californian.

"Interesting. A roomful of psychics, and not one of you used the word *murderer* to describe him." Nick clicked to the next image, which showed the same young man in an orange jumpsuit. "Who said Californian?"

Kate raised her hand. "I felt like he was near water, sand, a beach. So, Californian."

"Corey McDonald went to San Jose State. And so did she." The next image showed a pretty brunette with big brown eyes. "Marlena Hyden." Nick turned to the class once again. "Initial impressions?"

"Gone," Ava said flatly.

Nick closed his laptop. "Corey McDonald, a nineteen-year-old kid with no criminal record, was convicted of the murder of his ex-girlfriend, Marlena Hyden. McDonald maintains his innocence, and so does his family.

"That's where all of you come in." Nick scanned the room. "An appellate court will review McDonald's case. That's on the docket three months from today. You'll divide into two teams and perform a psychic analysis of the case. Then one representative from each team will accompany me to interview Corey at San Quentin in the weeks leading up to hearing. Look for anything that might have been overlooked during the first trial. There was a lot of media attention on this case, a lot of pressure to put it to bed quickly. If the investigating DA and local cops got it wrong, push us toward the right perpetrator."

Nick scanned the room. "Each group will get the same information, but essentially, it's a race against the clock—and each other—to find anything we missed and make sure justice is done."

Henry was already whispering to Kate. Even though Teddy and Kate had formed a convenient alliance after their first exam, Teddy knew how the teams would shake out. Misfits vs. Alphas. And the Alphas had a claircognizant, two clairvoyants, a telepath, someone who received messages through dreams, and a medium. The Misfits had a weirdo who could sometimes predict someone's death, a free spirit who could mostly talk to animals (both on this side and the next, to be fair), someone who was so crippled by her ability to read emotions that she'd just had a nervous breakdown, a bad boy with the ability to set things on fire, an awkward psychometrist, and a telepath who could barely control her own powers. Which team was going to win again?

"There's an extra incentive to solving the case," Nick said. "In addition to seeing justice done, the star student on the winning team will get a private tour of the FBI field office in San Francisco."

Teddy couldn't care less about the tour. Sure, she was sick of losing to the Alphas, but now she had a chance to do something important.

Dara raised her hand. "When do we start?"

"Now."

CHAPTER TWENTY-EIGHT

THE MISFITS SPENT TWO PAINFUL WEEKS GOING through every piece of paperwork associated with the case. None of them had gleaned any insight from the astral plane, so they were determined to mine the physical one and learn the case inside and out.

Here was what they knew: a jogger had discovered Marlena Hyden's body in a marsh along a wetland trail roughly twenty miles from San Jose State. Since the body had stayed in the water for so long, the coroner could not definitively determine the cause of death; in court, he said that he believed the bruising around Marlena's neck indicated she'd been strangled, but physical evidence was inconclusive. It was the perfect case for psychics.

Here was what they guessed: Corey's shifting account of his whereabouts the night of Marlena's disappearance, physical evidence found in his car, and testimony given by dormitory residents that he and Marlena had fought before her death had led to his conviction. The DA had sold the murder as a crime of passion. The night of Marlena's death, the DA claimed, Corey had snapped.

What they needed—and none of them saw a way around it—was to examine the evidence kits.

After trials, Nick explained, journalists and third parties were sometimes allowed to go through pertinent physical evidence. He made a call, pushing hard for the district court to release kits from both the prosecution and the defense. Ten days later, as Nick handed out gloves, he warned the recruits about possible contamination of the evidence, something that had been drilled into them in Forensics.

"Nothing we find here can be submitted as proof to the appellate court anyway," Nick said. "But it might lead to new evidence that can."

Each team had two hours to inspect the items under Nick's supervision. The Alphas won a coin toss (supposedly fair and square, though Teddy suspected that Kate knew the right call beforehand) and chose to go first.

The evidence included: a knife taken from Corey's tackle box; a photograph of the passenger seat of Corey's car; fibers from the car itself; residue of Marlena's blood; Marlena's lipstick, sunglasses, and a pair of plastic flip-flops, all found in Corey's car; additional photos of hair, fingerprints, and clothing fiber samples, also found in Corey's car, in Corey's and Marlena's rooms, on Marlena's body, and on Corey's person; beer bottles recovered from the Dumpster outside the dorm with traces of Corey's and Marlena's DNA.

In addition to the kits, each team was provided with hair and clothing samples belonging to Corey and Marlena, as well as an intimate possession from each, which their families had donated to aid in the psychic investigation. From Marlena, a sterling ring set with an opalescent moonstone. From Corey, a copy of *Romeo and Juliet* that he was reading when he was arrested, which Teddy found both tragic and ironic.

The problem was that psychic gifts didn't exactly work on command—or at least the Misfits' didn't. Which they were reminded of when Nick finally called them to the library to inspect the kits.

"I have a bad feeling about this knife," Jillian said, dropping it as soon as she picked it up. "It's caused a lot of death."

"Yeah, to fish. All the blood found on the knife was fish blood," Pyro said. "Just because the police found a knife doesn't mean it's the murder weapon. There's nothing on the coroner's report that indicates trauma relating to knife wounds."

Pyro, despite having no psychic abilities that would reveal new evidence, had turned out to be a major asset to their team. As a former police officer, he knew more about procedure than all of them combined.

"What's the point of this?" Jeremy said, pushing back his chair. Everyone hoped that he, as a psychometrist, would only have to hold Marlena's or Corey's personal items to crack the case open. But he hadn't had any luck getting a clear read on the evidence.

"We just need something to go on before the interview at San Quentin," Jillian said.

"I bet the Alphas figured it out this morning," Dara said.

"Maybe they know something we don't," Pyro said.

"Or maybe they're working together as a group," Teddy suggested, "instead of bickering, like we are."

Teddy surveyed the team. Pyro looked like he was about to punch someone; Jeremy wasn't far behind. Molly was chewing a fingernail, almost like she wasn't listening to the conversation. Teddy had assumed that Molly's powers as an empath would have helped them understand Corey's emotional state leading up to the crime, but so far, she'd said barely a word.

"Why don't we divide up the kits and work separately for a bit?" Teddy asked. She looked at her watch. "Dinner's in an hour. With any luck, we won't have to lie when we tell Ni— Agent Stavros that we're making progress on the case."

Molly looked up. "What?"

Dara sighed. "I'm sorry, did we interrupt you?"

Molly smiled. "I'm sure we can figure this out if we work together."

Pyro stood, the tips of his gloves smoking. "Just please, someone, do something."

"It's not like your powers come in handy here," Jeremy said as he reached for the copy of *Romeo and Juliet*.

"We're all frustrated," Teddy said. "We don't need to take it out on each other."

She grabbed a few photographs and wove through a row of books toward a small table in the corner of the library. She settled in, eager for solitude. But after a minute or two, she saw Molly flop down a few seats away.

Teddy had thought she knew Molly well enough—but the girl she'd met on the ferry didn't seem like the girl who'd hacked Eversley's computer, or the girl who'd attacked her in the exam, or the girl who'd returned to Whitfield acting like a Stepford wife. This Molly seemed distracted, out of sorts. Teddy silently cursed. When she'd been a loner in Vegas, life had been easier. She hadn't needed to give a shit about other people, to talk about feelings all the time. She blamed Clint. Screw empathy.

"Hey," Teddy said softly. "Everything okay?"

"Just tired." Molly smiled again. "These new exercises."

"Are they worth it?" Teddy asked. "Even though they're keeping people's emotions out, I can't help but think they're keeping other stuff out, too."

Molly looked confused. "What do you mean?"

"You're not picking up on things you used to. You haven't mentioned anything about the case—"

"Not everything is about the case, Teddy."

"*That's* not what I mean. Look," Teddy started, "Jeremy told me about what happened last year."

Molly chewed her lip. "I'm looking for a clean slate. Same as you."

"But is it worth jeopardizing your health?"

"I . . ." Molly said.

Teddy studied the faded blue carpet on the library floor, trying to find the right words. She didn't know how to voice what she was feeling. Concern, of course, but also frustration, maybe even suspicion. Months ago, Molly would have known without Teddy even having to try.

Dara wove through the stacks toward them, her signature silver bangles clinking. "Hurry," she said. "Jillian's got something."

Jillian hunched over the table, her face so pale it looked practically white. Pyro stood next to her, his arms out as if he planned to catch her in case she fell over.

"She slipped Marlena's ring onto her finger, and *this* happened," Dara said.

Jillian heaved as if trying to catch her breath after running one of Boyd's obstacle courses. Her hands traveled to her neck, clawing at something invisible there. In a high, thready voice not her own, she whispered: "I can't breathe."

Teddy lurched forward. "We've got to—"

Pyro caught her arm before Teddy could shake Jillian out of the trance. "*Marlena* can't breathe," he said. Then his gaze shot to Dara. "Do you think we can ask her questions?"

Dara nodded. "I saw something like this once in my grandmother's shop."

Pyro leaned forward. "We want to help you, Marlena. Nod if you're listening."

Jillian gasped. She was struggling for air.

"Someone strangled you," Pyro said. "Was it Corey?"

Jillian's eyes rolled back in her head. Her body trembled as she drew shallow, labored breaths.

"Was it Corey?" Pyro asked again.

Jillian stopped breathing.

Teddy rushed forward, grabbing her by the shoulders. She lifted Jillian's blond curls and pushed two fingers to her neck to check for a pulse, then waited before she felt the faint beat of Jillian's heart. Jillian opened her eyes and gasped. "Did I fall asleep or something?" she said.

Pyro placed a hand on Jillian's shoulder. "Nice work. Jillian, you just communed with Marlena."

"I did?"

Every step forward felt like a step backward. Sure, Jillian had connected with Marlena, but that hadn't made the way any clearer. Teddy had been so sure at the start of the assignment that casework would be straightforward. Follow the clues. Find the bad guy. But the more they studied the facts, the murkier they seemed.

Teddy glanced nervously from Jillian to the other Misfits. "So, we're sure that Marlena was strangled. Even if the coroner wasn't. That's something," she said.

* * *

The Misfits' lucky streak continued the next day, when they returned to the library to reexamine the kits. They split up again, this time each choosing a different clue from each kit. It wasn't long before Teddy looked up to find Jeremy quietly standing over her desk, a grin on his face.

"I've got something," he said, tossing the copy of *Romeo and Juliet* on top of her crime-scene photos.

"What?" she asked.

"He didn't do it," Jeremy said. "Corey is innocent."

"How can you be so sure?" Jillian demanded. The group had gathered around them.

"I held the book before, but I didn't get a clear picture of Corey from it. Or what I got was all muddled. So I went through the book page by page. I mean, look at Jillian. She went all in, right? I read each annotation. No flashes or anything, but I got a feeling: whoever wrote these notes didn't kill anyone."

Teddy slumped back, silently processing. Dara swung around to look at Jillian. "What do you think? You channeled Marlena. Is Jeremy right?"

Jillian's brow furrowed. She caught her lower lip between her teeth. "I'm not sure. I only know *how* she died."

"Well, I'm sure," Jeremy said. "So now we need to figure out who did do it."

Pyro scoffed. "A feeling? Right. What we need to do to prove he's innocent is establish his time line. Make sure he has a solid alibi. That's something his attorney failed to do in court. It left the jury open to suspicion to convict him. We should look through his Facebook photos of that night again." Pyro rifled through some printouts documenting Corey's social media activity in the moments leading up to Marlena's murder, including a picture of him looking like any other clean-cut college kid: UCLA Bruins hat, ripped jeans, white shirt.

"This is all we have," Dara said. "It must be enough to get a read on Corey."

"Teddy will have to figure it out," Pyro said.

At the end of the assignment, one person from each team was going to San Quentin to question Corey McDonald. She knew, like she knew how a player next to her was about to fold, like she understood all the unknown things that came to her known, that she would be the one making the trip.

Teddy looked at the copy of the book that Jeremy had left on the desk. She would need to know as much about Corey as possible to survive a trip into his mind. She just hoped Hollis Whitfield was a fan of Elizabethan playwrights, as she headed into the stacks to search under *S* for Shakespeare.

As Nick gathered the kits for safekeeping, Teddy handed him the Whitfield copy. "Don't forget the book," she said while stuffing Corey's copy in her tote bag.

*   *   *

Later, Teddy sat in bed with Corey McDonald's copy of Shakespeare's play. She'd never been one for poetry in high school, but she began to reread the text, quickly falling into the story. A dog-eared page caught her attention: "These violent delights have violent ends." The friar speaking to Romeo. The passage was circled, highlighted. Teddy shivered. Did Corey know what was coming? Cramped notations in pencil and ink in the margins. Underlined passages. Notes for an essay in the back. If she could find out how this kid's mind worked, maybe she could figure out how to gather his thoughts and memories into a structure she could navigate. She had to find his memory of that night. She fell asleep with the book on her stomach. She had dreamed of the yellow house in the nights since the midyear exam, but each time she reached to turn the doorknob, she found the chipped green front door locked. When she peered into the darkened windows, it looked as though no one was home.

Tonight the dream began in the way it always did. As Teddy walked up the steps, she saw that the porch was covered in shards of glass. She looked up. A window was broken, the door ajar. She stepped inside.

If before it had looked like someone was packing for a move, now the house looked completely abandoned. The little table was over-turned; the picture of Clint and her parents was gone. Teddy made her way through the rooms, searching for something, anything. There had to be a reason she'd gotten inside tonight.

She paused in a bedroom to the left of the hallway. Dust covered the wooden floorboards, and cobwebs laced every corner. Another dead end. She returned to the entryway, pausing by the door. She righted the little table, noticing a piece of paper she hadn't seen before. Scribbled on torn white paper was a message in lean, loopy handwriting and blue ink: *Be careful.*

Teddy sat up in her bed, knocking the book to the floor. When she bent to pick it up, she noticed a piece of paper flutter to the ground. Script. Blue pen. The note from her dream. How had it gotten in here? She must have missed it before.

CHAPTER TWENTY-NINE

COREY MCDONALD'S HEARING LOOMED—THREE MONTHS away, then two, then one—but otherwise, life at Whitfield continued as it had before. The Misfits survived Boyd's cruel and unusual torture, completed Dunn's psychic exercises, listened to lectures on police procedure, firearms, and forensics. There was one class that Teddy skipped: Empathy 101.

Teddy decided to use her free time to practice telekinesis. Progress had been hard earned and slow going. Teddy understood that her telekinetic feats so far—the door, General Maddux's wineglass—had been fueled by heightened emotions: anger, specifically. She would need to master her feelings in order to prove Clint wrong.

She could now float a Ping-Pong ball around an empty classroom in Fort McDowell, but a gentle breeze could do the same. She'd recently entered a staring competition with a paper clip. If she was ever going to bend a bullet, she'd have to tackle metal objects.

One brick at a time.

After a particularly painful session, Teddy returned to her room, threw her stuff down, and grabbed her towel, hoping for a quick shower before dinner. Jillian had other plans. She perched on the end of Teddy's bed. "You missed a really interesting lecture today in Professor Corbett's class," she said.

"I'll have to get a copy of your notes," Teddy said as she unlaced her combat boots.

Jillian stood up. "God, you're such a drama queen."

"Excuse me?"

"Clint ends your tutorials because he thinks you might hurt yourself, and instead of talking to him, or even to me, you decide to ignore it."

Teddy shrugged, hoping if she ignored that, too, Jillian would shut up.

"Did you even listen in Empathy 101? It's not all about you. We're all struggling to master our psychic abilities. Since I've arrived at Whitfield, Ava has teased me for communing with animals. And then the one time I make a connection with an actual person, it's a girl who was choked to death. I was terrified. And you didn't even ask me how I felt."

Teddy slipped on her shower shoes. She didn't want to be having this conversation right now.

"And what about Fred?"

"Fred?"

"My hamster?" Jillian's eyes were watery. "Who's about to die? I told you when I came back after Christmas."

Teddy had never really had friends like Jillian before—friends who knew so much about her, who understood parts of her that she didn't or couldn't express. She flushed. She felt trapped, claustrophobic. She didn't want to deal with Jillian or her hamster. She swapped her shower shoes for sneakers. "I need some air," Teddy said.

"You're just running away from this? Friends argue, Teddy. It shows that you care enough about other people when you're willing to fight for them."

Teddy heard the logic, but she preferred the first option: she was going to run as far as she could get on a very small island. Which really was not very far at all.

*　　*　　*

Teddy could complete the six-mile loop in just under an hour, which guaranteed that Jillian would be at dinner when Teddy returned to the room.

Before coming to Whitfield, she'd never been much of a runner, but now she actually enjoyed the activity. She liked the island's sloping vistas, quiet coves, historic buildings, and abandoned quarries. Once she found her groove, her body settled into a state that was almost meditative. Her thoughts emptied, leaving her aware of nothing but her breathing—until footsteps behind her intruded on her solitude. She cut a glance over her shoulder. Nick. For a moment, she considered speeding up.

"Hey," he said. He appeared at her side in running shorts and a baggy sweatshirt. His dark hair was damp and swept back from his face. He looked altogether different from the Special Agent Stavros who taught Casework. Different even from the guy she'd been alone with in the file room. Different but good. Really good. Probably not dissimilar from the way he might look stepping out of a shower. Here was the distraction Teddy needed.

"Got a minute?" he asked. "Clearance just came through for the McDonald visit. We're looking at next week for the one-on-one."

She kept running, risking a glance at him.

"How's the case going?" he asked.

"We have some leads," Teddy said, thinking back to Jillian's spiritual communication with Marlena, as well as Jeremy's assertion of Corey's innocence. Unfortunately, she hadn't had a breakthrough since she'd "borrowed" Corey's copy of *Romeo and Juliet*. And now she had only a week to figure it out. "Who are the Alphas sending to San Quentin?" she asked, panting from the steep slope they were now running on.

"Probably Kate Atkins." He was out of breath, too. "I assume your team will chose you?"

"Why would you assume that?"

"Because you stand out."

She stopped running and bent to catch her breath. "Don't do that," she said. He stopped, too.

"Do what?"

"Be nice to me." Especially after that fight with Jillian. She just wanted to be alone. She didn't want to deal with people and their *feelings*.

"Teddy—"

"I mean it, Nick." She let out a long breath.

He nodded. "I'm not trying to make this difficult." He held up his hands and took a step back. "I'm not doing it on purpose."

"Are you sure about that?"

"Look," he said, "it's hard for me, too. Okay? Is that what you want to hear?"

"It's a start."

"Point is, we're going to have to find a way to work together. And as long as I'm a teacher and you're a student—"

"Strictly professional," she said.

"I like to think we can be friends," he said.

She watched a bead of sweat drip down his neck into his T-shirt. Despite herself, she imagined the rest of its journey down his chest, abdomen . . .

She'd proved today that she didn't know how to be a good friend. Part of her wished that she hadn't bailed after Jillian had asked her about Clint. That she'd stayed to fight, even though it had been uncomfortable. She promised herself that next time she would.

"Okay," she said. "Friends."

"As a friend," Nick began when they'd settled back into their run, "I wanted to talk to you about why you've been skipping Corbett's classes."

This again.

"Make sure you go to the next one, okay?"

"Fine," Teddy said. "No more talking. Just running."

Nick smiled, flashing that killer dimple, and Teddy managed to stifle a groan. "See if you can keep up, friend."

Oh, she'd keep up, all right.

CHAPTER THIRTY

THE WEEK PASSED TOO QUICKLY. ON THE MORNING of the trip to San Quentin, when Teddy stopped in the main office to pick up a pass to leave the island, the secretary handed her a note. "Professor Corbett wants to see you before you go."

Teddy looked at the clock above the secretary's desk. It was 8:51 a.m.

"He knows you're leaving at nine."

"Thanks," Teddy said, trudging up the two flights of stairs to Clint's office. This was the most important day of her psychic career so far, and Clint Corbett was going to make her late.

To say that she'd been avoiding Clint would be putting it mildly. Everyone had noticed that she had skipped his monthly Empathy 101 class. Since the midyear exam, other than passing him without a word on campus, she had completely and totally ignored him. Her stomach twisted as she made the familiar journey down the hallway to his office. She checked to make sure her shield was up, sending another surge of power just to be safe, then knocked once.

"Come in."

Inside, his office looked the same: books strewn about, papers everywhere. The chalkboard in the corner held evidence of a puzzle to be worked out, something about mass and velocity. The screw encased in glass, which Teddy now knew came from Sector Three, was on his desk.

"You wanted to see me," Teddy said.

He looked up at her. "I heard you were going to San Quentin this morning with Agent Stavros and Kate. I assume you're going to use astral telepathy to enter McDonald's mind."

So this conversation was going to be all business. Nothing about what had happened between them. Teddy could keep it professional, too. "Yes."

"Are you prepared?"

Teddy clenched her fists, trying not show any outward signs of emotion. She wanted to prove to Clint that she had her feelings in check. The truth was, no, she didn't feel prepared. But if they were going to beat the Alphas and help Corey and Marlena, she had to at least try.

The Misfits hadn't gained any more insight since they had reviewed the kits. They were confident, from Jillian's communion, that Marlena had been strangled and, from Jeremy's psychometry, that Corey was innocent. Teddy had read *Romeo and Juliet* ten times since she had swapped the book. Her team thought that once she was inside his head, she'd be able to use his memories to find new evidence that would exonerate Corey—set an airtight alibi, identify another suspect. Then they could focus on finding the real killer.

She was counting on Clint's organizational strategy to help her. She was nervous that she would get lost inside Corey's head, and the precious minutes she had in front of him would be wasted. Though she had seen random snapshots in Molly's head, she'd never used the house inside anyone's head but Clint's. She'd never had to search for a memory, either. She didn't know if she'd be able to synthesize what she knew about McDonald into a concrete structure, even. She reached for *Romeo and Juliet,* which she had tucked into her backpack that morning for luck.

From reading Corey's notes, she'd learned that he was a smart and thoughtful kid. Observant. And it was obvious he'd loved Marlena.

Every line about Juliet had been highlighted. The famous speech about seeing Juliet for the first time had so many notations, Teddy could barely read it.

Clint took off his glasses. "Teddy, this is about more than a competition between classmates. You're doing real work now. This is why you're at Whitfield. To help people."

Teddy didn't know when it had happened, but as she'd lost herself in the details of the case, the assignment had become about far more than winning. Marlena and Corey were real to her—to all of them. She had watched the team work until their nerves frayed. Jillian, Jeremy, Pyro, too. They had to help because they could help. As Clint had said all those months ago, they had to show up. "I know," Teddy said.

Clint put his glasses back on. "Then all I can say is good luck."

Teddy knew she'd been dismissed, but she had more to say. "So, we haven't spoken in months. You know I've been missing your class. And all you want to do is make sure I know how important this case is?"

Clint looked at her. "Did you want to talk about something else?"

Of course she wanted to talk about something else. But the ferry was leaving any minute. "That's not fair."

"Life isn't fair, Teddy. But you have the chance to make it just. This is your job. So do it." He returned to the file. "You're going to miss your ride. I'll see you in class this afternoon."

*　　*　　*

After the ferry ride, Teddy found herself in the backseat of a government-issue Crown Vic, speeding southeast on Highway 101, through Marin County's rolling hills. Any moment it felt like spring would take hold and the landscape would be green and lush, scattered with wildflowers. But at this time of year, everything looked brown and bare.

Nick had spent most of the car ride briefing them on what to expect once they arrived at San Quentin—how to move, how to talk, how to conduct themselves should the alarms go off during their visit. The only item they were permitted to carry inside was their identification, Nick explained; that was why he hadn't brought his laptop, which he usually carried everywhere. Teddy made a mental note to leave the book in the car.

They exited the highway and drew to a stop at the prison's first security checkpoint. The guard on duty checked their IDs and allowed them to pass. They drove through secured metal gates, past twin perimeters of towering chain-link fences topped with looped razor wire. Nick parked, and they walked toward the main entrance. Comparing herself to the prison's massive scale, Teddy felt small. Maybe that was the point. She was going into a facility of thousands of people, with thousands of thoughts, memories, stories. She took a deep breath, gathering her strength. Her mental shield needed to be stronger than ever.

Nick paused before they entered. "Ready?" he asked them.

He held open the door and ushered them inside. More screenings, more ID scans. Nick checked his weapon and holster. They were processed through a metal detector, followed by a security-wand once-over. A female correctional officer patted down Teddy and Kate; a male CO frisked Nick.

Next they were ushered one at a time through a series of heavy iron-bar doors.

"Turn and face me." A CO sat in a small room tucked between the doors, situated behind a bulletproof sheet of clear acrylic. "Hands up. Show me your ID."

Teddy complied.

"Clear," the CO called out. The next iron door rolled open, propelling Teddy deeper into the heart of San Quentin.

Teddy had known the prison would be crowded. It housed more than four thousand inmates, roughly a thousand more than it had been designed to accommodate. As conscientious as she'd been with her mental defenses before stepping inside San Quentin, they weren't enough. As soon as she entered the prison, Teddy felt accosted by psychic impressions, coming so fast that she lost her breath. What was different about this place? The desperation? The despair? It had been a while since she'd been around so many people who weren't psychic. The anxiety that had tortured Teddy her entire life took hold of her body: her stomach churned, her heart raced, her vision swam. She needed to get herself under control. She saw Kate recoil as well, stumbling backward. For a split second their eyes met, and a moment of understanding passed between them. Teddy sent another surge of power to her wall. She took another breath. Remembered that she had a job to do. And that Kate was trying to do it better.

A pair of armed correctional officers escorted them to a row of attorney-client conference rooms near the entrance. Teddy counted five rooms, all of which were occupied. As the COs took up positions on opposite ends of the narrow hallway, Nick pulled Teddy and Kate aside.

"You'll each have thirty minutes alone with McDonald," he said.

Well, not quite alone. As an additional safety measure, Nick would accompany each of them into the conference room in turn. He assured them that he wouldn't interfere with their interviews in any way. This was their show.

In a coin toss, the Misfits had won the privilege of interviewing McDonald first. When the door to the last conference room opened, a CO gestured to her. Teddy walked inside. Nick followed.

When Teddy saw Corey, he looked different than the clean-cut boy in the evidence pictures: shaggy pale brown hair fell in his eyes, and his blue chambray shirt hung loose over his shoulders.

The door closed behind her. As when she'd connected with Clint during the exam, she knew she would have to lower her wall if she wanted to reach Corey telepathically. She felt vulnerable without it up these days, especially in a place like this. She wouldn't be able to rely on her usual lie-detecting skills, either—even in this room, one-on-one, her body felt like it was in hyperdrive. She'd have only her telepathy from this point forward.

"Hi," she said. "I'm Teddy Cannon." A chain connected Corey's wrists to the belt fastened around his waist. It rattled as he shifted in his seat.

"I'm Corey," he said. "But you knew that already."

She pulled out the chair opposite him and sat down. "Hi, Corey." She smiled, even though she couldn't dismiss the chance that he'd killed his girlfriend. It made her sick. "I'm here to ask you some questions, see if we can figure a way to get you out of here."

In the days leading up to the visit, she'd thought a lot about how she'd handle her time. She knew that she wanted to be up-front with him. Tell him she was psychic. She'd never had to tell anyone that before. There weren't any rules against outing herself, just about mentioning Whitfield. So, Teddy took a breath and began. "Corey, do you know what a psychic is?"

"A psychic? Sure. Someone who stares into a crystal ball, reads palms, that sort of thing."

"Not exactly," she returned. "I don't own a crystal ball, and I have no intention of reading your palm. But if you tell me what happened the night Marlena Hyden disappeared, I might be able to help."

His brow furrowed. "Do my parents know you're here?"

"Actually, yeah. They do."

"A psychic?" He slumped back in his chair. "So the attorney thing didn't . . ." He studied the ceiling. "God, they must be desperate. My dad's a scientist, you know that? He doesn't believe in any of this."

Corey scooted back his chair and lurched his upper body forward. For one foolish, panicked instant, Teddy thought he was lunging for her. Instead, Corey slammed his elbows on the table. "Damn," he said, as if her presence suddenly made his situation clear: his parents and his attorney had taken it as far as they could.

The best possible outcome of the meeting was for Teddy to identify where Corey had been on the night of the murder. If she could put his mind on that train of thought, maybe it would make it easier for her to find the memory of that night. "Let's try to start at the beginning, Corey. Can you tell me what happened the last time you saw Marlena?" She tried to sound gentle. Kind. Kinder and gentler than she ever had in her entire life, that was for sure.

"I told them, told everyone. A dozen times. I was drunk. If I remembered, I would've had a solid alibi. I'm not an idiot."

She hadn't expected tears or anything, but she certainly hadn't expected attitude. Teddy leaned forward in her chair. "Maybe I can help find that memory for you. Walk me through that night."

"Marlena was angry with me," Corey said. "That wasn't new."

"Did you two fight a lot?" Teddy took a breath, centered herself. Focused on keeping Corey talking. The better her sense of him, the more prepared she'd be when she entered his mind.

"We had our ups and downs, just like any couple."

"I get that," Teddy said. "Trust me." Building rapport could help. She remembered all of Clint's empathy lessons. Put herself in Corey's place. "Look, Corey. I'm on your side here," she said. "Can you try to remember where you were that night?"

This was the crux of his case: his defense could never establish a concrete time line. He hadn't had his phone on him—he said he'd lost it at a party earlier that night—so they couldn't track his location via cell towers. There'd been no GPS in his car. His friends hadn't seen him after he left the dorms. Corey had shown up at Marlena's room early in the night, been seen in his own room alone near dawn. But there was a whole lot of time in between when he wasn't accounted for.

"I dunno. I went to see Marlena, we talked, we hung out. Drove around."

This was something. He'd never admitted that they'd been in the car together, even though several of Marlena's personal effects had been in his possession.

"I didn't want to tell the cops we got in the car because I was drunk. I knew I shouldn't have been driving."

Teddy began to push into his consciousness, the inky darkness unfolding before her. He had no wall, so Teddy entered easily. The image before her was hazy, out of focus. She thought it looked like a Victorian, two stories, white siding, a big bay window. It flickered once or twice before disappearing back into nothingness.

The car. "Did something happen in the car, Corey? There were traces of blood—"

"I can explain that," he said. "She cut her finger in my tackle box, when she was looking for a bottle opener. It didn't seem like a big deal at the time. Must have gotten in the car, too."

This was going nowhere. The door to Corey's house, to Corey's astral self, was still closed. From the corner of her eye, she saw Nick raise his hands. *Ten minutes.* Time had gone too fast. She might as well change tacks. The book. She should ask him about the book.

"I read your book," she said.

"What book?"

"The one your parents gave me. *Romeo and Juliet*?"

He tried to rub his wrists underneath his handcuffs. "Oh, yeah. It's cool."

In her mind's eye, she saw only darkness. This line of questioning was another dead end. If she could talk about his essay, maybe. Or how Marlena reminded him of Juliet?

"You remember the part when—" she began to say, but suddenly, she felt the breath knocked out of her. Panic surged through her. She felt the presence wrap around her mind, tightening like a vise. Her wall was down, she was defenseless. Then a voice rang through her head: *Ask to see his handwriting.*

When she looked up, Nick was at her side. "Are you okay?"

"Yeah, just a headache," she said, rubbing her temples. "Can I have some water?"

Who the hell are you, and what are you doing in my head? she said.

All in good time, Theodora, the voice replied.

She jerked, trying to shake herself free.

Listen. I might be able to help.

Teddy shivered. An echo of the words she'd said to Corey mere moments ago. Nick brought her a bottle of water. "You have about five minutes left."

Teddy felt her stomach drop. Five minutes? That was all? "Okay." She took a sip and tried to concentrate. "Corey, you said you and Marlena got in the car. Did you go down to the wetlands?"

He crossed his arms. "No, I've never been down there."

Ask to see his handwriting, the voice said again.

"So, you didn't go to the wetlands?"

"No, I said I've never been there."

"Teddy, we need to wrap this up," Nick said from behind her.

"Hold on a second."

Ask, the voice said.

What did she have to lose? "Nick, can I borrow a pen and paper?" Almost as suddenly as it had entered her mind, the presence retreated.

"Teddy, you're out of time. Where are you going with this?"

"Please, just another minute."

Nick was at her side, handing her a lined yellow notepad and a pen he'd lifted from his breast pocket.

"Corey, can you write something for me, please?" She slid the paper across the desk and placed the pen in his hands. "I know it's hard with the, um"—she tilted her head—"handcuffs."

"What do you want me to write?" Corey asked.

"Anything. Your name. Your address. Who you want to win the World Series." Teddy watched as the pen made short strokes. "Wait—did you buy your copy of *Romeo and Juliet* used?"

He shrugged. "It's cheaper." He finished the sentence and pushed the paper and pen back to Teddy.

"Were there notes in the book already? When you bought it, I mean."

"Now that you mention it, yeah. It made it really hard to read."

That was why Jeremy couldn't get a read on Corey. The book had multiple owners. The notes hadn't been his. Hadn't been his comments, his thoughts. She'd based her whole profile on another person.

Jeremy's psychometric read was right. The person who'd written the notes in the book hadn't killed Marlena Hyden. But that person wasn't Corey McDonald.

Because the handwriting didn't match at all.

"Teddy, you're really out of time," Nick said, coming toward her chair.

She hadn't found the memory. Hadn't established a time line. An alibi. She wasn't even sure that Corey was innocent. Every assumption they'd made was wrong.

She'd failed. More, she'd failed Marlena.

Teddy stood, wordlessly allowing herself to be escorted from the room. Her entire body was trembling. Her throat burned. Her limbs felt weak, and her head throbbed. She slowly eased herself onto the bench where Kate had been sitting.

Nick hesitated. It was clear that he wanted to ask her what the hell had just happened, but he had to return to the room to supervise Kate. "You going to be okay out here by yourself?"

Teddy attempted a smile and cut a glance at the two heavily armed correctional officers stationed at either end of the hallway. "It's Kate's turn."

Once the door closed behind them, Teddy drew in another shaky breath and attempted to center her thoughts.

Someone had entered her mind when her walls were down, then proceeded to point out all the flaws in their logic, which now seemed glaringly obvious. But the only two people who'd been in the room were Nick and Corey, neither of whom was psychic.

Her throat felt so dry she couldn't swallow. She'd left the bottle Nick had given her in the interview room. She stood and approached one of the COs. "Excuse me, is there somewhere I could get water?"

The man ignored her. He stared straight ahead, Buckingham Palace guard–style.

She clenched her fists and tried again. "Look. I'm not going to wander away. I just want—"

She stopped as recognition set in. His eyes were black, pupils wide, as big as his irises. He wasn't ignoring her. And neither was the guard at the other end of the hallway, whose face bore an identical expression. The same desperately blank expression that Sergei and the Bellagio pit boss had worn the night Clint had mentally influenced them to walk away; the same expression Molly had worn in the warehouse.

Teddy felt the hair stand up on the back of her neck. Someone inside San Quentin was mentally influencing the guards. She had to tell Nick. Before she could stand and make her way back to the conference room, the door adjacent to Corey McDonald's drifted open.

A slight, neatly dressed older man stepped out. He gestured in Teddy's direction.

"Ms. Cannon," he said, holding open the door for her. "You're right on time. My client will see you now."

CHAPTER THIRTY-ONE

"MS. CANNON?" THE LAWYER REPEATED.

Teddy stared at the man as her brain scrambled for a response.

This was San Quentin, home to California's most hardened violent offenders. And she was supposed to leave a hallway where (at least in theory, even if they were under mental influence) she was protected by two armed guards and enter a private conference room with an unknown inmate? Teddy understood it was a bad idea. And yet she knew that whoever was in the other room had her number.

Teddy closed her eyes and slowed her breathing. The man inside was already in her head. Instead of trying to block his psychic advance, she welcomed it. *What do you want from me?*

The answer came almost immediately: *Wrong question.*

"Ms. Cannon?" the lawyer repeated.

Teddy took a step forward. The lawyer ushered her inside and then took her place in the hallway, closing the door behind him.

Teddy's gaze shot to the man who had summoned her. Just like Corey McDonald, he sat cuffed behind an institutional metal desk. But that was where the similarity ended. This man, whoever he was, was lean and wiry. Narrow nose, sharp cheekbones. A faint pink scar ran along the left side of his jaw. Eyes so dark they looked black. Something about him struck Teddy as vaguely familiar, but if she had met him before, she knew she would have remembered those eyes.

"Who are you?" she said.

"Wrong question again. Don't you want to ask who killed Marlena Hyden?"

Teddy regarded him warily. "You were in my head."

"I was."

"To lead me to discover that the notes weren't Corey's. To lead me to think that he's guilty of murdering Marlena."

"Yes." His answer was simple.

"But I still don't have proof."

"Well, not yet."

How wrong the Misfits had been. They had believed McDonald to be innocent—until this man intervened.

"Sometimes the justice system gets it right the first time." He paused, rattling the chain attached to his handcuffs. "And sometimes it doesn't."

Teddy forced her attention to the man before her, understanding that she'd been summoned for a reason. "Who are you?" she asked again.

"My name is Derek Yates." He watched her for a beat, looking for something—a glimmer of recognition, perhaps—before his expression tightened. "You don't even know who I am. You know even less than I thought you would."

"About what?"

"About all of us. Me, your parents—Marysue and Richard Delaney. Clint."

Marysue and Richard. Her parents. It was the first time she'd heard their names. "You knew my parents?" She slumped into the chair across from him.

"I met you once, too. But you wouldn't remember."

"Prove it," she said.

With his wrists still shackled together, he managed to reach into the pocket of his shirt and produce a worn black-and-white photograph. He set it on the table between them and pushed it toward her. Teddy spared it a quick glance. Then she did a double take. It was the photograph she'd seen in her dream.

She stared at the man before her and understood why he had looked so familiar. She'd seen him in the picture. And what was more, she understood that the picture was real.

"I'm like you, Theodora. And your parents. Fighting for what's right. Only I stood up to the wrong person, defied orders. And now I'm here—with a life sentence for a murder I didn't commit."

"If you're fighting for what's right, how did you end up in prison?" she asked.

"Sometimes right and wrong aren't black and white." He leaned back in his chair. "Sometimes decisions can't be so morally . . . easy."

"Who put you here?"

He tapped his index finger to the photo, chains brushing together with each movement. "Someone who takes his morality very seriously."

Teddy looked at the picture. He was pointing to someone she knew. Clint. Her mind raced. *If Clint put this guy away, he must have been guilty.*

Yates's gravelly voice sounded in her head: *Corbett would love to believe that.*

His thin mouth became even thinner, and he continued aloud: "And falsified the evidence to do it."

Teddy looked down at Clint's faded image, his wide shoulders and easy grin forever captured in time.

"I don't believe you," she said. "Clint wouldn't . . . He'd never . . ." Though she wanted to believe that he was the last person on earth who would do anything so compromising, she had firsthand knowledge that he was capable of withholding information. Teddy reexamined the photograph, now realizing that if it was real and not a dream, Clint had kept an even bigger secret.

He didn't just know that her parents were psychic; he'd been their friend, and he'd kept that from her. She felt anger build inside her. Teddy glanced up at Yates, who sat back in his chair, looking patient, as if he had all the time in the world for this conversation.

"What do you know about Clint and my parents?" she asked.

"Quite a bit," he said. "Unlike Clint, I'll tell you. But first I need you to help me in return."

Teddy didn't yet know if she could or would help this man, but he had something she needed, and so she went along, at least for now. "Start at the beginning."

"I was ordered to kill an army general by the name of Keith Sheffield."

"Why?"

"His political and military views were in direct opposition to my organization's. He had to be eliminated."

"Assassinated."

"Use whatever term you like. The point is, I refused the order. No one expected that. I had been a good soldier until then, like the rest of them."

"The rest of who?" Teddy said. "Psychic assassins?"

He smiled. "You could call them that. I went from being an asset to an inconvenience. So I became the scapegoat. Someone else was brought in to do the job, and they framed me. Then Clint made it his personal mission to see that I was put away for the rest of my life."

Yates went on to explain that there was an FBI videotape exonerating him and proving that someone else had committed the murder. Clint had seen it and knew the truth but had deliberately hidden the tape.

"Why would Clint falsify evidence?" Teddy asked.

"Because he believes I'm dangerous."

"And why would he believe that?"

"Because I am." He said it plainly, like a fact. Like you'd say "It is sixty degrees outside" or "The sky is blue." Teddy didn't doubt the statement for a minute. Yates put his finger on the photograph again, tapping her father's face. "They thought your father was dangerous, too. That's why they killed him."

Teddy went cold. "I was told my parents died on the highway, in a multicar collision."

"Your father died at Sector Three."

Her father had been murdered. Teddy didn't think she could feel something for someone she had never met, but now she ached for all the memories she'd never have. She took a deep breath to steady herself. "*They* killed him? Who are they?"

"The people who ran Sector Three. Government people. Military people." Yates reached forward as if he wanted to hold Teddy's hand, but his chains caught him before he could touch her. He pulled his hand back, frustrated. "To them, we're weapons, to be used and discarded at will."

"I don't understand," Teddy said.

"You mean why would the government want to train psychics?" Yates let the question hang unanswered. It didn't need a response.

"So Sector Three also trained psychics for government positions?" Teddy asked.

Yates smiled. "At first that's what we were led to believe. It was a research facility, designed to help us control our gifts. But it was more like a laboratory, and we were the experiment."

"Are you saying that Whitfield—"

"I'm saying that things aren't always as they seem. It's easy to think that the people in charge have your best interests at heart. But whether it's Sector Three or Whitfield, there's always a bottom line. And trust me, your interests are not the bottom line."

Teddy ran through the list of things Clint refused to talk about: the theft of the blood samples; the missing students; her genetic history. And there was more: the insistence on student anonymity; the deliberately vague school website; the over-the-top security. All supposedly for their own protection.

"I know why your blood sample went missing."

"How do you know about that?"

His dark eyes glittered. "You are the child of two powerful psychics who once trained at Sector Three. You are of utmost importance to our organization."

Was he saying that his organization had stolen her blood?

"There were three couples who had children while we lived there. They'd all be around your age now."

That was the link that connected her, Brett, and Christine. They were all children of psychics, experimented on at Sector Three. "Why tell me all of this? What's the catch?"

"Help me get out of here. Once I'm free, I'll help you."

"I don't need your help."

"I can help you find her."

Teddy blinked. "Find who?" she asked.

Yates slid his hands off the table, and the sound of the scraping chains gave her goose bumps. "Your mother."

Teddy stared at him. She was tempted to tell him she knew exactly where her mother was—at home in Las Vegas. Then she realized he wasn't talking about the mother who had raised her. "My mother is dead."

"I can assure you that Marysue Delaney is very much alive." Yates cocked his head. "And I'm willing to wager my freedom that somewhere deep down, you know that, too."

Teddy thought of the yellow house, the woman at the stove and her lullaby. She narrowed her eyes. "If she's alive, why didn't she come back for me?"

"And put you at risk? She was protecting you. The only way to do that was to give you a new name, a new family, a new home."

Before Teddy could ask another question, Yates lifted his finger to his lips. He turned his head to one side as though alert to voices she couldn't hear.

"Your friend Kate is finishing with McDonald now. You need to go." He pulled a business card from his shirt pocket and set it atop the photo. "My attorney's contact information. The location of the FBI video file I need is written on the back. You should be able to access it on Agent Stavros's hard drive."

She didn't bother asking how he knew Nick's name.

"Forward the video to my attorney. He'll take care of the rest."

Teddy heard chairs scraping from the room next door. She rose and headed toward the door. She didn't want Yates to think she'd give in too easily, though in her heart, she knew that she'd do anything for more information about her birth parents.

"Ask Corey where his Bruins hat is," Yates said.

She didn't question him. Right now she'd do anything he asked.

CHAPTER THIRTY-TWO

"I MADE IT CLEAR FROM THE START THAT YOU'D EACH have thirty minutes to talk to him." Nick said.

"This isn't just a dumb competition," Teddy said. "I need five minutes." Well, she hoped she'd be able to do it in that amount of time. She wasn't sure how long it would take. She just knew she needed to convince Nick to let her back into that room.

"Let her talk to him," said Kate. She had circles under her eyes, and her skin was pale. She looked like all the fight had been sucked out of her.

"What did you say, Atkins?" Nick asked.

"Teddy's right," Kate said. "What if I said that I had a flash of claircognizance when I was in there and I saw that Teddy going back in was the key to closing this case?"

"Did you?"

Kate shrugged. "Only one way to know." When Nick turned toward a guard stationed by the door, Kate winked at Teddy.

Nick pulled Teddy aside. He lifted his right hand as if he wanted to pat her arm, then stopped. He cleared his throat. "Same strategy you had before. He shared more with you than Atkins." Teddy nodded.

Corey was still sitting at the table when she and Nick walked in. He looked up, surprised. "I thought we were finished."

"I just had another question to ask, if that's okay?" Teddy said, trying to make her voice syrupy-sweet.

"Yeah, sure." He smiled at her.

She summoned up his Facebook profile picture in her mind's eye, remembering the Bruins hat low on his head. "So, you know how I said I can help find that memory for you?"

She closed her eyes and reached out to Corey's mind, sinking into the inky darkness. She saw the white Victorian house again, the details sharper than before: now she noticed that the paint was scuffed on the wooden siding; the floorboards were broken on the porch; the windows were dusty.

"Yeah," Corey said.

"I need you to try really hard. You had a few beers, right?"

"Yeah," Corey said.

In her mind's eye, Teddy walked closer to the house, up the creaky stairs. She knew who Corey was now, a mystery no longer. Before she even placed her hand on the handle, it swung open.

"She made such a big deal over a few beers."

Inside the house, Teddy turned and saw an old-fashioned linoleum kitchen, a small living room with a lumpy denim couch and a large TV. "A few beers. That's nothing. I get it, Corey."

Teddy walked toward the TV and turned it on. She flipped through the channels, through memories: Corey fishing with his father, looking through a copy of *Romeo and Juliet* in a classroom. Finally, she saw Marlena, and she watched as the night played out differently than he described it. Corey was yelling.

"Did you try to explain that to her?"

Corey raised his hands, cuffs catching against the table. "I don't remember."

Teddy watched the TV screen: Corey grabbed Marlena by the wrist. She pulled away. Then his hands were around her neck.

"Maybe she wasn't a very good listener," Teddy said.

Corey didn't say anything more.

In her mind's eye, Teddy walked closer to the TV. Marlena clawed at the air, Corey's truck, Corey. She couldn't breathe. Just like Jillian in the library.

"Then what happened?" Teddy said.

"I don't remember."

And suddenly, she was there, living the moment as Corey was. She felt the humid air on her skin. The warm night surrounded her. Marlena was on the ground now. Then he was hauling her into his truck. Driving her to the wetlands. Dumping her into the water. Teddy looked to her left, saw the Bruins hat fall off of Corey's head and into a bank of tall spike rush by the water.

Teddy shook her head, breaking the connection. She was in one place now. Looking into the eyes of a murderer.

"So why the Bruins? They're UCLA's team, not yours." Teddy knew all the California sports teams like the back of her hand. Not that the gambling knowledge had served her until now. "You were wearing the hat that night, right? We have the picture from Facebook."

Corey swallowed. "I like the team. That's not a crime."

"It is a crime if we find the hat in the wetlands, Corey. Which we will." Teddy pushed her chair back, legs scraping against the floor. She stood up to leave.

He sprang forward, jerking the chains with him over the table. "I didn't—it was an accident. I didn't mean to kill her."

The room went silent. All three of them realizing what he'd just admitted.

"No, I didn't mean to say that. I didn't." Corey looked from Teddy to Nick. "Hey, you guys told me that you were here to help. My dad hired you. My lawyer would've been here otherwise. This isn't . . . This shouldn't count."

She didn't need to see how the rest of it played out. Her heart was breaking—both for Marlena and for the Corey whom she'd thought she knew. The boy she'd thought was innocent, stuck in San Quentin, until she'd actually met him and looked into his soul.

CHAPTER THIRTY-THREE

TEDDY SAT SILENTLY IN THE FRONT SEAT OF NICK'S car. As she glanced out the window, she didn't see the San Francisco Bay; instead, the wetlands from Corey's memory surfaced in her mind's eye—and Marlena's face as Corey's hands wrapped around her throat. Teddy's own hands started to shake, and she slid them underneath her thighs to still them. When she tried to get Corey's memory out of her head, other images rushed to replace it: Yates in handcuffs, the photograph, the Sector Three symbol. She may have solved one case today, but she would have to sort through a past she still didn't understand—her own.

When they reached the San Francisco pier, Teddy shut the car door and boarded the ferry without a word.

"Teddy, you okay?" Nick's voice interrupted her thoughts. She hadn't even realized they had arrived on Angel Island. She made her way down to the dock. Nick followed. Kate was well on her way back to campus.

April played havoc with the normally placid bay. Waves churned against the rocky cliffs. Teddy had expected Nick to wonder whether she was all right. She hadn't expected him to ask. Nor was she prepared to see such genuine concern in his eyes. It threw her.

"Teddy?"

She chewed her bottom lip, not sure where to begin. Or, for that matter, if she should say anything at all. But the temptation to tell someone else what had happened—or at least part of what had happened—was too strong to resist.

"What did you see?" he pressed. "Do you remember?"

She'd never seen a dead body, let alone a murder. What she knew would haunt her forever: seeing the fear in Marlena's eyes just . . . cease to exist. She would have expected death to be gradual, not sudden. One moment Marlena was there, fighting, alive. The next, she wasn't.

Teddy wasn't conscious of moving toward Nick. Or maybe he was the one who moved toward her. Somehow her body was pressed up against his. And she just stayed there. His shoulders were broader than she'd imagined, the muscles beneath his shirt harder, more defined.

She finally pulled herself together and took a deliberate step back. "We already knew that Marlena was strangled to death," she said. "Jillian had that communion back in the library. But when I was with Corey, I accessed his memories. I . . ."

He studied her. "Yes?" he prompted.

Teddy struggled to put the experience into words. "I was right there with him and Marlena in the wetlands."

Nick's brow furrowed. "It's hard. I'd be lying if I said it doesn't get easier. That's the job, Teddy. When it gets easier, it's time to quit." He let out a breath. "I called in the tip. We have people tracking his hat. And officers working on a full confession with his lawyer present—" He paused. "I wanted to ask you back there. How'd you know about the handwriting? It was a neat trick."

Teddy stiffened. "Just a hunch." She didn't want to tell Nick that she had met a man named Derek Yates; she wanted to ask Nick about Yates without *telling* him about Yates. "I'm still in shock, honestly. We assumed he was innocent," she said. "For a time it seemed you did, too, otherwise we wouldn't have taken on the case."

Nick sighed. "I never like to see an innocent person put away. It's our job to be sure."

This was her opening. "So it's possible for an innocent man to be convicted of a crime he didn't commit?"

He gave a reluctant shrug. "Yeah. Of course. Cops screw up. Witnesses make mistakes. Juries get it wrong. It's not something anyone wants to happen, but—"

"What if they did?"

"What?"

"What if that's exactly what they wanted to happen?" She looked at him, wondering if she should go on. But she wanted to know. She needed to know. "What if evidence was altered in order to force a conviction? To lock away someone who knew something he shouldn't know?"

"Wait a minute, wait a minute." Nick held up his hands, palms facing out, like a traffic cop intent on slowing her down. "What you described between Corey and Marlena wasn't planned. Now you're saying that Corey was framed because he knew something he shouldn't?"

Teddy made a vague motion with her hand. "Not Corey. I'm talking in general terms."

His eyes narrowed. "No, you're not." Nick wasn't stupid. "Something else happened at San Quentin, didn't it?" he said, his voice harsh.

Again she felt the urge to unburden herself. Even stronger was the urge to ask for his help. Could she bet on Nick? She still wasn't sure.

Nick let out an exasperated sigh. "All right, fine. Don't tell me," he said. "Let me see if I can guess. Some inmate in there got to you somehow. Fed you some tale of woe. 'I didn't do it. I was framed.' Christ, Teddy. We're talking San Quentin here. Five percent of inmates openly brag about their crimes. The other ninety-five percent insist they're innocent bystanders who were set up by crooked cops and paid-off judges."

She leveled her chin. "So that never happens, huh?"

"Of course it happens. People get struck by lightning, too. Does that mean you run every time you hear thunder?"

She looked up. "Sky's clear. But thanks for the advice, Agent Stavros."

He caught her arm as she turned away. "Look, the justice system isn't perfect. I have no doubt I've messed up a few investigations, but never deliberately. The same is true for the rest of my colleagues."

"I'm sure," she said. "You're all a bunch of Eagle Scouts. No manipulation at all on your part, or Clint's, in getting me to come to Whitfield. But maybe that's a bad example." She wished she hadn't said it. She wanted to let it go, but after her conversation with Yates, she didn't know how.

A muscle twitched in his jaw. "Teddy—"

"Do you mind?" she said. He was still holding her arm. "I've got a class."

He released her. "Document what happened on the McDonald case. That's the investigation that matters. You'll find out soon enough that half of all crime-solving is paperwork."

She walked away from him as quickly as she could. She crossed the campus without slowing, her legs carrying her toward Fort McDowell. But once she was inside, she stopped. The thought of spending the next two hours listening to Clint Corbett lecture on empathy made her stomach churn. Even after her promise to stop skipping his class, she couldn't face it.

Instead, she turned down the hallway to Dunn's empty classroom. Teddy found herself studying a particularly complex diagram of the brain. What made her brain so different from someone else's, someone like Nick? Or Corey?

Footsteps interrupted her thoughts. Teddy turned around to see Dunn, who was shrugging a blazer over his *Science Rules* T-shirt. "Sorry, Professor, I was just—"

"Supposed to be in Empathy 101?" he said.

Teddy watched as he unpacked his bag at the front of the room. "I just got back from San Quentin with Agent Stavros." She looked down. "Felt like I wasn't really up to class after seeing the justice system up close."

Dunn nodded. "I understand."

She remembered the first days of school, when Dunn had spoken of mental attacks. Though the students had continued to work on strengthening their telepathic communication, they hadn't talked about mental influence since then. Had Yates influenced her, too? Made her come talk to him? Had she been played? But she'd seen the signs enough to know the symptoms. The dilated pupils, lost time, the distorted thoughts afterward.

"Professor," Teddy started. "May I ask you a theoretical question?"

Dunn put down a graph he was looking at and nodded. "Of course."

"You mentioned mental attacks last semester."

"I did."

"How do you know if . . ." Teddy began. "I'm not really sure how to put it."

"There are a lot of different kinds of mental attacks," Dunn said. He sat down behind his desk. "It's any kind of uninvited connection. Mental influence, for example, when you direct people to perform an action against their will." Like Clint had in Vegas. But that wasn't what Yates had done to her.

"Clint sometimes gets into my head. But it doesn't hurt."

Dunn pressed his hands together. "Go on."

Teddy nodded. "Can pain accompany telepathy or other forms of psychic communication? Like influence?" She thought of the viselike pain that had accompanied Yates's first words.

"Is this still purely hypothetical?"

Teddy looked away. She was sure that, like Clint, Dunn could tell what she was thinking, so she checked her wall, sent another jolt of power to be sure it held.

"Yes, there's certainly a way to make your presence known. That's why it's so important to have a strong wall or defense, which I know you've worked on with Professor Corbett," he said. "But here at Whitfield, we don't believe in using power like that. Even when we mount a mental attack."

"Thanks," Teddy said. "I should probably go back to class." She turned to leave, but Dunn stopped her.

"You know, technically, what you do is a mental attack."

"But I don't hurt people." Teddy thought about the way she slipped into people's minds. An invasion of privacy? Yes. But an attack?

"You may not intend to hurt people," Dunn said. "But sometimes when you try to force your way in, you leave scars. Like with Ms. Quinn."

"I never meant to hurt Molly." She'd barely been in control of her abilities back then. Teddy would apologize; they would argue; Molly would forgive her like Jillian had. That's what friends did.

Dunn nodded. "I know."

"She said that your techniques have helped her shut out students' feelings. She's not as, well, jumpy, as she used to be." Teddy looked down, rubbed her hands on her pants. "Almost like a different person." Molly had hung back as they worked the case. She may have been keeping others' emotions at bay, but she was keeping her own at bay, too. After their conversation in the library, Teddy hadn't pushed further, though she could have.

Dunn shuffled some papers on his desk. "Ms. Quinn hasn't shown up for her tutorial in weeks."

Every time Teddy thought she understood Molly, she discovered something that changed her perception. Molly had said Dunn's techniques were helping her, yet she'd been bailing on his sessions.

"My second-years are coming in soon. If you have any other questions about theoretical mental attacks, please let me know. But Teddy?"

"Yes?"

"This is a very serious and potentially dangerous realm of psychic study. Not one to be taken lightly."

Teddy left Dunn's classroom. She still wasn't ready to go to class. Everyone would want to know about her trip to San Quentin. She wasn't sure she could deliver that information without mentioning Yates.

Yates had been right about the handwriting. And the hat. Clearly he'd known her parents and Clint. There was a photograph to prove it. But could she trust that he was telling the truth about Whitfield? Or Clint's involvement in his setup? She needed evidence. Evidence she might have once she accessed the video file Yates had mentioned. Convenient that Teddy knew someone who was a certified CIA-level hacker.

*　*　*

It was dark when Teddy knocked on the door of Molly and Dara's dorm room. Inside, Molly sat on her bed, a laptop on her knees. Dara wasn't there.

"You're supposed to wait for a response before you enter someone's room," Molly said, closing the laptop.

"And we're supposed to be technology-free at Whitfield," Teddy said. "But I guess we're both rule-breakers, aren't we?" She'd meant it as a joke, but the words came out more harshly than she intended.

Molly ignored the question. "Where have you been all day? Everyone's been looking for you."

"Around," Teddy said. She had been so focused and careful in her conversation with Corey, but now, across from Molly, she floundered. She had to remind herself that this wasn't an interrogation. This was an apology, and she couldn't rely on any psychic tricks.

"Great talk," Molly said.

"Listen, I know I've been a bad friend," Teddy said. "But I'm working on it."

"I appreciate that, Teddy," Molly said. "But I think you should go." She stood up and moved as if to usher Teddy out the door.

Teddy had come for a few reasons; her motivations were not completely pure. It had been a lame apology, even she had to admit. But there was too much at stake. "Well," she said, "I need your help."

"I thought you came here because you were worried about me. Now you need a favor? Which one is it?" Molly crossed her arms.

Teddy could no longer see the world the way she had at the poker table. She used to know everyone's cards and would make her move accordingly. She'd raise when she would win the pot, fold when she would lose. Each decision calculated to her benefit. Being at Whitfield had changed that. Clint, Molly, Jillian, Pyro, even Nick had changed that. She wanted to be the person they told her she could be—someone who did the right thing, played well on a team, never left a teammate behind. But maybe she was better off alone.

She needed to leave this room with the USB drive Molly had used on Halloween. She would watch the surveillance video. If Yates were innocent, she would send the file to his lawyer. He would hold up his end of the bargain. She would find her mother and she would expose how Whitfield had been compromised. If Yates was telling the truth about that, then everyone around her was in danger. They would see that her actions had been in their interest, too.

"It's both. I know it sounds bad, but—you're the only one who can help me."

"Teddy, I can barely manage my own course load."

Teddy didn't want to have to pressure Molly. That was how she rationalized this. Pressure. Not blackmail. "You owe me. Especially after the exam."

Molly rubbed her wrists, as if easing an old hurt.

"Molly, I need a USB drive. The one you used in the lab on Halloween that allows you to access someone's computer. And then I need to duplicate a hard drive."

Molly bit her lip. "Teddy, I can't. If you get caught, they'll know it was me in the lab. You can't just clone a hard drive without—"

Teddy swallowed, steeling herself for what she would do next. It definitely wasn't a good-friend move. "I know you've been skipping your sessions with Professor Dunn. So whatever line of horseshit you've been peddling about feeling better because of his exercises is a lie. I also know that you left school because you attacked someone last year. Just like you attacked me." Molly's eyes watered, and Teddy knew she understood that what Teddy had said was meant as a threat; if Molly wanted Teddy to keep her secrets, she had to turn over the USB drive. Teddy tried to keep her voice even. She didn't want to be moved by Molly's display. "I know it's not your fault, Molly. You're going through stuff. But so am I."

"You're blackmailing me?" Molly said.

"I'm giving you the chance to help. And in return, I'm going to help you."

Molly's chin began to quiver. "Teddy, I can't."

"I'll probably need to borrow your computer, too," Teddy said. "Just for a day or so."

Molly stood up, silent. For a second, Teddy wasn't sure if she would hand it over. After what felt like an eternity, Molly opened a drawer in her nightstand. Her voice was quiet but clear. "I'm assuming you don't know what you're looking for. So you'll need at least five minutes to copy the hard drive onto the disk." She handed both the laptop and the USB drive to Teddy.

"I'll give everything back when I'm done." She'd blackmailed a friend. Was she supposed to feel different now? Jeremy's words from that Empathy 101 class long ago echoed in her ear: *Sometimes the end justifies the means.* Teddy swallowed. What she was doing was right. It had to be. "I wish it didn't have to be like this."

"Yeah, sure. That's what friends are for." Molly walked to her desk, scrawled down a note, and handed it to Teddy. "Here's the password."

Teddy took it, then turned and made her way out the door. As she was leaving, Molly spoke: "You think you're the one acting noble. But the truth is you just do whatever you want, Teddy. You don't take anyone else into consideration. You don't even look behind to see who you've left in your wake."

Teddy didn't turn around. "I'll explain it later if I can," she said. She didn't say she was sorry because—deep down—she wasn't.

CHAPTER THIRTY-FOUR

IF SHE WAITED EVEN A DAY, TEDDY WASN'T SURE SHE'D be able to go through with what had to happen next. Armed with Molly's USB drive, she walked around the corner of Harris Hall and headed between campus buildings in the direction of faculty housing. She'd first considered sneaking into Nick's room when he wasn't there, grabbing his computer, and putting Molly's USB drive to quick use. But Nick nearly always kept his laptop in the canvas messenger bag he carried with him to class, so that plan wouldn't work. Nor did she have enough skill—or, frankly, nerve—to sneak into his room while he slept.

She practiced her script as she walked along the coastal path toward the small cluster of buildings where the faculty lived. *I know it's late. But I want to finish up my paperwork for the McDonald case. I can't find the forensics report, and I was wondering if you had a copy.*

She repeated it again and again, the words falling into rhythm with her steps. Not many professors lived on campus, but for those who did, there were converted barracks from Angel Island's days as a military base. Teddy scanned each door for Nick's name.

His was the last on the row. "I know it's late," she said under her breath. She could hear the faint sound of the television within, the shuffle of socked feet. She knocked.

Nick swung open his door, and his eyes widened in surprise.

"Teddy?" He looked beyond her, perhaps to see if she had come alone. "What's wrong?"

Her mind went blank. The words she'd been practicing were suddenly gone.

"What are you doing here?"

"It's late," she said, trying to stick to the script.

Nick stuck his head out the door, doing a quick canvass of the area, then grabbed her arm. "Come inside before anyone sees you."

And then she was inside.

He was wearing his athletic clothes, and his hair was damp, giving her the impression that he'd just returned from a late-night run. He smelled like cinnamon—Old Spice.

"McDonald case," she said, the words coming back to her now. Why did he make her so nervous? Pyro didn't make her nervous, with his bravado and cheesy one-liners. That, Teddy knew how to handle. But Nick? "I wanted to finish the paperwork for the case while it was still fresh in my mind. I—"

Nick turned to organize the files that were spread out along his coffee table. As he did, his T-shirt rose to reveal a stretch of smooth, muscular skin. His back was paler than she'd thought it would be, considering they lived in California. He probably worked too much to go to the beach. The illicitness of viewing skin she wasn't supposed to see, and discovering something personal about him, stopped her in her tracks. "I misplaced my copy of the forensics report." She paused as he turned to face her. "Do you have a copy?"

Nick came back toward Teddy. "You walked all the way down here to ask about a file?" He looked at his watch. "At eleven o'clock at night?"

"Yes?" Teddy said. Even she was unsure about it now. It had seemed logical before.

"Do you want something to drink?"

"Wh-what?" No, she didn't want a drink. She wanted the report. He was supposed to go get the report. She was supposed to find the laptop, use Molly's USB drive.

"A drink." He went into a kitchenette tucked into the corner. Teddy took the minute to study her surroundings. Atop a narrow desk, pushed against one wall, was Nick's laptop, on and open. She let out a breath. This could actually still work.

"Don't worry, nothing alcoholic. Water, coffee, juice?" he said.

"What kind of juice?" She looked around the rest of the apartment. Behind a door that was slightly ajar, she glimpsed a bed, neatly made with a navy blue comforter. A second door was closed. A few clean plates sat in a drying rack next to the sink. A coffee cup sat next to the paperwork table. The television was broadcasting an NBA game.

"Orange."

"Okay, sure." Pyro had never offered her juice. She'd never given him the chance. Nick was her teacher. Yet here she was in his apartment.

He went to the fridge, took out a Golden State Warriors mug, and filled it with OJ. Their fingers brushed as she reached for it. "Thanks," she said.

"So why are you really here, Teddy?"

She looked around the apartment. The laptop. That's why she was really here. But she couldn't say that. "McDonald's forensics report."

"And when I get it," he said, "you'll go?"

"Yes." Teddy said.

"You didn't come here because you wanted to talk about what happened today? Between you and McDonald?" His brown eyes searched hers. She knew he wanted her to share. To say that she felt shaken by Corey's confession. But it wasn't Corey's confession that was rattling her.

"I came for the paperwork, Nick."

"I'll get it for you, then. I've got copies in my office. I should probably change my shirt, too." He smiled. "Have a seat. I'll be right back."

This was actually going to work. Her heart thudded in her chest, but she forced a smile. "Thanks."

Nick walked toward the second door.

Don't look at his ass. Focus, Cannon.

The moment the door closed behind him, she raced toward his laptop. She dug Molly's flash drive from her pocket and plugged it in. The screensaver on Nick's computer sputtered, flickered on and off, then went black. The machine gave a whirling, fluttery noise, as if an internal fan had clicked on high. Molly's code flooded the screen— page after page of what looked like pure binary nonsense—as a million windows came up. For a moment, Teddy wondered if maybe the drive was a virus and not a clone. Then a progress bar popped up on the screen, showing *Stavros Hard Drive*. Molly hadn't been playing her. Teddy's heart sped right along with the little wheel as she strained to hear the sound of Nick's return.

She clicked through prompt after prompt. *Please,* she thought, *let him have trouble finding the papers.* Finally, the progress bar reached 100 percent. Teddy jerked the flash drive from the port and thrust it back in her pocket. The door swung open behind her.

"Got the report." He threw the paperwork down on the coffee table. He had pulled on a worn FBI sweatshirt, frayed around the cuffs. No skin to be seen.

Teddy stuffed her hands in her pockets, ran her thumb over the USB drive. "Thanks. Guess I better be going."

She watched the muscles in his jaw work. He looked down at his hands, avoiding her gaze. "What if we met under different circumstances? What if I really was plain ol' Nick?"

"And my name really was TeAnne?"

"I'm being serious."

"So am I," she said. "But I'm not TeAnne. I'm Teddy Cannon,

student at the Whitfield Institute for Law Enforcement Training and Development."

"You could have waited until morning for that report."

Her mission was done. She should be out the door. Back to her dorm room, on Molly's blackmail-borrowed laptop, sifting through the files to find the one that proved Yates's innocence. Instead, she asked: "What are you saying?"

"I'm saying," Nick said, taking a step closer, so close that he could reach out and touch her if he wanted to, "that I wish it were different. Don't you?"

Yes, of course she did. In that moment, more than anything, Teddy wanted things to be different. She wished that Nick really were plain. Or old. But he had the ass of a minor Greek god, and she felt safe in his arms. He'd been with her that morning when she'd seen Corey McDonald take Marlena Hyden's life. He listened to her when she talked, and encouraged her ideas. He seemed steady, and normal, and real. Like he could be something solid and forever.

But it was none of those things that made her want him more desperately than she'd wanted anyone before. In that moment, more than anything, Teddy wanted to *be* different. She wanted to be the kind of person who wouldn't take advantage of Nick. Or Molly. She didn't want to leave people in her wake.

And just like that, the moment spun on its axis. Nick brushed a lock of hair from her eyes. The tenderness of the gesture nearly made her swoon. Actually swoon.

He kissed the tip of her nose, the corner of her mouth, the hollow of her throat.

He caught her around the waist and, with a strength she had underestimated, lifted her up. Literally swept her off her feet as he carried her to his bed. And she let him, though he now moved with agonizing slowness. A button loosened. A kiss. A brush of his fingers against her newly exposed skin. Nick moved lower and lower, no part of her body unworthy of his touch. First her collarbone. Then the upper swell of her breasts. Her ribs and the soft curve of her hips. All received the same tender, lavish attention.

"We shouldn't be doing this," he said.

"I know," she said. "I don't even like cops."

"Teddy?"

"Yeah?"

He whispered into her ear: "Shut up."

CHAPTER THIRTY-FIVE

AT SIX O'CLOCK THE NEXT MORNING, WHILE HEAVY drifts of fog blanketed the campus and the sun was faint on the eastern skyline, Teddy followed the path toward the dorms. She'd crept out of Nick's room while he was still asleep. Later, she hoped to slink into her own room for a change of clothes without an inquisition from Jillian. She had returned only for Molly's laptop. And now she was slinking into a stall of a mostly deserted bathroom on her floor.

Teddy locked the door and sat on the edge of the toilet. She balanced Molly's computer on her lap. She tried not to think about the way Nick's hands had felt around her waist and as they traveled down. It had been a mistake to sleep with Nick.

She plugged in the thumb drive and typed in Molly's password: MightyQ1989. The laptop beeped: *Incorrect password*.

Teddy tried again and received the same result. She tried in all lowercase and then in all uppercase. *Incorrect password*. Had Molly somehow set her up? Acquiesced in person but created a technological obstacle? She'd been played for a fool again.

Teddy shut the laptop and trudged downstairs to Molly's room. She wanted to bang on the door, but she couldn't risk waking any of the other students. So she gave three slow, careful knocks. She waited a minute and did it again. At last she heard rustling from inside the room, and the door opened. Molly was in pajamas, her hair messed and her eyes barely open. "What's wrong?" she whispered.

Teddy peered at Dara's bed.

"She's at the gym," Molly said.

Teddy shut the door behind her. "You gave me the wrong password," she said.

"What?" Molly looked confused.

"For your laptop."

"No, I didn't."

"MightyQ1989," Teddy said. "I tried it half a dozen times and couldn't get in."

"MightyQ1988," Molly corrected. She held her hand out for the laptop.

Teddy hesitated. "No tricks?" Had this been Molly's play to see what Teddy was up to? The only way to track the information? Either way, Teddy had no choice but to trust Molly now. She needed what was on that laptop. She'd come too far to turn back.

Molly held her hands up in a gesture of surrender. "No tricks."

Molly turned the computer around, and Teddy followed the commands to access the USB drive. It worked. The home page of Molly's computer suddenly looked like Nick's.

Teddy scanned the names of all of Nick's files, clicking on anything that looked like it might be related to Yates. She tsked and sighed through every click. All she learned was that Nick had eclectic tastes in music (Ray Charles, Beyoncé) and an obsession with the Golden State Warriors.

"It's not here," Teddy said. "The file's not here." She slammed the laptop closed, held her hands over her eyes. She had to think. What moves did she have left? None. And that was when she started to cry.

It wasn't a pretty cry. It was an ugly, messy cry. The heaving, can't-catch-your-breath, please-make-it-stop kind of cry.

"If you tell me what you're looking for, maybe I can help," Molly said.

"Why would you help me?" Teddy said, wiping her nose. "I black-mailed you yesterday."

Molly sat down next to Teddy on the bed. "I'd rather not help you. But I'd also like you to leave my room at some point." She sighed. "If there's anything I've learned in my time at Whitfield, it's that you can't survive here on your own. Sometimes you need to ask for help. And you seem desperate. What's on the drive?"

Teddy swallowed against a hard lump. "I'm trying to find a file."

"Tell me. If it has to do with hidden data, I can get it."

And so, without saying a word, Teddy passed Molly the slip of paper Yates had given her.

Molly glanced at the paper, then froze. Her eyes went wide. She stared at the alphanumeric code on the paper, then her gaze shot to Teddy. "Do you even know what this is?"

"Of course. It's an FBI video file."

"No. Not just an FBI video file. A highly classified file." She shook her head. "I assumed you just wanted to see if Nick had a girlfriend he hadn't told you about." Suddenly, Molly was all business. It made it easier to focus on the video file instead of whatever was going on between them.

"How did you know this was Nick's hard drive?" Teddy asked.

"Please."

Teddy let out a breath. "Okay, number one—that's totally insult-ing. Jealous snooping isn't my style. Number two—someone told me the file would be on Nick's laptop."

"Someone? Teddy, do you understand what you're messing with here?"

Teddy ignored the question. "So how do I go about finding that file? Or are you telling me it's impossible?"

Molly bristled at that. "Nothing's impossible. If it's in a computer, I can get it. It's just a question of difficulty."

"Meaning?"

"Look, I recognize that code because I've bumped up against similar sequences. Occasionally, agents will download highly classified files onto their personal computers, even though it's strictly against protocol—for obvious reasons. Nick doesn't strike me as the kind of guy who would do something like that."

"So where are those files stored?"

"On air-gapped computers in secure federal buildings."

"Translation?"

"Air-gapped means the physical computer isn't connected to the Internet. It's like a vault. In theory, these highly secure, classified files can be retrieved only by agents with security clearance."

Teddy felt her shoulders sag. Yates had made it sound so easy. "You said in theory."

"In theory because you need someone good." Molly said. "But if I'm going to do this, I'll need to know everything—how you got this, why you need it—"

"That seems unnecessary," Teddy said.

"I can't hack blindfolded."

Teddy had gone all in before. But going all in at a Vegas poker table? You risked money. You risked your reputation, your ego; if you were like Teddy, you risked your parents' house and the ire of a Russian Mob boss named Sergei. But this was going all in like she'd never done before. Molly was asking her to give everything—her past, present, future.

Teddy thought about walking out the door and forgetting the whole thing. She could go back to a life of just focusing on school. Her deal with Clint. Keep her nose clean. Get her money. But Yates had told her that her birth mother was alive and that he could help find her. And that was something she simply couldn't walk away from.

So she told Molly the whole story, about meeting Derek Yates at San Quentin, his mental attack, his insistence on his innocence—and his claim that Clint had been involved in falsifying the evidence that got him there. She told Molly about her parents, and Sector Three, and how they and Clint and Yates had known one another at the military facility. How Yates suspected that Whitfield had been compromised by his organization—that he believed the missing blood samples were proof of it. That they shouldn't trust everything they learned at Whitfield; that the school itself was set up for ulterior motives. When she finished, Teddy braced herself for a lecture.

Instead, Molly looked deeply troubled. She stood and paced the length of the room. At last she turned and looked at Teddy. "Retrieving that file isn't impossible," she said. "But it's not something you and I can pull off on our own."

She went on to describe the necessary steps, which would involve breaking in to an FBI building—it was a California case, so the file was likely stored locally—hacking the agency's internal server, and downloading remote spying technology. In other words, it would be a lot harder than talking her way into a professor's room and plugging a flash drive into a laptop.

Molly gave a decisive nod. "Here's the bottom line: we put everything in front of the rest of the group and decide how to move forward. You need their help, too."

Teddy let out a ragged breath. She'd just done the hardest thing of her life. Put total trust in someone else. Told her everything. And now she was going to have to do it all over again. Believe in the unseeable once more and trust four more people with all her secrets.

* * *

In Casework later that day, when Nick announced that the Misfits had solved the crime, Teddy hardly cared that the Alphas looked miserable. She had bigger things to worry about. She barely registered when Nick announced that the prize would go to Teddy as the team MVP. She had won a tour of the FBI facility in downtown San Francisco.

Dara nudged her shoulder. "Molly told me this morning that you wanted us to all meet up tonight? Your dorm room?"

"Yeah," Teddy said, shaking off her stupor. "Tonight." After tonight, everything would be different.

Students began to file out of the room, and Teddy grabbed her bag, but before she could leave, Nick pulled her aside. "Hold on a minute, would you, Teddy?"

Teddy's heart lurched. She forced herself to meet Nick's eyes—which she had studiously avoided from the moment she'd entered his class.

"You left something behind yesterday," he said.

For a second, Teddy thought he might lean in to kiss her cheek. Instead, he lifted the manila folder containing McDonald's forensics report. "You still need this?"

She'd left his place in such a rush that morning, she'd completely forgotten the paperwork. "Oh. Um, yes, thanks."

He studied her. Guilt stabbed at her insides. She'd slept with Nick—one of the first guys in a long time with whom she could actually picture herself—then taken off without a word. After she'd demolished his privacy by hacking in to his hard drive.

"Everything all right, Teddy?" He lowered his voice. There was suspicion in his tone. He was, after all, an investigator. And Teddy figured there were pieces of information that weren't adding up for him.

"I'm not a morning person," she said. She couldn't bear to think what might happen if Nick discovered what she had done. The kicker was that her feelings were real. She liked him. The sucker punch was that she needed the Yates file anyway.

Out of the corner of her eye, Teddy caught Ava practically falling out of her chair to eavesdrop. Nick noticed, too, and quickly changed the subject.

"We found Corey's Bruins hat. This morning. Guess you really earned that prize."

She didn't feel like a winner. "Yeah, guess I did."

CHAPTER THIRTY-SIX

ONE BY ONE THE MISFITS ENTERED TEDDY'S DORM room, until the six of them were sitting on beds and chairs and the floor. Teddy felt more nervous than she'd been that day she had bet it all at the Bellagio. Except tonight, her friends would be the ones to make the gamble. This was what it meant to ask for help. Sure, she'd technically asked for help over the last semester. Before this morning, those pleas had been transactional—each party had something to gain or to lose. But why would these people, who were relative strangers only mere months ago, risk their standing at Whitfield for her? Teddy looked around the room. They were waiting for her to speak. Her tongue felt heavy, her mouth dry.

Eventually, Jillian broke the silence. "Sorry I was held up after dinner. There was a bird I had to see about another bird. So, is this about McDonald?"

"It's about what happened when I went to San Quentin," Teddy said. She glanced at Molly, sitting cross-legged on Jillian's desk. Molly nodded as if encouraging Teddy to continue.

Teddy took a deep breath. She started at the beginning: What had happened when she entered the prison. How Derek Yates had pushed into her head. How he'd told her to ask about Corey's handwriting and ultimately pointed her to the clue about Corey's Bruins hat. How he'd mentally influenced the correctional officers so he could meet Teddy face-to-face. How Yates had trained at Sector Three—a program that had gone disastrously awry—alongside Clint, and how they had gone their separate ways: Clint, to Whitfield, and Yates to a secret organization of psychics who assassinated world leaders. He hadn't been too clear on the particulars of his work, but when he'd refused to kill again, they'd set him up. And then Clint had tracked him down and withheld evidence that proved Yates's innocence.

Teddy left out the part about her parents being at Sector Three. Part of her hoped that if she presented the story without personal involvement, they'd be more inclined to help; if she sold the story without emotions, they might agree on facts alone. They should help Yates because something was happening at Whitfield. She told them that Yates believed his organization was behind the theft on Halloween. But the fact that Whitfield had their blood at all, according to Yates, suggested that the government would use psychics for secret purposes. Something about Yates's words from that day cut her to the bone: *To them, we're weapons, to be used and discarded at will.*

Jillian tucked a tangled curl behind her ear and looked at Teddy. "Why didn't you tell us sooner?" she asked.

"I didn't want to involve you in this mess if I could help it."

Dara stood up to pace the crowded room but quickly recognized the futility of even trying—the space was barely large enough to accommodate them all. She sat back down. "My grandmother was right all along about Sector Three."

"What did you really think—the government wanted to help us develop our psychic powers, no strings attached?" Pyro asked. He let out a low laugh. "Yeah, right."

"If that's what you think," Jeremy said, "then why are you here?"

"I need to learn to control my abilities," Pyro said, slapping one palm against his chest. "But I didn't sign up for indentured servitude."

"So what do we do now?" Dara asked.

"We need the file Yates told me about," Teddy said. "That's where we start."

Jillian blinked. "I thought you already tried. The video isn't on Nick's laptop, right?"

"It isn't," Teddy said. "But that doesn't mean the FBI doesn't have it."

All eyes turned toward Molly; she seemed uncomfortable, picking at the hem of her sweater. "So, I guess we're going to hack the FBI," she said.

"No freaking way," Pyro said. "Generally, I think you're all out of your goddamn minds, but you're *really* out of your goddamn mind."

"Just listen before you make a decision," Molly said. She spoke now with a confidence that Teddy hadn't seen from her in weeks. Even when Teddy had been pushing her to hand over the hard drive, she'd seemed on the breaking point, but now Molly seemed focused, calm. She walked the Misfits through a rough plan. The video file resided on an air-gapped computer located somewhere within the FBI building. Extracting that file was possible only if they could get inside. They wouldn't need physical contact with the actual computer, just proximity. With the right hacking programs and tech devices, as well as a crew stationed nearby to handle the transmissions, they could pull it off.

"Last time I checked, even breaking in to the FBI building is a federal crime. As in five years to life," Pyro said.

Molly shook her head. "You're forgetting something. We won the McDonald challenge. Teddy gets a personal tour of the San Francisco FBI building."

"So technically, we're not breaking in at all," Teddy said.

Jillian shook her head "Either way, it's wrong. If we get caught, we'll go to jail."

"Not jail," Pyro said. "Federal penitentiary."

"So you'd rather, what, forget this whole thing?" Teddy asked. "Maybe you can do that. But I don't want this place to turn into the next Sector Three. And if I can do something to help a psychic—" She still wasn't telling them the all the reasons she needed to do this. She felt for her parents' picture in her pocket.

"Help a criminal, you mean," Pyro said.

"No," Teddy said. "A psychic who was treated as a weapon, not as a human. That doesn't bother you, Pyro?" She directed this line of reasoning at him, since his ability could easily be turned destructive. "It doesn't make a difference to any of you that we've been misled by the guy who's teaching us Empathy 101? He broke his cardinal rule— he tampered with evidence to benefit the outcome of a case."

At that, Pyro fell silent.

"Aren't there legal ways to get the information?" Jillian asked. "Couldn't we use the Freedom of Information Act and formally petition—"

"That could take years, and that's if we ever see it at all," Teddy said.

"Putting in the request would also reveal that we know something we shouldn't," Molly added. "That could end up being even more dangerous than what I'm suggesting."

At that, even Jillian fell silent.

"No," Pyro said. "So, Clint lied. Everyone lies. I can't risk my whole career for some washed-up crazy assassin in prison. Not happening."

Teddy ran her fingers along the edge of the picture in her pocket, hesitated. Another secret. This one, something private, a part of her that she had only started to understand. Something she wasn't ready to share. Her friends didn't have the same things at stake. But if it was going to convince them, maybe this information would help. Teddy removed the photo from her pocket.

"This is Yates," she said, putting it on the table and pointing a finger. "And you recognize Clint." She looked up to make sure she had everyone's attention. "And these are my birth parents. This picture was taken at Sector Three, where they met. Yates told me that my father was murdered because he resisted the government's demands.

And my mother is out there still, hiding from the people who were responsible for it. You know that blood samples went missing this year. They belonged to three individuals with specific genetic markers. Individuals whose parents were both psychics who had trained at Sector Three. Yates believed they were specifically targeted by his organization."

Teddy looked around the room. Jillian was still twirling her hair; Pyro was shifting back and forth on the balls of his feet; Molly had begun to pick at her sweater again, her confidence gone as suddenly as it came; Dara was rubbing her hands together; and Jeremy was staring at Teddy, unblinking.

"Just drop another bombshell, why don't you?" Dara said.

Teddy looked down at the photograph. Had her parents known when she was born that she'd be psychic? "The three blood samples that were taken belonged to Brett Evans, Christine Federico . . . and me."

Pyro stood, his eyes flashing dark. "When?"

"What?" Teddy said.

"When did you find out?" He stared at her, his facial features hard. The flame tattoos on his neck had flickered to life.

"A little after Halloween, I guess."

"Teddy, you could be in danger," Jillian said.

"You've known for months and you didn't tell us." Pyro ran his hands through his hair. "I knew you had trust issues, but this . . . Jesus. Something could have happened to you."

Hearing it from him made it feel that much more real. "I know," she whispered.

Again the room fell silent. Teddy was surprised that Jeremy was the first to speak. "Well, I guess we're breaking in to an FBI computer."

"What?" Dara said. "You're joking, right?"

"I mean, it seems like the only logical option," Jeremy said. "Teddy is in trouble. She asked for our help." He stood up.

Teddy was surprised that it was Jeremy jumping to her defense first. She looked between him and Molly, but Molly was only nodding along to Jeremy's words.

"The boy makes a point. I guess I'm in, too," Dara said.

"I'm already in," Molly said.

"Look at what's been happening around here. Three blood samples were stolen. Two recruits went missing. Teddy's saying she could be next," Jillian said.

Pyro still looked like he was going to set something on fire. "You've kept this to yourself for too long, Teddy."

If she didn't know better, she would have said that he looked almost hurt. "I'm sorry. I didn't know if I could trust you." She saw the fire in his eyes turn dim. "We need you," she said.

He waited. They all waited. In the moments of silence, Teddy considered the man she'd dismissed as a player. She'd been the one to see only what was on the surface. Everything he'd done and told her about himself—his dedication to his partner's family, his inability to leave Molly behind—had shown him to be deeply loyal. Someone who could love fiercely. Someone who, once he found what he wanted, wouldn't be that willing to let it go. She had been the one unable to let him in. Maybe it wasn't Pyro who had set the terms of their relationship but her.

His body tensed and he squared his shoulders, his decision made. "Of course you need me," he said.

"Is that a yes?" Dara asked.

They waited as Pyro seemed to measure his words, the outcome. "You think I'd let you punks go without me?" He stood. "But we'd better not get caught. Federal prisons are fireproof."

CHAPTER THIRTY-SEVEN

IN THE HEIST MOVIES TEDDY HAD WATCHED WITH her dad—the ones that usually took place in Vegas—schemes fell in place pretty quickly. Plans were established, materials gathered, key players recruited, locations scouted, and the mission executed. What movies never portrayed was the waiting. The Misfits soon realized that heists demanded an excruciating amount of waiting. And Teddy Cannon? Not the most patient person in the world.

The visit to FBI headquarters was scheduled at the end of the semester. Which left Teddy with weeks of pretending like everything was normal, weeks of classes where she acted as though nothing had changed.

Instead, she focused on the plan. Went over every step in her head, went through every location, every variable, every possibility. Jeremy would transport them to and from San Francisco on his boat. Dara and Molly would camp in a hotel room on the top floor. While Molly ran the tech portion of the break-in, Dara would facilitate communication between the teams. Jillian—with all the birds of San Francisco as backup—would stay on the ground as their eyes. Pyro would provide ground transport, surveillance, and muscle, if they needed it. Which Teddy hoped to God they didn't.

But the whole plan hinged on her. She needed to enter the FBI offices, log on to Nick's computer, and leave the premises before any FBI agents noticed that the team had broken about a dozen laws right under their noses.

The first obstacle to overcome: mental influence. If the plan went sideways, she might need to convince someone to keep quiet. And for that, she needed Jeremy.

Jeremy waited outside of Fort McDowell, hands in his pockets. Teddy still found Jeremy difficult to predict. At times, he seemed overanalytical; at others, completely disinterested. His support had surprised her, but she had to stop worrying about the team. She had to embrace this new thing called trust—no, she had to surrender to it.

"Hey," she said.

"Remember," he said, "I told you I wasn't any good at this."

They walked to an empty room on the top floor of Fort McDowell. These rooms reminded her of the study carrels in Stanford's library—not that she had gotten far in her coursework there.

Jeremy pulled two chairs over. "It's like what we do with Dunn," he said. "Except you don't ask, you demand. I hate that part. It makes me feel sick."

Teddy took a deep breath. Her eyes scanned the room, settling on the window behind him. She'd ask—no, demand—that Jeremy open the window.

"Ready?" he asked.

She'd never been inside Jeremy's mind. It looked different than the inky blackness she waded through in others' minds, which was navy in some places, black in others, like velvet. The inside of Jeremy's mind felt like negative space, pitch-black and dense. *Open the window,* Teddy said. She felt bile rise in the back of her throat.

No, Jeremy said.

Open the window, she repeated. Her voice echoed around in her head and his. She tried to focus on the command, but her thoughts wandered back to the night weeks earlier when Jeremy, cross-legged on the floor of her dorm room, had been the first to agree to help.

She blinked, and she was standing there again in her mind's eye, watching her friends watching her. The images came fast and furious now. Without an organizational technique, without a house, she had no way to control her astral telepathy. It was just like what had happened with Molly in Dunn's class. Teddy lost her breath trying to keep up: Jeremy as a kid, in his mother's arms, reading a book; Jeremy watching the Twin Towers fall; Jeremy crying in his bed, alone; Jeremy teaching himself to ride a bike; Jeremy studying with tutors, papers scattered across a desk; Jeremy, always alone; then Jeremy embracing Molly on the shore of Angel Island; Jeremy, with the other Misfits in the dining hall; Jeremy on his speedboat, crossing the bay—

And then a wall, smooth and cold, slammed up in front of her eyes with such force that Teddy fell off her chair. Teddy's skin felt arctic, and not because she'd successfully commanded Jeremy to open the window.

"I think you've got the general idea," Jeremy said. His voice was shaking. Teddy couldn't tell if he was upset or angry.

Teddy pulled herself up. "Jeremy, I didn't mean to—" He'd been trying to help her, and she'd screwed everything up.

"What's going on in here?" a booming voice asked. Clint Corbett stood in the doorway of the small classroom. Immediately, Teddy surged her wall into place.

"I reserved the room, Professor Corbett," Jeremy said. "We're finished, anyway." He grabbed his bag and left without giving Teddy another glance.

She'd been avoiding Clint for months, and now here he was, feet away. The distance between them felt like miles. They were separated by everything he'd refused to discuss: the theft, her parents, Sector Three. She might as well have been standing on the other side of Angel Island—or even back in Vegas.

"You haven't been coming to class," he said, though his question—why?—remained unasked.

Teddy had expected Clint to be angry. To be on her ass about ditching. She was practically daring him to kick her out of Whitfield. Yet he hadn't. She gripped the wooden desk. She was so angry with him.

"Maybe we should both sit down. And you can explain yourself."

"I don't think that I'm the one who needs to explain myself," she said, releasing her grip on the desk. She took the photo out of her pocket; she'd been carrying it around since the day Yates had handed it to her in San Quentin. She laid it on the desk.

"Where did you get this?" he asked, slack-jawed.

"I dreamed about it first," Teddy said. She cleared her throat, knowing she couldn't mention Yates. If she did, Clint would surely intervene—transfer him, or burn the file, or something. She sent another surge of power to her wall. "And then it came in the mail a few weeks ago," she lied.

Clint's brow wrinkled. "No return address? No note?"

"No," Teddy said. "But I know those are my parents. And that's you with them."

Clint sighed. "Teddy, this would have been a distraction."

"You knew them! You knew my parents and you never told me!"

Of all the things that Clint had kept from her, this one hurt the most. If she had sat across from him in his Taurus in Vegas and he had said: *I knew your birth parents, they were psychic,* she would have told him to sign her up right then.

Finally, Clint said, "We were young when we first met. Younger than you are now—"

"Where?" Teddy said. "Where did you meet?" She wanted to see if he would put all his cards on the table.

"At a government training facility."

"Do you mean a school like Whitfield or something different?"

"It was a high-security military facility. The primary purpose was to teach desert combat techniques to troops who would be deployed overseas." He winced as if remembering something painful. "The psychic training was ancillary to the facility's primary directive, genetic experimentation. There was little oversight, no real direction or control. No accountability. I think that was the venture's downfall. Ultimately, it pioneered genetic research on psychics."

"Sector Three," Teddy said.

Clint's eyes met hers. "How do you know about Sector Three?"

"Rumors floating around school." She couldn't tell him that Yates thought something similar might be happening at Whitfield. Another thing that Clint had kept from her. Another thing she was keeping from him.

He cleared his throat. "Your father was an enormously talented telepath. He passed that ability on to you. It doesn't always happen like that. Psychic abilities skip generations and even manifest in people who have no family history."

"And my mother?"

"An astral traveler. It's likely that she's the source of your astral power," Clint continued. "In altered states, your mother's astral body could visit other planes. Like dreams." He leaned forward. "You said you saw this picture in your dream. Where?"

"A yellow house. I thought I might've— It sounds stupid now."

"That's where your parents lived on base. You were born there."

She'd been dreaming of home.

Clint began with names, Marysue and Richard Delaney, names she knew already, thanks to Yates. He went on to describe the high-security military training base where they had met. The base located in a remote section of Nevada desert. It was comprised of three sections: Sector One was devoted to combat training. Sector Two was designated for psychic training; men and women with special skills had been gathered there to hone their innate abilities.

Clint explained that the researchers who had been brought in to administer the program had scoffed at the idea of psychic abilities. "They referred to us as fleas," he said.

Teddy frowned. "Fleas?"

"You know, the old joke. A military scientist tells a flea to jump and records how high it jumps. He cuts off a leg, repeats the command, records the height of the jump. The experiment is repeated three more times, until the flea has no legs at all, and a final command to jump is given. When the flea doesn't move, the scientist records the following: *Flea without legs is deaf.*" He shook his head. "They thought we'd end up the punch line to some military joke."

Instead, the psychics—Clint, her parents, and the others there— had proved beyond doubt that extrasensory perception was not only real but could be actively cultivated.

It was inspiring, at the beginning. They were energized by the work they were doing. They thought they were the good guys, fighting for a cause. Then Richard and Marysue had married.

Clint stopped.

"What?" she said in a voice that was cracked and dry. She had been afraid to interrupt, afraid of losing a single detail of her parents' story.

"At that point," Clint finally continued, "two things happened. They expanded the program to include another sector—Three. They recruited the best of our group to form an elite psychic corps. I was planning to join, but I had to go home and take care of my father in Las Vegas, and I accepted a position with the Las Vegas PD instead. I left the facility."

"Did my parents join Sector Three?"

"Your father. Richard was better than any of us. The things he could do with his mind. He could crush a piece of metal in a blink of his eye." Clint shook his head. "But it was more than that. He was a natural leader, the kind of guy who just drew people to him. Your father might have changed the world."

"What happened to him?"

"I wasn't there, Teddy. I left months before it got bad. There are only whispers . . ." Clint paused. "Sector Three changed him. I don't know what happened inside those walls, but it wasn't good. Richard became paranoid, obsessive . . . violent."

That wasn't what Yates had said.

"Your mother was pregnant with you. You were born on base. A few days later, your father led a coup against the officers in charge of Sector Three. Somehow he'd broken into the arsenal and stolen semiautomatic rifles, ammunitions, grenades, everything he needed to start his own private war—on a military base." He shook his head as if still in shock about the outcome of events. "Naturally, they returned fire. Richard was killed.

"About a month later," Clint continued, "at a little after three in the morning, I heard a knock on my door. It was your mother. She was frantic, Teddy. Nothing like the woman I knew. She shoved you in my arms and told me to take care of you. She said she'd be back for you as soon as it was safe." He stood and moved to the window.

On clear days, you could see the brilliant orange of the Golden Gate Bridge from this spot. But today wasn't clear. Great billowing drifts of fog obscured everything.

"And?" she said.

Clint turned. "And nothing. I never heard from her again."

"She never—"

"I never heard from her again," he said. "I went back to the base, but Sector Three was destroyed. It looked like there had been a massive explosion."

Teddy's stomach twisted. That matched the landscape that she'd seen months ago in Clint's memory of the desert. She felt trapped in the classroom. As if the story of her parents, of her past, were too big to fit into the small room. She stood, but there was nowhere for her to go. "Why didn't you tell me any of this before?"

"I wanted to," Clint said. "But every time I tried, I thought, *If she finds out now, she won't want to come to Whitfield.* Or *It will distract her from her studies.* Or *It might influence the outcome of her exam.*" He sat back in his chair. "I owed it to your parents to look after you," he said. "And that's what I did. I wanted to wait until the right time to tell you."

The anger was back. "There isn't a right time," Teddy said. "Every day you waited made it worse."

He nodded, rubbed his hands on his pants legs. "I used every contact I had in law enforcement to try to find her. Every psychic contact, too." He shook his head. "I traced every Jane Doe that came across my desk. Missing persons, hospitals, arrests. Nothing."

But she wasn't gone—at least not according to Yates. "Okay," Teddy said.

"Okay? That's it?"

"What am I supposed to say? You want me to make you feel better about yourself. Make it seem like you did the right thing. You tried to find her. Guess what: you didn't." Because despite everything he had just said, he still was keeping things from her: about the theft, about Yates, about what was really happening at Whitfield.

"Teddy, I—"

"You know what?" Teddy said. "I'll take a page out of Boyd's book on this one: sometimes trying isn't good enough."

CHAPTER THIRTY-EIGHT

TEDDY WENT OVER THE PLAN IN HER HEAD FOR THE millionth time, partly to prevent her mind from spinning into what-ifs: *What if the boat doesn't start? What if the USB doesn't work? What if my mental influence doesn't hold?*

After the brief session with Jeremy, Teddy had gone to the Cantina to "practice" mental influence on unsuspecting customers. And every time she'd tried to force someone to bend to her will, she felt that same horrible feeling, the bile at the back of her throat. She'd had to spend whole minutes with her hands on her knees, breathing just to steady herself, after commanding someone to turn left instead of right. It had worked. But with nerves and pressure added to the mix? Suggesting that a drunk person change direction and an FBI agent look the other way were entirely different ball games.

She went over the sequence of events one more time. *One: Molly, Dara, Pyro, and Jillian get day passes from the front office and leave Angel Island to set up at the Embassy Hotel, across the street from the FBI offices. Check.*

Two: Ditch the ferry. Jeremy drives his speedboat to Pier 39 with Teddy. Check.

Teddy kept her eyes on the iconic Golden Gate Bridge in the distance, juxtaposed with the mountain backdrop. For Teddy, the view just never got old. Jeremy coasted into a slip he had rented in the bustling marina. Teddy was glad to see how busy it was—that meant their coming and going wouldn't be noticeable among the crowds of spring visitors.

Teddy took a deep breath and looked around, imagining returning to this spot after a successful mission. Her brilliant exit strategy? Convincing Nick that she was coming down with food poisoning. It sounded more like getting out of a bad date than a highly secure government facility. Pyro would pick up a car and park it near the FBI building, ready for them all to jump in the moment Molly located the video file with the damning footage. Pyro would drive them back to the pier. They would board Jeremy's speedboat and return to Angel Island immediately.

Simple.

At least Teddy told herself it would be simple. Over and over. Funny how that didn't seem to settle her nerves any.

Teddy checked her phone. It was ten after three. She was meeting Nick at four in the lobby of the FBI offices. Teddy looked up and saw Jeremy staring at his phone, too. Molly had shared the smuggled devices so they could communicate over the course of the day. Though they could link up psychically, none of them had tried to sync with more than one person over great distances before. Going digital rather than psychical was logical.

"Should you be doing that while the engine's on?"

"Sorry." He stuffed his phone back in his pocket, cut the engine, and secured the lines. Teddy had started toward the taxi stand when she realized he was tailing her.

"What are you doing?" she asked. He had been standoffish since that lesson, even though he'd assured her that he felt fine.

"Going with you, of course."

Teddy gritted her teeth. "You know that's not the plan," she said.

"What good am I, just sitting here?"

"You're the getaway driver. It's a lot of good to have you sitting here."

"What if you need someone else for mental influence? I could—"

"I've got it," she interrupted.

"I want to go in there instead of waiting on the boat. I can't wait somewhere and do nothing if something bad happens."

"Nothing bad is going to happen," Teddy said. "We all know the plan. We're all going to look out for each other."

He looked down, playing with the keys to the boat. "You can't promise that. And if something happens to Molly again, and I'm not there to . . ."

Teddy put her hand on his shoulder. "She'll be fine, Jeremy. She's staying in a hotel room. She's not going to be in any action." He stiffened. She removed her hand. He obviously didn't want her comfort. "If we want this to work," she continued, "we all need to stick to the plan. Your role is critical. You stay with the boat. Okay?"

* * *

Teddy left Jeremy by the dock and hailed a taxi. It hurried her away from Fisherman's Wharf and past the noisy cable cars that clanged along Hyde Street through the historic district of San Francisco.

Eight stomach-churning minutes and twenty dollars later, the driver dropped her at the Embassy Hotel. Pyro sat in the lobby, casually reading a paper. He stood and greeted Teddy with a peck on the cheek. They were just another average couple visiting San Fran on vacation.

Teddy forced a smile. "Everything okay?"

"Room's ready. All checked in." He took her hand and guided her into the elevator. But instead of pressing the button for the top floor, he hit three.

"Hey," Teddy said, "I thought we—"

He squeezed her hand. His gaze flicked toward a camera located in the ceiling, near the upper-right corner. She waited until he'd ushered her into a third-floor suite, where Dara, Jillian, and Molly were already inside, to voice her concern: "I thought we needed a room on the top floor to pull this off."

The three women stood near the window, huddled around a table with Molly's tech paraphernalia: two laptops, an old-school radio, a cell phone, a hard drive, and a bunch of other wires and devices Teddy didn't recognize.

Dara crossed her arms. She was clearly pissed. "I booked a top-floor room. But the hotel screwed up the reservation. This was the best they could do."

"At least we're still facing south," said Jillian.

Dara tilted her head toward the window. "Take a look. There's Nick's office."

Teddy glanced at the tinted facade of the FBI building. "How can you tell which one?"

Pyro picked up a pair of Steiner special-ops binoculars—swiped from school, no doubt—and handed them to her. "Sixth floor, third window from the left."

Teddy lifted the infrared binoculars to her eyes and adjusted the lenses. Through the slits in his office window blinds, she spotted Nick, feet propped up on his desk.

She set down the binoculars and transferred her attention to Molly. "How's it going?"

Molly didn't bother to look up. "I'm trying to find some way to compensate for our position. We may be too low, depending on the amplitude and frequency of the radio waves. Problem is, there's no way to know for certain until you start transmitting."

"That's why we were supposed to have a room on the top floor," Pyro said through his teeth. He wasn't directly accusing Dara of being incompetent, but Teddy assumed she got the message.

"I know that," she said, her voice rising. "That's why I *booked* a room on the top floor."

"Wait a minute." Teddy's throat went dry. Weeks of planning undermined by a reservation glitch? "Does that mean this won't work?"

"Don't worry about it," Molly said, her fingers flying over her keyboard. "It just means I need to recalibrate some of my numbers to compensate for our current position. If I could actually focus while I do that, it would be a huge help. So, hey, everybody? Shut up."

Molly would hook in to the hotel Wi-Fi. From there, she would download malware from the Darknet onto a flash drive.

"I've got it," Molly said. She passed the drive to Teddy. "You remember what to do?"

Teddy would surreptitiously slip the flash drive into Nick's computer, which was hardwired in to the FBI's main air-gapped server. The flash drive would then upload a virus that would turn on the computer's FM-radio frequencies. As Teddy's smartphone was equipped with a built-in FM radio, all she had to do was leave her phone near Nick's computer. That would let Molly use the FM frequencies to remotely hack in to Nick's computer, directly access the air-gapped server, and grab the video file.

"And if I need more time?" Molly said.

"Dara will text me," Teddy said. "I'll keep an eye on my phone."

Molly nodded. "Remember, agents in that building routinely monitor the main server. We won't be able to hide what we're doing for long. Once we signal you that we have the video file, get the hell out of there."

"I will." It couldn't happen fast enough.

"And while all that's going on," Dara added, motioning to the window, "I'll keep an eye on Nick's office. Jillian and Pyro will be on the street level, patrolling the exterior of the building. If anything looks weird, we'll text you."

"It's time," Pyro said. "Nick's probably waiting."

Teddy looked at her watch: 3:54 p.m. She smoothed down her crisp white blouse and navy slacks, which she had worn instead of her usual jeans, T-shirt, and combat boots. She had wanted to avoid detection on security footage if it came to that (which she hoped it wouldn't). But there was a small part of her that also wanted to, well, look nice. For Nick. When the thought had formed in her mind, Teddy had tried to push it away. She was a lot of things—but nice? She wasn't nice. She didn't want to be nice. So why did she want Nick to think she was?

"Can I talk to you for second?" Dara said.

"Is this still about the room thing? Molly says she has it handled." Teddy brushed some lint from her blouse.

"Um, not quite." Dara looked at Teddy's shirt and then said in a louder voice, "Teddy, you ripped your shirt. I'll loan you mine. Come change in the bathroom."

"I didn't—" Teddy began, but Dara was pulling her into the small hotel bathroom.

"I didn't want to freak out in front of everyone," she said. "I think I had a death warning."

"You think?" Teddy said. The list of what-ifs grew by one: *What if I'm putting someone's life in danger?*

Dara played with the silver bracelets on her wrist. "I'm not sure. I just saw a rope snapping. But we don't have any rope. That's not a part of the plan. I'm sorry, Teddy. It's not a science. I don't understand until it's happening. Maybe it's about someone two thousand miles away."

"If it's someone two thousand miles away, then why are you telling me?"

Dara continued to fumble with the bracelets. "Because I saw you standing over the body."

Teddy would have thought that with news like this, her heart would go into overdrive; instead, it stopped. "Are you saying that someone will die?" How far would she go to get this information? She had bent a few rules, but would she—could she—take that risk? She looked around the small, yellowing hotel bathroom. It felt like a cell. "But just because you see it doesn't mean it happens. You've seen things before that didn't happen."

"But I couldn't not tell you."

There was banging on the door and Pyro's voice. "Okay, ladies, time's up."

Teddy's heart kicked in again. She opened the door. *Another item on the checklist,* Teddy thought. *Make sure no one dies.*

"You're still wearing your shirt," Pyro said.

"Oh, yeah," Teddy said. Pyro raised one eyebrow. She added, "I fixed it." She slipped the flash drive and the cell phone into a small black clutch. It wasn't too late to back out.

"Remember. We got you, Teddy," Jillian said. "If what Yates said about his organization coming for you next is right, then we have to do this. Someone's coming for one of us. That means they're coming for us all."

Teddy knew the plan. But that didn't mean she was ready. She hadn't had enough time to practice mental influence. Hadn't had enough time to come to terms with the fact that she was lying to Nick once again. No, not lying to him, tricking him. Putting his job on the line. And Dara's vision. The bile rose in Teddy's throat. She hadn't even tried to influence anyone and she already felt sick. But as she looked around at her friends and realized what they were risking for her, she knew there was only one thing she could say, even if she wasn't sure she believed it herself: "I'm ready."

CHAPTER THIRTY-NINE

TEDDY WIPED HER HANDS ON HER SLACKS AND WALKED through the doors of the San Francisco FBI headquarters. The building was a monument to concrete and glass. There were no flashing lights, no slot machines ringing, no smell of booze in the air, but she was still playing to win.

She was supposed to meet Nick in the lobby. She'd received those instructions from the secretary in the front office before she'd left campus that morning with her day pass. Teddy was sure Nick would've liked to tell her directly, but she had avoided being alone with him since That Night.

Because she felt bad. For manipulating him, yes. But mostly because she'd gotten something she'd wanted for all the wrong reasons. She now sounded like a story in *Chicken Soup for the Messed-up Millennial Psychic Soul*. Once Teddy would have written it off. Given herself props for bagging a guy like Nick.

She smiled when she looked up to see Nick waiting by the reception desk, dressed in the standard FBI suit.

"You're here," he said, the left corner of his mouth ticking up slightly. God, she wanted to kiss him right there. But that wasn't part of the plan.

She took out the piece of paper with the note from the secretary. "As directed."

Nick cleared his throat, shifted on the balls of his feet. All tells,

Teddy knew. He was nervous. "I was thinking maybe we could talk before we start?"

Teddy sucked in a breath. They couldn't talk. If they talked, Teddy wasn't sure she could go through with this, as much as she wanted one more moment with plain ol' Nick. She looked around the lobby, playing up the nerves she was already feeling. "Do you think that's a good idea?"

Nick followed Teddy's gaze. "I guess you're right." He reached for her hand, then stopped himself. "If you'll follow me, Ms. Cannon."

They checked in with a security guard, who scanned her ID, snapped her photo, and issued a visitor's pass. The security guard waved Nick ahead and directed Teddy through a metal detector. No problem there. She wasn't carrying a weapon.

Next, however, came the X-ray machine. This was where things could get sticky. Teddy knew that visitors were not permitted to bring cell phones or other electronic devices into the building. This would be her first test. Teddy placed her clutch on the moving belt and braced herself.

"Hey, Nick!" a man called over from the elevators a few feet away. "Did you hear we finally got a call from Lambert?"

Nick turned to Teddy. "One second," he said.

She couldn't have asked for better timing.

Teddy watched as the security guard flicked the button to pause the belt once her purse was inside the scanner. Fixing an expression of polite interest on her face, she reached out to his mind. *Nothing here,* she said. *Scan clear. Move on.*

When someone fought against her influence, she felt like she was swimming against a current. The inky darkness of the security guard's mind churned like an ocean before a storm. He was resisting her command. She swallowed the taste of bile.

Nothing here. Scan clear. Move on.

The last wave crashed and the ocean settled, now smooth as glass.

The security guard's face slackened, and his pupils expanded. He flicked the button again, sending her purse out the other end of the X-ray machine. Teddy watched his pupils return to their normal size.

"Thanks," she said as she walked slowly toward Nick. Out of the corner of her eye, she saw the security guard rub his temple as if he had a headache.

Check.

She joined Nick at the elevator, still uneasy from the effort. Teddy toyed with her clutch, her fingers tracing the outline of her cell phone.

"I thought we'd start at the crime lab," he said. "That's probably the most interesting place here."

As much as Teddy actually wanted to see forensic equipment, she had a mission, and time was running out. "We could start with your office," she said. She chewed her bottom lip. There were only so many moves she could make. "I was thinking about what you said earlier. Maybe we should talk."

He stared at her. Two minutes ago, she'd been trying to keep it professional. And now . . . if she were a guy, she'd think girls were crazy, too.

"What changed in the two minutes since I went to talk to Bradley?"

She sighed. "Nothing. Everything. I don't know, I've never done this before."

"Done what before?" Nick asked.

A bell pinged and the elevator door slid open. Teddy stepped inside, her hand hovering at the number pad. "Gone on a tour of the FBI? Tried a relationship with someone I actually liked?"

"So you like cops now, huh?" The left side of Nick's mouth curved up again. He followed her into the elevator. "Sixth floor."

Luckily, she was saved from any further awkward conversation as two other people entered the elevator. When the doors opened on the sixth floor, she followed Nick down the hall. He ushered her inside his office, his hand barely grazing the small of her back. As soon as the door was closed, Teddy crossed the room to Nick's desk. She casually set down her clutch. All she had to do was insert the flash drive in his computer and upload the malware.

But now that she was actually in Nick's office, Teddy understood that this would be harder than she had thought. She would have to convince Nick to leave her alone in the room—either by means of her own wiles or by mental influence.

"So, you want to explain what this is all about?" he asked. He took his suit jacket off and hung it on a peg behind his door. He crossed his arms over his chest, causing his shirt to bunch over his biceps.

Teddy's stomach lurched. Carefully, she said, "What do you mean?"

"They teach us stuff at Quantico, you know. But I don't have to be an FBI agent to see that you're scared."

Of course she was scared. She was scared this whole thing would backfire at any second, in the dozens of ways she had imagined and the millions of ways she could never anticipate. Teddy took a deep breath. If she was going to influence him, the time was now.

"We moved too fast the other night," Nick said. He uncrossed his arms, shifted again on the balls of his feet. "I take responsibility for that. What's going on between you and me, and my position at school—"

His words stopped her short. What was he saying? That he wanted to try to make this work? Or that it was a bad idea? For a split second, the what-ifs circling in her mind pivoted. *What if we could be together?*

Of course, that option had quit being an option the night she hacked in to his laptop and copied his hard drive. Even less of an option now, with her friends staked out in a suite across the street and a purse full of malware.

There was a knock, and the agent from the lobby peered around the door. "Hey, Nick, Lambert's just out of an interrogation and picked up something. You have a minute?"

Nick turned toward Teddy. "Sorry," he said. "I won't be too long."

Teddy should have been elated. Maybe not a bona fide miracle but close enough: Lambert had given her a window to hack Nick's computer. And she'd avoided using mental influence to do it. So why did she feel so disappointed? "No problem," Teddy assured him. "Take your time."

She practically dove for his computer the second the door closed. She shoved the flash drive into the USB port. Seconds later, her cell phone buzzed. Dara would confirm once Molly had downloaded the virus.

Download complete.

Check.

They were back on track.

She moved toward the window and scanned the street below. She spotted Pyro in a navy hoodie, smoking a cigarette outside a café. Overhead, she saw a seagull swoop in an irregular pattern. She wondered if it was a sign from Jillian.

Her cell phone buzzed again. She opened her purse to check for the message from Dara: Position too low. Buy more time.

Teddy looked out the window toward the Embassy Hotel where Dara and Molly waited. She imagined Molly bent over her laptop as Dara paced and talked and texted. *Buy more time.* How much more time? Ten minutes? An hour? Teddy began to respond when a movement at the edge of her vision caught her attention: two figures climbing the Embassy Hotel's fire escape. Molly and Dara were headed to the roof.

This was not a part of the plan. Teddy typed: What are you doing??? She hit send and glanced back out the window only to see Molly swing onto the hotel roof just as a figure in a navy hoodie launched up the fire escape after them.

This was definitely not part of the plan. In the span of two minutes, three things had gone wrong. Her phone buzzed once more: Under control.

Teddy glanced back out the window. Dara and Teddy hadn't noticed the third figure, which must have been Pyro. But what if it wasn't Pyro? Because whoever it was certainly didn't move like Pyro. No. It had to be him. But just in case . . .

Someone on the roof. Teddy stared at her phone. No response. She looked across the street.

Two seconds later, her phone began to buzz. A call from Dara. Could she risk answering it? If Dara was calling, it had to be serious. Had she seen something else?

Before she could pick up, the door opened and Nick reentered the room. "How did you get that past security?"

"Wait a minute. I'm not supposed to have it in here? Sorry, I didn't know. I mean, I know they're not allowed at Whitfield, but I figured it was okay. So . . . no cell phones in your office? Is that a rule?"

"Something like that, yeah. The security guard didn't catch it?"

"He didn't say anything." Teddy shrugged. "I guess the FBI isn't any better than the TSA when it comes to scanning things."

Nick looked her up and down, eyes narrowed. But if his eyes were on her, they wouldn't be on her USB drive. She had to stick to the plan as best she could. They'd extensively covered situations like this in Boyd's class. If every member of a team reacted blindly as events unfolded, missions would dissolve into nothing but chaos. The first text she'd received from Dara had asked for more time: that was the directive.

When Teddy had walked into the lobby, she'd never thought her last play would be to talk about her feelings. To take a leaf from Clint Corbett's book. But that was exactly what she did. "You were right. I'm scared. I don't know how to act around you. And it's not because you're my teacher." She struggled to articulate what it was she felt. "I don't date. I don't do relationships. I don't let people in, Nick. But I want to try with you, if—"

A shrill overhead alarm cut her off. The noise and the sudden panic made Teddy think of Whitfield's midyear exam. But this wasn't an obstacle course. This was real life.

"Stay right here. Don't move." Nick turned and left the room. The sound of loud voices filled the corridor.

Teddy's gaze returned to the roof—Dara and Molly, perched on the lip of the building, rope gathered around their waists. *Why not just go down the fire escape?* This so, so wasn't a part of the plan. Molly hated heights.

What if Dara's vision . . .

She couldn't finish that thought.

Teddy jerked the flash drive out of the port and tossed it in her clutch, absolutely certain she was about to be busted. Someone had caught Molly hacking the air-gapped computer and traced the breach back to Nick's computer.

She watched as her two friends scaled the side of the hotel into a quiet alley two stories down. They were about halfway down by now, Dara making better progress. Teddy watched as Molly stopped her descent.

Teddy felt the snap of the rope as if it had lashed her entire body. One second Molly was hanging, and the next she was falling. In heist movies, this kind of thing happened in slow motion. The hero had time to do something. All Teddy could do was watch.

Nick burst back into the room. "You've got to leave the building, Teddy. Now."

"Leave? What?" She couldn't process what was happening. She couldn't think. Molly. Molly had fallen. Dara had tried to warn her, and she had gone ahead anyway.

"Teddy. You have to focus." He grabbed her arm. "Someone called in a bomb threat. The building's being evacuated."

A bomb threat? Teddy felt her heart drop into her stomach. Had

Dara called and done that to buy time? A signal to get Teddy out of the building? They were so far off-plan that Teddy had no idea what to do next. She desperately needed to check her phone. Make contact. Get back to the hotel room. Regroup.

"There's a bar in the hotel across the street," Nick said. "Wait for me. We're not finished talking."

Teddy's heart dropped six stories to street level, where moments ago everything still seemed possible.

CHAPTER FORTY

TEDDY JOINED THE STREAM OF EMPLOYEES AND VISI-
tors filing out of the FBI building. She blinked, trying to rid her mind
of the image of Molly's fall. When she opened her eyes, she surveyed
the chaos. People running and shouting. Flashing lights and loud-
speakers. Police officers warning everyone to stand back. In the midst
of all this, Teddy saw two men wearing vests that said *Bomb Squad*,
leading German shepherds toward the building. Teddy shook off her
panic. She needed to focus if she didn't want to call attention to herself.

Who had phoned in the bomb threat? That wasn't adding up. It
was too much of a coincidence. She remembered what Nick had told
the class when they started their casework: *Never dismiss coincidences.*

They had almost secured the file when the alarm had gone off. She
clung to the hope that Dara had been the one to create the diversion.
She texted: All okay??? Molly???

The second Teddy pressed send, her phone lit up with a call.

"Teddy." Dara's voice was ragged. "I tried to stop her, but she insisted—"

"I saw. Is she—?" Teddy couldn't say the words.

"She's unconscious," Dara said. "Pyro found a pulse. But we have
to get her to a hospital."

"Where are you?"

"The alley behind the hotel. We're all here. Pyro, Jillian . . . and

Molly. Jeremy, too. I don't know how he found us, but I'm glad he did. He got us off the roof when the FBI closed the hotel. Fire escape and everything. He's the one who had rappelling gear. But—"

"I'm on my way." Molly was alive. She was still alive.

"Teddy, it's bad. Really bad. There are agents everywhere. Cops, too."

"That's what happens when you call in a bomb threat."

"I didn't! God, why would I do that?"

"I thought maybe to buy more time." She hesitated a second before she asked Dara one last question. The question she didn't want to ask, the one that would make the mission salvageable. What was the point of risking everything if they hadn't gotten what they'd come for? "Dara—did Molly locate the video file?"

Dara paused. "She did."

Teddy let out a sigh of relief. "I'll be there soon."

"Teddy, there's something I have to tell you—"

"It can wait. We have the file, we have Molly—"

"Molly dropped her laptop when she fell. The file . . . it's gone."

*   *   *

Teddy wove through the crowd, down Polk Street, and around the back of the Embassy Hotel. The file was gone. All that planning, all that work, had been for nothing. And the cost had been so great. Molly had survived the fall, but did Dara's vision predict later complications? It was as if the wails of police sirens and fire trucks went silent. The only sound Teddy heard was her heart, thudding to the repeated question: *What have I done?*

A pair of rough man's hands grabbed her, shaking her out of her stupor. Teddy struggled against his hands and landed an elbow in his chest. He was yelling, but Teddy still couldn't register individual words, couldn't understand what he was saying. He released her. And suddenly, the world was back to full volume.

"Teddy, relax. It's me."

Pyro.

Teddy looked and saw Dara standing nearby, fidgeting with her silver bracelets. Jeremy was sitting near a fire escape, his face blank. Then Teddy saw Jillian, face blotchy, stooped over Molly. Molly on the ground of the alley. Pyro's navy hoodie, stuffed underneath her head as a pillow. Her head was bleeding, her wrist already swollen.

Oh, God.

Teddy bent down closer, reached out to touch Molly's face.

"We didn't want to move her," Dara said. "But Pyro checked. Broken wrist. And she hit her head, but—"

"We have to get out of here now," Pyro said. "The longer we wait, the harder it's going to be."

Teddy's gaze was on Molly. Her pale face, her broken body.

"Teddy," Pyro said.

"What?"

Teddy knew she should be focusing on next steps, but she still was struggling to understand what happened, how it had all gone wrong. "Did you call this in?" Teddy said.

"Hell, no," said Pyro. "You think we wanted this kind of shit storm? Cops everywhere? We were trying to keep a low profile."

"So someone called a bomb threat to both the hotel and the FBI building?"

"Probably not some random asshole, though," Pyro put in.

Other than the Misfits, the only person who knew that Teddy had planned to retrieve the file was Yates. But he didn't know when or how. And it was in his interest that the mission succeed.

Teddy forced her thoughts back to the immediate crisis. They couldn't sneak into the hotel room. Staying in the alley until the threat passed wasn't an option, either. Eventually, someone—hotel security, a cop, or an FBI agent—would spot them. Each second they wasted put their safety and Molly's life in danger. They needed to get out of the alley and onto the boat as quickly as possible.

"There are a couple of police officers at the other end of the alley," Pyro said. He turned to Teddy. "Do you think you can convince them nothing's happening?"

Teddy nodded. She'd never influenced two people at once before, but she could try. She had to.

"See that Dumpster in the parking lot?" Pyro said. "How about making it fly with a little telekinesis? Provide a distraction?"

She could move paper clips. But a four-thousand-pound trash heap on reserve psychic energy? Teddy shook her head. A fire, especially in the midst of a bomb threat, would be a distraction that would pull the cops' attention. "I think I'll defer to you on this one."

Pyro nodded. "Wanted to give you first dibs. I'll light it up as soon as you're in position." He turned to Dara, Jeremy, and Jillian. "Car's parked at the corner of Eddy and Larkin. Burgundy Hyundai sedan. Key's over the visor. I'll carry Molly. Dara, you drive. Then we get the hell out of here. Everybody got it?" His eyes shifted to Jeremy, who stood frozen. "Jeremy, you with us?"

Jeremy's eyes snapped to Pyro. "Yes, I—" he swallowed. "Yes."

"I can provide a distraction, too," Jillian said, pointing to the sky. "Seagulls."

"Okay, then," Pyro said. "Let's move."

Teddy nodded. Her body was waking up. A shot of adrenaline coursed through her, the good kind, not the kind that had stopped her in her tracks when she'd exited the FBI building. They could do this—together. They had to. For Molly.

Pyro turned his attention to the Dumpster. Within seconds, she heard the shouts: *Fire! Explosives! Clear the area!* Teddy's gaze shot to the cops stationed at the other end of the alley. Their attention was fixed on the Dumpster, which had erupted in flames, but she couldn't take a chance that their gazes might waver. She felt the bile at the back of her throat. *Don't turn around. Watch the fire.*

She imagined splitting herself in two: half of herself reaching toward one man, the other half toward the other. One of the cops was more acquiescent. She felt the mind of the man on the left go calm, while the mind of the man on the right thrashed against her will, the darkness of his mind cresting. She remembered how Clint had guided the guards and Sergei away from their hiding place all those months ago. She should have asked him how before she'd discovered she couldn't trust him.

Don't turn around, she commanded. *Watch the fire.*

She saw Pyro pick Molly up and begin to run out of the alley, Dara, Jeremy, and Jillian racing behind him. Teddy redoubled her efforts to direct the cops' eyes away from her friends.

The one cop's mind wouldn't settle. She was drenched in sweat, her slacks sticking to her thighs. She wanted to fall to the ground, collapse, give up. She was drained.

"Stop!" one of the cops shouted, turning toward her friends. "Police!"

A flock of seagulls swooped down into the alley, cawing and beating their wings as though fighting over scraps of food. Jillian. The birds were shielding the Misfits from the police officer's view.

Teddy didn't wait for another chance. She sprinted out of the alley and around the corner toward Eddy Street. Later, she couldn't remember how she made it through the mass of people, cops, FBI agents, firemen. She couldn't remember opening the door to the Hyundai, piling into the backseat, or Dara peeling away from the curb, racing toward the harbor. All she remembered was Molly's bloody face in her lap.

CHAPTER FORTY-ONE

TEDDY BRUSHED MOLLY'S HAIR BACK FROM HER FORE-head, watching Molly's eyes flutter as if she were dreaming. Next to Teddy, Jeremy held Molly's hand in his own. He ran his thumb over her fingers again and again. Before, when Teddy had screwed up, it had been her ass on the line; she'd been the one to take the risk. But today she'd walked into the FBI building, and Molly had been the one to get hurt.

Teddy ran through the past hour in her mind, trying to find the precise moment their plan had fallen apart. How had they messed up the hotel reservation? Who had called in the bomb threat? Why had Jeremy left the boat? Especially after Teddy had explicitly told him to stay put.

Teddy cast a glance at Jeremy. It was only then that she noticed he was wearing a navy hoodie similar to the one Pyro wore.

"It was you on the roof, wasn't it?"

Jeremy shook his head as if coming out of a trance. "I'm sorry?"

"Why didn't you stay at the docks?"

Jeremy swallowed. "I, I just—"

"Teddy," Jillian said. "Let it go, we've all been through a lot."

But Teddy couldn't let it go. "Dara said you had rappelling gear, too. How did you know? Tell me."

Jeremy looked down at Molly's unmoving form. "I just had this feeling. I couldn't leave her alone, not when I could do something to help her."

"Turn here," Pyro said. "We'll dump the vehicle and walk to the dock." Dara maneuvered the car and cut the engine. Pyro opened the back door and lifted Molly into his arms.

"We have to get her to a hospital," Teddy said.

"No hospital," Pyro said. "If we take her to the hospital, there'll be a police report." He shifted Molly higher in his arms.

Molly groaned, stirring. "I don't want to go to the hospital." She leaned in to Pyro's shoulder.

"Molly!" Teddy cried. "Is she awake?"

Pyro ran the back of his hand against her forehead. "She's slipping in and out. We'll take her to the infirmary when we're on the island. Jeremy, can you handle the boat?"

Jeremy nodded, fumbling for the keys from his pocket.

They hiked the two blocks to the marina. Teddy remembered thinking that it was the perfect San Francisco day. Not a cloud in the sky. Pretty pastel Victorians gleamed in the afternoon sunlight. Tourists meandered up and down steep sidewalks, stopping in outdoor cafés and browsing in cute shops. Teddy took it all in with a sense of disbelief. Impossible to conceive that something so awful could be happening in the midst of such picture-postcard beauty.

*   *   *

The infirmary was deserted except for one lone nurse on duty—the stocky and efficient Nurse Bell—and an upperclassman with a migraine. When the group entered, Nurse Bell snapped into action, guiding Pyro, who carried Molly, to a private room. Once Pyro had gently settled Molly onto a bed, they were shooed into the infirmary's waiting room.

After what felt like forever, Nurse Bell returned. "She's stable for the moment, but she'll need treatment. I've paged Dr. Eversley." Her gaze swept around the room. "What happened?"

A beat while they exchanged uneasy glances. Finally, Pyro volunteered, "She fell. Her wrist is broken. Contusions to the head and body. No other broken bones."

"I didn't ask for a diagnosis," Nurse Bell replied. "I'm fully capable of assessing her injuries."

The Misfits stayed silent.

"How long has she been in and out of consciousness?"

"About two hours," Teddy said. She knew it sounded bad. She felt like the worst sort of person.

Nurse Bell looked between them. The moment stretched. "And you're coming to me only now?"

"We were in San Francisco," Teddy said. "We were—"

"Hiking," Dara said. "She fell hiking."

"And you didn't think to bring her to the emergency room?"

"She doesn't have insurance," Jeremy said, speaking for the first time since they'd boarded the boat back to the island. "She begged us not to take her to the hospital."

Nurse Bell released a lengthy sigh. No words accompanied it, but her opinion of the way they'd handled Molly's injury was clear. "I will alert Professor Corbett to these events. Now I have to take care of your friend."

Her stomach tied in knots, Teddy asked, "Should we wait?"

Nurse Bell paused. "There are many things you should have done. Loitering in my waiting room isn't one of them."

*   *   *

The Misfits trudged together toward Harris Hall. No one spoke. It was easier not to. Fog had begun to sweep over school grounds, shrouding the normally tranquil Zen garden in a gray mist.

Teddy stopped at the steps of the dorm. She looked at Dara. Someone had to summon the courage to say the words on everyone's minds. "Did you see—" she began.

Dara shook her head. "The future can change."

"Molly's *not* going to die," Jeremy said. He stated it as a fact, when all of the Misfits knew that the future was always murky, constant only in its inconstancy.

Jillian brushed his shoulder. "It's okay, Jeremy."

"*Okay?* How is any of this okay?" He jerked away from Jillian's touch and turned on Teddy. "This is all your fault. If you hadn't wanted to go, none of this would have happened."

"Jeremy, you don't mean that. We decided this as a team," Jillian said.

Nice of Jillian to come to her defense, Teddy supposed, but completely unnecessary. Jeremy was right. Everything that had happened was her fault. She didn't try to defend herself. She couldn't.

"If Teddy had just thought about what might—" Jeremy said.

"That's enough, Jeremy! Molly wanted to get that video file. She wanted to go on the roof. And she was the one who wanted to go down that line. You followed us. It wasn't a particularly challenging descent. It was an accident. She got hurt. And that sucks. But it was her choice," Jillian said.

"Is there any chance that this could have been worth it? Any way of recovering the hard drive?" Pyro asked.

Dara lifted the backpack with the broken laptop. "It's shattered. And I looked through the debris. The hard drive was missing. When the computer hit the pavement, it must have skidded beneath something in the alley."

After everything they'd been through, they had nothing to show for it. They'd left the island that morning hoping to right a wrong. They'd been so confident they could pull it off. Free Yates, stop Whitfield from turning into another Sector Three, and . . . Teddy swallowed hard as she realized what else: find her mother. Suddenly, she saw their plan for what it was—foolhardy, selfish, shortsighted—and Teddy felt sick.

CHAPTER FORTY-TWO

TEDDY LAY ON THE TWIN BED IN HER DORM ROOM, waiting for news of Molly's condition. She rolled the Ping-Pong ball Clint had given her between her fingers. The wall clock ticked off the seconds. Teddy had never noticed it before; now it was all she could hear. Those steady ticks reminded her of how she hadn't been quick enough in Nick's office or, later, in the alley.

"You're tormenting yourself," Jillian said. "It's not like you pushed Molly off the roof, Teddy. It's not your fault."

Teddy ignored her. Of course it was her fault. No one was going to convince her otherwise. "Part of me feels like I should start packing now," she said. She rolled onto her side, reaching for the purse she'd used earlier that day. She dumped the contents onto her bed, including the cell phone that Molly had given her. She felt strange having a phone again; she'd become used to living in the moment, tech-free. Her heart twisted. The screen indicated one new message. Teddy pushed a button and read it: Just in case.

Just in case . . . what? As Teddy filled in the rest, she couldn't help but think the worst. *Just in case something happens to me.*

"What is it?" Jillian asked.

"A message from Molly. There's an attachment, too. Must have come in before I left."

Jillian leaped from her bed and stood over Teddy's shoulder. "Open it."

Teddy pressed the alphanumeric link. Disbelief and incredulity warred for dominance in her mind as she watched a folder containing two video files appear on the cell phone screen.

She clicked the first. The phone went momentarily dark. A small white arrow appeared, and Teddy pressed it. Then a black-and-white video image filled the screen, revealing a grainy surveillance shot of a crowded sidewalk. No sound. Men and women walking with umbrellas flexed open to shield themselves from rain. Tall buildings loomed around them. It could have been any large metropolitan city. Teddy noted the time and date stamp floating in the lower-right corner: August 17, 08:21. Six years ago.

Teddy's breath caught. This was it. The proof they'd been after.

The video rolled on. A uniformed hotel doorman stepped from beneath an awning and signaled for a cab. Three men followed. The first was slight of build, dressed in full military regalia. The general whom Yates had been ordered to kill. The two men trailing him were dressed in suits, though their physique didn't fit their attire. They had broad chests, long arms, and stubby legs. Gorillas in suits. Teddy pegged them as bodyguards. One of them held an umbrella over the first man's head, while the other scanned the street for signs of trouble.

A cab rolled to the curb and stopped. Just as the doorman swung open the passenger door, a fourth man rushed forward. The angle of the camera captured him only briefly. He was a short man with a round face and heavy facial hair. Even though the quality was poor, one thing was for certain: he was not Derek Yates. The short man bumped into the general—hard—then leaped into the cab, slamming the door shut as the cab sped off.

The general staggered backward, and his bodyguards caught him under the arms to prevent him falling. At first it appeared no more than a bit of urban incivility caught on film. A passerby rudely stealing someone else's cab. But then the general pressed his right hand against his chest as his bodyguards lowered him to the ground. A dark stain spread down his shirt. Blood seeped through his fingers. He hadn't been pushed out of the way; he'd been stabbed.

Then the video ended.

"That was not Derek Yates," Teddy said.

"Click the next file," Jillian said.

This video was higher quality. A police interrogation room, stark but brightly lit. A young, uniformed police officer stood near the door. A man sat in handcuffs at a small metal table. "That's Yates," Teddy explained to Jillian.

Before she could say more, the door to the interrogation room opened, and Clint, dressed in a shirt and tie with a detective's badge clipped to his breast pocket, stood before the table. This video was also time-stamped: August 20, 23:07. Three days after the murder of the general.

Yates spoke. "You know I wasn't there."

"Then why does the murder weapon have your fingerprints all over it?"

"Come now, Clint." Yates gave a brief, sardonic smile.

Clint placed a hunting knife, sealed in a clear plastic bag, on the table. "Are you saying this isn't your knife?"

"Of course it is."

"But you—"

"That knife was stolen from me."

It was Clint's turn to smile. "Someone stole your knife and dropped it at the scene of the murder? That's your story?"

"You've known me a long time. Would I leave prints behind?"

"They wanted you out of the way, so they framed you. Set you up for murder."

"That's right."

"Give me a name, then. You don't owe them your loyalty. Not anymore. Tell me who's behind this. Who have you been working for?"

Yates's entire body stiffened. Softly, he said, "You know I can't do that."

"Can't? Or won't?" Clint rubbed his chin in frustration. "I'll help you if I can, Derek. But you have to give me something to go on."

"I'm afraid that's simply not possible."

Clint shoved back a chair and sat. Both men were silent, and Teddy understood that they were communicating not with their voices but with their minds. Yates went pale, and his whole body shook.

"Sign the confession," Clint said, his voice even as he slid a piece of paper and a pen toward Yates.

"Don't do this," Yates wheezed.

"He's mentally influencing him," Teddy said to Jillian, aghast. "Forcing him to sign that confession."

She pulled Yates's card from her pocket and found the address for his attorney. She was going to be expelled from Whitfield in any case. At least she could right one wrong before then.

"Everything Yates said was true," she murmured.

Which meant that Teddy didn't want to stay at Whitfield anyway.

CHAPTER FORTY-THREE

TEDDY HAD KNOWN CLINT WOULD WANT TO SPEAK to them. She just didn't expect the summons to arrive so quickly. Less than ten minutes after she and Jillian hit end on the video, a knock sounded at their door. Teddy opened it to find a second-year recruit standing in the hallway: Clint wanted to see them in his office. Now.

Teddy, though psychically, physically, and mentally exhausted, jolted her wall into place, shoring up whatever remaining currents of power she had available. But even as she did it, she realized how pointless the exercise was. If he wanted information, all he had to do was look into any of her friends' minds and he'd see everything.

No sense putting off the inevitable.

Teddy and Jillian arrived to find Dara, Pyro, and Jeremy already there. She would have liked time to share Molly's video with her friends before she confronted Clint about its contents, but that wasn't the hand she'd been dealt. It didn't matter. One way or another, she was going to see this through.

Clint's office, a room that had been Teddy's refuge, wasn't spacious. With all six of them crammed inside, it felt like a holding cell. Dara and Jillian sat in chairs facing Clint's desk; Teddy and Jeremy stood by a tall metal filing cabinet; Pyro hovered near the door. Before she could stop herself, Teddy's gaze flew to the desk, to the glass dome beneath which rested the screw with the Sector Three symbol stamped on the head.

"Molly was transferred to a hospital," Clint began. "She has a grade-three concussion. She's conscious now, but brain injuries are complex, and her prognosis isn't clear. Bottom line, the doctors don't know how it will impact Molly's life going forward. We don't know how it will impact her psychic abilities. All we can do is give her time and hope she fully recovers."

He studied each of them in turn: Jillian, Dara, Pyro, Jeremy. Teddy had a swift and sudden understanding of the phrase *His antenna went up*. She could see him thinking, considering, weighing, probing each of them for information. He turned his attention to her. His eyes narrowed, and she raised the voltage on the electric fence that kept her thoughts private.

"Next," Clint said, "as each of you are aware, you committed several felonies. You hacked the FBI mainframe and corrupted a confidential file. The charges that could be leveled against you include criminal trespass, conspiracy, cyberattack on a government institution, and computer fraud. And that's just the beginning."

If Clint knew, Nick knew. Nick more than knew. Nick was probably the one who'd told him. Teddy couldn't think about what that meant.

"So . . . are we under arrest?" Dara said.

"No." Clint leaned back in his chair. "Not today. The Whitfield Institute and the FBI have a very productive relationship. A relationship that nobody wants to see undermined by your stunt. And as you can imagine, the FBI is not eager to admit that its files were breached by a group of lightweights too ignorant to avoid detection on the goddamn surveillance cameras."

He shifted forward in his seat, drilling his forefinger into his desk. *"However,"* he continued, "the evidence collected against you will remain in the possession of the FBI. And there's no statute of limitations on some of these felonies, so if any of you ever tries a stunt like this again, I'm confident that you will be prosecuted to the full extent of the law."

Now Teddy would spend the rest of her career wondering if tomorrow would be the day the FBI would come knocking. Why did she always get herself into these situations? She thought she was doing the right thing—no, she knew she was doing the right thing—so why did she always end up worse off than when she started?

"And as of this moment," Clint continued, "you're all on probation. Break one rule between now and graduation, and you'll all be expelled."

Teddy clenched her fists at her sides, silently seething. How dare he act so self-righteous? Yes, they'd acted stupidly. But Clint had ruined the life of an innocent man. Sent Yates to San Quentin for a crime he didn't commit.

Unable to stand it one second longer, Teddy spoke. "Before you go any further, there's something you should see. Something Molly risked her life to obtain." She handed her cell phone across the desk. "Press play."

The video links cycled through one more time. "What was it you told us, Professor Corbett?" Teddy pretended to think. "'A psychic can never use his power to tamper with evidence or testimony to benefit the outcome of a case.' I've forwarded the link to Yates's attorney. The video clearly shows someone else committing the murder. Yates was convicted based on a coerced confession. Key evidence that was suppressed. That should be enough to get him a new trial."

"That's why—" Clint stopped himself. Shook his head. "How did you—"

"Know where to look?" Teddy realized there was only one way to play this: with the truth. She took a step forward, drew back her shoulders, and met Clint's eyes. She said, "When I went to interview Corey McDonald in San Quentin, I met a prisoner named Derek Yates."

Once she started, Teddy couldn't stop talking. She tried to slow her rush of words, but it all came pouring out. Everything Yates had told her about Sector Three, how the government had experimented on psychics, how her father had fought back, how her mother was still alive. How Clint had forced a false confession—an accusation the videotape had painfully borne out.

She spun around, intending to launch herself out the door and never come back, but Clint's words stopped her: "If you leave now, you'll never know the truth."

"The truth?" she echoed. Her throat felt raw. "The video documents the truth. Coming from you, that's—"

"Teddy," Clint interjected. "There were reasons for what I did. Reasons that I don't have to justify. Reasons you don't understand—"

"Reasons? There's no justification for what I saw on that tape."

He shifted in his chair, obviously uncomfortable. "There are things I haven't told you, but I wasn't certain if they were true . . ." He trailed off, looking over Teddy's shoulder as though staring at some distant image only he could see. "I wasn't there. I've already told you that. But I had friends on base, people I trusted. There were rumors about psychics who were being pushed too far. Subjected to endless psychological tests and physical trials meant to turn them into something they were never meant to be. Psychic soldiers. Killing machines, all empathy destroyed. I heard that your father fought back—that he led an uprising against the people behind the experiments. That would certainly be consistent with the Richard I knew." He paused, seemingly lost in thought. "The point is," he finally continued, shaking his head, "the few psychics who survived Sector Three vanished. Including your mother. And a year or two later, a series of inexplicable events began."

"What do you mean?" Pyro asked.

Clint started as if suddenly remembering there were others in the room. "Assassinations, kidnappings, bombings. Operations executed in broad daylight and with distinct political agendas. Everything that happened had at least one psychic element to it: mental manipulation, clairvoyance, telepathy, *something*."

"And you thought these psychics were the ones who escaped Sector Three?" Dara said.

"Yes. Someone was still manipulating them into serving a twisted agenda."

"You assumed Yates was one of them?" Teddy asked.

"He was with them, I'm sure of it. He'd been involved in at least four cases that I knew of, each more brutal than the last, but I didn't have enough evidence to tie him to them." Clint shook his head, looked at her. "But I wasn't after Yates. I knew what he'd undergone at Sector Three. The Yates I knew was never a killer. He wouldn't have hurt anyone."

"But you put him away despite that. He was your *friend*," Teddy said.

"My friend was gone. He'd been gone for years." Clint rubbed his forehead. "I had no option. I decided that if I couldn't get to the people at the top, I'd start at the bottom. Start arresting psychics like Yates who I believed were being used as weapons. That way I could shut down the entire operation once and for all."

"But that didn't work, did it?" Pyro said.

Clint shook his head.

"So when the government started a new school?" Teddy asked.

"I had to be involved. Because I vowed to never let something like Sector Three happen again."

Silence filled the room. Teddy and her friends attempted to process what they'd just heard.

"But what about the blood tests?" Jillian asked. "We're still research subjects. How is that any different?"

"Yes. We're research subjects. But Whitfield conducts genetic studies, not clinical trials. No student will be subjected to experimental drugs or treatments. At Sector Three, psychics were tortured. Recruits are safe here. I've seen to that."

"Tell that to Brett Evans and Christine Federico," Pyro scoffed.

"We have no reason to believe that their absence is the result of foul play."

"But doesn't it seem a little coincidental?" Pyro countered. "If I were the detective on this case, I'd be looking into whether a vigilante group who used powerful psychics to achieve their ends might be interested in kidnapping such individuals."

"We don't think they were kidnapped," Clint said. "We think they may have been recruited by—"

"When can we see Molly?" Jeremy interrupted. Teddy noticed that Jeremy was getting fidgety, as if he'd had enough of the conversation.

"I'll keep you apprised of her recovery," Clint returned. Apparently, he'd had enough as well. He stood. "Whitfield Institute doesn't keep recruits against their will. If any one of you no longer feels safe here, or no longer believes in the work we're doing, you're free to leave. I hope none of you makes that choice." When none of them made a move to leave the office, Clint dismissed them, saying, "You're free to return to your dorms. But no leaving the island without express written permission from me."

On the way out of the room, Teddy tried to catch Jeremy in the hall, but he begged off, saying that he had heard a storm was blowing in and he had to secure his boat.

CHAPTER FORTY-FOUR

WHEN NO ONE SAW JEREMY ON SUNDAY, TEDDY ASsumed he'd left campus to visit Molly in the hospital, even though Clint had expressly forbidden it. But when Jeremy didn't show up for classes Monday morning, it was clear something was up. A quick visit to his dorm room confirmed it. His clothes were gone. So were the few personal belongings he'd brought with him. No explanation. No goodbye. The rest of the Misfits were left to wonder whether he had lost his faith in Whitfield Institute or was just too shaken by Molly's injury to stick around.

In the weeks that followed, the team splintered. Rather than bringing them together, the botched mission and the devastation that had followed sent them on different paths. No harsh words were spoken or blame assigned, but a fissure divided them just the same. Pyro set off dozens of fire alarms with as many different girls. Jillian wandered the island's footpaths, engaging in long conversations with squawking, chirping birds. Dara stayed in her room, writing letters to her grandmother about the characteristic peculiarities of death predictions. And Teddy, reeling from the loss of her friends and the camaraderie they'd enjoyed, again turned to schoolwork, trying to compartmentalize her worry about Molly's condition and to swallow the guilt she now felt. No change had been reported: Molly remained under the care of physicians at the hospital in San Francisco. Teddy felt she should be with Molly, supporting her friend's recovery, rather than staying on campus preparing for exams that would take place in the second week of June. She knew there was nothing she could do to help. But the nagging sense of inadequacy just wouldn't quit.

After she'd forwarded the file to Yates's lawyer, Teddy had hoped for news. An email, a phone call, a letter—any word from Yates that he would honor his promise to help her find her mother. But the days passed and she heard nothing.

So Teddy worked harder. She hadn't been strong enough during the mission; her influence hadn't held; she hadn't been able to control her telekinesis. With considerable effort, she'd mastered just one feat: directing the path of Ping-Pong balls and paper clips.

All those months ago, Clint had said that if she worked hard enough, she might bend a bullet. If she remembered correctly, the process would involve manipulating time. Or something.

Recalling that conversation, she was filled with self-recrimination. If she had mastered that sooner, as Clint once hoped, could she have changed the trajectory of Molly's fall?

The question kept her up at night.

*   *   *

She couldn't ask Clint for help; she was determined to find a solution on her own. Instead of giving up in frustration, as she once might have done, she spent her days in the library, scouring the shelves for anything that might guide her, though she knew she should be studying for her exams.

One day she discovered a slim pamphlet written in the 1920s by a man named Swami Panchadasi. He explained that bending a bullet wasn't just about moving an object but about slowing time. Or, rather, about transcending time. He encouraged the reader to accept the idea that the past, present, and future occurred simultaneously, not discretely. It was a concept that Teddy had only just grasped in astral telepathy—she could sift through someone's mind to access a lifetime's worth of memories. But its implications for astral telekinesis eluded her.

In Seership, Dunn looked both east and west to understand psychic phenomena. Teddy put down the Panchadasi pamphlet and picked up a textbook on astral quantum mechanics. In a short passage titled "The Theory of Astral Telekinesis," it described two principles that clarified Panchadasi's assertion. It explained the movement of subatomic particles as they "jumped" around in time. Teddy—any human, really—was composed of millions and millions subatomic particles, so she could also jump around in time. The textbook continued by describing the universe as probabilistic, not deterministic. Past events, those that had been observed, were fixed, but future events, which had not been observed, existed in "a state of probability," where many outcomes were still possible . . . until one became most probable as time passed. The wiser the clairvoyants, the more likely they were to select the most probable outcome. (Teddy wondered: had Dara seen only a possible outcome for Molly's fall, and was that why she had survived?)

Teddy understood the theory of an astral telekinetic being able to jump around in time to influence an outcome. But she still didn't see how to put it into practice. Neither the textbook nor the pamphlet had provided any practical way to do that. So she took a page from the professors at Whitfield, copying their methods: if she tuned in to people's minds by imagining a walkie-talkie, and she sorted through their memories by imagining a house, she would devise a metaphor to control time.

She needed a device that would capture events second by second. She'd taken a film class in high school, and they'd used real film—not digital—to document action frame by frame. Teddy cut and pasted celluloid in the school's lone editing dock to make dinky films about the kids at the local 7-Eleven. If she imagined time like an editing dock, she could run through events at the speed of her choosing.

And so Teddy started to visit the lower shooting range, where up-perclassmen practiced marksmanship. She stood on the sidelines, pretending to watch but instead focusing on extending her astral self out through her physical body, while simultaneously trying to slow the movements of the world around her.

Gunshots always broke her concentration.

Panchadasi had warned that it took great practice and even greater patience to "become a being of a simultaneous universe." Patience had never been Teddy's strong suit. But that didn't prevent her from returning to the range again and again.

May begrudgingly gave way to June, but the fog didn't dissipate, and still there was no news from Yates. The sky was perpetually gray, the horizon blurred against the sea.

On a rare cloudless morning in early June, only one other student turned up at the range—a third-year named Max Waldman. One of the school's best marksmen. He gave her a curt nod, then slipped on his protective hearing gear and shooting goggles. He lifted his weapon, checked the chamber, then assumed a firing stance and eyed his target: a paper cutout of a man with his arms resting at his sides, his feet shoulder-width apart.

Teddy stood to one side. She applied the lessons she'd been practicing for weeks. She focused on the scene in front of her. Watched Waldman squint as he sighted his mark. Heard the click of the trigger and the sharp explosion as the bullet left the chamber. She reminded herself that since time itself wasn't linear, she could take all the time she wanted. *I am a being of a simultaneous universe.* She recited the line from the text over and over, like a mantra.

She saw the world around her as if in slow motion. The wind caressing pine needles through a nearby tree. The undulating pattern of a bird's wing above. Teddy saw Waldman's shot, and she imagined reaching out her astral hand to nudge the bullet, while also holding the film deck still. Her head throbbed. She felt the deck speeding up beneath her fingers. She was losing her grip. The bird's wings were speeding up.

Then it was over. She was back in her body, back on the physical plane. Teddy looked at Waldman's target. The bullet hole was nowhere near the head or the heart, where Waldman would have aimed. It was at the very bottom, just outside the target's left foot.

"Don't flatter yourself, Cannon. Even the best marksmen miss from time to time."

She whirled around. "Nick."

For a moment, she could only stare. In the weeks following the debacle at the FBI offices, she had seen Nick around campus. But the icy glare he had sent her way whenever he caught her looking in his direction had silenced her more effectively than anything he might have said.

She understood. She'd behaved horribly.

Still. Here he was. Close enough to touch. And since he hadn't immediately turned and walked away, she chose to interpret that as a sign that he might finally be willing to listen to her apology. Not forgive her—that was ages away, if they ever got that far. But at least he might be willing to hear her out.

"Nick. About what happened—"

"You can't be serious." He turned slightly, his expression one of disdain. "You're something else if you think I'm going to listen to your excuses."

His words cut deep, but she deserved them. "I'm sorry, Nick. That's all I wanted you to know. If I thought I'd had any other choice—"

"Right." He laughed. "That's exactly what I'd expect you to say."

"What?"

"You had to lie to me, steal my files, break in to the FBI computer. You had no other choice."

Teddy faltered but forced herself to go on. "I blew it. I know that. But what was between us was real. I felt it, and you did, too."

He stared at her, his gaze cooler than she'd ever seen it. "Was," he said. "Past tense. You like to gamble. You took a risk."

She watched him stride away without looking back.

*   *   *

In bed that night, Teddy tossed and turned as she replayed her meeting with Nick in her mind. It was well past two in the morning before she finally drifted off to asleep. She dreamed of the yellow house. Teddy pounded on the door, screaming for her mother to let her in.

CHAPTER FORTY-FIVE

IF TEDDY HAD THOUGHT MIDYEAR EXAMS WERE tough, finals were another thing altogether. Twice as long and twice as hard. Teddy felt like she'd run several marathons on the astral plane over the last twenty-four hours. Each of the skills she'd learned this year were tested in a series of written and practical exercises. Only the last one—an oral exam—remained.

She entered the same small classroom in Fort McDowell where she'd taken her entrance exam all those months ago. She half expected to find Clint waiting for her, smirking, but Dunn and Boyd sat in the two chairs on the other side of the table. She didn't know if she felt relieved or upset by Clint's absence.

"So," Dunn began, clasping his hands in front of him. "It's been quite a year, Ms. Cannon."

"I'll say," Boyd said, shuffling some papers.

Dunn shot her a look, then returned his attention to Teddy. "This portion of the final exam is simple. Explain to us the most important skill you've mastered this year, and then demonstrate it."

Teddy reflected on her time at Whitfield. Six months of school and she hadn't mastered *anything*, exactly. She could make a paper clip zoom across the desk, but nothing heavier; she wondered if that was a notable display of telekinesis, given that she had once blown a door off its hinges. Damned if she was going to let Dunn and Boyd know about her experiments on the shooting range. And while she might breach Dunn or Boyd's mind, if she infiltrated their consciousness, she couldn't be certain she'd locate a memory that would confirm her tenuous hold on astral telepathy. She could start an auditory telepathic connection, but so could everyone else in her class. Teddy felt she had been called on her hand at poker with nothing to show. She cleared her throat. "Mastered?"

"Yes." Dunn nodded. "Mastered."

Teddy thought about how she'd made it through the year. She couldn't have completed the midterm without Kate. She couldn't have solved the Corey McDonald case without the Misfits—even, she reluctantly had to admit, Jeremy. She couldn't have found the video without Molly. Molly, who was still in the hospital. And she couldn't have done any of it without Clint, who had taught her so much, then abandoned her when she needed him most. *Be vulnerable,* he'd said.

"I still have a lot to learn," Teddy said. "When I first came to Whitfield—" She stopped, thinking of the first obstacle course when she'd abandoned Molly on the wall. "I only looked out for myself. I didn't think that anyone would look out for me." She thought of the stupid arguments she'd had with Jillian and the not-so-stupid arguments she'd had with Molly. Teddy sighed. "I guess the skill I've learned the most is that I have to trust my team. I know that's probably the wrong answer," she said, glancing from Boyd to Dunn. "It's probably supposed to be something psychic, right? But that's the honest answer." *That's the vulnerable answer,* Teddy thought.

Boyd cleared her throat. "I think we're done here, Cannon. Results will be posted tomorrow."

* * *

Everyone wanted to celebrate. Teddy thought it was premature, as they didn't yet know if any of them had passed the final exam. But the others walked down to the Cantina, and she went with them.

"Hey, Cannon," Kate said as Teddy approached the wooden bar.

"World's not ending . . . yet. There's still something to celebrate." Kate clinked her margarita glass to Teddy's.

"Very funny."

"Seriously, you look like you just found out your puppy died."

"I feel like it." Teddy drained her drink.

Kate looked down at the wooden bar. "So, I—" She hesitated, which was unlike Kate. "I think I'm supposed to tell you something. It doesn't make any sense to me. But I told you if I got anything about Jeremy, I would tell you." She rattled the ice in her glass. "Claircognizance is strange. You wake up and you just know something in your bones. Like you've always known it, and you don't know how or why. But I think I'm supposed to tell you that he cut the rope. On purpose. You'll know what it means."

He cut the . . . what? Teddy's mind whirred as the pieces suddenly, horribly clicked into place. Jeremy was the one who'd brought the rapelling gear. Jeremy had been on the roof when he wasn't supposed to be. The only reason to tamper with Molly's gear would be to prevent her from sending out the video. Which would mean he'd been the one to call in the bomb threats to the hotel and FBI headquarters. To change their room reservation. But why? He'd appeared shocked and devastated in the alley after Molly's fall, but had that been an act? It didn't add up. He'd been the one to encourage the group toward breaking in to the FBI to secure the evidence that would free Yates.

Teddy's thoughts lurched forward, making other connections. The obstacle course at midyear. He'd also been in the lab on the night when the samples went missing. Yates believed that whoever took the blood samples had ties to his organization. Jeremy, with his boat, had unfettered access off-island; he'd be able to transport the samples without anyone at Whitfield knowing. Teddy had seen it, too, when she'd looked into Molly's mind. The doctor's bag, the boat that night on Halloween. They'd been smuggling the samples off-campus.

And then he'd used his boat to sneak away after Molly had—

Molly. An icy chill rushed down Teddy's spine. He'd tried to kill Molly, but he hadn't finished the job.

Kate turned as Ava called to her, gesturing her to the dance floor. "I'm sorry about what happened this year. To your friends."

Teddy was already out of her seat, halfway to the door. "Thanks," she called over her shoulder. "I have to go."

She had to get to Molly.

Jillian, Dara, and Pyro were standing by the water, laughing and playing ring toss. "We need to check on Molly," Teddy said urgently. "Kate just told me that Jeremy was the one who sabotaged her line."

Their laughter died. The gulf that had grown between them over the last few weeks collapsed; it was as if they were once again back in the alley, united by their grief. "Wait," Pyro said. "Kate said what? How would she—"

Ignoring him, Teddy turned to Dara. "Do you remember anything strange about that afternoon? Did you see Jeremy with a knife?"

"A knife?" Dara shook her head. "No. I mean, he hooked us into our gear. Told me to go down the line on the right and Molly on the left—Oh my God. You think he really did that? Why would he want to hurt Molly? I thought he loved her."

Teddy's mind raced. She didn't know, but she was going to find out. "When was the last time anyone heard from Molly?"

"Dunn visited her yesterday," Jillian said.

"We need to go to the hospital, we need to warn—"

"Calm down," Pyro said, rubbing his hands down her arms. "Let's think logically. You're accusing Jeremy of something awful. I didn't like the kid, and he was weird as hell, but that doesn't mean he tried to kill someone."

Teddy shook him off. She didn't want to be calm. She wanted to *do* something. "If what Kate told me is true, Molly is in danger."

"We can use the phone behind the bar," Jillian suggested. "Call the hospital. See if they can put a security detail on her room until we get there."

Perfect. Action. Teddy went to the bar and asked to borrow the phone. She dialed the number for the UCSF Hospital, a number she'd called so often to check on Molly's condition that she had it memorized. "Seventh floor. Neurology Unit," she said when a hospital receptionist answered.

"Thank you, I'll transfer your call."

A click and a dull hum echoed through the line as the call was connected. Ringing. Teddy waited what felt like forever until a duty nurse picked up. "Neurology Unit. Nurse Williams speaking."

"Hello. I'm calling to check on a patient. Molly Quinn. Is there someone—"

"Did you say Molly Quinn?"

"Yes. Is she okay?" Teddy blurted, then quickly checked herself. This wasn't a call to check on her condition; she'd find how Molly was faring once she got there. In the meantime: "I'm afraid she might be in trouble. Is there any way to post security near her room, just to make sure nothing happens to her until we get there?"

"Security? For Miss Quinn?" The woman sounded taken aback.

"Yes. Just for a few—"

"I don't know what this is about, but I'm afraid I can't help you."

"Then connect me to someone who can."

"Miss— Who am I speaking with?"

"I need to be connected with hospital security. Now."

"Miss, you don't understand. Molly Quinn checked herself out about ten minutes ago."

Teddy paused, stunned. "She left?" she finally managed. "Did she say where she was going?"

"I'm afraid it's not our policy to ask. Someone came to collect her, and that was it. She left pretty quickly."

Teddy's stomach clenched. "Who was it?" she said. "A man? Thin, midtwenties, dark hair and glasses—"

"No. Not a man. A woman."

"A woman?" Teddy's head spun. She didn't remember Molly mentioning family, but she must have had someone who looked after her. "A relative?"

"A relative? Possibly, but they certainly didn't look alike. This woman was very tall, with white-blond hair."

Teddy thanked the woman and hung up. Too late. If she'd just reached out to Molly sooner . . . And said what? She didn't have any answers. Just a growing sense of unease. The more she thought about it, the clearer it became that something wasn't right. Another Misfit gone.

* * *

She had to tell Clint. They hadn't had a conversation, just the two of them, since that awful night in his office, but a student's safety was at stake.

She didn't have to go far to find him. Clint stood on the quad, watching workers secure the lines to an enormous white tent that had been erected on the field. "I have to talk to you—" she started.

"I wanted to talk to you, too," he said. "Derek Yates escaped custody yesterday after his court hearing."

Teddy reeled. Of all the things Clint might have said, not even the most gifted psychic could have predicted that. "*What?* That doesn't make sense," she finally managed. "He was being granted a new trial. He's innocent. Why would he run?"

"Either he was convinced, based on his prior experience with the justice system, that he wouldn't receive due process . . . or he was afraid that his former organization would come after him."

"So," Teddy said. "This whole thing was about creating an opportunity for a prison break?"

"More like a courtroom break."

For weeks, Teddy had struggled to decide if she'd done the right thing in releasing the videotapes. Yes, Yates might have been part of a group who committed heinous crimes. But he hadn't been guilty of the crime he'd been convicted of. He was entitled to due process, just like anyone else. So her actions had been justified. But there was no denying that she'd set loose a dangerous man. That meant she was responsible for whatever Derek Yates might do next. She forced herself to ask, "Was anyone hurt?"

"No. Not at the courthouse, at least."

She let out a breath. "How did he escape?"

"The same way Derek Yates does anything: mental influence."

"Where will he go?"

Clint squinted at the tent. He was silent for so long that Teddy thought he wouldn't answer. Finally, he replied, "The Derek Yates I knew didn't like loose ends. Hard to imagine he would leave unfinished business behind, particularly if he had a score to settle."

Teddy's heart began to gallop. In other words, settling the score with the once trusted friend whose deliberate mishandling of evidence had led to Yates's incarceration. Now she wondered if she'd become a loose end, too. Or if she was just a piece in the game all along. If, from the beginning, Yates had used her as a conduit to Clint.

"Yates might try to come to campus. Especially tomorrow, when there'll be visitors. Crowds provide good cover. Commotion. Distraction," Clint said. "And with Yates comes the possibility of his old friends. And Teddy—there's a chance he'll come looking for you now, too."

She nodded. "If he shows up on campus, we'll be ready for him."

Clint shook his head. "Whatever you're thinking, stop it. Now."

"But I—"

"I mean it, Teddy. No more misguided heroics. You're on probation. One more screwup and I'll have to expel you."

He turned, walking over to kick the tent pegs before Teddy even had the chance to share her suspicions about Jeremy.

CHAPTER FORTY-SIX

SUNLIGHT STREAMED IN THROUGH THE DORM WIN-
dow, hammering at the back of Teddy's eyes. She squinted to block it
out, but the attempt was useless. Teddy preferred to creep slowly into
daily consciousness, but now, even dragging a blanket over her head
didn't help. Jillian had flung wide the makeshift draperies to greet the
new day. One of Teddy's top roommate annoyances.

"Teddy, I'd really thought you'd learn to sync your circadian
rhythms by now," Jillian said, letting out a long *ohm*. "Exam grades
should be up. Want to go check after breakfast? Then we can get ready
for the graduation ceremony."

"Jesus H. Christ, Jillian. If you are naked right now, I don't know
what I'm going to do." Teddy pulled a pillow over her head.

"You're going to miss me," Jillian said. "You're going to miss me
a whole lot."

*　*　*

As Teddy and Jillian walked downstairs for breakfast, they passed a
bulletin board that hung in the lobby of Harris Hall, advertising various Reiki healing groups and tarot readings. Pinned in the center was
the list of final exam results. Dara stood in front of it, her head low.
Teddy immediately thought the worst: that Dara hadn't passed. And
if Dara hadn't passed . . .

"Hey," Teddy said. "Everything okay?" She gestured to the bulletin board.

"I passed," Dara said. "Barely. The Casework final was killer."

True. Nick's exam had indeed been torture. Page after page of questions on FBI procedure, interrogation techniques, methods of dealing with cybercrimes, and criminal justice ethics. A final exam so difficult that Teddy couldn't help but believe it had been made especially difficult in retaliation to the Misfits' antics at the FBI.

Teddy shook her head. "You had me worried, Dara."

"What? Oh, sorry. It's just . . . I can't get this warning out of my head."

"Warning? What do you mean?"

"It keeps shifting. I can't make out what happens and to whom."

After Dara's last vision, Teddy promised to take each and every one of her predictions seriously. Particularly in light of the disturbing news Clint had shared the day before. "Maybe I can help," she said. "What do you see?"

Dara frowned. Closed her eyes and concentrated. "I see the quad. And the white tent. Lots of people there. A crowd. Music playing."

"That doesn't sound like a death vision," Jillian cut in. "That sounds like graduation."

Teddy shot her roommate a look.

"Then," Dara continued, "something goes wrong. But I can't see what it is. I don't hear gunfire; there's no bomb. One minute everything looks fine; the next, people start screaming, panicking, running in all directions. There's someone there, some shifting figure." She shook her head and chewed her bottom lip. "It doesn't make sense. I think someone's going to die, but I don't know who. Or how. The more I try to pin down exactly what's happening, the more the image fades."

Dara stopped speaking, and the three of them stood in silence.

"We need to tell Clint," Jillian said. "Get him to cancel."

"He won't cancel," Teddy said. "We've already got too many people on campus. How would it look if a school that trains students to work with police agencies, FBI, CIA, and every other top-notch security agency in the country can't provide security for its own event?"

"So," Jillian said, "what do we do?"

Teddy looked at Dara. "Do you see Yates at the ceremony?"

Dara shook her head.

"Wait a minute," Jillian said. "*Yates?* Did you say Yates? Why would Yates be here?"

"He escaped custody yesterday." Jillian and Dara stared at Teddy in horror as she relayed the information Clint had shared the day before.

"So Clint thinks he might come here?" Dara said, her voice climbing up two octaves.

"I didn't say that. Clint didn't say that. But it is a possibility, so let's not be caught with our guard down, all right?"

Dara and Jillian exchanged an uneasy nod, then their gazes shifted to the thick yew bushes in the Zen garden, as though they expected Yates to jump out from behind them at any second.

Teddy released an exasperated sigh and said, "We'll let Clint know. Tell him what you saw, even if it's not definitive. Forewarned is forearmed, right?"

The stomp of boots interrupted their conversation. A stiff palm landed hard against Teddy's back. "You passed, recruit. Don't look so glum," Boyd said. "We're supposed to be celebrating today. And you more than most. You're still here."

Teddy forced a smile. Still here. But for how much longer? Despite what Dara had seen in her vision, Teddy harbored a certain dread that Yates was on his way. To take care of loose ends or make good on his promise, Teddy couldn't be sure which. Either way, she knew it wouldn't be good.

* * *

The graduation ceremony began exactly as scheduled, at fourteen hundred hours, two o'clock civilian time. Teddy shuffled into a row of folding chairs next to Jillian, Dara, and Pyro. She craned her head around as she did so, trying to spot Clint. A little over three hours had passed since Dara had shared her death vision, and in that time Teddy had tried to track Clint down, to no avail. He'd been unavailable all morning, in a meeting with campus security. Afterward, it seemed that everywhere she went, she trailed one step behind him—his office, the groundskeepers' building, the ferry building, even the catering tent. She kept missing him.

A string quartet seated at the foot of the stage lifted their bows and began to softly play, clearly to draw the crowd's attention to the ceremony. But Teddy took the opportunity to lean across Jillian's lap and whisper to Pyro, "Dara had a death warning."

"When? Just now?"

"No. Earlier this morning."

Dara briefly explained her shifting vision and her supreme frustration that she still couldn't pin it down.

"Just be sure you stay alert," Teddy said to the others. "It could be Yates, anyone."

Pyro's brows shot skyward at the mention of Yates's name, but as the ceremony was now under way—Whitfield stood at the podium to make his opening remarks—he let it pass without further comment.

Jillian, however, wasn't quite as content to stay silent. She leaned toward Teddy and whispered, "I've let the seagulls know."

Better than nothing, Teddy supposed. But she couldn't help but feel like a sitting duck herself. The best she could do was continue to scan the audience for Yates or anyone who looked out of place.

To her relief, the ceremony went on without incident. Whitfield Institute's newest graduating class left the stage, diplomas in hand. Teddy stood on the western edge of the tent and watched as recruits, alumnae, government liaisons, and faculty milled about by the refreshment table. Caterers moved among the crowd, distributing bottled water and flutes of champagne.

Finally, she spotted Clint and moved toward him. They had spent the year parrying information, both of them giving just enough so that one always felt like the other had the upper hand. But lives could be at stake now. She filled him in on Dara's death warning, enjoying the subtle satisfaction of being open and honest. No more games to play. Nothing else to hide. Unfortunately, there was no action for Clint to take, either. The grounds were as secure as he could make them. But at least they were on the same page for once.

Short of remaining alert, Teddy had done all she could reasonably be expected to do, and she discovered she was starving. Dara's death warning had killed her appetite that morning, and she'd skipped lunch looking for Clint. Now she was more than ready to join her friends at the buffet.

"I know this sounds crazy, but I think I saw Brett Evans by the bar a few minutes ago. But when I looked back, he was gone. I mean, I thought it was him. But I'm not sure," Jillian said, her eyes widened. "Unless—you don't think I can see ghosts now, do you?"

"I saw him, too," Pyro said, popping a mini-quiche into his mouth. "So, definitely not dead."

"He's here?" Dara said. "Weird. Why'd he come back?"

Pyro shrugged. "Who knows. Maybe he regrets dropping out the way he did. Or maybe he has a friend who's graduating."

"Should we tell Clint?" Dara asked.

Teddy nodded. "I'll go. I just talked to him," she said. She wove through the crowd, heading toward the stage. She spotted Clint's broad form not too far away, his back to her, deep in conversation with a woman Teddy didn't recognize.

She'd darted around a group of graduates who'd clearly enjoyed a bit more than their share of the champagne when she felt a hand clamp down on her forearm. Teddy jerked back, but she'd been caught off-balance. Whoever had grabbed her pulled her behind a flap in the tent wall.

"Surprised to see me, darlin'?"

Brett Evans. But he looked different. The laid-back Texas cowboy she'd met her first night at Whitfield was leaner, harder. His hair was cut in a military style. His easygoing smile veered more toward a leer than a grin. And then the smile faded altogether. He tightened his grip on her arm.

"Brett, you're hurting me."

"Take me to Yates and no one will get hurt."

Yates? Brett wanted Yates?

Teddy shook her head, her thoughts spinning wildly. "He's not here. I haven't seen him."

"Then where is he?"

"Where . . . I don't know. How would I know?"

"Don't lie to me, Teddy." He gave her forearm another vicious squeeze.

"Brett, what's this about? What are you doing?"

"We're supposed to track him through you. Those were our orders." Brett used his free hand to pull a gun from his back pocket. "I'll use force if I have to, Teddy. I don't want to, but I will. When it comes to Yates, the end justifies the means."

Jeremy had said the same thing all those months ago. Memories suddenly flooded her: discordant moments that hadn't seemed important at the time slammed together with a new and disturbing force. Jeremy talking to Brett before Halloween. Jeremy giving Brett a recruiting pitch for his organization just before he'd secured the blood samples. Because Brett, like Teddy and Christine, was a child of Sector Three psychics.

So Brett and Jeremy were stepping in, ready to take Yates's place in his former organization. What had Clint called them? Vigilantes? Psychic soldiers?

Teddy shook the thought away. The terminology didn't matter. She had to get help. One of the Misfits would certainly realize she was missing. "Let me go, Brett. Someone will notice I'm gone. And when they see you, they'll—"

"They'll what? Welcome a prodigal student with open arms? Of course they will. And frankly, it'll be hours before anyone notices you're gone. That's why I'm here and why Jeremy's making himself useful somewhere else on campus."

Jeremy was on Angel Island. "Where—"

"Teddy?" Clint asked. "Is that you?"

Relief surged through her. She'd never been so glad to hear Clint's voice.

Clint stood just inches away, on the other side of the tent wall. Before she could cry out for help, Brett jerked her roughly against him. Quietly, he intoned, "Say one word and you'll go first." He lifted his gun, pressed the barrel against her cheek.

Dara's warning snapped into place. The tent. The ceremony. The crowd. The figure wasn't Yates. It was Brett.

Brett tightened his grip on his gun. Flicked off the safety. Then, to Teddy's horror, he turned the gun and aimed it directly at the tent wall, exactly where Clint stood, completely unaware of the danger he faced.

Teddy sucked in a breath, striving to calm her wildly beating heart. She'd trained for situations like this. She knew what to do. What she *had* to do. She concentrated on the film deck in her mind, the feeling of the metal reels in her hand.

Brett pulled the trigger. A puff of smoke accompanied the bullet as it left the barrel of the gun.

There was no clear vision because the future wasn't fixed. Because Teddy was there, too, and she had a chance to change the outcome.

Slowly, slowly. Slow everything down. I am a being of a simultaneous universe.

She watched a breeze cradle a leaf, slowing its descent to the point where it appeared frozen in midair. An ant, crawling over a discarded crust of bread, slowed to the point where any movement it made was virtually undetectable.

Teddy watched the bullet as it sliced through the air. She focused on extending her astral self toward the piece of deadly metal as if she could knock the bullet off course. Panic gripped her, and she felt the film reels speed up. She was losing her grip on time. The bullet was hurtling toward Clint's chest. It was two feet away, now one.

With all the energy she had left, she reached out her astral hand and felt her fingers touch hot metal. Horror gripped her as she heard Clint give a grunt of pain. His body fell against the wall of the tent, then collapsed on the ground. Then the reels, and time, spun out of her control.

Teddy jerked free of Brett's grasp as the sound of the gun blast caused chaos to erupt around them. Dimly, she was aware of screaming, running, crashing glass as guests overturned trays and tables in their rush to flee.

She threw herself against the tent wall, and landed on the ground beside Clint. The bullet had missed his heart but hit his shoulder. Still, he was alive. Brett hadn't killed him.

"Stop him," Clint said, breathing hard. "Don't let him leave the island."

Teddy felt the brush of cold steel against her palm and looked down to see Clint pushing his gun at her. "Go, Teddy. *Now*."

Teddy grabbed the gun and ran.

*　　*　　*

All around her, the reception dissolved into mayhem. Boyd stood at the center of it all, issuing orders.

Brett had said that Jeremy was here. If Jeremy had come to Angel Island, he'd come by boat. And Teddy knew exactly where that boat was docked. Spying Jillian, she yelled out, "Jeremy's boat! Get help and meet me there!"

Jillian nodded and took off in the opposite direction.

Unwilling to waste the seconds it would take to wait for her friends, Teddy raced past Harris Hall, then past the infirmary. She hurled herself over a low stone wall, stumbling, sliding, plunging down the steep incline that led to the jogging path. She edged toward a cliff that towered above the cove.

Jeremy's speedboat bobbed on the incoming tide. But the boat itself was empty.

Clint's gun still clenched in one hand, Teddy braced her hands on her knees and gulped in air as she considered her options.

It was a sharp descent—almost vertical—from her current position to the cove. A bit farther along the path was a switchback trail leading down to the water, but that took—

She heard the sound of pounding feet and skittering pebbles. She turned to level her weapon directly at Brett's chest as he came barreling around the corner, his own gun loose by his side.

"Drop your weapon," she ordered.

"What the—"

"Drop your weapon now!" She clicked off the safety and tightened her grip. Her hands were slick with blood and sweat, but they didn't shake. The tension of her finger against the trigger was whisper-thin.

Moving with exaggerated care, Brett extended his arms from his sides, palms facing Teddy, and let the gun slip from his hand.

"Kick it toward me," she said.

He did. Keeping her gaze fixed on Brett, she gave it another kick, sending it skidding behind her.

"It doesn't have to be this way, Teddy." Jeremy. He walked, unarmed, to stand next to Brett.

She was outnumbered, even if armed. Her advantage was so slight as to be almost nonexistent. Teddy was poised over a cliff with her gun pointed at Brett and Jeremy, but she had no way to subdue either of them. The only thing she could do now was stall until Jillian, Pyro, and Dara arrived.

"What are you doing, Jeremy?" she asked, buying time.

He gestured to the space between them. "We shouldn't be enemies. We're working toward the same goal. We both want to use our psychic gifts to keep people safe."

"*Safe?*" Teddy's anger flared. She couldn't help but think of Molly's safety. He hadn't protected her.

"Yes, Teddy. We keep this country safe. We think big-picture. Yates was a traitor. I had to do everything I could to make sure he stayed in prison. He abandoned the cause."

She thought about the surveillance video she'd seen. A man had been murdered on a busy city sidewalk, without a trial, without a judge, without a jury. "You're talking about assassinations."

Jeremy shook his head. "You don't understand. Yates let personal feelings get in the way."

"What about Molly? You didn't have personal feelings for her?"

At that Jeremy ducked his chin, avoiding Teddy's eyes. "I recruited her myself," Jeremy said. "But her loyalty wavered. I had to intervene. I meant to destroy the laptop. I thought she'd drop it. Not . . . "

"We helped Molly," Brett said, picking up where Jeremy left off. "She hated sensing people's emotions all the time. Made her feel crazy as a bullbat. The Patriot Corps fixed her up. And in return—"

Jeremy shot Brett a glance, silencing him.

"You helped Molly?"

Molly was working with Jeremy?

Teddy ran over the events in her head: the hacking of Eversley's computer at Halloween; the attack in the warehouse. Teddy felt like she'd been blindsided. Of course Molly was a member of the Patriot Corps. Her behavior had always been erratic. Irregular. Like she was hiding something. "Is that why she came back from winter break so altered? Did your group do something to her? Experiment on her? Like they did on psychics in Sector Three? Was that before or after you made her attack me in the warehouse?"

Teddy heard a noise from behind her. Jillian.

Thank God.

But then a burst of searing pain shot through the base of her skull as something rock-hard slammed against her head. Teddy fell forward, landing on her hands and knees. Clint's gun, knocked from her grip, skittered across the rocky ledge.

Pinpricks of light danced in front of her eyes. She gritted her teeth, determined to hold on to consciousness.

"Stay down," a female voice ordered. Not Jillian.

Teddy blinked. Christine Federico swam into focus, her toned arms flexed, Clint's gun now firmly in her grip.

Whitfield Institute's two missing recruits were missing no longer. Teddy tried to gather the strength to telekinetically rip the gun from Christine's grip, but the attempt was futile. After bending the bullet, she barely had enough energy to move her physical body, let alone her astral one.

Teddy tried to stand, but Christine swung the barrel of the gun directly at her. "I said, don't move." Her finger found the trigger. "We're wasting time."

Jeremy stepped between them. "No," he said. "We have orders to protect her. Marysue—"

Teddy's head snapped up at the mention of her mother's name. Everything Yates had promised her. "How do you know my mother?"

"Your mother's with us, Teddy," Jeremy said. "Do you know what I would give for more time with my mother? Anything." He bent down on the ground so he was eye-level with her. "If you join us, you could see her again. If you only knew what we could do together. If you only knew your potential."

Her potential. For recruitment. She was the third name on that list. Brett. Christine. And Teddy. Three children of psychics, experimented on at Sector Three.

Before he could continue, she saw a burst of light from the corner of her eye. Suddenly, the scrub brush beside her was on fire. Jeremy stood and spun right, looking for the source of the attack. As he did, a seagull swooped down, diving at Christine's head.

My friends, Teddy thought through the pain. *They're here.*

"Hands where I can see them," Nick said.

From behind her, Teddy felt another burst of heat as Pyro launched another attack of fire at Jeremy. Then Jeremy leaped off the cliff into the churning waters below, followed by Christine and Brett. Pyro sprinted down the trail after them, but the boat's motor roared to life before he could reach them.

Nick helped Teddy to her feet but said nothing. Teddy wanted to thank him, but he turned back to campus, presumably to repair the damage of their misguided heroics before she could.

From the top of the cliff, Teddy, Jillian, and Dara watched the boat peel away, waves in its wake.

They'd gotten away.

CHAPTER FORTY-SEVEN

JUST AFTER DAYBREAK, THE COAST GUARD SPOTTED Jeremy Lee's abandoned speedboat drifting near Alcatraz Island. No sign of Jeremy, Brett, or Christine. Still no word from Molly.

Those facts weighed on Teddy's mind as she made her way back to UCSF—the same hospital that had treated Molly—on her way to visit Clint. But nothing weighed as heavily on her mind as the opportunity she had lost: to find her mother. Yates knew where she was. Jeremy knew, too. Both had vanished. If Teddy wanted to look for her, she wouldn't have any idea where to start. And she had the feeling that the organization her mother was somehow involved with knew how to hide people and keep them hidden.

Teddy knocked on Clint's door and stepped inside only to pull up short at the sight of Rosemary Boyd standing by his bedside.

The sergeant acknowledged Teddy's presence with a brisk nod, and Teddy waited for her to say something about what had happened the day before, maybe even praise her for saving Clint's life. But she simply grumbled something about the inefficiency of the hospital staff, and Teddy understood that it was as close as Boyd could come to expressing affection for a colleague.

Clint turned his head toward Teddy. "I'm glad you came." Their eyes met and held. What had passed between them couldn't be fixed with four words. Or a single look. But it was a start.

Boyd said nothing, in fact had turned her back on them to stare out the window. It was as if she sensed an emotional moment was transpiring in her presence, and it was too much for her to bear.

To Teddy's relief, Clint didn't look too worse for the wear. His left shoulder was bandaged, and his other arm was hooked up to a blood pressure cuff. An IV needle was threaded into his wrist. But other than that, he appeared fine. Terrifying to think how close he'd come to dying. Dara's vision could have proved correct. The idea that Teddy had saved Clint's life—by using her astral telekinetic ability, no less—was overwhelming. She still hadn't fully processed it.

"You're going to be okay, huh?" she asked.

Clint attempted a shrug, then grimaced. "I might not be able to toss a football for a while," he said. "But my shoulder will be fine."

"You did good, Cannon," Boyd said, as she turned back from the window. "Stuck to your training."

Teddy looked at her. Was she getting a compliment from Boyd? "Training?"

"That's what we learn to do in law enforcement and in the military. Protect and serve. We obviously trained you right. Something clicked into place for you to step up to save Corbett." She set a meaningful stare on Teddy. "You weren't just looking out for yourself in that tent, Cannon."

Boyd turned to go. Teddy braced herself for another slap on the back as Boyd passed her. But instead, Boyd just squeezed Teddy's shoulder. Teddy wasn't sure whether she preferred Boyd's praise or punishment. The door clicked behind her.

"Any news from Molly?" Teddy asked.

Clint shifted, adjusting his position on the pillows behind him. "We have no idea where she is."

"But you think she's with"—Teddy paused, struggling to remember what Brett had called it—"the Patriot Corps?"

Clint nodded. "We don't think she went voluntarily."

At the end, Molly had fought against the Patriot Corps's interests;

otherwise, she wouldn't have sent the file to Teddy. *Just in case.* Just in case they tried to kill her? Teddy felt sick. "I can't help feeling responsible," she said. "I knew something was off all year."

"I missed it, too," Clint said. He sighed. "I think Molly was trying to protect you. Wanted to save you from them in the end. But Jeremy had other ideas."

Teddy's heart broke a little more as she thought about how far Molly had gone to protect her, when she had failed so badly to protect Molly.

"It's just a theory," Clint continued, "but it adds up."

"And now she's gone and I'm still here," Teddy said.

"We'll find her," Clint said. "She's not lost forever."

"Not like you thought my mother was," Teddy said.

"If Marysue is alive," Clint said, "we'll find her. I promise."

There was a knock at the door. "Not interrupting a Hallmark moment, am I?" Nick slipped into the room, looking more handsome than ever in a charcoal gray suit.

"It's fine," Teddy said. "I was just leaving." She'd been avoiding him since he'd shown up with the rest of the Misfits on the cliff's edge. With any luck, she wouldn't see him again until next year. She offered Clint a quick smile and squeezed his arm.

Clint winced. "That would have been a Hallmark moment, Teddy, if you'd gone for my uninjured arm."

"Sorry," Teddy said. She grabbed her leather jacket and moved to the door.

"I'll walk you out," Nick said. "Just in case."

"I'm a big girl. I'll be fine."

She left the room and made her way down the hospital corridor only to have Nick follow. "Teddy, wait."

She spun around. "What do you want? Another apology? You've made it clear you don't want to hear it. So—"

"No. I don't want another apology."

She shook her head. "Look, let's just forget about everything, okay? Pretend like it never happened. Next year it'll be like a fresh start. Deal?" She stuck out her hand to shake.

"I'd like that."

When she looked at him, she wanted to believe him. With every fiber of her being she resisted the urge to read his mind.

He took her hand in his. Rough fingertips grazed her skin. His eyes locked on hers. "Nick Stavros, FBI. Some people know me as just plain ol' Nick." He smiled, revealing that dimple.

She wanted things to be different. She wanted to be different. But she wasn't. She was just herself. She cleared her throat. "Theodora Cannon. Stanford dropout, former gambling addict, current student at the Whitfield Institute for Law Enforcement Training and Development. Once owed over a quarter million dollars to a Russian loan shark. Astral telepath and telekinetic. Misfit. I used to live in my parents' garage in Las Vegas. My birth parents were psychics, and the government experimented on them and killed my father. My mother is still alive but may be working for a vigilante political psychic assassination squad. Some people call me Teddy for short. But those who know me really well call me TeAnne."

*　　*　　*

Later that night on Angel Island, Teddy sat with her friends at the Cantina, waiting for the last ferry to take them to San Francisco. From there, they'd all enjoy a little time off until returning to school the following year. Soon, with some help, Teddy would try to unlock the puzzle of the Patriot Corps. She would try to figure out how to find Molly and her mother. But for now, all she wanted to do was knock back a cold beer on a warm summer night with three friends who had taught her that even misfits have a place.

"Excuse me." A guy with a red baseball came up to their table. "Are you Teddy?"

"What's it to you?" Pyro asked, laughing, taking a swig of his beer.

"Some guy asked me to give you this," he said, handing Teddy a folded piece of white paper.

"What guy?" Dara said.

The stranger shrugged and returned to the bar.

Teddy opened the crisp white paper, folded neatly in half. Inside, the writing was blocky, bold, large. Scrawled across the page in thick black ink:

I always keep my word.

See you soon, Theodora.

Until then.